# Studs

## Kathy Wilson

# Dedication

This book is dedicated to my dear, departed friend, Glenn Bob, aka Glen Nabor.

Glen was raised in a humongous family on a humungous farm in the Midwest. As a result, he had a slow, quiet, gentle way about him and was always kind in his thoughts and actions toward others.

Glen and I worked in the Contractor Sales division of a very large building material conglomerate in a suburb of Seattle. He was given the addition of "Bob" to his name by our citified manager, who thought Glen's countrified mannerisms were somehow humorous. The "Bob" part caught on and soon everyone who worked in that department became a part of the "Bob" family. That included me, and I became Kathy Bob.

Even though we worked together for only three years, we formed a friendship that lasted over 30 years. I valued our friendship dearly and was devastated to learn of his sudden death in 2016. I had told him that I was writing a book and that he was in it. Although I had been working intermittently on the book for about fifteen years, it was never complete enough for me to share it with anyone, including Glenn Bob. He never got to read this book. After his death I was inspired to dedicate it to him, and that was the motivation I needed to finally finish it.

I'm sure Glenn Bob would have enjoyed it and he'd hope everyone else who reads it would do the same.

# Chapter 1

"Hey, girl. I got a wunnerful opportunity for you," Gene boomed into the phone. He sounded suspiciously upbeat. It wasn't like him to be so cheerful - or so loud - early in the morning. It was 8am and that easily qualified as gawdawful early in the morning in my book. I felt all prickly on the back of my neck – a sure sign something very unpleasant was headed my way.

"What's that, Gene?" I replied reluctantly, holding the phone arm's length away from my ear. My ears started ringing when they were exposed to loud noises such as sonic booms, dynamite blasts, and Gene's telephone voice.

His voice was as big as he was. "Beefy" was the kindest word to describe him. He had probably played football in high school, but now he was way beyond playing any kind of sports. He got enough exercise just toting his big belly around all day.

"You've been doing such a wunnerful job of estimating that I've got too much work. I've plumb run out of Project Supes." Project Superintendents, to the rest of the intelligent world.

"Well, that's good news. I'm glad I'm doing such a good job for you," I hinted for a compliment but my hint slid right over Gene's bald head.

"Yup. I got me a job up in Stanville and I need someone to run the job. That's you, girl."

Was he ever going to remember I had a name and stop calling me "girl"? In my head I yelled at him, "My name is KATLIN! KATLIN GREENE!"

"I've never run an entire job, *Gene*", I emphasized his name, hoping that he'd get the hint. "You know that my actual on-site experience in construction is limited to a couple of years working as a carpenter and five years as a roofing contractor. I

1

don't have the expertise to run an entire job, especially a commercial job. My background is 99% residential... or don't you remember? I only started doing commercial when I came to work for you three months ago as your estimator."

"Hell, girl. You can do it. There's nuthin' to it. And the pay's a lot better than being an estimator."

Did I hear him say the pay was better? "Talk to me," I replied, trying to sound only slightly interested.

"It pays twice what you're gettin' now. And since the job's kinda far for you to drive every day, I'll spring for a place for you to stay during the week."

He sure knew the way to my heart. Twice what I was being paid now! That was more money than I'd ever made in my whole life! It was a fortune... or at least it seemed like it to me. And he was going to give me a place to stay, too! His unusual generosity should have set off some alarms in my head, but I think they were short circuited by the visions I was having of him throwing huge wads of money at me.

"Well... I don't know. Let me think about it." I was still trying to sound disinterested in the hopes that he wouldn't pick up on how eager I truly was. He was very good at sensing when he had the upper hand in negotiations and he always took advantage of his position. "Yeah. Okay. I guess I'll do it for you. But I'm still not so sure I can actually do the job. What if I run into trouble?"

"I'll be up there once a week and the rest of the time I'm only a phone call away. Don't worry. You'll do just fine. Be at the office at six Monday morning and we'll drive up to the job together. I'll tell you more about it then." He banged the receiver down.

Did I hear him clearly? Did he really say "six Monday morning?" He couldn't possibly mean 6 am. That meant I'd have to get up in the middle of the night to get to his office. It had to be some kind of cruel joke he was playing on me. A new version of redneck humor.

Let's get something clear right now: I am not one of those weirdos who jump out of bed at four in the morning, bright-eyed and chirpy, ready to skippy-do into the day. Nine or thereabout was a much more civilized hour to begin one's day, in my estimation. Even at that decent hour I liked to ease into wakefulness with a few quarts of coffee to get me motivated enough to actually face the world.

Without warning, dark doubts began to seep in around the edges of my mind. The creeping vines of reality began to choke off the gleeful vision of all that money I'd be getting in my new high-paying job. The reality of having to get up early in the morning was almost a law of the construction world. But that was only a minor inconvenience compared to the real cause of my growing fear – supervising a commercial construction project.

It was one thing to estimate materials and labor from plans and then get bids from subcontractors. That was the easy part. The difficult part was actually getting the dang thing built and making it look acceptably similar enough to the architect's drawings so it would pass the multitude of required inspections.

As if that wasn't enough, commercial construction had to be built within budget. Each project was bid on by a pack of contractors, hungry for the contract. The lowest bidder always got the project, unless one of the contractors was a member of the owner's family, either blood or cultural. The challenge that every contractor faced was to bid low enough to get the contract for the job, yet high enough to realize a profit, thus making it possible for them to continue in business for another few months.

And just as a little added extra excitement in any commercial project, there were time constraints spelled out in the contract between the owner and the contractor, with extreme financial penalties should the contractor fail to meet said time limits. The project had to be completed within the very specific period of time or some highly expensive per diem penalties were automatically activated. It wasn't uncommon for this little technicality to put a contractor out of business.

All this, and more, fell on the responsible shoulders of the Project Superintendent.

In this particular case that would be me.

And there was one other glaring item: a person of the female persuasion was not a common occurrence in the manly world of construction, and especially in the management area of construction.

That person of the female persuasion would also be me.

From past experiences as a carpenter and a roofing contractor, I couldn't even begin to imagine the many opportunities in which I'd get to prove my knowledge, abilities, talents, *and* authority as the Supe on this job.

I could only hope that everything I'd learned during my past experiences in regards to dealing with the male construction animal would help me as I took on this outrageous job opportunity with all the special challenges it would no doubt provide.

Hoo boy.

*Now* what had I gotten myself into?

# Chapter 2

Somehow I managed to make it to Gene's home office at the appointed time of 6am on Monday. Actually, his girlfriend Ginnie owned the house. Sometimes I wondered about that. How much credibility can a person who is in the housing industry have if they don't own their own house? Realtors, building contractors, mortgage officers, and the like somehow lose believability when they rent. Or worse, live in their girlfriend's house.

I dragged myself up the stairs of the front porch and found the doorbell. I punched it and was rewarded with the howls of a whiney country Western song.

Gene threw the front door wide open and greeted me with a big bear hug. "Hey, girl. C'mon in. Whaddya think of our new doorbell? We got over a hunnert songs on it that we can change it to. All of our favorite Country and Western songs. Ain't that great?"

*Ghastly was more like it*, I thought. *Especially* at this uncivilized hour.

"Hi, Gene. Ginnie." I'd gotten up way too early and had yet to imbibe my requisite gallon or so of coffee to be any more conversational than that. I sat down at the dining room table, which currently was being used as an office desk, to wait for whatever was next. Hopefully it was coffee. And lots of it.

Ginnie was almost as big as Gene, but much nicer looking. For one thing, her mustache was much less noticeable than his. Their hair was the same color, but she had lots more of it. This wasn't too difficult to manage since Gene's ring of hair barely came up to the edge of his grubby baseball cap. When he took his cap off, the back of his head looked a lot like the planet Saturn.

Ginnie smiled at me from the kitchen where she began talking to Gene in a manner typically used with first-graders. After a few minutes of discussion between the two of them about miscellaneous work-related stuff and a few un-work-related things, Gene turned his attention to me.

"Here's what we'll do. You leave your truck here and follow me in Ol' Blue up to the job site. We'll go over things once we get up there and get you settled. I'll bring you back and then tomorrow you can drive up there in your own rig and start the job. Today I'll just show you the job site and you can start to get the hang of things."

"Sure. Sounds good to me. Got any coffee?" I probably should have had a lot more coffee before I got to Gene's, but then again sometimes it's a good thing not to be too aware of one's surroundings. Or the situation at hand.

Gene poured me a cup of coffee so weak it could have been tea. At this rate, I was going to have to drink three or four gallons just to get the caffeine level in my bloodstream up to normal. Probably one of these days I'd teach him how to build a manly cup of coffee so he, too, could experience what being totally alive was like... in a caffeine-induced way, that is.

"Let's head on out the back and I'll introduce you to Ol' Blue," he grinned at me with a twinkle in his eye.

I hated when he got that twinkle in his eye. It always meant something horrendous was about to happen to me.

The grin on his face got even wider as he turned to walk toward the old, falling-down barn where he stored leftover building materials from his jobs, equipment he wasn't currently using, and machinery he was going to fix one of these days.

We sauntered around to the back of the barn where an old, beat-up camper sat on top of a pickup truck that should have been retired from service eons ago. The camper had rusted itself solidly onto the back of the truck, which was a good thing since the tie-down clamps were now just clumps of fuzzy white oxidized aluminum. Like a couple that's been married for decades, as the truck and camper had aged together, they'd begun to look more and more alike. It was difficult to imagine what color either of them had been originally. Since Gene called this unit Ol' Blue, I figured one, or both, had at one time been some shade of blue.

The truck was big for a pick-up. With its dual rear wheels, I guessed it was probably a one ton. The heft was probably needed to carry around a camper as big as this one. The front of the camper stuck out over the top of the truck cab enough to effectively protect the windshield and half the hood from sun, rain, and whatever else might fall from the sky. The back of the camper extended beyond the truck bed by at least three feet. I hoped there were some fold-down aluminum steps to get into this thing. I could just see myself walking out of the camper, all bleary-eyed first thing in the morning, and walking on air for a nanosecond before dropping to the earth like a boulder.

"Here. Have a look-see." Gene invited as he tried unsuccessfully to open the door. He started pulling harder, grunting as he pulled. Finally putting all his considerable weight into the effort. he was able to break the door free from where it had rusted to the door frame. "Might need to spray a little penetrating oil on those door hinges," he mumbled mostly to himself, but loud enough so I could hear his badly disguised suggestion that it was up to me to fix the sticky door.

I'd never been this close to a camper before. I never could understand the point of even temporarily living in something so cramped when there are perfectly good hotels everywhere.

As I climbed into it, I discovered that despite how monstrous it looked from the outside, the interior was claustrophobically small. And super efficient. Every inch was used for something... and often multiple somethings. The bathroom was a single unit – sink, toilet, and shower. It was a dream come true for multi-taskers. You could sit on the toilet and do your duty while you brush your teeth and take a shower. I could see how this could save a person precious time in the morning. The dinette table was designed to seat four adults, or two Gene-sized people. Theoretically it converted into a full size bed, but only for six year old kids or midgets. The bed was "upstairs", which meant it was stuffed into the miniscule space over the cab of the truck.

"So, this is what I'm going to use for the office?" I asked hoping that he was going to rent a nice, normal motel room with a real bathroom for me in Stanville.

"Yup. Office *and* your home away from home. Wunnerful, ain't it?"

I took a few deep breaths to calm myself so I wouldn't scream something like, "Are you *nuts*? I'm not living in this... this... thing." Once I'd taken enough deep breaths to put myself in a hyperventilated state, I calmly replied through clenched teeth "Yeah. Wunnerful. Just wunnerful."

"Well, we better get going. We're burning daylight. The foundation sub is meeting us at nine this morning. Ol' Blue hasn't been run for a while, so we better get goin' so we can take it a little easy on the old guy."

"Do you think this thing is safe to actually drive on public roads?"

"Huh? Oh. HARHARHARHAR," he laughed appreciatively, his belly bouncing up and down with each "har." "That's a good one," he said as a few more guffaws erupted from him and then faded away. "Go ahead and get in. Here's the key. Ol' Blue should start right up."

There was no point in telling Gene that I wasn't the one making the joke. He *had* to be kidding about actually driving this rust pile down the freeway. As an added challenge, we had to take a ferry across Puget Sound just to get to the freeway and all vehicles had to be turned off while the ferry was under way. What if this pile of corrosion and rust wouldn't start when the ferry docked and we couldn't drive it off the ferry? I'd seen before how humiliating it was for people when the ferry crew had to push their crippled car off the ferry and all the other passengers looked on, smugly grateful it wasn't them.

"Gene, just in case there's some trouble with Ol' Blue getting off the ferry, I think you should drive it off. I think it needs a real man to handle it."

"Whatsa matter, girl? You afraid you can't handle this big ol' rig?" he looked at me quizzically.

8

"Yeah. Yeah, that's it. I can't handle it. You being a man, all mechanical and stuff, it would be better if you do it. I'll drive your car to the Park N Ride at the top of the hill. When you get there we can change vehicles," I said, hoping I sounded more casual about the whole Ol' Blue ferry ordeal than I felt.

"Okay. But just this once. You gotta learn how to handle this rig because I ain't comin' up to Stanville just to drive it to the trailer dump," he said disgustedly.

Trailer dump? What the heck was that? Was it like a garbage dump for old, dead campers and trailers? Was it possible that I'd be so lucky as to get to drive this rolling wreck to the special place where terminally rusted RVs went to die? Maybe there was hope after all. I'd find out later. Right now I didn't want Gene to think I was a complete moron by asking him what a "trailer dump" was.

"Let's git movin'. Git in and start 'er up," he ordered.

Like a whupped puppy, I slunk into the front seat of Ol' Blue and turned the key. Drat. It started right up.

I pulled out onto the highway and floorboarded the gas pedal. This effort resulted in Ol' Blue reaching the local speed limit of 35 mph in only a little over a mile and a half. It was then I noticed that in order to keep all six tires on the asphalt, I needed to use some extremely proactive steering methodology. The camper made the truck top-heavy, causing Ol' Blue to sway back and forth like a fat old woman lumbering down a grocery store aisle, staggering first in one direction and then in some other random direction.

I was comforted in knowing that Gene would have no problem finding me as I drove down the highway. As Ol' Blue and I trundled along the road, the copious amounts of thick black smoke that were belching from the exhaust left an obvious trail.

Finally, we reached the ferry dock, Ol' Blue and I. Gene was right in front of me in the waiting line, sitting comfortably and looking as if he were on a luxury cruise. His car – well, actually Ginnie's car – was probably the original source of the term "land yacht. It was an older Lincoln convertible, white with navy trim and decorated in a nautical theme with little chrome anchors cleverly attached to it in strategic places. I wasn't sure which was more embarrassing to drive – Ol' Blue or the land yacht.

I kept Ol' Blue idling until we were directed onto the ferry, despite glares from a few people holding their noses in the cars next to me. As soon as I was directed onto the ferry and got Ol' Blue parked on the deck, I jumped out, found Gene, and pushed the keys for the hideous truck at him. I held my hand out for his car keys, which he reluctantly dropped into my waiting palm. It seemed he wasn't too overjoyed at having to drive his beloved Ol' Blue either.

Ferries are a way of life for anyone living on the Olympic Peninsula in Washington. Unlike many of the locals, though, I love riding on the ferries. This particular adventure was over way too soon and before I knew it, I had arrived at the top of the hill where Gene and I were to trade vehicles.

The hour drive up the freeway to Stanville took an hour and a half, but otherwise was fairly unexceptional. That is if you discount all the strange looks, hand signals of obvious meaning, and unintelligible comments I got from people who passed me in their boring, normal cars. I didn't even get sea-sick from the swaying of Ol' Blue as it lumbered down the highway at the daring speed of almost 45 mph. I discovered quite early in my relationship with Ol' Blue that speeds faster than that caused it to have an extreme waddle, often causing it to suddenly veer one way or another, sometimes into another lane of traffic. This was not a desirable feature, in my estimation.

We finally arrived at the jobsite, and I parked on some flat dirt next to where Gene had parked the land yacht. As I jumped out of Ol' Blue, grateful to have arrived with nothing important falling off of it during the trip, I took a few moments to survey the building site.

As jobsites go, this one looked fairly unimposing to me. Simple, even. But then, looks can often be deceiving, as I've often discovered.

# Chapter 3

I found Gene kicking at the dirt on the edge of a narrow ditch. We stood there for a few minutes, slowly rotating like pigs on a BBQ spit, as we looked at the job site in its entirety. There wasn't much to see at this stage of the construction. A pile of dirt with a trench around it where the store was to be built, the old run-down house and garage that had to be torn down or moved, and the swampy area in between the two was about all there was.

"Where the heck is that guy? He said he'd meet me here at 9:30. I don't have all day to wait around for subcontractors to decide if they're gonna show up," Gene grumbled.

"Who is this guy?" I asked.

"The foundation sub. We agreed to meet here this morning. He should be here by now," he said, kicking at the dirt again, more aggressively this time.

"I'm sure he'll be here soon. Maybe he got delayed at another job or something. Just relax," I said soothingly to Gene.

"Don't tell me to relax. He should be here by now. We're ready to start construction and he bygawd better get here soon or I'll fire him before he even starts the job," Gene growled at me.

This was a side of Gene I'd never seen before. He'd always been Mr. Nice Guy, always smiling and congenial. Where did this Mr. Mad Guy come from? Maybe he needed more coffee, too.

"While we wait for this guy, why don't you show me where you want Ol' blue parked. Then you can help me get the camper set up and show me where things are and how they work," I suggested, trying to distract him from his growing anger with the tardy foundation sub.

"Yeah, that's a good idea," he said and turned to walk over to where I'd parked the truck. I stumbled along after him, watching the uneven ground for potholes. When he abruptly stopped I almost ran into him. One shouldn't tailgate, even when walking.

"Here oughta be good," he said waving his arms around to indicate the space where he wanted Ol' Blue. "It's real close to the pay phone, so when the phone guy comes he can just string a wire from the pay phone over to the truck," he said.

*"Can it possibly get any classier?"* I thought. "Great idea," I said out loud. No sense in getting Gene riled up any more than he already was. I jumped in Ol' Blue and maneuvered the lump of rust around to approximately the position he'd indicated.

"That's good," he shouted. "Park 'er right there. C'mon, let's go over to the house and I'll introduce you to Maude and Henry."

"Who are Maude and Henry?" I asked.

"They're the couple who live in the old house. You might say they're the 'managers' of this here little gas station," Gene informed me.

I looked more closely at the house that was squeezed onto a small corner of the property and, sure enough, two ancient gas pumps stood outside the front of the house. The small yard may have once been a bit of green lawn with a few flowers, but now was oil-soaked gravel with two rusty old gas pumps. The front bedroom of the tiny house had been converted into some kind of office and cashier booth.

"Maude and Henry get free housing plus a small salary in return for taking the customer's money after they've pumped their own gas," Gene explained to me as we walked over to the back of the house. He banged loudly enough on the back door to make it bend inward with each knock. "Maude's a bit hard of hearing and Henry's always got the TV blaring," he offered as an explanation when he noticed me looking at him with big eyes. I was feeling a little skittish around him right now. After all, less than two minutes ago he'd been about one degree under exploding about the concrete sub. His moods seemed to come and go as quickly as the sun behind wind-blown clouds.

# Studs

Just then the door slowly creaked open and a round, doughy face appeared. "Hiya, Gene. This must be the gal you was telling me about. What'd you say her name was?" she asked Gene while giving me the once-over.

"I'm Katlin," I informed her.

"Glad to meet ya," Maude slurred at me through thick, flapping lips unblocked by any visible teeth. Her unkempt hair was of a color somewhere between fireplace-ash grey and dingy white. The dress she had on perfectly matched some brightly flowered fabric I'd seen in a Bag-O-Rags I'd bought at a discount store. The rags were much cleaner, though.

"Hello, Maude. Nice to meet you, too," I said politely, shaking hands with her.

"Henry. HENRY! Come meet the nice girl who's going to build the new store. HENREEEE!" She yelled at her husband, who, along with something furry, was dozing in a recliner.

"Hunh? Maude, you don't have to yell. I can hear ya plain as day," Henry barely spoke loudly enough to be heard over the TV. He was so thin there was room for him and several other people in the ratty old Naugahyde recliner. Everything about him was beige – his skin, what was left of his stringy hair, his teeth. He even wore some sort of beige shirt and pants that could possibly have been a uniform of some kind once upon a time.

Just then, the furry thing next to him began to move and a black nose appeared from one end. "Meet Fuzzles, our widdle puppy-wuddy," Maude gushed. "Fuzzles meet Katlin, a new friend." Fuzzles suddenly realized there were new people in the room, people who might have treats and who might want to fondle his furry little body. He began wriggling so exuberantly that he slid out of his cradle in Henry's arms and fell on the floor. Embarrassed, he began to pee.

"What a cute little doggie," I managed to croak out. I hate dogs. They stink, they put their noses where they don't belong, they bark loudly and too often continually, usually at the most inopportune times. Plus they leave piles of brown smelly stuff where I inevitably step.

"Oh yes, he's our pride and joy. Isn't he, Henry. Our widdle snookie-wookums," she crooned to the dog while pretending to talk to her husband.

"Well, we better be getting back to the job site, right, Gene?" I said moving closer to the back door. "We don't want to miss the foundation sub," I suggested meaningfully.

"Oh, right. Well, we'll see you later. Nice to see you again," Gene said politely. It almost seemed as if two or more people lived inside of him. He could be mean as a cornered snake and then turn around and in a flash be a real sweetie, then just as quickly erupt in a lava flow of anger.

We walked in silence back to where Ol' Blue was parked, both immersed in our own thoughts. My thoughts were stuck on Maude and Henry. Hopefully I'd be too busy to build much of a friendship with them. I mean, face it. We had very little in common, starting with doggie love on their part. Ick.

Just then a cloud of dust roared around the corner, brakes screaming in agony as they tried to halt whatever was making the dust storm. From somewhere inside the dust cloud came the sound of a truck door creaking and groaning its unwillingness to move as someone tried to open it. Finally, a scrawny, disheveled man with an amazing likeness to one of those rubber dead chickens threw open the door and emerged from the truck. He walked a few steps, then just stood, slowly and steadily looking at the trench around the pile of dirt, unmoving until I began to wonder if he was still alive.

"Hey, Larry," Gene suddenly bellowed, startling both me and the rubber chicken man. "Over here," he yelled as he waved his arm, motioning for this new person to come toward us. "It's Larry," he said out of the side of his mouth. Like that name told me anything.

Larry slowly strode over to us, picking his way over the dirt and rocks piled in the center of the rectangular ditch.

"Hi, Gene. Sorry I'm late but I had phone calls and stuff. You know how it is," he said in a tone of voice that confided knowledge of the intricate ways of the manly world of construction-type business.

"Yeah. It happens. When are you going to start laying the rebar?" Gene asked Larry. Rebar, I knew, was construction lingo for reinforcing metal bars used to keep concrete from breaking up.

Aha. A clue. Rubber chicken guy must be the foundation sub.

"Well, let's see. Today's Monday. I can probably start first thing tomorrow. How's that?"

"That's great. You need anything from me?"

"Nope. I got a copy of the foundation plan and I can get the rebar delivered this afternoon. We're all set."

He and Gene just stood there, sticking their toes in the dirt and spitting occasionally, in the time-honored Male Bonding Ritual, Contractor Version.

I was beginning to feel invisible. This was just great. So far, my first and only subcontractor didn't seem to know of my existence. I loudly cleared my throat.

"Oh, yeah," Gene turned to me, suddenly remembering I was standing alongside him. "This here's Katlin. She's my Project Supe. Be nice to her, now," he winked at Larry, sharing some sort of private man code. "Katlin, this is Larry Luntz, your foundation sub."

"Glad to meet ya," Larry stuck his hand out for me to shake. There were calluses on his hand, a good sign. But his limp handshake was shaky and his eyes were awfully red. Not good signs. He looked very much like the wreck of a truck that he drove - in dire need of intense body work due to long term neglect and abuse.

"Hi, Larry. Good to meet you, too," I said, not really sure if I meant it.

"Okay. Everything's set, then. Right?" Gene inserted himself between Larry and me.

"Yep. We're all set to start tomorrow morning first thing," Larry confirmed.

"Great. Anything you need, just talk to Katlin, here," Gene said, then turned to walk back to his car. He concluded this conversation as abruptly as he did his phone conversations.

"Before you go, Larry, how do I get in touch with you in case something comes up? Do you have a business card?" I asked. Maybe Gene had given me his phone number in the thick file of papers for this job, but then again he was often a little casual about details.

"I don't have a phone, but evenings I'll be at the tavern. It's my office," he chuckled at his own wittiness.

Great. So I was going to have to deal with Don't Call Us We'll Call You Construction Company. "Yeah. Ok. See you tomorrow, Larry. First thing," I said in what I hoped was a Construction Supe tone of voice.

Larry catapulted himself back into the mass of dirt and dents that long ago had started life as a shiny pickup truck and roared off.

Granted, this was my first experience as a Project Superintendent, but I was pretty sure things were supposed to be more organized than they had been so far. Crazy thoughts began rattling around inside my head. I had big bad qualms about Larry, the concrete subcontractor. I didn't know if there were any other subs Gene had committed work to, and if there were, who they might be. In a flash the horrible realization came to me that I didn't know what I was doing and I didn't know what anybody else was doing, either. Nor did I even know if *they* knew what they were doing. This was not a promising start in my new career as Project Superintendent.

"Um, Gene? Do you have a signed contract with Larry?" I asked him as we walked back to Ol Blue.

"No. Why do you ask?"

"Oh, I don't know. I guess I just thought it might be a good idea, under the circumstances."

"Nah. A handshake's good with me," he replied.

Okay. So there was no contract between Larry and him. Even I, the greenest, most inexperienced Project Superintendent in the entire history of the construction industry, knew better than that. This was not good. I hoped Gene hadn't seen my mouth fall open when he informed me that there was no contract. I have absolutely no control over what my face does and take no responsibility for what shows up on it.

"Uh huh. Well then. Is there a list of the other subcontractors you've hired in that pile of paperwork Ginnie gave me?" I asked hopefully.

He stopped walking and turned to look me in the eyes for emphasis as he delivered the bad news. "There are no other subcontractors except for the usual electrical and plumbing guys I use. It's your job to hire the people you need," he explained slowly in an obvious effort at being patient with my obvious ignorance of the duties and responsibilities of his Project Supes.

It was at that exact moment that I discovered it was going to be up to me to find all the rest of the subcontractors I'd need - the framer, sheetrocker, roofer, flooring installer, acoustical ceiling installer, painter, glass installer, and who knew how many other subs. This all should have been arranged long before I showed up on the job to start construction. *Now* was not a good time to be trying to find subcontractors for this project.

He turned and continued walking until we reached the car. "Well, our work is done here," he announced proudly as he scanned the jobsite. What was he thinking? It wasn't as if we'd actually accomplished anything. I began to wonder if he might be just a half a bubble off level.

"Get in. I gotta get back to the office," he ordered.

We were driving onto the ferry when Gene dropped another surprise on me.

"By the way," he casually mentioned, "I've signed you up for a class in project management."

*Now* he signed me up for a project management class? I was beginning to suspect that Gene ran his company according to The Management by Crisis Theory.

"When am I going to have time to go to this class?" I asked.

"Relax. It's only one evening – next Tuesday. You can leave the job early. It's in Bellevue so you'll need to leave the job about two or so. Not a problem," he said with more confidence than I felt. He obviously didn't know rush hour traffic around the Seattle area like I did.

"Fine. Sounds good. I can use a little bit of touch-up in my project management skills," I countered with only a slight hint of sarcasm. A single three hour class was not going to magically turn me into a proficient Project Superintendent. I should have taken this class - and lots more - weeks, months, *years* ago.

At his place, we said our good-byes with him promising to be readily available should I need him for anything.

I went home to pack a few things for the week ahead and then drove right back to the job site. I'd be sleeping in my new home away from home that night. Each morning when I awoke, I'd have the world's shortest commute to work – about five steps from bunk to bumper.

It was late when I arrived at the job site, or as I'd begun to think of it, Casa del Construction. I threw my belongings into the back of the camper and climbed in after them. Luckily I didn't have a lot of belongings because there wasn't a whole lot of room to put them. One plastic garbage sack filled with clean clothes, one paper grocery sack with necessities such as soap, a toothbrush, and a few items of a personal nature were all the necessities I needed. I stashed the bag of clothes in some kind of cabinet, put the other sack on the 3" of counter space in the "kitchen", unrolled my sleeping bag in the upstairs Master Bedroom suite, tossed my pillow up after it, and I was set.

After a delicious and nutritious dinner of corn chips, clam dip, and a couple beers, it was beddie-bye time for this Construction Project Superintendent.

# Chapter 4

"What's the ceiling doing so close to my face?" I wondered. Okay. So I wasn't exactly thinking coherently. That's just how I am first thing when I wake up. I closed my eyes, hoping I was actually still asleep and just dreaming that the ceiling in my bedroom was mere inches from my nose.

Wait a minute. Where the heck was I?

I stealthily felt around the bed, afraid to turn my head to see if there was anyone else in bed with me. Nope. Good news: I was alone in bed. Bad news: I was alone in bed. Oh well. "Might as well get up," I told myself.

I rolled over and fell out of bed as I always did, hitting the floor. However, somebody must have moved my bed during the night, because the floor was at least 20 feet farther down than it should have been. Well, okay. Maybe six or eight feet. But it sure felt like 20 when I landed.

Carefully, I looked around, moving only my eyeballs in case I'd broken something of great importance. This was definitely not my bedroom. It looked more like a tiny child's playhouse. Little stove, little refrigerator, little table, little cabinets, little windows. And the bed, where I'd just recently been so safely tucked away, was up a little ladder.

What was this place and how did I get here? Oh wait. It was all coming back to me.

This miniature house was Ol' Blue and it was going to be my home, office, and Command Central for the next several months while I oversaw the building of a combo mini-mart and gas station. O joy of joys.

Now that I knew where I was, the next priority was to make sure everything in my body was still working. Ever so slowly I began moving things that were farthest from the main part of my body – toes, and fingers, then legs and arms. So far, so good. Everything seemed to be working. I carefully stood up, ready for my first day on my new job.

Well, almost ready. Since I was still dressed in my summer uniform – cutoff jeans and a tshirt – all I had to do to get ready for the day was brush my teeth and hair.

I found my bag-o-clothes and pawed through it until I found the implements I so desperately wanted – toothbrush, toothpaste, hairbrush and wash cloth. Holding onto them as if they were life preservers, I entered the Master Bath. I could hardly wait to scrub the fur off my teeth. With happy anticipation I applied the toothpaste to my toothbrush, turned the handle on the faucet ...and kept turning the handle. What the heck was going on? No water was coming out of the faucet even though I'd turned it to Full Blast setting.

Well, I'd just call Gene. He'd be able to tell me what's wrong and how to fix it. Then suddenly I remembered that I didn't have a phone. The phone had yet to be hooked up to the camper. That was one of those Project Superintendent jobs for me to figure out.

There was nothing left for me to do but humbly knock on Maude and Henry's door and beg them for some water.

Quickly as I could, I trotted over to their back door and knocked gingerly. No response. Oh yeah. I forgot Maude was hard of hearing. I stepped back a bit, the better to get a good swing as I banged a few times on the door. Finally I could hear Maude's muffled voice telling me that she was coming. After a few minutes I banged again.

"Yeah, I'm coming," she yelled again. I jumped back in surprise as she creaked the door open.

"Hi, Maude," I said sheepishly. "I don't seem to have any water in the camper and I was wondering if I could use your bathroom to brush my teeth and wash my face."

"Oh, honey, sure you can. C'mon in. Don't mind the mess. Just step over these here newspapers. The bathroom's right down here," she pointed me down a dark hallway.

Somehow I managed to navigate through the narrow tunnel of ancient newspapers and magazines to find the bathroom door and light switch. A few minutes later I emerged, feeling like a new woman. Well, at least a woman without furry teeth.

"Thanks so much, Maude. There must be something broken on the camper. Do you suppose I could impose on you to use your phone and call Gene to tell him about this?" I asked her.

"Well, sure you can. Just write the phone number down on this here form so's we can get paid from the gas company for your call. They charge us for long distance calls unless they's business," she said as she handed me a stub of a pencil.

"Not exactly your high budget operation," I mumbled to myself, knowing that Maude couldn't hear me. I dialed Gene's number and waited for what seemed like an infinite length of time, during which Maude was standing directly in front of me, staring at me.

Finally Ginnie answered the phone. "G & G Construction. How may I help you," her voice had never sounded so sweet to me.

I turned my back to Maude, giving myself the illusion of privacy. "Hi, Ginnie. This is Katlin. I'm up on the job site and I can't seem to get the water to work in the camper. Is Gene around? Maybe he knows what's wrong with it."

"I can tell you what's wrong with it," she replied, sounding just a little testy. "I told him to get that ol' thing ready for you, but he kept procrastinating and procrastinating. He never filled up the water tank. Now you're up there and probably nothing will work because everything's empty. That man can drive a woman to drink. Here's what you have to do. Get a garden hose and hook it up to the faucet on the outside of the old house. Never mind what that old couple say about it. They aren't paying for the water, even though they'll probably gripe like they are. They may even have a hose you can borrow. Then go around to the left side of the camper. There's a little door. Just open it and you'll see where you can hook up the water."

"Wow. Thanks so much, Ginnie. I've never used a camper before so this is all new to me," I said gratefully.

"Well, there's probably more you'll discover. Just give me a call. It's my old camper so I know pretty much everything that needs to be done. Did he show you how to use the stove?" she asked.

"No, but it can't be that hard. Just turn the knobs and light the burner with a match, right?" I asked hopefully.

"Yeah, IF there's any propane gas in the tank. Well, I guess you'll find out. Good luck. Call me if you need me," and she hung up.

I turned around to thank Maude for the use of her phone, and almost bumped into her nose. I'd forgotten she was standing watch over me as I used her phone.

"Thanks, Maude," I said as graciously as I could while backing away from her. "It looks like there's going to be a bit of an adjustment period for me while I get everything sorted out and hooked up."

"That's okay, honey. You just come over anytime you need anything. We're happy to help," she said, sounding as if she truly meant it. I was beginning to change my first impression of these people as Maude's genuine offer to help gave me a glimpse of her true nature. She reminded me of geodes I'd seen in rock shops. Rough and ugly on the outside, but inside they were filled with incredibly beautiful, brilliant crystals.

"Oh. That reminds me. Ginnie... you know, Gene's girlfriend? She said that I could hook a garden hose up to your water for the camper. She said you don't pay for the water. Is that right?"

"Lemme think." There was a pause that seemed to drag on longer than it probably did before she spoke again. I guess it took her a while to do her thinking. "Yep. I think Thomas Oil pays for our water and our electricity."

"They pay for your electricity, too? If so, then maybe I could string an extension cord over here to get power to the camper. Otherwise I won't be able to see a thing at night inside that thing."

"Fine with me. Don't cost us nothin'," Maude generously offered.

"Um. You wouldn't happen to have an extra garden hose and an extension cord lying around, would you," I asked, hoping I wasn't taking too much advantage of her good and generous nature.

"Henry's probably got one out back somewhere. HENRY!" she yelled at me. Henry, it seemed, was in the room directly behind me.

"What now, Maude," Henry replied in his perpetually weary-sounding voice. I wasn't sure if he was always tired or if he used this voice in an attempt to discourage repeated requests from Maude to do some sort of chore.

"Do we have an extry garden hose and electrical cord for Katlin, here," she yelled again. I moved aside so as to be out of the way of any further wifely communications directed at Henry.

"Dunno."

"Well, git up and go look for them," she ordered, then turned to me. "Honestly, that man is useless. I only keep him around because I feel sorta sorry for him. We been married 47 years and not oncet has he done any work without me telling him to get movin'."

Aha. So this was the secret of marriage longevity. Husband badgering.

"Well, uh, thanks for your help, Maude. I better get back over to the camper and, um, check on the plans before the foundation subcontractor gets here," I mumbled as I edged toward the door. "I'll come back later and see if Henry found the hose and cord." I made as graceful an exit as I could.

On the way back to the camper, I wondered what other little challenges might surprise me on this job as Project Superintendent.

I wondered, too, if others who held this position had similar experiences. Probably not. It wasn't just any Project Superintendent who got to live in an ancient, rusty camper with no phone, water, or electricity, smack dab in the middle of a dusty job site in Stanville.

# Chapter 5

As I strolled from Maude's house back to the camper, I glanced toward the mound of dirt that marked the pad where the store was to be built. Something was moving. Being a good little Supe, I decided to detour over that way and find out what it was. Probably just kids playing in the dirt, and I'd have to chase them off, which didn't please me. Some of my most pleasant memories as a child were playing with my little cars in the dirt, making roads and tunnels. I could understand how kids would be drawn to this mountainous pile of dirt.

I was astounded to see it wasn't kids at all. It was Larry!

"Larry! You're here!" I said, my joy and relief at seeing him obvious even to him.

"Yep. Said I would," he said without stopping his work. He was tying baling wire, or tie wire as it's known in the construction industry, around long pieces of rebar to hold them in place while the concrete was poured into the footings and walls.

Normally building the footings would have been a separate operation from building the foundation walls, but I was tight for time so I made an executive decision to do both walls and footings at the same time. To make it even more interesting, the walls were 8' high. The bottom half of the walls would eventually be backfilled and under dirt. The top 4' was supposed to stave off any flood waters that might roll in from one or both of the rivers that were on either side of the job site.

As badly as Larry's hands were shaking from what I suspected was a hangover, I figured it was a good thing he wasn't operating anything more dangerous than pliers and wire cutters. I didn't much care how shaky his work was as long as it passed the inspection which needed to be done before the concrete was poured.

"You better call the cement company and get concrete scheduled for a pour in two days. I'll be done with the footings tomorrow," he informed me as he continued to work. I was fascinated with the way his Adam's apple bounced up and down in his scrawny neck when he talked. It looked like someone was playing with a yo-yo in his throat.

"Uh, yeah. I'll do that," I said, dragging my attention away from the throat yo-yo back to the conversation we were having. "By the way, what did you say was the name of that company where you like to get your concrete," I asked, slyly tricking him into giving me the information I needed while trying to not appear even more dumb than I felt.

He answered without looking up at me. "I didn't. But it's Acme."

So much for my sly trick. "Great. Thanks. I'll call them right away."

Before I called them, however, I had to figure out how much concrete to order. Luckily, Gene had left me the set of plans and specs, along with some other paperwork which I hadn't had time to go through yet. Maybe the list of materials that some other estimator had figured was in there and I'd only have to locate that information and call it in.

I started to walk back to the camper, when Larry stopped me. "You better call the building inspector to get his OK before the concrete pour," he yelled. I waved my acknowledgement at him, acting like I already knew that, as I continued walking to the camper. What did he think I was, stupid or something?

I hoped the building inspector's name and phone number, along with the building permit, were in the mess of papers somewhere. When I got back to the camper I was relieved to find the building permit on top of a pile of papers. That little problem was half solved. A knock on the camper door solved the rest of it.

I swung the camper door open wide and saw an extremely portly man backpeddling as fast as he could. As he obviously just realized, camper doors swing outward – a space-saving feature no doubt.

# Studs

"Sorry. Can I help you?" I asked.

"Old Henry said the Project Superintendent was in here," he replied, nodding toward the house so I'd know which Old Henry he was referring to.

"Yes. That's me. I'm the Project Superintendent."

He looked me up and down while I reciprocated.

I guess I wasn't what he was expecting. A man with a crew cut wearing a flannel shirt, jeans, and work boots, was probably more along the lines of his expectations of what a proper Project Superintendent should look like. Instead, what he was seeing was a woman with shoulder-length hair the color of burgundy wine wearing very short cut-off jeans, a tshirt imprinted with "The Lady's Sewing Circle and Terrorist Society", and flip-flops.

I wasn't sure what I was looking at. He was an older gent, probably close to retirement age, dressed in dark, polyester no-iron/no wrinkle slacks and black, thick-soled cop shoes. His white, short-sleeved nylon shirt was stretched so tight over his belly I was afraid the buttons would pop off and go flying at any minute. He was an inch or two over 6' and seemed to be almost as wide as he was tall. He had the face of a farmer – big, red apples for cheeks and squint lines radiating from his eyes.

"I see," he said after forcibly gathering his wits about him. "Well, I'm Phil Mikelson, the building inspector for Stanville, and I'd like to see your building permit, soils evaluation, and compaction test results," he said in a voice that managed to combine friendliness with official overtones. He'd probably had years to perfect the combination.

"Here's the building permit," I said as I grabbed it from the top of the dinette table where I had everything spread out. "What's a soils evaluation?"

His hand stopped in midair as it was moving to grab the building permit. His mouth went slack for a moment before he could overcome his amazement at my monumental lack of intelligence and completely non-existent competence. "It's the environmental engineer's report for the soil compaction."

"Oh. I see. Um. What's soil compaction?" I asked, almost afraid he'd haul me off to jail for criminal stupidity.

"That pile of dirt," he said pointing toward where Larry was working, "was hauled in here. It's not what you call your 'native soil.' Digging it up, hauling it here, dumping, and dozing fluffs it up. It needs to be compacted until it's dense enough for you to put your building on. Otherwise your store might just possibly sink into the ground until only the roof is visible," he patiently explained to me in tones usually heard from kindergarten teachers.

"Would you like to come in while I look through the paperwork I was given for this job? I just got here today and haven't had a chance to see what I was given. I can offer you cold lemonade," I babbled. Again, I heard the familiar refrain of my mantra, "What have I gotten myself into" as it echoed through my head.

"Lemonade would be nice. It's rather a hot day already, isn't it?" Phil said as he climbed up into the cramped interior of my home office. I backed up, giving him room to squeeze his bulk into the camper. As he settled himself in the dinette, he looked at me curiously. "How did you get this job?" he asked, amazingly without any trace of sarcasm.

I told him my long story as we sat and enjoyed our bottles of icy lemonade. Either he was a patient listener or he wasn't anxious to get back to the office.

"Well, I'll help you all I can. I live just across the bridge on the island," he said, pointing to the long, concrete bridge that linked the mainland to Camas Island. "I drive past here every day. I'll stop by occasionally to see how you're doing. If you need me for a specific inspection, you can call me at this number and I'll stop by on my way home in the afternoon or on my way to work in the morning," he said as he handed me his business card. "Maybe we can enjoy another lemonade together," he hinted. I made a mental note to buy a case or two of the sweet drink. One can never be too nice to building inspectors.

"Thank you so much for your help. I'll find out the name of the company who did the soils testing and get those compaction tests to you before we start the concrete pour," I said, truly grateful to him for being so helpful and for not putting a "stop work" red flag on the project.

"By the way, if you want to know the best place to eat around here, it's the Daisy Café, just over one block and up two. You'll know it by all the cars in the parking lot. My wife, Mavis, owns it and she's the best cook in this county," he said with pride, puffing his already sizeable chest out even more.

"*Ah. That explains much*," I thought, discreetly glancing at his girth. Aloud I said, "Again, I thank you. I'm sure I'm not going to want to do much cooking in this tin can. I always appreciate good cooking."

"Be sure and have a piece of pie after your meal. My Mavis makes pies you'd sell your soul for. I should know. I'm walking proof of how good her pies and her cooking are," he said with a twinkle in his eye, patting his "walking proof".

"Oh, and one more thing," he continued. "If you want to avoid an expensive fine by OSHA, you'll save your shorts for the beach. You need to wear full length jeans, a long-sleeved shirt, and work boots. I know, I know," he said holding up his hands to ward off a comment I hadn't even begun yet. "It's summer and too hot for work boots and long sleeved shirts. But I'm telling you, OSHA can not only fine you, they can shut your job down."

"Thanks for the warning. I sure don't need a fine nor do I want to get on the wrong side of the OSHA inspector... or any other inspectors," I said meaningfully.

I already liked this man. I was grateful for his kindness and generosity. His offer to stop by on his way home from work was going to be of undeniable help to me. Unlike the way most building inspectors worked, I wouldn't have to wait for days or even weeks to have him schedule inspections for the various portions of the job. I felt comforted knowing that any questions about permits and inspections I might have would probably be easily and willingly answered by this kind man.

After Phil drove off, once again I trundled up to Maude and Henry's to use their phone. The first call would be to the phone company to have my own phone installed. The second call would be to Gene. I had to find out about those soils engineer's reports.

Maude answered the door several minutes after I'd banged loudly on it. The stacks of newspapers and magazines they'd been saving for years, just in case they might someday need them, had scrunched the width of the hallways into paths that barely allowed her to pass. Henry, being not much more than skin over bones, had no trouble moving through the narrow trails. But Maude was more sizeable and it took her some effort to squeeze through some of the more narrow passageways.

"Well, hello there! Long time, no see!" she croaked with laughter at her little joke. Her voice reminded me of someone. Who was it? Oh, yeah. Ma Kettle.

"Hi again, Maude. Sorry to bother you again so soon, but may I use your phone? I want to call the phone company and have them set me up with my own phone. And I have a kind of emergency on the job site," I explained.

Her face lit up with the prospect of hearing some disastrous news about the job site. Real life drama was always much more interesting than the contrived plots on the soap operas she watched. "Come in, come in. You know where the phone is. Just remember to write your phone numbers down. I'll make us a little snack and we can have a little girlie chat when you're done," she said.

"*Probably aerosol cheese and stale saltine crackers*," I said quietly to myself, not even making my lips move. The thought made my mouth go dry and my stomach scrunch up. "Maybe another time, Maude", I said loudly enough for her to hear. "I have to get back to the camper and go through some paperwork to catch up on this job." It was the best lame excuse I could come up with on such short notice.

"Okay. Another time, I guess," she said, crestfallen. "I just took some chocolate chip cookies out of the oven and they're still warm.

Chocolate chip cookies!! I'd give my ex-mother-in-law's right arm for chocolate chip cookies. "Well, maybe I'll have a few minutes after I make these calls," I offered generously.

"Okay! Tomorrow I'll make my famous cinnamon oatmeal cookies and we can have us some girl time over cookies and coffee," she said.

"Oatmeal cookies. Yum," I said, wiping away the drool from the corners of my mouth. What was wrong with Henry? How could he be so skinny with a wife who baked cookies every day?

I turned back to the chores at hand, beginning with the phone company. I've always hated dealing with mega-corporations and governmental departments. The people who work in places like that have no creativity. They do what they're told to do and no more. I think some of them get a fiendish delight from telling customers how many ways they *can't* help them. I was expecting something similar when I called the phone company and wasn't disappointed.

"I'll need an address for the phone hook-up. 'The camper by the pay phone in the parking lot by the new mini-mart' is not an address," the woman who controlled the destiny of my phone informed me.

"Look. This is a construction site. There is no address for the building. There isn't even a building yet," I explained.

"I'm sorry," she said in that sing-song way that's so annoying. I could tell by the smirk in her voice that she really wasn't sorry. "There's nothing I can do." I heard a faint snicker after she said this last bit, I swear.

Arghh! I hate it when people tell me there's nothing they can do. It forces me to do immoral acts, like lying. "Just a moment," I said sweetly to her.

"Maude!" I yelled. "What's the address here?"

"4719 Stanville Camas Road."

"Thanks."

"Okay. You win. Here's the address. 4719 Stanville Camas Road. Will that work?" I asked.

"We're showing a phone already at that address," she continued, heroically continuing to carry out her mission of being as non-helpful as possible. I firmly believe the phone company sends them to classes to learn this.

"Yes. That's true. We want another phone line installed."' Well, it wasn't completely a lie.

"One moment," she intoned nasally. To her credit, she did not put me on hold. I heard some computer keys clacking before she returned her attention to me. "I have the installation set up. The installer will be out on Thursday to install your new phone line. Will someone be there?" she asked, always the efficient phone company employee.

"Yes. Someone will be here all day," I assured her.

We signed off with her spouting the usual formal and insincere "thank you for doing business with your local phone company" stuff.

Oboy. Only a couple more days and I'd have my own phone. Life was getting better by the minute. Now to call Gene and ask about the soils reports. I figured it should only take a couple of minutes since either he or Ginnie probably had the information conveniently within reach.

# Chapter 6

"G and G Construction," Ginnie finally answered the phone after several rings.

"Hi, Ginnie. It's me, Katlin. I have a slight problem. Is Gene there?"

"No, he had a meeting with the people at Thomas Oil. I think he's got another one of these mini-marts to build. Isn't that fabulous?"

"Well, yeah, except he's already so short-handed, where will he find people to do the work?"

"Well, you just better hurry up and build that one up in Stanville so you can do another one."

"Thanks for the vote of confidence, but I think I'll see how this one goes before I commit to another one. I've already run into a problem. Maybe you can help me."

"What is it, honey?" Didn't anyone at G and G remember I had a name?

"The building inspector stopped by the jobsite today and asked for the soils engineer's reports. I can't find them in the paperwork Gene gave me. Do you have them there?" I asked.

"No, I don't. And you won't find them anywhere in that mess of papers he gave you. I told that man that he couldn't cut corners like that. I told him he'd end up having to pay in the end. I told him," she added for emphasis.

A small, cold pebble of dread was starting to form in my stomach. "What are you talking about?" I asked as my jaws began to tighten.

"He knew all that dirt had to be compacted and tested, but he figured a podunk town like Stanville wouldn't have a building inspector who would be as strict or as savvy as one in a big city, like Seattle," she answered.

"So, are you telling me that he never had the soil compacted?" I asked, my voice beginning to get all screechy like it does when I stress out. The cold pebble was rapidly growing into a boulder.

"Yep, that's pretty much it. You might want to call Thomas Oil and talk to the project architect there. His name is Bob Something. Here's the number," and she rattled off the phone number for the oil company's headquarters in Tacoma.

"Thanks, Ginnie. I'll give them a call and see what help they can give me." If any, I thought to myself. I quickly hung up the phone and dialed the number she'd given me.

"Thomas Oil," a nasal female voice informed me.

"May I speak to the project architect for the store in Stanville? I think his name is Bob," I offered helpfully. They probably only had about 75 Bobs working there.

"Thank you. I'll connect you now," she intoned.

*Only one Bob? Must not be a very big company*, I mused to myself while I waited on hold.

"Bob here," said a wheezy male voice.

"Hi, Bob. This is Katlin Greene, the project Superintendent at the Stanville job. I just ran into a little problem and I hope you can help me," I said.

"Wellllll, I don't know. I'm just the architect and...," he whined as he began to back-peddle.

"It's really a simple thing," I interrupted before he could put me on hold while he thought of someone else to transfer me and my problem to. "You see, the building inspector came by today and he asked me for the soil compaction reports. I don't have them and I thought maybe you would," I said hopefully.

"No, I wouldn't have such a thing. I only have the construction drawings. You'd need to talk to the designing engineer at the engineering company for that," he sounded much relieved now that the problem appeared to be in someone else's department.

"Who is the engineer? Do you have the phone number of the company?" I asked him. I was beginning to feel like Alice down the rabbit hole, wandering from one unreal scenario to another.

"I think I've got it... yes, here it is. Ready?" he asked and then carefully gave me the information, asking me to repeat it back to him so he could make sure I got it right. Bob, ever the careful, detail-oriented architect, absolutely did *not* want to be responsible for *any* errors, no matter how small or insignificant they might be. And that obviously included giving out phone numbers.

"Thanks, Bob. I appreciate this." I hung up and dialed the engineering firm that had originally done the soils tests for this project.

"Worldwide Geotechnological Engineering," said a pleasant female voice. What a difference from the receptionist at Thomas Oil. *This* company probably paid decent wages, resulting in a classier level of employee.

"Hello, this is Katlin Greene. I'm the Project Superintendent for the mini-mart that Thomas Oil is building in Stanville. I need to talk to the engineer who did the original soils tests," I explained, trying to sound as professional as she did.

"Thank you. That would be Bob. I'll connect you," and she was gone.

*Another Bob? Maybe Bob is a favorite name for architects, engineers, and others of that ilk*, I amused myself with the thought while I was once again on hold.

"Hello. This is Bob. How can I help you," a gentle friendly voice said.

I went through my story while he quietly listened.

"Oh, yes. I remember that job. I did the preliminary soils evaluation on it but never heard back from anyone, so I thought they'd abandoned the project. There were six or seven lifts of 12", each of imported soil that had to be compacted," he said.

"I've got the foundation sub here ready to pour concrete in two days and the building inspector wants to see my compaction reports from you. Now you're telling me the compaction was never done? What can I do?" I said, trying desperately not to whine.

"The bottom line is that the soil needs to be of a certain density. Typically, that's done in one of two ways. The most common method is the one you're asking about – compacting the soil mechanically. The other method is to bring the soil in, grade it, and let it set for a minimum of a year, during which time nature will take care of the compaction," he explained.

"Well, the first method didn't happen and the second isn't going to. I don't have a year to sit around and wait for the soil to compact all by itself. I just got started on this job yesterday and the company I work for has a contract to complete the project within 90 days. If I can't start construction this week we'll never be able to make up the lost time. My boss will end up paying a hefty fine for each day the project isn't done beyond the completion date in the contract and he'll never get another job from Thomas Oil," I explained, the stress of the situation beginning to make my voice to sound all screechy.

"Tell you what I'll do. I'll send one of my guys out tomorrow morning first thing and he can retest the soil to see what the compaction is right now. We did those original tests about six months ago. The soil should be somewhat more compacted now. After I get the new numbers I'll have a better idea of what options you have," he said, sounding like a doctor who wants to test for everything before he ventures to give an opinion as to which treatment he's going to torture his patient with.

"Thanks. I really appreciate this. I'll talk to your guy tomorrow," and we both hung up.

I really needed a chocolate chip cookie. Bad. Maude was looking more and more like she just might become my best friend in the whole world. I put a friendly smile on my face and turned around to tell Maude I was ready for our little tete-a-tete. She was more than ready, and shoved a mug of hot, steaming coffee toward me with one hand, and with the other set a plateful of cookies on my lap.

It only took me five minutes to down the first two cups of Maude's coffee. It was just the way I like it... so black and thick you could use it to pave roads. All I can say about her cookies is that I've never met a chocolate chip cookie I didn't like, but hers came close to being the first. It must have taken her years to perfect the technique of getting the edges burnt to just the right shade of ebony while the middle of the cookie was still half raw. If this was an example of the rest of her cooking, the mystery of Henry's svelte figure was solved.

*She probably doesn't have much in the way of visitors*, I guessed from the way and she cleverly detained me with her coffee, cookies, and constant jabbering. I busied myself with downing her coffee and chewing on the baked part of her cookies, feeding the raw parts to Fuzzles under the table. Finally, I extricated myself from her company and walked over toward the building site to tell Larry about the latest predicament.

I didn't see him right away, so I figured he must be working on the other side of the dirt mound. After walking around the mound twice, searching for him in the trench, I finally had to acknowledge that Larry wasn't there. He must have worked all of about, oh, maybe an hour. Well, he could run but he couldn't hide. I knew where to find him.

I hopped in my truck and drove to the tavern. Like most taverns in small towns, the Lucky Horseshoe Bar and Grill opened at 8 in the morning to catch the early trade. It was mid-morning and the bar was already busy with those who needed "some hair of the dog that bit them". The bar was filled with the old boys on Social Security who had a life-long habit of rising early and the workers who had just gotten off the graveyard shift at the local animal rendering plant and lived an upside-down life. But Larry wasn't with them. Not this morning, anyway.

Well, I'd go looking for him later tonight. Right now I had plenty of other issues to work on. Like finding a framing subcontractor, for one. I'd need the framers to get started within the next two weeks. I also needed to get the lumber list from whoever did the estimating for this job and get the materials ordered. I hoped there was such a list. Otherwise, I'd end up having to calculate the materials – an unnecessary and time-wasting duplication of effort.

I also had some other, more important things to do. I needed to get some groceries. There wasn't even one single stale potato chip in the camper and I wasn't going to spend every evening in the only eatery in town that was open after 4pm – the smoke-filled Lucky Horseshoe Bar and Grill. Eating their greasy microwaved hamburgers could be hazardous to my health. Or even worse, I could be forced to eat their simulated pizza, manufactured from a crust of cardboard, topped with white gluey cheese and orange grease. Nor could I live on Maude's cookies and lethal coffee for breakfast.

It took five minutes to find the only grocery store in Stanville, fifteen minutes to get the few groceries I could store in the eensy "kitchen" of my Casa de Construction, and another five minutes to drive all the way back to the job site.

After carefully storing my few groceries, I figured I'd spent enough time on being domestic. Next I wanted take care of my "home improvements." I still had no water and no power. I had a hunch I was going to learn more about the fine art of Husband Badgering very soon.

I walked over to Maude and Henry's, knocking loudly on the back door for Maude's benefit. During the time it took for Maude to navigate through the forest of old newspapers, I let my gaze wander, looking around at the neighborhood. How had I managed to miss the fact that an ice cream shop was right across the street? Things were looking up in Stanville. Just then Maude opened the creaky door and her face wrinkled up in a smile when she saw me.

"Hi Maude. I was just wondering if Henry had found the garden hose and electrical cord like we talked about earlier. I can haul them over to the camper and hook them up if he's too busy," Too busy. Right. Too busy watching TV with the volume turned up to decibels that would drown out the sound of jets breaking the sound barrier.

"Lemme check for ya. HENREEEEEE!!," she howled toward the front of the house. After a few moments there was no response. "I better go see what that man's up to. You just stay right here and I'll be right back," she assured me.

By the time she got back with Henry in tow I would have had enough time scarf down three cookies, if she'd offered them to me.

"Henry's going to help you hook up your water and electricity, aren't you, Henry?" she directed this last at him with the meanest look I've ever seen on a human face. It made me kinda wonder about the origins of her species.

"Yes, Maude," Henry sighed with a great act of martyrdom. He must have been exhausted from flipping channels all day.

Henry and I walked to the side of the house where a little falling-down shed was cleverly hidden amidst bramble bushes that had completely grown over the entire end of the house. Going into the shed was sort of like entering another world through a magical forest.

Henry rummaged through several piles of dusty stuff before he found one end of an electrical extension cord. "Here. Pull on this," he mumbled as he handed me the end of the cord.

I did as he ordered and things began to move in the piles of dust and rust where the end of the cord was showing. It was wound around everything it seemed. As I pulled on the cord, it was freeing more and more things from the pile. Stuff was tumbling every which way, releasing years of accumulated dust and crud. By the time I'd gathered the entire thing all in one big, gnarly mass, I could barely see through the cloud of ancient dirt, spider skeletons, and petrified mouse poop.

"Henry? Are you in here? Have you found the garden hose yet?" I asked.

No response.

I backed out of the shed with the mangled electrical cord and looked around. No Henry. Well, at least I could hook up to electricity and be that much more civilized. I found an electrical outlet on the outside of the house, plugged the cord in and began walking backwards toward the camper, laying the cord carefully on the ground as I went. I got to within 20' of the camper before I ran out of cord. I must admit that I did utter some very bad language at that point.

Now I had two choices. Move the camper closer to the house or go to the hardware store and buy a longer extension cord. I chose the latter.

Before I made the trip to the store I thought it prudent to find out if I was going to need to purchase a garden hose as well. I walked back to the house, looking around for Henry as I got closer. That man sure was good at disappearing. I dove back into the shed, able to see into it better now that the dust had once again settled into a soft blanket over everything. I looked for something resembling the shape of a garden hose. No luck. *Maybe it was stored outside*, I thought. At least it would be easier to breathe outside of this decrepit shed.

After walking entirely around the house as I looked for the garden hose, I found it. I grabbed onto it and yanked. My reward was about 6" of rotten hose. Mentally I added "garden hose" to my shopping list.

The trip to the hardware store netted me the items I needed to bring my Casa del Construction up to somewhat livable conditions. In no time at all I had everything hooked up so I could enjoy the modern conveniences of water and electricity. It almost brought tears of joy to my eyes.

I'd had a very full first day on the job. If every day was going to be like this one, I'd fall over dead from stress-induced exhaustion in less than a week. I'd accomplished enough for one day, I decided, and drove to the Lucky Horseshoe where I fully intended to treat myself to a delicious and nutritious dinner of sodium, cholesterol, and numerous unpronounceable preservatives, all washed down with cheap, skanky beer.

I'd no sooner walked in the door when I noticed one of the pairs of eyes studying me belonged to my lost foundation subcontractor. As I walked toward him he somehow managed to shrink even smaller than his usual scrawny size in an effort to become invisible and avoid an embarrassing tongue lashing.

"Larry, I'm so glad I found you," I gushed at him, knocking him completely off balance.

# Studs

"H-hi, Katlin. Nice to see you, too," he lied.

"I want to tell you that we've run into a little glitch and you won't be getting your concrete in two days."

"Oh. That's too bad," he lied again. At the rate he was going with the job, he wouldn't be ready for concrete this century. I was really beginning to dislike this runt. Unfortunately, I had to find a way to work with him until his portion of the project was completed, which I dearly hoped would be very soon.

"It'll probably be the end of this week or the first of next week. You can still finish installing the rebar for the footings so you're ready when we get the go-ahead."

"Sure. I'll do that. I'll be there first thing tomorrow morning."

I don't tolerate people lying to me very well. *I might just have to shoot him and put him out of his misery if he's lying again*, I thought.

"Good. See you then," I chirped at him as I walked to the end of the bar and found a stool as far away from him as I could get. I'd be on him like a coat of paint all day tomorrow, making sure he stayed on the site and finished getting the footings ready for inspection and concrete. *If* he showed up, that is.

# Chapter 7

Way too early the next morning I discovered that there was no need of an alarm clock in Casa de Construction. At dawn, or thereabouts, huge trucks from the nearby rendering plant began rumbling by within inches of my new home on wheels, shaking me out of my slumber.

As I had learned from Phil, the entire area surrounding the job site was on an ancient river delta and the ground had the basic consistency of Jell-O pudding. Dump trucks, farm machinery and the like passing by on the main road in front of the job site made the entire site jiggle like a fat man's belly when he laughs.

There was no sleeping in on this job evidently, so I dragged myself out of my cozy little nest and down the stairs into my "kitchen". My head felt groggy. I'd only had one beer at the bar the night before. That was hardly enough to give me a hangover, so I decided it must have been the simulated food.

I squeezed into the shower, thinking it would help me clear my head. One blast of cold water and I was instantly awake. I shot out of there like a spitwad from a snapped rubber band. Goodie. My first challenge of the day had arrived. I had obviously missed some little detail when I hooked up the water to the camper.

The good news was that now at least I could brush my teeth in the privacy of my own bathroom. And my head wasn't so groggy now, either. The bad news was that, even though I had no hot water in the shower, I did have a shower and now had no excuse to run over to Maude for coffee and cookies.

But wait! I'd seen a little espresso stand next to a real estate office on the highway just outside of town as I was driving in. Now seemed like an opportune time to visit Stanville's only coffee shop. Pulling on my OSHA approved uniform ( full length jeans and a t-shirt) I jumped in my truck and raced out to The Oasis, a life-saving refuge in my coffee-deprived desert. And what a paradise this little espresso stand turned out to be. The coffee was as black and thick as used 90 weight motor oil and the home-made cookies were the size of garbage can lids. Things were looking up in Stanville.

Slowly driving back to the site, happily munching on my cookie-of-the-day (Pumpkin Spice with cream cheese frosting, generously sprinkled with crunchy candied ginger) and slurping my thick, rich coffee, I was thinking life couldn't get much better than this when suddenly it did. As I pulled into the space next to the camper, I noticed the van from the engineering company parked by the dirt mound. I sauntered over that way, so immersed in the joys of cookie and coffee that I nearly ran face-first into the soils tester.

"Hi there. You must be Katlin. I'm Stan from Worldwide Geotechnological Engineering. Bob sent me out to re-test the soils on this project," he said, sticking his hand out for me to shake.

"Hi. Glad you could come out so quickly," I replied, stuffing the rest of my cookie into my mouth so I could be polite and shake his hand. "What have you found?"

"So far, a big pile of dirt," he said breaking into great guffaws of laughter. Seeing I wasn't joining in, he sobered up. "Sorry. Engineer-type humor. Actually I haven't had a chance to get started yet. I just got here and was scoping out the job. I'll set up my equipment and take the samples. Then I'll have to take them back to the lab to process them."

"Sooooo, when do you think you might be able to get me some information about the soil density?" I asked as I watched him lug about two and a half tons of engineerish stuff to the dirt pile.

"Probably tomorrow. I'll call you as soon as I know for sure. What's your phone number?"

"Um. I don't have one yet. How about if I call your office tomorrow morning and get the results?" I said, feeling about as unprofessional as Larry the Lush, who also had no phone.

"That'll work. Here's my card. It won't take long to take the samples. If I hurry I might even be able to get the results this afternoon," he offered.

"That'd be great. Thanks," I said and I turned to go back to the camper. I had more work to do and now that I'd jolted my system awake with an overload of caffeine and sugar, I was ready to tackle anything.

I'd no sooner gotten settled at the combo dinette/office desk when there was a knock on the camper door. This time I knew to open it slowly so I didn't coldcock the person on the other side. It was the phone installer! Happy days!

"Boy, am I glad to see you! You're a day early!" I practically yelled at him in my caffeinated excitement.

"Yeah. The schedulers never do get it right. The old woman in the house said you want the phone installed here. She's kidding, right?" he eyed me suspiciously as he asked.

"She's not kidding. I'm the Project Superintendent of this job and I need a phone here in my job office," I explained, knowing it sounded better than it looked.

"There's a problem," he said. "I can't hook up a phone to a truck."

"This isn't just a truck. It's got a camper on it. This is my office and I need a phone in it."

"Yeah. I get that. But I can't install a phone in something that might drive off. If that happened, it could pull all the connections out of the phone vault, not to mention it could also pull the entire box along with it," he said pronouncing each word slowly and distinctly, as if I had trouble understanding the English language. I could tell by the regular flexing and unflexing of his jaw muscles that his patience was becoming overtaxed at having to explain these simple facts to me. "That would disrupt a lot of people's phone service and make them very, very unhappy," he finished his explanation.

"Oh. Gotcha. Well there's got to be some way to get me a phone," I began to whine.

"Why don't you just use this pay phone?" he asked, indicating the phone booth I'd parked Ol' Blue next to.

"Oh, yeah, that'd work real good. All I need is a really big bag of quarters and I'm in business. And if someone wanted to use the phone, I could simply inform them that it's my office phone and send them on their way," I said sarcastically.

"Yeah, I see what you mean." After a few minutes of silence, during which both of us gave deep thought to the problem, he suddenly sprang to life. "How about if I hook you up with a long extension cord. Then when you need to drive this thing off, you can just unplug your phone from the cord and go?"

"You're a genius!" I almost wanted to hug him. He'd definitely redeemed himself in my eyes. *Now all I needed was a phone*, I thought to myself. Another one of those small oversights that it seemed were so common when one worked for Gene. "Now all I need is a phone," I repeated my thought out loud to him.

"They've got a sale on phones right now at the hardware store. You go get one and I'll finish up here. I'll leave the cord coiled up behind this phone booth. You'll be all set by the time you get back from the store."

"A million thanks," I offered with genuine sincerity as I stepped out of the camper. "I can't tell you how much I appreciate this."

He smiled at me, as pleased with himself as he could be. He'd solved the pretty little lady's problem and looked as proud as a knight who'd just slain a dragon.

I jumped in my truck to head to the hardware store once again. It was one of those small older stores that seemed to have every kind of ho-dad, doomaflinky, or gee-gaw a person might need for any kind of home repair that reared its ugly head. Most of the people who worked there were lifers, having begun their career before they'd even graduated from high school. If these jaunts to the store kept up, in no time I'd feel like I was one of them.

By the time I returned, the phone guy was gone and so was Stan, the soil tester. I sent a brief prayer to the construction gods, imploring that they make sure both had done their jobs well in my absence.

45

I found the phone cord coiled up just where it was supposed to be and plugged my new phone into it. I was almost afraid to pick up the receiver. If there was no dial tone, it could be just enough to tip me over the edge and send me screaming down the highway toward my safe and sane home back on the farm. With a quick but meaningful glance heavenward, I lifted the receiver and put it to my ear.

HALLELUIAH! The blessed droning of dial tone kissed my ear. I had my very own connection to the outside world! I had a phone! I was Somebody!

Hurriedly I unwound the entire length of the cord and brought it and the phone into the camper, setting the phone on my dinette desk. My first call was to Gene or Ginnie or whoever would answer the phone at the office to let them know I had my own phone and give them the number. But wait. What was my number? The phone guy forgot to tell me what it was. Bad words issued from my mouth as I stormed outside and slammed the camper door. It was no use scanning the horizon, hoping to see the phone company truck. It was long gone. I spun around, ready to stomp back into the camper and call the phone company to yell at someone when I noticed some paper wadded in the door handle.

"Probably a disconnect notice from the phone company, the way things are going," I muttered angrily to myself as I unwadded it. Nope. It wasn't a disconnect notice. It was the official notice from the phone company, no doubt left by the phone installer, thanking me for being a valued customer and notifying me that my phone was connected. I turned the paper over, and there in big, bold, black type was my very own phone number. Life was just getting better and better.

Holding the precious piece of paper in my hand, I re-entered the camper, this time more sedately. Grabbing the phone I called G and G Construction Headquarters.

"G and G Construction," Ginnie answered.

"Ginnie! Guess what? I've got my phone installed!" I practically yelled at her in my excitement of being connected to the outside world.

"Well, that's great news, honey. That was fast. I expected we'd have to contact you through that meddlesome Maude for at least a couple of weeks. What's your number?"

I carefully recited the number for her. "As long as I have you on the phone I may as well bring you up to date on what's been happening around here."

After updating her on the events at my end, my next call was to the local lumber yard to get recommendations for framing subcontractors.

I called the local building supply and asked for the Contractor Sales Department. After a short wait on hold, blessedly without Country *or* Western music, I was connected to one of the salesmen.

Evidently asking for names of framing subs who were not only good and reliable, but who were also available at the height of the construction season was cause for great merriment at this particular lumber yard.

"You want *what*? Little lady, do you realize what time of year this is? There ain't *any* framing contractors available... not even bad ones. Call back around November. There might be a few out of work by then," the salesman informed me between sputters of uncontrollable laughter. I could hear the chortling in the background from the other guys in the department. I'd not be ordering any building materials from them in the near future if I could help it. Besides the fact that he made the fatal mistake of calling me Little Lady, I do not tolerate public humiliation. I hung up on him as his insulting snickers were fading out.

Immediately I called Beacon Building Materials in Bellevue, where I'd worked before I went to work for Gene. I'd been one of the top salespeople in the Contractor Sales Division of that large and highly successful company. But that's another story.

The receptionist connected me to the Contractor Sales office quickly and efficiently.

"Glenn Bob here," a familiar voice answered.

"Hey, Glenn Bob. This is Katlin Bob," I replied, using the additional name of Bob that all of us in the department had adopted as an inside joke.

"Hey, Katlin Bob! To what do I owe the honor of this call?" Glenn Bob asked.

"I need a framing contractor," I began. As I filled him in on the whole story, he patiently listened. He was long on patience, having had years to perfect it, watching the corn grow back on the farm in Iowa. Or was it Ohio? I could never remember which.

"Hmmmm. Let me ask around. Gimme your phone number and I'll call you back in a few minutes," he replied.

Glenn Bob was not only the epitome of patience, his word was gold. I knew he'd call back when he said he would, unlike so many other people who use that promise as a ruse for escape. It was only a few minutes and my new phone rang. In my enthusiasm to call people, I hadn't given any thought to how I'd answer it. It should be official, but G and G Construction was already taken by the "main office". Maybe "Stanville Construction Site". No, not specific enough. I had to think of something before the caller gave up. Oh hell.

"Hello?" I said.

"Hey, Katlin Bob. I think I found you someone. Remember Roger O'Donnell?" he asked.

"Oh yeah. That guy who used to work in contractor sales at the competition. What about him?"

"Well, he got divorced, quit his job, and went into business for hisself as a framing contractor. Guess that's what he was doing before he took up selling lumber. His dad was a builder and taught him the business. Carl Bob, here in the office, is one of his best friends, and he says Roger knows what he's doing and is pretty good. He's just getting started and business is kinda slow for him yet, so right now he's got an opening in his schedule. You interested?" he asked unnecessarily.

"You bet! What's his number?"

# Studs

Glenn Bob rattled off a couple of phone numbers and I thanked him profusely. We chatted about general catch-up stuff before we hung up. Now *that* was the way to treat a Project Superintendent, especially one of great importance and esteem, such as myself.

Next I called Roger. I wondered if he'd remember me. We'd only met once or twice at Beacon. Both times he was there to meet with his friend, Carl Bob, who was now the manager of the department. I figured he'd be out somewhere working and I'd probably just get his answering machine, but to my surprise he picked up on the second ring.

"O'Donnell Construction," he answered gruffly.

"Hi Roger. I don't know if you remember me, Katlin Greene from Beacon?" I began. "I was in..."

"Yeah. I remember you. What can I do for you?" he interrupted me.

"Well, I'm Project Superintendent on a job in Stanville, and I'm looking for a framing sub. You were recommended to me," I continued.

We briefly discussed the job and agreed to meet the next Monday night at a cocktail lounge midway between Stanville, where I was, and Bellevue where he lived. A face-to-face meeting is always best when discussing details of project, I always say. Besides, it would give me an opportunity to show him the plans and specs, and hopefully we'd be able to come to agreement on a number for his price to frame the building. The fact that he was tall, ruggedly handsome, and had eyes of liquid chocolate had nothing to do with my happy anticipation of our meeting. I might just get a framing subcontractor real soon and I had a maybe kinda sorta date.

I wondered if I dared to test the limits of my improving luck with a call to the soils engineer. Oh, what the hell.

"Worldwide Geotechnological Engineering," the receptionist answered.

"Hello, this is Katlin from the Stanville project for Thomas Oil. Is Stan there?" I asked.

"One moment, please, and I'll connect you," she said with precise efficiency.

Stan answered almost immediately.

"Hi Stan. It's Katlin from the Stanville job. Have you discovered anything yet about the soils compaction?" I asked.

"Actually, your timing couldn't be better. I just now got the results," he said, and then gave me a string of the new numbers.

"This means nothing to me, Stan. I'm not an engineer. Tell me in basic English what they mean."

"Well, they're better than I expected but not as good as they need to be. If you're willing, there's something you can try. It's been real dry lately, and the lack of moisture tends to make the dirt fluff up. You might get some sprinklers and set them out on the pad for a few hours. Don't let the dirt get too wet or it'll turn to mud. I'll come out again in the morning and take samples to see if the watering gives us more density," he instructed me.

"Ok. I'll see you tomorrow, bright and early. Bring coffee," I instructed back at him.

Goodie. Another trip to the hardware store, this time for sprinklers and more garden hoses. Somehow I had never envisioned that my job description as Project Superintendent would include watering a pile of dirt. I imagined it would be more along the lines of me standing in the midst of a group of devastatingly handsome, muscular, studly men, pointing at something on the plans and then pointing them toward the work I wanted them to do. "Dirt Waterer" seemed out of place in my vision.

After another quick trip to my favorite hardware store, and coincidentally the only one within a two hour drive, I placed the sprinklers on the dirt pad, hooked the hoses up to the house, and turned the water on. It looked like a mini farm with irrigation sprinklers. I crossed my fingers and toes, hoping this would work.

# Studs

I admired my mini-irrigation system for a few more minutes, then went back to the Ol' Blue. It was way past dinner-time and my cookies and coffee had long since worn off. A bowl of chili sounded downright yummy and since I just happened to have a six-pack of canned super-hot chili con carne, I was all set for dinner in my new home.

The kitchen in the camper was miniature, but efficient. The stove was right next to the sink which was right over the tiny fridge. I could actually cook, serve, eat, and clean up... all while conveniently sitting at the dinette. I found some matches and turned on the gas for one of the burners, then lit the match and held it somewhere near the burner edge. As a safety measure, I closed my eyes in case something blew up. Much to my relief, I heard a gentle "foom" and when I opened my eyes, there was a beautiful blue ring of flames around the burner.

Quickly I opened one of the cans of chili in the six-pack I'd bought, spooned it into a tiny pot, and set it on the burner. Maybe this wasn't going to be so bad, I thought as I popped open a beer and went outside to drink it while I waited for my chili to heat. After an amazingly short period of time I smelled something and it wasn't the delicious smell of hot chili. I hurried back into the camper and discovered that what looked like steam coming from the pot was actually smoke. I'd burned my first meal in Casa de Construction.

Cooking With Gas Lesson #1: Gas burners are a great deal hotter than a electric burners. Anything placed on a gas range cooks in an amazingly short time - much quicker than electrical stoves, which were the only kind I'd ever cooked on. Although I didn't know it at the time, my second lesson in Cooking With Gas was coming up very shortly. It would prove to be even more exciting than Lesson #1.

I spooned the unburned chili off the top, scarfed it down, drained my beer, and went outside to check on my dirt watering. I'd deal with the black chili that was welded to the bottom of the pot later.

The sprinklers had been going for about an hour and it looked pretty wet to me, so I turned the water off. I sure hoped this worked because if it didn't, I was quite sure Gene wasn't going to like the alternatives. Waiting a year for nature to compact the dirt naturally would cost G and G Construction a fortune in penalties for not honoring the completion time in their contract with the oil company. Plus there was the possibility that Gene would be blacklisted by them, barred from ever doing another project for Thomas Oil. The alternative - hauling off the existing dirt and replacing it the right way - was the better of the two alternatives, but still very expensive, which made it not a very attractive option also.

Turning to go back to the camper, I saw the familiar round figure of my favorite building inspector.

"Hey, Phil. Over here!" I yelled at him. He waved back and patiently waited for me to walk toward him. He was not a man to waste energy in unnecessary exertion.

"How are you doing with the soils reports?" he got right to the point.

"I think I'm making progress. The soils tester was here yesterday and told me to wet down the dirt to help compact it. He's going to give me the results of his tests tomorrow. We'll know more then," I said.

"Well, let's hope that works. I'll stop by on my way home tomorrow. By the way, my wife said to tell you to stop by for a piece of pie... on her. I think she wants to get you hooked on her good cooking," he said with a wink as he turned around and walked toward his car.

I watched him as he got in and drove off. What a sweet guy. His wife was lucky to have such a man to share her life with.

I walked back to Casa de Construction and entered the Great Room. A quick glance at the aftermath of my dinner was all the evidence I needed to decide I was going to simplify my life by tossing the burnt chili pot into the dumpster behind the house and buy a new pot tomorrow. Housework is so easy if you do it right.

That done, I settled into the dinette with the paperwork Gene had given me for this project. As any good Project Superintended should do, I needed to study the specs and familiarize myself with this particular project. The fact that any other good Project Superintendent would have done this little chore weeks before the job began didn't daunt me in the least. At the time, I was too naïve to know any better, but that wasn't going to last for long.

It was late and it'd been going through the plans and specs for several hours. I was in a state of overwhelm, the main symptom of which included talking to myself and expecting intelligent responses in return. Suddenly, I discovered an oddity. "What the hell is a flood gate?" I asked myself. I had no answer. So much for intelligent responses. I decided to come back to it later.

So far I understood how the store was to be constructed, as per the 147 pages of plans and 596 pages of specifications. How, I wondered, could a simple rectangular building no bigger than 40' x 60' with only one room, if you didn't count the dinky bathroom, generate so much detail for the construction of said building?

Well, sure, there were some oddities about this particular store. It had a "floating" concrete slab floor, for one thing. Unlike the typical construction of a building with a concrete slab floor, the floor in the plans for this building was unattached to anything. Not the walls. Not the footings. Nothing. No where. "So what is going to keep it from moving up and down on this weird gelatinized dirt," I asked myself. Again, I had no answer. I sat for a while, trying to envision the floor rising and falling like an elevator, with customers having to step up or down to enter and exit the store, depending upon where the floor was at the moment.

After I'd had enough fun with the floating floor, I returned to the flood gate thingy. That contraption had me completely baffled. I could see how it was to be built, but what I didn't understand was how it worked. The flood gate was little more than a thick slab of plywood with u-shaped metal around all four edges to give it strength and stability. It looked like there were side rails built into the front door jamb and this flood gate was to be inserted into the rails in case of flood.

*What minimum wage employee is going to risk injuring themselves, not to mention taking a chance on death by drowning in a flood, just to take the time to insert a 300 pound steel-reinforced sheet of plywood into the door jamb?* I asked myself. Was it possible there existed such a dedicated person who would jeopardize their life in order to save unknown quantities of potato chips, jars of pepperoni sticks, and lottery tickets from certain, soggy death?

It was more than my overworked brain could handle. Time to shut down. I needed rest in order to be ready for my next big, exciting day of being a Project Supe in Stanville.

# Chapter 8

Living inches away from a pay phone had its advantages, one of which was that I never felt alone. Another was that I never lacked for entertainment. The phoneless people of Stanville used this particular pay phone day and night. I soon learned there were "rush hours", usually very early in the pre-dawn morning, when I wanted to sleep, and very late at night, when I wanted to sleep.

I could clearly hear one side of the conversation, and sometimes more if the person on the other end of the line was angry, drunk, or both. I was quickly getting the low-down on many of the town locals.

However, after a late night cozied up to a set of plans and specs, I would have preferred to not be awakened at dawn by a semi-drunk rendering plant worker explaining to his better half why he hadn't come home last night.

"Honey, it's true, I swear. I had to work a double shift at the plant. You know I'd rather be home in bed with you," was the last thing I heard before Mr. Lying-through-his-teeth slammed the phone into the receiver, escaped to his car, and roared away. Evidently the Mrs. wasn't buying his pathetic story.

I slid out of my cozy nest and climbed down the ladder, heading toward the Master Bath to take the world's quickest shower. I still hadn't figured out how to get hot water to the bathroom, so my showers were more of a quick in-and-out dash. Even though it was the hottest part of summer in the Pacific Northwest, with temperatures hovering around a steamy 65°, I preferred the temperature of my shower water closer to scalding.

After my brief shower in which some water actually did manage to hit my body, I realized I wasn't feeling quite up to par. My head felt like it was filled with steel wool and my mouth tasted like I'd drunk motor oil the night before. I hoped I wasn't coming down with something. It's bad enough to be sick, but to be sick in an ugly old camper, all alone, no one to take care of me and cater to my every need... just thinking about it was making me feel worse. I needed to get my mind off how bad I felt, and work was just the thing.

The plans and specs were still laying exactly where I'd left them the night before... strewn all over the dinette. Since there was no place for me to sit down to cook a decent breakfast, I opted for Plan B – coffee and cookies at The Oasis. There was no point in kidding myself that I was capable of doing anything or thinking clearly until I had my first jolt of coffee. Maybe even my second or third jolts.

The Oasis Espresso filled half of a building that was, in total, about the size of a large dumpster. The other half was occupied by the only real estate office in town – Paradise Real Estate Company. This unlikely, but highly successful, duo of enterprises was owned by Cherie ("It's pronounced Sha Ree", she pointedly told me. "It's French, ya know.") Burnham, a shrewd wheeler-dealer disguised as a floozy. I suspected she used her looks as a diversionary tactic in business negotiations. I could see how it might be difficult for a man to keep his mind on the business at hand when faced with mile-high, foofy bleached blond hair, talons painted blood red, and cleavage that rivaled The Grand Canyon.

She may have had a pert little figure in high school, but now she'd reached a matronly age and was of a, shall we say, more substantial size. Although she bragged to all within hearing range that she still wore the same size clothing as when she was in high school, it must have taken her quite a while each morning to shoe-horn her bulk into those "high school" size clothes. I honestly didn't know that polyester stretch pants could stretch that much. Sometimes modern technology is simply amazing.

The Oasis was fast becoming my favorite place in the whole world. Not only did Cherie provide raucous, raunchy entertainment with her gossip about local people and events, her daily feature was a different gourmet cookie almost the size of a hula hoop. Today's special was Oatmeal Raisin with a Maple Glaze. It made getting up in the morning worthwhile.

Just being in the presence of such glorious cookies and wondrous coffee was making me feel lots better. My head was clearing and the first bite of cookie cleansed my mouth of that foul taste.

Once back at Casa de Construction, I was forced to face the reality of a pile of dirt that was too fluffy to build on. Stan had arrived by the time I got back with what was left of my cookie, and was busy taking dirt samples.

"Hey, Stan! Good to see you. How are things looking?" I almost chirped. Huge amounts of caffeine and sugar have been known to make me almost cheery in the morning. Almost. Besides, I was relieved to see that I'd timed my arrived so that I wouldn't have to help him lug those tons of equipment to the sample site. Even better, he'd taken his soils tests.

"Hi, Katlin. Well, the dirt's looking better, but I won't know for sure if the numbers are good enough until I get back to the lab and run the tests."

"Sounds like we're making progress, anyway," I said hopefully.

"Yeah, it's getting better, but it's still got a ways to go. We'll see if this watering did the job. You can call me later this afternoon," he said as he carefully placed the last of his apparatus in his truck. That's the difference between contractors and engineers. Contractors *throw* their tools in the back of their truck, along with their empty beer cans, leftover materials from various jobs, and their dog.

"Oh, that reminds me. I have a phone now. Here's the number," I said, grabbing for his clipboard and pen to write my new phone number on the report for this job. He grabbed it away from me and handed me a tablet of sticky notes to write on so I wouldn't muss up his tidy report.

"That's good. I'll call you later today," Stan said as he got into his truck to drive back to the engineer-land of WorldWide Geotechnological, Inc.

*Pleaseohpleaseohplease let the test results show the numbers I need,* I prayed to the Construction Gods as I walked back to Ol' Blue.

Just then I heard the singular squeal that comes only from air brakes on a semi-truck. I turned to find myself almost nose-to-nose with a shiny chrome grill about the size of a billboard. I stepped back a bit and to the side, ready to share some special language that I'd learned when I was a logger with this rude driver of this rig.

"Where's the project supe? I gotta delivery for him," the driver said before I could take a breath.

"I'm it," I said with a wide grin and a perverse sense of pleasure. I waited for his face to fall off in shock and was extremely satisfied when it did. "What do you have for me?" I asked sweetly.

"I've got the canopy. Where do ya want it?" he replied after the few moments he needed to put his face back together.

"The canopy? The huge one that goes over the gas pumps that aren't installed yet?" I squeaked.

"Yep, that's the one," he grinned down at me, enjoying way too much the difficulty this new problem was causing me.

"It's a little bit premature, as you can see," I indicated by swinging my arm around, inviting him to take a look at the job site, which consisted of a pile of dirt too fluffy to build on. The truth was, I wouldn't need this delivery for another 45 days. *If*, that is, everything went as per schedule, which so far it wasn't. "I have no idea where you can dump it. No matter where you put it now, I'll end up having to move it, and probably more than once."

"Not my problem, little lady," he informed me. "Thomas Oil ordered the delivery and I just do as I'm told."

*Little lady, huh?* I thought of several things I could tell him to do with the canopy, but doubted if he was physically capable of doing any of them. "Just drop the load over there behind that little shed," I directed him, hoping that the chosen place would be one of the more unused portions of the site.

Finally, I made it back to Ol' Blue and settled in to study the deadly soils report Gene had left with the rest of the paperwork mess. Somehow I just knew there was a solution to the problem this report was causing. After an hour or so in which I practically memorized the entire thing, I still didn't understand a bit of it. It was just strings of numbers and symbols in some language only engineers or ancient Greeks could read.

Since I'd made no progress on finding the answer to this problem in the soils report, I decided to tackle the plans and specs. Maybe the answer was hiding in there somewhere.

Soon I found myself in the state of expanded awareness that always happens to me when I dive into a set of plans and begin to mentally see the project in three dimensions, envisioning it as if it's being built right before my eyes. Like this job, for instance. While I was studying the foundation section of the plans, I was seeing the concrete being poured over the rebar in the foundation, then the concrete for the floor being poured and finished. As I turned from the foundation page to the framing plan, I began to see the concrete blocks being set so carefully in alignment as the walls grew…. wait a minute!

Concrete blocks? This was a stick framed building. What were concrete blocks doing on the plans?

Excitedly I looked in the specs to see if there was mention of the method of wall construction. Yep. Concrete block.

Holding my breath, I searched through the plans and specs for any hand written notes that would indicate a change. The rule of priority in construction is that hand-written notes overrule printed specifications and printed specifications overrule drawn plans. There was nothing anywhere that even remotely indicated a change from concrete block to stick framing.

This was excellent! It was better than excellent. It was a miracle!!

Excitedly, I called Bob-the-Architect at Thomas Oil.

"Bob!" I almost shouted at him in my excitement, catching myself just in time. I didn't want to scare the poor, timid thing. "Katlin up here in Stanville. Hey. The plans and specs I have for this building show concrete block. But I understood that it's to be stick framed. In fact, that's how it was bid and that bid was accepted by Thomas Oil. My question is, which is correct? Concrete block or stick frame?"

"Oh. You must have the old set of plans. We changed that a few months ago. It's to be stick framed, all right," he wheezed at me.

"How do I get a set of current plans and specs? I'm thinking I just might need them," I said sarcastically. In my excitement I forgot that Bob had no sense of humor.

"Lance said he's coming up tomorrow to take a look at the job. I'll send them up with him."

Oh great. Lance was the District Manager and I didn't need him nosing around at this point. I'd rather he waited until I had something to show him besides a pile of fluffy dirt.

"Good," I managed to squeeze out between clenched teeth. At this rate, I hoped I didn't end up breaking all my teeth off in my extreme efforts to keep from screaming at people. "By the way, isn't a concrete block building heavier than a stick framed building?"

"Oh, certainly."

"Do you know how to figure out the difference in weight between the two for this building? It may be critical to getting the soils compaction approved. If you can't do it, probably Worldwide GeoTech has someone there who can do it," I innocently mentioned. One thing I've learned when dealing with those on the lower rung of authority. Ask them if they are capable of actually doing what you want them to do. Their ego will always take over and answer "Yes I can do that!"

"Of course I can. If you'll wait just a moment I'll have that figure for you," he said haughtily.

He came back on the phone sooner than I expected. "Here's the numbers. Write them down exactly as I tell you," he said brusquely.

I did as he said, repeating them carefully to him. I was hardly able to contain my excitement. "Thank you so much, Bob. You may have just been instrumental in saving this project from certain death. I don't know what I'd do without your help," I gushed at him.

60

"You're welcome. If you need anything else, you just call me," he said much more warmly, now that I'd shown proper respect for him and his talents.

I'd better be careful with him, I thought to myself. I might need his help again on this project.

As soon as we hung up I called Worldwide Geotech and asked the receptionist if I could talk to Bob. Talking to her was like shopping at Nordstrom. It always gave me a sense of being among the elite.

"Bob here," he answered quickly.

"Hi Bob. This is Katlin from the Thomas Oil project in Stanville. Something's come up and I think it may solve our problem," I began. Then I told him about my discovery and gave him the new numbers from the other Bob.

"Good work, Katlin. Stan just got back an hour ago and has been running the numbers on the tests for you. Let me see if he's done. Hold, please."

I had barely started my hum-along with their on-hold music when Bob broke in on my private concert. "Great news, Katlin. The combination of watering the dirt and the new numbers put you right where you need to be," he said with a smile in his voice.

My knees went weak. "Really? You have no idea how wonderful this is. I'll need a report or something for the building inspector, I think," I suggested.

"Certainly. I'll dictate a letter to my secretary right now and get it in the mail tonight."

"Um. Actually, I need it right away. Could I just come by the office and pick it up?"

"Sure, if you want to drive down here. We close at 5:00 so you better get going now," he cautioned me.

"I'm on my way. Don't close until I get there!" I almost yelled before I slammed the receiver down.

I made it to their office with seconds to spare. The receptionist knew without me telling her what I was after. It must have had something to do with the frantic look in my eyes and how I slid to a halt in front of her desk, almost tumbling over it and into her lap.

"Thanks," I said gratefully to her. "You and Bob will surely go to Engineer Heaven for this wondrous deed you've done today."

She delicately tee-heed as she handed me the envelope with the letter. I tore it open and quickly scanned it to make sure it had the requisite information and approval language. It did.

I floated back to my truck on my Happy Cloud. My thoughts were as light as the meringue cookies at The Oasis. Maybe this Project Superintendent gig wasn't going to be so bad after all. If this was as awful as it was going to get, I could easily handle any and all challenges that came my way. Super Duper Supe. That was me!

Deliriously happy thoughts like that kept me amused on the drive all the way back to Stanville. As I drove through the town I thought of stopping by the Lucky Horseshoe for one of their world famous chiliburger gut bombs – a greasy hamburger patty so thin you could almost see through it, nestled on a piece of bread made from the finest chemicals money could buy, covered liberally with cheap, out-of-date canned chili. On second thought, maybe not.

However, it reminded me that I should check up on Larry the Lush, as I was beginning to fondly think of him.

As I drove by the tavern, sure enough I spotted the nose of his truck sticking out from behind the back of the tavern. There was a small area in the tight alleyway behind the bar where the professional drinkers tried to hide their vehicles from their bosses, wives, and/or girlfriends. It was indicative of the level of intelligence of this group that they truly believed no one knew they did this.

I quickly found a parking place and strode into the bar. Larry was hunched over his beer, furiously scratching at a cardboard ticket in the futile hopes of winning the lottery so he wouldn't be forced to work for a living. I walked quietly up to his rounded back and stood there for a moment before announcing my presence.

"HEY, LARRY," I said loud enough to be heard over the nasal tones of some country western crying-in-your-beer song that was playing on the juke box. I was delighted to see Larry jump up and quickly turn around. In his beered-up state he forgot to unwind his feet from the barstool legs. He tipped over with a loud crash, much to the amusement of everyone in the bar. *He must do this a lot,* I thought, *since no one seemed to be in much of a hurry to help him.*

"Oh. Hi Katlin," he said looking up at me as he laid on his back on the floor, the barstool resting uncomfortably, I hoped, on his front, his legs still contorted around the barstool.

"We got the okay from the soils engineers to go ahead with the foundation. The building inspector will be onsite first thing tomorrow morning to sign off on it, so you better have your ass on the job by daybreak and tying up rebar like your life depended on it. Because it does," I said as I leaned over and peered down at him. I learned long ago that in order to be heard by certain people you need to speak their language. I figured Larry would clearly get my meaning.

"Yessir. I mean, ma'am. I'll be there be 6am," he almost saluted.

"If you aren't, I'll be knockin' down the door on your sleazy apartment and dragging your skinny ass out of bed. You got me?" I added for emphasis.

"I'll be there. I promise," he whimpered.

I turned and strode back out, feeling the looks of awe following me from all of the good ol' boys as I pushed open the door and let it slam shut forcefully behind me. Once I was in my truck, I let out a shuddering breath and took a moment to let my hands stop shaking. I should have been an actor. Being tough and mean didn't come naturally to me and when I was forced into it, I felt drained afterward. Even if it did feel kinda good at the time.

By the time I got back to Ol' Blue it was late... too late to call Gene. "Well, I'll just call him in the morning and tell him how his Project Supe is a super heroine. Just wait until he hears about how I saved the day! He'll probably give me a raise."

Those thoughts, and others just as irrational, kept me company all through the evening as I ate my delicious and nutritious dinner of microwaved popcorn and beer. Thoughts of my prowess as the smartest and most clever Project Supe were still rattling around in my head as I finally fell into my cozy bed and fell into sleep, exhausted and deliciously happy.

# Chapter 9

"Yeah?" Gene growled into the phone.

"Gene! It's Katlin!" I chirped. "I wanted to catch you before you left for work."

"Well, you did that, all right. It's damn near the middle of the night."

"Oooooh. Sounds like somebody hasn't had their coffee yet," I sing-sung to him.

"Coffee, hell. Katlin, you know what time it is?"

"Well of course I do. I'm not stupid, you know. It's 5:09," I informed him. Honestly, you'd think the man could afford a working alarm clock.

"In the future, kindly wait until 6am before you begin your social calls to me. Now, what's up," he grouched.

"Well, you'll be pleased to know that I've solved the problem with the soils compaction," I began, ready to share every glorious detail of my superior intelligence and extraordinary problem-solving talent with him.

"Good. I'll be up later today. See you then." And he slammed his phone down.

How rude. After I'd made a point of getting up bright and early so I could share the good news with him. Just as soon as I'd been jiggled awake by the first rendering plant truck passing by, I'd crawled out of my cozy cubby-hole bed. Despite the fact that I had a splitting headache, probably from shocking my body by getting up so early, I had thought only of Gene's best interests. I honestly thought it would help to start his day off right to hear the wonderful news I had for him, and I had felt all warm and fuzzy at the thought. Now I didn't give an ounce of belly button lint.

After I'd had time to think about it I decided that, in the interest of being fair, I'd probably caught him at a bad time. Maybe he and Ginnie were having a little playtime. I'd wait until he came up to the job to regale him with my wondrous tale. In the meantime, I decided to reward myself at The Oasis. I got one shoe on before I realized it wasn't open yet.

As I sat at my dinette, groggily musing over my situation, I noticed my thinking was rather slow. I felt like I'd been at the bar drinking all night, but I'd only had one beer last night with my popcorn entree. If it was the flu, it was the morning flu. The morning flu. Oh no. That was impossible. I hadn't come within kissing distance of any guys within the last two months. It had to be something else. Maybe the fumes from the rendering plant. It had smelled pretty bad in the camper when I got up in the morning, but I attributed it to my lousy diet upsetting my digestive system, causing certain natural gases to be released into my sleeping bag.

Gradually, I became aware of another strange and unpleasant odor. *Somebody* needed to take a shower. Badly. I looked around for whoever that person might be. Finding no one else I could blame, I decided it must be me. My brain seemed to be taking a long time to shift into gear this morning.

Well, brain or no brain, it was time to take a trip to the nearest state park and avail myself of their dime-a-minute hot shower. Evidently my 15 second showers of ice-cold water weren't having much effect on my personal hygiene. I tossed a few necessities into a paper bag, jumped in my truck and drove out to the only park I knew about – the one on Camas Island.

It's amazing how a nice, long, hot shower can change your perspective on life. Suddenly everything seemed shinier, brighter. As I drove back out of the park I noticed all kinds of things I hadn't seen before when I was trying to peer through the fumes arising from my armpits and other bodily crevices. Like, for instance, I hadn't seen the bright red and white sign that showed a cute little trailer icon. As I got closer, I could read the words under it. "Trailer Dump." Funny. It didn't *look* like a cemetery for old RVs.

# Studs

At the entrance to the park, I stopped to ask the lady park ranger what the trailer dump was used for. What she told me was so disgusting I almost lost my appetite for my morning cookies. I decided she was playing a macabre joke on me and drove off to The Oasis for my breakfast – three megahuge coffees, extra caffeine, if you please, and two cookies de jour. Today's treat was Chocolate Chip Pecan with tiny chocolate marshmallows delicately sprinkled on top.

As I pulled into the job site, I noticed Larry's truck parked alongside the dirt pile. Either he'd slept in it or he really had gotten up at the crack of dawn to get to work. I guessed the latter because he almost had all the rebar set and tied up. I stood on the side of the trench, watching him work. He finally noticed me and turned a whupped puppydog look on me. It wasn't pathetic enough to make me feel any kindlier toward him.

"You going to be done with that today?" I asked him.

"Yeah, I should be done by noon," he said hopefully, like I was going to pat him on the head for begin such a good boy.

"Good," was all I gave him back, and turned to walk back to Command Headquarters. I got only a few feet before I was stopped by the curtain of dust my favorite building inspector's car made as it pulled up next to Ol' Blue.

"Hi, Phil," I greeted him as soon as he struggled free of the confines of the compact car. It must have been all the county could afford, and it was about one size to small for Phil.

"How ya doing today?" he greeted me back.

"Things are much better. If you stopped by last night like you said, I'm sorry I wasn't here. But the reason for my absence is exciting. I have some very good news," I began, and told him the entire story, beginning with the discovering of the discrepancy showing concrete block on the plans when the building was actually to be made of wood. I didn't spare any details, and he was properly attentive and even appreciative when I was done with my tale.

"Well, I must say you're one clever little lady," he said. "I don't know many older, more experienced project superintendents who would have been smart enough to catch that."

His compliments covered me like warm sunshine and I didn't even mind him calling me "little lady." We walked back to Ol' Blue together so I could give him the letter from Worldwide Geotechnological.

"Where's your building permit? I'll sign off on the footings so you can do your pour. When I stopped by last night it looked like Larry was almost done and I've seen enough of his work through the years to see that he knows what he's doing. I won't always be this lenient," he said in a voice trying hard to sound stern. "You've had a rough start and I can see that you're trying to do the right thing, so I'll go easy on you this one time. Remember, I need to sign off on the foundation walls, too, before you pour them. I'll make a copy of this and put it in the file at the office. If you're here when I go by tonight on my way home, I'll drop it off. Otherwise I'll see you Monday," he said.

"Thanks for all your help. I really appreciate it," I said. I could tell he sensed the genuineness of my gratitude for his help. The smile that widened his face and the sudden embarrassment that turned his cheeks cherry red were dead giveaways.

"It's my job," he mumbled as he inked his initials on the building permit.

"I don't know how late I'll be here today. My boss and his girlfriend are coming up to look at the job. Not much to see that's different then when he was here on Monday, but he's the boss. I'll probably be late on Monday because I have to stop at his office before I drive up here. But I'll be here in the afternoon when you go home," I informed him.

"See you then," he winked at me as he said this and then walked back to his car, whistling a chirpy little tune.

I glanced at my watch and saw it was normal business hours, so I called G & G Construction again, this time to talk to Ginnie.

"Ginnie," I said as soon as she picked up the phone," this is Katlin. I have something to ask you about the camper. The horrid park ranger person at the state park told me something unbelievably disgusting and I want the real story from you." As I told her the revolting things the park rangerette had told me, she began laughing. This was not the response I expected. She must have misunderstood, so I began my unbelievable tale again, which only made her laugh all the louder and harder.

"Honey, that's just part of camper life" she wheezed when she was able to catch her breath and talk again. "What goes in, must come out. It's not so bad, really. You just have to make sure that you stand back and a little bit to the side when you first unhook the hose. Sometimes pressure builds up a bit and, well, you just make sure you bring some towels with you when you take Ol' Blue to the dump. In fact, you might want to dump that tank *before* you take your shower," she said, trying to hold down her snorts of laughter.

"Oh," was all I could think of to say. My mind started doing that scary thing it does when I'm faced with unpleasantness. It became creative. Maybe I could pay someone to do it for me. Or bat my eyelashes at some hapless man and get him to do the trailer dump thing. Oh gawd. Batting my eyelashes? What was I thinking? I had stooped to the lowest level of womanhood. Of course I could do this thing on my own. Ginnie had done it, hadn't she?

"Of course, I always got Gene to do it for me," she said, breaking in on my thoughts. Well, there went that brave hope. "Maybe you can find someone to help you with it when you go to the park."

"Yeah. Maybe. Oh, one other thing. I don't have any hot water. What do you suppose could be causing that?"

"Did you light the pilot light under the water heater?" she asked.

"Um. What's a pilot light?"

"Haven't you ever used gas before?" she asked, sounding a little annoyed.

"No. I've always had electricity and I've never even *been* in a camper before," I admitted.

69

"Oh, good lord. Why didn't somebody tell me. Listen, I'll come up there with Gene today and show you what you need to know about the camper. Gene should have shown you, but some days that man just doesn't seem to have a brain in his head. It's almost like he goes to another planet or something for a few days. When he goes into one of those moods he's more useless than tits on a noodle."

"Thanks, Ginnie. You're a wonderful help and I really appreciate it," I said, truly grateful that she existed. What a pickle I'd be in if it wasn't for her. I'd have no water, no electricity, no heat, and I'd hate to think what would happen if I hadn't found out what a trailer dump was. Visions sprang into my mind... vivid images of the tank bulging with raw sewage, pressure building and building until it burst, sending gooey, smelly god-knows-what all over the place as it exploded. "Thanks, again," I said, beginning to gag as I rang off.

Maybe I could get Ginnie to go with me to the trailer dump tomorrow and I could watch as she showed me how to manage this disgusting task. Yeah. We could do some girl bonding over the poop chute. Much better than shopping or doing lunch or some other girlie stuff.

As I played with that thought, tossing it around in my head for amusement, there was a discreet knock on the door. One thing about this job, it sure wasn't boring. I never knew who I'd be entertaining next in my miniature home and office. I gently swung the door open, having learned about camper doors with the building inspector, and was greeted by red... everywhere.

The man standing in front of me had thick, seemingly uncontrollable hair in that bright shade of red typically used for safety equipment. The longish strands in his massive mane were pointing every which way. The red didn't stop there. It bled down into his ruddy face, which was framed by a neatly trimmed beard a few shades lighter than his hair. His shirt was red flannel, covered by a red plaid wool jacket. I was disappointed to find blue jeans. I half expected to see red all the way to his toes.

"Howdy. Maude said you're the Project Supe for this here job. My name's Red.," he said. Gosh, I never would have guessed. "Red O'Leary."

Red was tall. So tall that while I was inside the camper and he stood on the ground we were almost eye-level.

"Hello. I'm Katlin Greene. How can I help you?" I asked.

"Well, I heerd you're gonna be building this here mini-mart and new gas station. I figure that old house and garage are gonna have to either be torn down or hauled off. Am I right or am I right?" he asked in a staccato voice sounding more like a used car salesman than a…. whatever he was.

"Yes, I suppose you're right," I agreed.

"I move houses," he said as he handed me a home-made business card decorated with red glitter and a sticker of a shiny red star centered at the top. Sure enough, it said right on the card, "Red O'Leary, House Mover".

"I figure it's gonna be easier and faster to move the house and garage than it would be to tear them down. 'Course you could always donate them to the fire department and let those guys burn 'em down. But they sometimes take a while to get around to it. There's permits to get and all. I'll bet you're on a tight schedule. Am I right or am I right?" he continued.

"You're absolutely right," I agreed, beginning to enjoy this conversation. He talked so fast it was like his mouth was on fire.

"Well, I can get that garage moved in a day or so for ya. That'll give you more room. Tight little job site, ain't it," he asked, not expecting me to answer. He continued on quickly before I could interrupt him. "Looks like materials are already starting to stack up," he said meaningfully, nodding toward the pile of cardboard boxes that contained the canopy.

"Yes, once again you're right."

"Tell ya what I'm gonna do for ya. I'll move that garage and won't charge you a thing. That's right. You won't owe me a penny. And instead of charging you my usual reasonable and competitively priced fee to move that run-down old house, I'll haul it away just for the materials in it. I might oughta be able to salvage some of the old siding and such. People are always looking for cheap lumber, and used is as cheap as it gets."

This guy was gooooood! I happened to know that old, weathered lumber was in great demand from high-end architects and contractors who were building replica "estate homes". Cheap used lumber, my pink ass. He was going to make a quite a nice profit off that dilapidated old garage, selling the used wood as "antique barn lumber".

He was right about one thing. I did need the extra space - for parking all my guest's rigs if nothing else. I quickly made the executive decision. "That sounds good to me. When can you move it?"

"Me and my crew will be here first thing Monday morning. We'll get 'er outta here probably in a day or two," he proudly announced.

"Great. Thanks for stopping by. You've solved one of my problems. Now if only all the rest of them were so easy to solve…. but I guess that's why I get paid the big bucks," I hoped he appreciated my construction humor. He did. I was rewarded by him slapping his knee and letting loose with a couple of guffaws.

"See ya Monday morning," he said cheerily, and loped back to his truck – a bright, fire engine red pickup, of course.

I returned to the dinette that I expansively called my office. Now I could call the concrete company and order the "mud" for the footings for Monday. That little chore took all of five minutes. *What else could I do to be productive and earn my wages,* I casually wondered. I began rummaging through the pile of papers to see what else I needed to take care of. There was a knock on the door before I could find out. As I slowly opened the door, being careful not to deck whoever was on the other side of it, I saw tight jeans, broad shoulders, and a gorgeously rugged, tanned face.

It was the Marlboro Man!

Mentally, I did a quick personal inventory. Hair brushed? Check. Face washed? Check. Deodorant? Check. Teeth brushed? Check. I was ready for this.

"Ohhh, helloo. May I help you?" I crooned in my sexiest imitation of Marilyn Monroe.

72

"Howdy. Name's Lance Lawrence and I'm the District Manager for Thomas Oil," he announced.

"Glad to meet you. I'm Katlin Greene, Project Superintendent," I tacked on the title after my name, hoping it gave me a little more prestige. Ol' Blue did nothing to improve my public image and a girl needs all the help she can get in certain circumstances. "Won't you please come in?" I offered, moving aside so he could squeeze by, making sure he had only enough room so he'd have to brush against me. I'll admit it – sometimes I can be a little devious.

"Here's the plans that Bob sent up from the main office," he said handing the rolled up plans to me as he looked around. He was so tall, even without his cowboy hat, he had to keep his head ducked or he'd scrape his scalp on the ceiling of Ol' Blue. "Nice place ya got here. Real convenient. Everything you need within arm's reach," he said, being overly generous and kind in his remarks about Ol' Blue.

"Yes. Convenient. Would you like to see the job site?" I asked, becoming more uncomfortable by the minute. Just standing next to him was making my eyebrows sweat. "Do you come here often?" I blurted out, then froze in mortification. Part of my charming personality is that there's no quality control between what goes on inside my brain and what comes out of my mouth.

"Well, I'm usually up here once a month or so to check on how the stores in my area are doing. I like to see them in person... check out the condition of the store, the people who're working, and just take a good look around in general. It makes it more difficult for the store managers to pad their reports." He stepped out of the camper and held out his hand to me. What a gentleman. If I hadn't been staring so intently at his unbelievably deep blue eyes I might have seen the slight creasing around the corners of his lush mouth as he suppressed his smile at my awkward comment.

And then he aimed his killer eyes at me and smiled. "But now, I'll probably be coming up here to Stanville a lot more often."

Gulp.

"Good," I said as I took his hand and stepped out of the camper. He didn't move back to give me any room, and we just stood there with less space than an ant hair between us. He looked intently into my eyes with a knowing grin on his gorgeous face. My ear lobes were starting to sweat.

"Since there's not much to look at here on the jobsite, I suppose you'll want to go over to Maude and Henry's to check out the operation," I said stupidly. Now he'd have an excuse to leave. Just when we were having so much fun. I wanted to slap myself, but as close as we were, I'd probably miss and hit him instead.

"You're right, I should do that. How about you come with me and we'll get to know each other a little better," he invited with an inviting wink.

"Okay," I said, using the full extent of my brain power to come up with even that lame response. My brain had said "adios" the instant my eyes had registered his rugged beauty. I'd always been a sucker for a guy in cowboy boots, tight jeans, and a big, um, belt buckle.

He let go of my hand and we walked together across the lot to the old house. I wondered if Lance warned his store managers of his impending visit or if he just dropped in unannounced in order to surprise them.

"I like to make unscheduled visits to my store managers in order to surprise them. Keeps them on their toes," he answered my unspoken question.

I looked at him and realized he must have read my face. Another of those curious traits I'm blessed with is that whatever I'm thinking shows in my face, as if I had a ticker tape of my thoughts marching across my forehead.

We arrived at Maude's back door much too soon. She flung the door open before we even had a chance to bang on it.

"Lance! I knew you'd be here today. I could feel it in my bones. I made your favorite cookies – fudge chocolate chip," she said in a coy, little-girl voice. This man had an amazing effect on women, no matter what their age, it seemed. "Oh. Hello, Katlin.

How are you today? I haven't seen you around lately," she said in a whole other tone of voice, this one dripping in icicles.

"I finally got my phone hooked up and didn't want to bother you and Henry any more than necessary," I explained unnecessarily. Neither Lance or Maude seemed to care. They'd moved into the kitchen and Lance was busy chomping on a huge cookie as Maude watched him with adoring eyes, holding out the plate with the pile of cookies toward him. They were stacked so high I was afraid they'd topple over hit the floor. Once anything hit that floor, it was a goner. It'd be swallowed up by the years of accumulated dirt, disgusting doggie things, and spilled, mummified food so thick it looked like a bas relief pattern in the linoleum. I hated to think of those beautiful cookies coming to such a dismal end, so I stood with my hands out, ready to save the lives of any falling cookies.

Just then a loud BANG BANG BANG shocked me out of my deep thinking.

"Arf. Arf. Arfarfarfarf," Fuzzles replied to the door. It was like having a furry animated door bell.

"Wonder who that could be," muttered Maude, with just a bit of irritation. She seemed to be a bit frustrated that her time with Lance was to be shared with so many others. She waddled down the narrow hallway, navigating smoothly past some of the larger piles of newspapers, and opened the door. "Ginnie! Gene! What a surprise. I didn't know you were coming up today. I would have baked some extra cookies if I'd known." It wasn't like she didn't have enough cookies now. The tower of cookies she'd stuck in front of Lance would feed half the town of Stanville.

"Hi, Maude. Is Katlin here? She's not at the camper or out on the job site," Gene inquired.

"Hi Gene. Hi Ginnie. Glad to see you made it," I said, wedging myself between Maud and a stack of newspapers. I was truly glad to see them. It seemed Lance had replaced me as a love object with fudge chocolate chip cookies. There was little point in me hanging around, watching while Maude made goo-goo eyes at him. "Let's go to Ol' Blue. We can go over things there, where we have room to spread out the paperwork."

Ginnie chatted on about nothing in particular while we walked the short distance back to Ol' Blue. They'd parked the land yacht a discreet distance away, as if Ol' Blue's pathetic condition might be contagious to other vehicles. We climbed into the camper and squeezed into the dinette – Ginnie and I on one side and Gene all by himself on the other.

"Here's something to keep you out of trouble," he said as he tossed a set of plans on the table. "Although it looks like you'd have to work pretty hard to find any trouble to get into around this Podunk town," he added with a smirk.

"What's this?" I asked, ignoring his pathetic attempt at humor. It didn't help that his observation was all too accurate.

"Another set of plans from Thomas Oil for another store. They like the work I'm doing on their mini-marts and want me to do more of them. That's fine with me. So, I need you to do the take-off and estimate on this one by the bid date, which is about couple of weeks away, I think."

"A couple of weeks? What if I can't get the bids back from the subs by then?"

"Don't worry about it. They're all pretty much the same. If you can't get a sub to bid on time, I'll just plug in a number from one of their old bids."

"Gene, they're not all the same. Take a look around here. We have a house and a garage to move. That's not on the plans. Who knows what other little surprises will arise on this job. Have you gone to the job site and taken a look at it?"

"Nah. Don't need to. It's in the city, so utilities are right there and the land's probably flat as this table. Why would I need to go take a look at the job site?"

How had this man managed to stay in business as long as he had? I'd learned years before, when I was a roofing contractor, that job sites always needed to be carefully inspected *before* bidding the job.

I'd once lost big money on a roofing job because I didn't inspect the existing roof that we were to tear off and replace. Hidden under the top layer were two other layers of composition roofing, and then the big nasty surprise – a layer of wood shingles. All this needed to be removed and hauled to the dump, incurring hefty dump fees. Then plywood had to be installed over the spaced boards that the shingles had been nailed to. The cost of the extra dump fees, hauling fees, plywood, and labor to install the plywood had put me in the hole financially for quite a long time. It was little surprises like this that were found only by careful on-site inspections.

"Okay, Gene. You're the boss," I acquiesced, though reluctantly.

"Um, I don't mean to interrupt this business talk, but what smells so danged awful?" Ginnie asked, wrinkling up her nose, along with some other parts of her face.

Gene took a couple of deep whiffs and jumped up. "That's propane! Don't anyone light up a cigarette!" he shouted as he jumped out of the camper in one giant step, saving himself first. Ginnie and I followed almost as quickly.

"Where's it coming from? You had the gas system checked in Ol' Blue before you brought it up here, didn't you?" Ginnie asked Gene, giving him the barest hint of The Look.

"Well, no, I didn't," he admitted, looking down at the ground. "But I meant to."

"That's not doing Katlin any good now, is it?" She turned to me and said in a sympathetically gooey voice, "Good thing you don't smoke, Honey. You'd be fried to a crisp by now."

Just what I wanted to hear.

"Where's it coming from?" I asked Gene, panic starting to make my voice get shrieky.

He inched back into the camper and began sniffing around. When he got to the stove and opened the oven to take a whiff, he almost gagged.

Propane, I was to learn later, doesn't have a smell. In order to alert users of the deadly gas when they have a leak, a horrid odor akin to rotten egg and beer farts is added to the gas. Originally a nice floral scent was added, but people liked it, ignored the fact that the deadly gas was leaking into their living space, and began getting blown up left and right. Somebody finally got smart and added a stench that no one could tolerate for long.

"It's coming from the oven," he announced in between gagging and coughing.

"But the oven isn't even on. I couldn't get it to work," I said.

"What do you mean, you couldn't get it to work? Didn't you light the pilot light?" Ginnie asked me.

"What's a pilot light?" I asked.

"Oh lordy. We better turn off the gas at the bottle and air this place out. While we're waiting I'll tell you all about cookin' with gas," she said.

Ginnie patiently taught me about pilot lights and other facts of life with propane. I learned that once propane gas is turned on at the bottle or tank, it flows to and through the pilot lights. If they aren't lit, the gas just keeps on flowing until something happens to stop it. Like an explosion.

There were three pilot lights that had been filling the camper with propane gas all night long. As it turned out, I was very lucky that I'd kept a small window in the Master Bedroom Suite open. Had I not, I would have been asphyxiated during the night. I was luckier still that my bed was at the top of the camper. Propane, I learned further, is heavier than air so the majority of it stayed near the floor. No wonder I was feeling groggy and not quite with it in the morning. It was a miracle I hadn't been killed dead.

Ginnie chatted on while the camper aired out and I got control of my emotions. It isn't very often that I come this close to being dead. I could feel the need for a cookie coming upon me, but it would have to wait until Gene and Ginnie had gone. We had business to take care of, now that there was no danger of my being blown to smithereens in my sleep.

When the gas had mostly cleared out of the camper, Ginnie sent Gene in to light the pilot light on the burners and in the oven. I suspect she sent him into the camper before it was completely aired out in the secret hope that he'd get his eyebrows singed off or have some other minor catastrophe to teach him a lesson. Fortunately, or unfortunately, depending on whether you were Gene or Ginnie, nothing happened. He lit the pilot light in the oven, on the stove, and finally on the water heater, which meant that I'd be able to take hot showers in the convenience and privacy of my own bath. Life in Ol' Blue was getting almost civilized.

"Now can we get back to business?" Gene asked in a rather surly tone.

*This must be one of his bad days,* I thought. *Or maybe he's been fighting with Ginnie again. She can be pretty strong-willed and doesn't let him push her around, like he does other people.*

We all climbed back in the camper, settled back into the dinette and Gene continued where he'd left off before we were so rudely interrupted with the potential of my impending death. He barked orders to me on what he wanted done as I hurriedly made notes of them. "And don't forget we've got that Project Superintendent class on Tuesday," he reminded me. I made a note to appease him, but the truth was, I hadn't forgotten. I was looking forward to it, hoping I'd learn something that would help ease me through this mess I'd gotten myself into.

Gene and Ginnie left, their visit having taken up no more than half an hour at the outside. As they pulled away, I realized that neither had shown me how to do the poop chute thing. Well, it couldn't be that difficult.

More importantly, I'd had no chance to regale the two of them with the story of how my amazing intelligence, brilliant wit, and superb problem-solving talents had saved this project from certain doom because of the too-fluffy dirt. It was a toss-up as to which was more upsetting to me – almost getting killed by propane or not being able to tell my boss what a super hero I was.

I looked for Lance's truck, but he must have escaped the cookie crumb covered clutches of Maude while Gene and Ginnie had me imprisoned in Ol' Blue. I wasn't too disappointed. I knew he'd be back... if for no other reason than it was his job. I hoped that wasn't all.

It was Friday, which meant that I could go home for the weekend. I was ready for my own bed, cooking on an electric stove, and a bathtub with hot water in which I could soak as long as I wanted. I just hoped that my friends who were housesitting for me would be gone when I arrived. I was exhausted mentally and needed some alone-time to do nothing. Not even think. I especially didn't want to feel obligated to be nice to people when all I wanted to do was reconnect with my animals, my home, and my bath tub.

# Chapter 10

Thank God for cowboy coffee. Although my house-sitting friends lived a citified version of the cowboy life, only real cowboy coffee touched their lips. It was easy to make. Coffee grounds were dumped in a pot, a little water poured over the pile, and the mess boiled for an hour or until a spoon stood upright in it. It was then poured into a mug and drunk, grounds and all.

I got all the way to Gene and Ginnie's place before my one cup of cowboy coffee began to wear off.

A vehement dislike for Monday mornings was beginning to grow inside me. Normally I didn't mind Mondays too much, but getting up in the middle of the night just so I could make it to Gene's by 6am was inhuman.

I crawled out of my truck, staggered up to the porch, and pushed the doorbell before I remembered they'd customized the ring. I was greeted by the whiney sounds of some broken-hearted rhinestone cowboy, wailing on about how he lost his girl, his dog, and his pickup truck. Why don't they ever sing about their cows? I mean, they *are* cowboys, aren't they?

Thankfully, Ginnie opened the door with a cup of steaming hot coffee in her hand.

"Oh, bless you my angel," I crooned to her as I grabbed it out of her hand and started to slurp it down. "Ack! What is that horrible taste?" I choked out after one large gulp.

"That would be coffee with three spoonfuls of sugar, which is just how I like *my* coffee," she said grabbing the cup back. "If you want *your* coffee, it's over there," she said pointing at the coffeemaker steaming away on the kitchen countertop.

"Sorry. I thought you were bringing me coffee," I said.

"Not even His Lordship, more commonly known as Gene, gets waited on around here. You want coffee, you get it yourself," she informed me.

Something was amiss. She wasn't usually this cranky, not even this early in the morning.

"Where is Gene? He's supposed to give me updates and instructions for the work this week," I said, nonchalantly looking around for clues as to what was going on.

"He's out of town for a few days. I'm to give you this... and this," she said, handing me a large envelope and a smaller one with my paycheck in it.

"Okay. Thanks. Guess I'll just head on up to the job site, then, if there's nothing else," I sort of hinted.

"No, there's nothing else. You call me if you need anything. If there's an emergency or anything that you can't handle, I can get a hold of Gene, but it's best to try and handle things yourself. He's really tied up right now," she said this last part almost to herself.

"Okay. I'll just be on my way then," I said, and left before I realized I didn't have any coffee. Well, there was always coffee on the ferry, if you could call it that. I usually had a difficult time keeping a straight face when I ordered it at the snack bar. Even though it was barely beige in color, it made up for the weak color with the strength of its vile taste, which was reminiscent of burning rubber. But, hey, it had caffeine in it and it would hold me until I got to The Oasis.

As I pulled on the ferry, I looked for any rigs I might recognize, indicating that some friends might be going to the city this morning. During the week the ferry was mostly full of locals and it was always a delightful surprise to discover friends aboard to share the ride with. During the weekends, we locals abandoned the ferry to the tourists.

Even though I saw no one I knew, the ride was fun. I loved watching the seagulls play in the updraft alongside the ferry. I don't know any other birds that have as much fun as seagulls.

# Studs

The drive up to Stanville seemed to go fast, and I was mighty happy to see The Oasis appear on the horizon as I drove into town. I parked, jumped out of my truck and almost ran into the shop.

"Hi, Cherie. What's the cookie of the day?" I asked her as she poured my giganto coffee.

"Death by Chocolate. It's half fudge cookie and half white chocolate cookie with dark chocolate frosting and a giant chocolate chip on top. Want one?' she asked unnecessarily.

"Better make it three. I'm going to be having a tough day today. I can just feel it in my bones. Three coffees, too, if you don't mind," I replied.

"Those cookies are going fast. Guess I'll have to make these again sometime. Even ol' Phil came in and got one. If his wife found out, she'd hit him up alongside the head with one of her skillets. She doesn't cater to his eating at any other place but that little café of hers. She's afraid some other woman will snag him with her cooking. That's the way she caught him, you know. Fattened him up for the kill, she did. Well, that'll be $14.76 including tax," she informed me.

A person sure got a lot for their money at The Oasis. Great coffee, unspeakably delicious cookies, and the juiciest gossip.

"Thanks, Cherie. See you tomorrow," I mumbled through a mouthful of chocolate and cookie. She was right. I could die happily from an overdose of these cookies.

I had a big day in front of me. Red was going to begin moving the garage, concrete for the footings was scheduled for a pour, and I had a date with Roger, the framing contractor. Well, I was categorizing it as a date. I wasn't sure what category he'd place it in, but I'd find out later.

As I drove up to the job site, Red was already at work with his crew. He was surrounded by mini-Reds, all in dirt color bib overalls and jackets. With their flaming red hair and the beige color of their work clothes, they looked like a bunch of giant walking matchsticks.

I parked my truck, jumped out, and walked over to the garage. The activity was starting to attract quite a large audience. There's not a lot to do in Stanville, and moving this garage was a big event. Mostly the group was made up of older retired guys who all looked like they ate often at The Daisy Café. Most wore both a belt *and* suspenders to keep their pants from sliding off the underside of their generously sized bellies. Like all sidewalk superintendents, they knew exactly how the project should be run. Anyone listening to their conversation for a bit would think it quite obvious they had recently retired from various construction trades. The truth was that most were long since retired from farming or the rendering plant.

"Hey, Red! How's it going?" I yelled at him over the noise of his workers yelling directions at each other, everyone in the crowd yakking, and the traffic.

"Hi, Katlin. So far, so good. We'll know more when we get it up in the air a bit. There's some dryrot that could make it a bit tricky, but I think we'll be okay." He turned around to the crew and whistled at them. Instantly, they all stopped what they were doing and gathered around him.

"This here's my wife, Ruby. Most everyone calls her Mrs. Red. My daughter, Scarlett, and my son, Red, Jr. Oh, and this here's my younger son - we call him Sparky," he proudly introduced each one to me. "There's more crew comin' along someday, but right now they need to grow up a little more before it's safe to bring them out to the jobs."

"Quite a nice crew you have right now, Red. I'm pleased to meet all of you. How many more are there?" I was properly impressed with his home-grown crew.

"Ruby and me got three more of our own, and my Scarlett has a two-year-old, so we've got plenty of crew for the future, don't we honey," he almost hummed with pleasure and pride as he put his arm around his wife.

"It looks like this is the social event of the year. Look at all the people who've come to watch this. And there's more coming. Will it be safe to have all these people around while you're raising the garage?" I asked.

"No problem. That's part of Sparky's job. Traffic control, and I don't mean cars. He looks harmless, but he's like a bull terrier when people cross his line. Don't you worry about those people getting in our way," he assured me.

"Well, that's a relief. You're drawing quite a crowd," I said.

"These people will get tired of standing around, watching us raise the building inch by inch. By noon they'll all be back to what they normally do. Watching TV or whatever," he confided to me, holding his hand up by his mouth so no one could read his lips. I doubted if most of the people in the crowd could read anything, let alone lips.

"Looks like you've got it all under control. I'll be in the camper if you need me for anything. Very nice to meet you all," I said, and I really meant it.

I got halfway to Ol' Blue before Red yelled at me to come back.

"Me and the wife would like to invite you as our guest to the annual all-you-can-eat crab feed at the IOOF Hall this Thursday," he announced, still with his arm around Ruby.

"Crab? I love crab! It's my most favorite seafood, right next to salmon," I squealed like a pig, which was probably what I was going to turn into come Thursday. The phrase "all-you-can-eat" in conjunction with fresh cracked crab has that effect on me. "Thank you for inviting me. I'd love to go," I almost squealed again.

"Ruby will give you the directions to our house. You can come out after work, say about 6, and we'll all go from there," he said.

"Great! I'm looking forward to it. Thank you," The crab feed was in three days. That gave me plenty of time to practice for it, and pretty much I figured the perfect place for strengthening my eating muscles would be The Daisy Café. If it was anything like most country cafes, the food was usually piled high on surf-board sized plates.

Before I transported all my week's supply of clean clothes and other miscellany designed to make my life in Ol' Blue more bearable, I thought it might be prudent to check on Larry's progress with the footings. The concrete truck was scheduled to appear at about 10am, only an hour away, and usually deliveries are scheduled pretty tightly at concrete plants.

I'd walked all around the perimeter of the footings twice before I finally gave in to reality – Larry wasn't on the job as he'd promised. There was nothing to do but go on a hunt for the little weasel.

But first things first. I needed to haul my clothes and other necessities in Ol' Blue. I wanted to finish stowing my few staples, such as a case of beer and eight or ten bags of various flavors of potato chips, before I took off on my "search and destroy mission".

Just as I was ready to jump in my truck and head for the Lucky Horseshoe, where I was confident I'd find Larry, a huge dust cloud squealed to a stop on the other side of the footings. As the dust gradually dissipated, Larry's truck became visible.

"Larry! Concrete's going to be here in less than an hour. You better be ready for it," I threatened as I got close enough to his truck to be heard.

"Huh? Oh, don't worry Katlin. Everything's ready, or just about. I've just got a bit more bracing and checking for plumb and grade and we're set," he said.

He jumped out of the truck, grabbed a few tools from the back of the truck and threw them toward the footings.

"Is anyone else going to be here today to help you?" I asked.

"Yeah. I got a couple of guys coming to help with the pour."

"Well, I'll leave you to your work. Remember, you have less than an hour to be ready," I warned him and turned to walk back to Ol' Blue. While I had a few moments I wanted to familiarize myself with the plans Gene had given me on Friday. I found it saved me time and errors if I went through the plans and specs before I started estimating the building materials. It gave me a better sense of the project as a whole.

I got about halfway through the book of specs when I heard honking and yelling coming from the street. I looked up to see a concrete pumping truck trying to get through the crowd watching Red's crew raising the garage.

"Hey! Hold up," I yelled at him as I ran toward the truck. When I finally beat my way through the crowd, I jumped up on the running board to talk to the driver. "Where do you think you're going?" I demanded.

"Right over there, next to those footings, if it's any of your concern," he fired back at me.

"I'm the Project Superintendent here and that makes it my concern," I informed him, not all too nicely. "Park it over there on the side street and let's go take a look at the site to see where you can park this thing," I ordered him.

He was so surprised to discover a woman Project Supe that it took all the bluster out of him and he politely did as he was told. I hung onto his side mirrors as I rode along on the running board.

I hoped I wasn't going to have a pissing match with every supplier, subcontractor, and truck driver on this job in order to get them to acknowledge my authority. It seemed to be getting easier, though. Maybe I was growing macho muscles. It was a good thing I was getting all this practice, because, as I was soon to find out, I was going to need all the macho I could muster up.

When he'd parked where I directed him, we got out and walked around, discussing the best location for his pump truck and where the concrete truck would best be situated.

"Those phone and electrical wires are hanging awfully low. I've got to be on this side of them so's I can raise the boom and not electrocute myself or anyone around me," he pointed out.

"Works for me. You should be able to pull right in here and then back straight out when you're done," I said pointing where I wanted him.

"Good enough," he said and got back in his truck to pull into position.

*One down, one more to go. And here it comes now*, I thought as the concrete truck stopped in the middle of the street in front of the job. As I ran toward the concrete truck, I glanced over at Larry to see how he was doing. He was pounding a stake in the ground to keep the attached 2x4 brace from slipping. I got to the concrete truck just as the driver jumped out of the truck cab.

"Hey! Over here," I yelled and waved at him.

He just stood there, watching me fight my way through the crowd to him. I braced myself for another opportunity to enlighten a driver about who I was and what that meant to him.

"I'm the Project Superintendent, Katlin. After the pump truck gets in place, you can go ahead and back in over there," I said, pointing to the place I wanted him to park his truck.

"I'm the driver of this truck, Missie, and I'm thinking I'd rather be on the other side of the pump truck," he challenged me.

*Missie?* That was a new one.

"The pump truck driver and I've already discussed this and I'm not going over the entire discussion again with you. Park it there, where I tell you, or take it back to the plant and tell your supervisor why you're returning with a full truck of undelivered concrete," I told him, looking directly and steadily at him.

There was a few moments of quiet while he contemplated his position and his choices.

"Where'd you say you want me to park?" he asked.

"Care to walk over there with me and I can show you?" I invited him.

Together we marched over to the pump truck and I showed him where to place his truck. I waited in place while he walked back to his truck, climbed up into the cab, and slowly maneuvered it precisely where I'd shown him to park it.

Both drivers got out of their rigs and were standing with me, watching Larry as he finished up. Every minute he kept these trucks waiting made me more anxious. The drivers didn't seem to care, though. Why should they? Both were paid by the hour. The longer Larry took, the more they got paid. I just hoped their respective companies didn't charge a time penalty like some of the bigger, more professional companies did.

Eventually Larry signaled he was ready and the two drivers went to work. The dance between the three of them was amazingly complex and exacting. The concrete driver regulated the rate of pour at just the right speed to keep the pump truck always loaded with the proper amount of concrete. Too much and it overflowed onto the ground, wasting expensive concrete. Too little and the pump truck would have to be stopped and primed again. It was intriguing to watch the pump truck driver deftly operate handles, levers, and buttons as he moved the boom around, cautiously avoiding the electrical wires. The pump truck driver guided the boom with the long hose smoothly so Larry could easily move around the footings to fill them level with the top of the form.

The pour went fine without any interference from me. I heaved a big sigh of relief when it was over, as I watched the two drivers washing the concrete off their trucks and tools. It had worked out fine... this time. Next time I'd know enough to stay on top of Larry so he'd be ready *before* the concrete truck arrived.

And next time I wouldn't have any arguments, shoving matches, or ego challenges from the truck drivers. I knew they couldn't wait to tell the rest of the guys back at their respective companies about the hardass woman who was the Project Supe on this job. Nothing like word-of-mouth advertising to smooth the way.

Larry was on the top of the forms, precariously balanced on the edges of the concrete forms, using some sort of giant eggbeater. I had to admire his courage – or lack of common sense. For footing he had only the 1 1/8" edge of the plywood forms. This wouldn't have been so scary, but the walls were over 8 feet high. If he lost his balance he could be seriously injured, and I couldn't afford to lose him right now.

"Larry! What are you doing up there?" I yelled.

"Getting' rid of any rock pockets so's you have a solid concrete footing wall. Otherwise you could have big voids where they's no concrete," he yelled back. I detected the slightest of sneers in his voice, as if I should have known all this.

"Yeah. I knew that. I just want to make sure you're being careful. I don't want you to get hurt."

"Well, ain't that real touching. Don't worry. I won't fall off this wall and break anything important."

"Especially don't break yourself. I don't have anyone to replace you," I muttered as I went back to Ol' Blue.

I could tell it was getting near lunch time by the rising volume of sound coming from my stomach. Larry was going to be busy for a while. He wouldn't dare leave the concrete until he'd gotten all the air bubbles out of the concrete and smoothed the surface to the grade line inside of the forms.

On my way to Ol' Blue I looked toward the garage and noticed that the crowd had diminished. Either Red had been right or the sidewalk supervisors were taking time for lunch. Red and his crew were munching on whatever was in the huge coolers they used for lunch boxes as they sat on stacks of lumber they'd brought for bracing under the house.

Things were under control and it looked like a good time for me to escape for lunch. I figured it was safe for me to go have lunch at The Daisy.

I had no problem finding The Daisy, since the business district of Stanville was about four blocks long and one street wide. I found a parking place, jumped out of my truck, and was instantly struck by the wonderful, mouth-watering smells of fried food, coffee, and onions. I paused at the door to wipe the drool from my face. I wanted to make a decent first impression on the good people of Stanville.

Phil was right. His wife's cooking was beyond excellent. French fries crispy on the outside, soft and fluffy on the inside. Hamburgers cooked to perfection and built the old fashioned way – bun toasted crisp on the grill, lettuce, thick tomato slice, American cheese, mayo, relish, and ketchup. In the interest of possible romance tonight with Roger, I reluctantly had the onion deleted from this mélange of hamburger mastery.

# Studs

I was just licking the last drops of greasy hamburger juices and condiments off my hands when a piece of lemon meringue pie appeared in front of me. It was enormous. The pan it was baked in must have been the size of a tractor tire rim. I had never seen meringue floating so high over pie filling. I could barely see over it.

"You must be Katlin," the pie said. "Phil's told me about the good job you're doing on the new store. We're all looking forward to having a real gas station in town, I can tell you. Oh, we'll all miss Maude and Henry, but it's time they moved into that retirement place they bought years ago. Henry's just getting too old to be working."

By now I'd figured it out that there was someone *behind* the pie talking to me. I leaned over a bit and spied an apple dumpling of a face topped with hair as white and frothy as whipped cream.

"Oh my, I'm forgetting my manners, aren't I? I'm Mavis, Phil's wife. I recognized you from Phil's description. You're just as purty as he said you were."

"Hi, Mavis. I'm delighted to meet you. Phil was absolutely right about the food here. That was the best hamburger that ever passed my lips. And those fries are heavenly," I gushed.

"Oh, pshaw," she actually said pshaw. "It's just good ol' country cookin'," she said, her cheeks turning rosy from her embarrassment.

"Well, I come from the country, and this is way better than anything I've ever eaten in one of our restaurants. You'll be seeing more of me," I said, hoping the "more of me" didn't mean I'd balloon to the size of Phil from eating her cooking.

"I'm glad to hear that. We serve up farmer's breakfast and lunch, but no dinner. You're on your own for that, honey," she informed me.

"I have to be on the job quite early, so I'll probably miss the farmer's breakfast, but you'll see me again at lunchtime for sure." Okay, so I lied about breakfast. But I wasn't giving up my cookie and coffee habit at The Oasis for any breakfast, I don't care how big or greasy it might be.

"The pie's on me as a welcome to Stanville," she said with a big smile.

"Wow! Thank you so much! You sure know the way to a person's heart," I said as I dug into the pie and almost swooned when the combination of flavors hit my mouth. I hoped the people sitting next to me didn't think from the noises coming from me that I was having furtive sex. This was unbelievably fabulous pie! No wonder Phil was as round as a champion hog at fair time.

"I better be getting back to the kitchen before something burns," she said and turned to go.

"Fngk oo oh mwa," I mumbled my thanks around a mouthful of lemon meringue heaven.

She just smiled knowingly and bustled back to her world of cooking.

When I had practically scraped the design off the plate in an attempt to get every last lemon pie molecule, I settled back with a satisfied sigh. After paying for my meal and leaving a generous tip, I waddled out to my truck and languidly drove back to the job site. I wouldn't be hungry for at least a day, so it was a good thing the crab feed wasn't tonight.

Things were quiet on the site, as I expected. There's a rhythm to construction. Things get busy and hectic for a while and then they slow down, sometimes almost seeming to stop. I think the slow periods exist for the sole purpose to make Project Superintendents paranoid, as they wait in the deathly quiet for the next onset of frenetic activity and with it, all the crises that make them wonder what the hell they're doing in this business.

Still having plenty of time before I had to get ready for my appointment/date with Roger, I decided to work some more on the take-off for the plans Gene had given me on Friday.

Two hours was all I could stand before I jumped up, scattering mechanical pencils, erasers, and various measuring tools all over the dining room of Casa de Construction. I hate the frustrating boredom of waiting for time to pass when I have an appointment, especially one with so much potential as this one. I changed clothes, brushed my hair, sniffed my armpits to make sure my deodorant was still working, swiped mascara all around my eyes, and grabbed my purse. As I grabbed for the door, it knocked loudly. I screamed and jumped back as Phil flung the door open.

"Are you okay? I heard you scream," he asked with great concern.

"No. I mean yes, I'm fine. You just scared me when you knocked," I explained. "Don't worry about it. Happens all the time," I said as I caught my breath.

"I see you got the concrete poured. It looks good, so I'll go ahead and sign off on the footings. I also see you had pie at my wife's café," he said, pointing to my hair.

I stepped into the master bath, and sure enough, I had missed some meringue and it had ended up in my hair. I almost licked it off, but stopped myself just in time. What would Phil think if he saw me sucking the meringue from his wife's pie out of my hair?

"Thanks for catching that," I said as I wet a wash cloth and wiped it off properly. "I have an important appointment in an hour and I want to make a good impression," I said.

"Well, you look fine now. Guess I'll be going since you have an appointment. I'll stop by in a couple of days to see how you're progressing with the trenching for the slab," he said in a fatherly way.

Trenching? What was he talking about?

"Okay, I'll see you then. Thanks for stopping by to put your official OK on the building permit for the footing walls, Phil. I really appreciate you coming by like this. It sure saves me a lot of hassle. And especially thanks for telling me about your wife's café. The lunch I had was scrumptious. I'll be back for more."

After he left, I decided to take a few moments and look at the plans and specs again to see if there might be a clue about what the trenching was about. It didn't take long to find it. The specs clearly stated that the plumbing and electrical had to be installed in trenches under the concrete slab floor. I had assumed the plumbers and electricians would take care of all their own work, which in my opinion included digging the trenches. Especially since they knew where they wanted them and there were no lines on the plans indicating where they went.

Even more especially because I hated dirt work of any kind, particularly if it meant I had to use a shovel. Now I wasn't sure whose responsibility they were. This was a question for Gene.

# Chapter 11

"G & G Construction," Ginnie answered.

"Hi, Ginnie. Is Gene back yet?"

"No, it'll probably be another day or so. What can I do ya for?"

"It's about the trenching under the slab in the building. Who does it?"

"Why, you do, honey. That's why Gene left those shovels with you. He did leave you some shovels, didn't he?" she asked, almost as an afterthought.

"Uh, no. I don't remember him leaving them around here. That's no big deal. I know where they sell them all day long. So, if I'm to dig the trenches, how will I know if I'm digging them in the right spots? Inquiring minds want to know and there's nothing in the plans showing where the trenches are supposed to be."

"Call the plumber and the electrician and have them come out and paint their trench lines on the ground. You do have their numbers, don't you?" she was getting smarter about asking me if I had what I needed. Good thing, too, because most of the time I had no clue as to what I needed.

"Yeah, their phone numbers are right here on the bid. I'll call them now. Thanks," I said, although I didn't really mean it. I wasn't looking forward to digging trenches. That was now first on the list of work that I didn't think should be included in my job description of Project Supe, right before Dirt Waterer.

"Oh, by the way, Gene didn't happen to have an excavating contractor lined up, did he?" I asked hopefully. I'd been so busy with getting Casa de Construction set up, hound-doggin' Larry, and dealing with the fluffy dirt issue that I'd completely forgotten about finding a dirt mover.

"Let me see... yeah. He's using Mark Hobak. Guess he's the one who did the dirtwork up there so far. Seems to know what he's doing and is pretty good at it."

She gave me his number, which I didn't have. Nor did I have an estimate or bid for the work from him. I was beginning to think that this project had two possible endings and neither one was good. Either it would get finished late and Gene would have to pay a hefty fine or he'd give it up as a lost cause, walk away from it, and my lofty position as Project Supe would evaporate.

After thanking Ginnie and hanging up, I called the plumber, then the electrician. They both were all too happy to come out and mark their lines on the dirt. I was mildly curious as to how they intended to paint dirt, but figured I'd find out soon enough. They both said they'd be on the job site at 8am tomorrow.

Next I called Mark Hobak.

"Hobak's Backhoe," boomed a cheery male voice on the other end of the phone line.

"Hi. Is this Mark Hobak?"

"Yep. You have the grand pleasure of talking to Mark Hobak himself," he happily informed me.

"Great. This is Katlin Greene. I'm the Project Supe for the minimart here in Stanville. I guess you've been doing the dirtwork here, is that correct?"

"Sure have. Whatcha need?"

"Well, Larry Luntz just is finishing up the foundation walls now as we speak, and I'm gonna need backfilling in a day or so. What's your schedule like?"

"You're in luck. I just happen to have a few days clear in my schedule. I can haul my equipment over there tomorrow and get the backfill done in a couple of days. Howzat?"

# Studs

"Actually, I'm in a bit of a time crunch and I'd really appreciate it if you could backfill Wednesday. And do you have a dump truck? Because I think we're going to be needing more dirt."

"Hmm. Maybe I should come over there and take a look at what you've done so far. I'll be there in a couple of minutes." And he hung up.

True to his word, it was only a few minutes before Mark roared onto the job site with his humungously macho pickup truck. It was only a tiny bit smaller than one of those monster trucks you see at county fairs. He parked next to Ol' Blue, dwarfing my home on wheels. Curious as to how he was going to disembark this giant machine, I watched as he climbed down six chrome steps to earth level.

If that saying about a big truck compensating a man for size in another department, Mark must have been compensating for all departments. When I walked up to greet him I realized he was short. *Really* short. He barely came up to my shoulder.

"You must be Katlin," he boomed at me, sticking his little hand out for me to shake. Such a big voice for such a little man.

"Y-yes. I am. And you must be Mark," I stammered trying to overcome my astonishment at the sight of this little man and his ginormous truck. From the size of his voice on the phone I had expected someone about twice as big.

"Well, looks like things are moving right along here," he said as he scanned the job site.

"Yes. Larry will be done with the foundation walls today. I'm figuring on letting the concrete cure most of tomorrow and then Larry can pull the forms tomorrow afternoon. Shouldn't take him long."

"Isn't that kinda rushing things? That concrete will still be pretty green."

"I know, but when I started this job it was already two weeks behind schedule. We've got to push in a few places in order to make up time. The concrete'll be cured enough for him to pull the forms off and for you to backfill... as long as you're gentle with it."

He smirked. "Honey, I'm always gentle."

I chose to ignore his innuendo. "Great. Then can you do it? And how much fill do you think you need to bring in?"

"Sure, I can do it. I'll have my backhoe here tomorrow afternoon. Probably we'll be needin' about six truckloads of fill. I'll get that here tomorrow before I bring the backhoe in."

"Perfect! Thank you so much." I was almost melting with gratitude and relief that Mark was able to respond so quickly. "See you tomorrow, then." He smiled, climbed back into his truck, and bounced out of the job site.

"*Better put Larry on red alert so that he gets his forms stripped tomorrow afternoon,*" a little voice warned me. Good idea.

He was still perched on the top of the foundation walls, putting the last of the finish on the mud inside to bring it to grade.

"Hey Larry," I yelled loudly enough so he'd hear me but not too loud. I didn't want to spook him into losing his balance and cause him to tumble off the wall.

"Oh, hi Katlin," he said very unenthusiastically. "I'm kinda busy. Without any help I'm just barely going to be able to finish this before my girlfriend comes to pick me up."

Girlfriend? The thought of him with a girlfriend temporarily froze my brain. I couldn't envision what type of woman who would want to be his girlfriend. Or even get within twenty feet of him, for that matter.

"Well, just make sure you do a good job. I don't want my framers complaining that the wall's so rough they can't work with it. Listen. I've got Mark Hobak coming Wednesday to backfill. He's bringing his backhoe here tomorrow and several loads of fill. I need you to be here at noon to strip the forms and I want them completely stripped by end of work day tomorrow."

"That's really pushing the concrete. It'll still be green ya know."

"Yes. I realize that. But it'll be set up enough. I don't have the luxury of waiting any longer. Just be here tomorrow and get it all stripped."

# Studs

"Okay," he said in his usual lackluster voice. It was as good as I could hope to get from him.

Before I got ready for my meeting with Roger, I had one more task to do: check on Red's progress with the garage.

I sauntered out toward the garage expecting that I'd have to fight my way through half the population of Stanville to get to Red. I was quite surprised to find only a few stragglers hanging out to watch the slow process of raising a building off its foundation, micron by micron.

"Hey, Red!" I yelled at him from a safe distance. I wasn't too anxious to have an old decrepit building accidently come tumbling down on me, especially one that no doubt was covered with mummified spiders, fossilized rat poop, and other disgusting, creepy stuff.

Red looked up from what he was doing, waved, and said something to Sparky, who took over whatever Red had been doing. "Hey, Katlin. You got here just in time. We're about to shut 'er down for the day."

"Oh. You said it would be done and gone today." Another learning experience in my new career of Project Supe: Never rely on promises from a used lumber salesman.

"We'll be done for sure tomorrow. It took a little longer than I expected, what with crowd control and all. We had to work a little slower than usual, too, because of the condition of this old, rotten building," he said, the excuses easily falling out of his mouth.

"Good thing. I'm looking forward to having more room around here. We'll be having lumber packages, refrigeration, and trusses delivered very soon and I'll need the space," I said. Actually, there was already plenty of room for the materials that would be delivered. The trusses would be set atop the walls with a crane and wouldn't even touch the ground. But a little extra pressure always helped to get the job done on time, I figured.

He nodded his head sagely as he looked around the job site. "We'll have this old broken-down building out of your way before you know it," he assured me.

We stood and looked at the old garage, now hovering on scaffolding about two feet over its foundation.

"Is it safe like that, just hanging in the air?" I asked him.

"Oh, sure. We've got pilings built under it to hold it up and it's perfectly balanced. It's as solid as if it were on the ground," he said with grand confidence.

"What about little kids getting under it to play. Could it fall on them and crush them to death?"

"Katlin. It's okay. I've been doing this for almost 40 years now and I've never had a building fall over and squash little kids, or anyone else. Rest easy. It's perfectly safe."

"Yes. Well, I have a natural talent as a worry wart. I'm quite good at it, actually."

"Yeah, so I see. Well, I'll be getting along now. We have a bit of things to tidy up before we call it a day. See you tomorrow," he said. I think I detected some relief in his voice as he made his getaway.

"Great. See you tomorrow. I have to go meet a framing sub now," I said importantly to his back.

He turned, tipped his hat to me, smiled, and continued walking back to help Sparky complete the last adjustment before they left for the day.

There was nothing left to do but go to my meeting with Roger. I was ready to burst with all the excitement about this meeting. Roger was tall, good looking, and lots of fun to be around. He'd always made a special point of saying "Hi" to me when I worked at Beacon. I hoped I could keep my speed under Warp 4 as I drove to the bar where we were meeting.

As I always do when I can't wait for the fun to start, I began without the other participants. I'd arrived at the bar an hour early, which just happened to be during their Happy Hour. Twofer drinks and all the rancid, extra salty peanuts you could eat.

The cocktail lounge was a typical after-work watering hole for carpenters, heavy equipment operators, loggers, and anyone else who wore jeans, flannel shirts, and steel-toed boots as their work uniform. Small tables, barely big enough for one ash tray and four drinks, were scattered around in no particular pattern. Sturdy wood chairs, the kind that don't break easily during bar fights, completed the décor. It was dark, smoky, and getting noisier as Happy Hour wore on.

I found a table in a corner, as far away from the jovial crowd as possible. I was hoping it was far enough away so Roger and I could hear each other. I also hoped the crowd stayed jovial. Fights had a habit of spontaneously breaking out in this kind of bar.

Roger arrived half an hour late, by which time I'd had two gin and tonics and was getting *very* happy. Peanuts, I was discovering, do not soak up alcohol very well. He stood just inside the door, trying to spot me through the cloud layer of smoke. I stuck my arm up and waved at him, but he didn't see me. I stood up and waved, but he still didn't see me. I cupped my hands around my mouth, making an improvised megaphone, and yelled, "ROGER!!"

That not only got his attention, but the attention of everyone else in the bar. Immediately, a male chorus singing "Raaaaahhhger" began, accompanied by hoots and whistles. It stopped after Roger made it to my table. I graciously thanked the choir and we both sat down as they howled with laughter, slapping each other on the back in appreciation of a fine joke, well delivered.

"Redneck humor," I said in an aside to Roger.

He grimaced and turned around to catch the bartender's attention with two fingers stuck up in the air, indicating in barroom language, "two more of the same".

"So, what have you got for me?" he said, getting right to the point as he turned back around to face me.

I handed him the rolled up plans, which he quickly unrolled and flipped to the framing page. He looked at it briefly and gave me a figure. *How, I wondered, could he come up with a price after looking at the plans for all of two minutes? He may be good, but there isn't a contractor alive who's good enough to give a bid after just a glimpse at the plans.*

"The price sounds good, but I have another bid coming in tomorrow," I lied. "I can let you know tomorrow evening if you get the job or not." Something didn't feel quite right and I wanted some time to sort it out when my head wasn't under the influence of a goodly quantity of alcohol and the studly nearness of Roger.

"I've got a busy scheduled and can fit this in, but I'll need to know by tomorrow for sure," he said.

Busy schedule? Not according to Glenn Bob. Of the two men, I trusted Glenn Bob a whole lot more than I did Roger. In fact, I was beginning to feel the warning prickles that are my personal liar detectors.

"How long will it take you to complete the framing, including setting the trusses and sheathing the roof?" I asked.

"One week. I'll have my complete crew on the job every day. I've got seven guys plus my dad who does supervisory work and also does some of the lighter framing," he explained.

"Sounds good to me. It'll be a couple of weeks before we're ready for framing. The footings and foundation walls were just poured today. The floor is next, then framing. Can you be ready to hop on it in a couple of weeks?"

"Yeah, that should work out fine for me. How about we celebrate our working together with another drink?" he asked as he began to run his foot up and down against my leg. I wasn't real sure if he was just swinging his leg and accidently made contact with my leg or if he was making some kind of move on me. I didn't care to find out. Something about him was making me uneasy, setting off alarms in my head.

He made a motion to the bartender for another round.

"No thanks, I better get back to the job. I've got a big day ahead of me tomorrow and still have phone calls to make tonight. Thanks for coming. I'll call you tomorrow and let you know for sure whether you'll be doing the framing," I said, standing up to leave.

He stood up too, and moved close to me, putting his arm around me and rubbing the palm of his hand on my bare arm in an attempt to make his intentions more obvious. Why do guys think that's a turn-on? It makes my skin hurt.

"Maybe we can get together again before I start the job," he said wiggling his eyebrows up and down so I'd be sure to catch his drift.

"Yeah, sure. Maybe," I said, pulling out of his grip. I grabbed the plans and my purse, leaving him to pay my bar bill, and walked outside and into fresh air. I inhaled deeply, greatly appreciating the air as it cleared my head.

Suddenly I felt very sober. This was not at all what I had expected. The sleaze-ball lied to me and then had tried to use sex to get the work. Okay, so maybe the thought had crossed my mind that we could have a bit of romance between us, but that had nothing to do with him getting the contract or not. He had just killed any chances of "us" *ever* happening. After his all-too-quick price and false allusions to being so very busy, which I knew were untruths, I didn't trust him. With me, nothing kills the tingle of romance for me quicker than dishonesty.

We might be able to work together, but we'd never be able to play together.

I drove thoughtfully and carefully back to Ol' Blue. Another romantic opportunity with yet another stud down the drain. Oh well.

# Chapter 12

The grogginess I felt the following morning had nothing to do with propane gas poisoning. It was completely self-inflicted. I'd had more than sufficient gin the previous night at the bar with Roger. Even sleeping in a bit didn't seem to help much. Maybe Cherie at the Oasis had a cookie that was not only delicious, but did double duty as a hangover cure. If not, I knew her coffee would wash the cobwebs out of my brain.

But wait. I had a shower with hot water now! That would do the trick!

I shed my negligee – an XXL men's cotton teeshirt – and stepped into the Master Bath. I turned on the hot water, blended it with just the right amount of cold for the perfect shower, and stepped into the stream of water. Heaven, just heaven.

For all of two minutes.

The sudden shock of icy water took my breath, leaving me without enough air in my lungs to scream sufficiently loud enough to express my pain. I must say, though, that it did seem to clear any residual gin out of my body instantly. I managed to rinse the soap out of my hair and off my body before I turned blue from the frigid water.

"What could have possibly gone wrong, *now*?" I asked the Camper Gods, looking heavenward, even though I wasn't completely sure they resided in that direction.

By the time I'd dried off and dressed, my teeth had stopped chattering so I could talk clearly enough to be understood. Immediately I placed a call to Ginnie, my camper guru.

"G and G..." she managed to say before I cut her off.

"Ginnie, the hot water isn't working in this metal beast you call a camper again. I barely had five seconds of hot water before it suddenly turned to ice. I'm lucky to be alive. I could have frozen to death in the shower," I whined at her.

She was silent for a few moments. Evidently she was trying to contain her laughter, which abruptly burst out of her in one huge roaring explosion.

"I don't understand how you can possibly think death by freezing water could be even the *least* bit hilarious," I said, sniffing indignantly.

"Haw haw haw ha heh heh. Sorry, honey. You're sure having yourself a time with that ol' camper, aren't you," she said when she could speak again without breaking into fits of giggles. "There's nothing wrong with the water heater. It's just that camper water heaters are kinda small. That one only holds two gallons. There's a technique you use when showering in a camper."

"I'd be very excited to hear this technique, Ginnie," I said, hoping she caught the sarcasm dripping off my every word.

"Here it is: you get in the shower and get wet. Then you turn the water off and lather up. Then you turn the water back on and rinse off. You better rinse off in a hurry cuz it'll be pretty obvious if you took too much time, as you probably figured out by now," she said, a few giggles escaping from where they'd been hiding in her mouth.

"Thanks. I'll keep that in mind," I said.

"Anything else I can help you with?" she offered.

"No, I think that'll be all for now. Wait, I do have one question. Why would you spend good money on something like Ol' Blue, even when it was all shiny and new, when you could stay in a perfectly good motel?" I asked. It was beyond any type of logic or reasoning I knew of as to why anyone would put themselves through the torture of living in a tin house the size of a small dumpster, even for a matter of just a few days, when civilized hotels and motels with all the hot water you could want exist everywhere.

"It's an adventure," she stated, as if that explained everything.

"Oh. I see. Well, thanks for the info. I'll talk to you later," I said, still completely baffled about the attraction some people had for campers and other primitive housing of that ilk.

I dressed hurriedly and performed my ablutions in record time, anticipating the life-giving coffee I was soon to be enjoying from The Oasis. Grabbing my purse and keys, I jumped out of Ol' Blue and nearly ran into one of two white vans.

The electrical and plumbing contractors had obviously arrived on the scene. Obvious because none of the other trades use white vans and no plumber or electrician would dream of using any other type of vehicle. I wandered over there to see what was going on.

"Hello. May I ask who you are and what you're doing?" I inquired politely.

As if it was choreographed, two men who had been bent over performing some sort of strange ritual straightened up at the same time and looked at me. One man finally stepped toward me.

"Yes,ma'am. I'm JJ Dollarman, your electrician. That young feller in the green plaid shirt is Don Hobob, your plumber. We got a call that you needed the trenches marked, so that's what we're doing," he explained. Although both men had substantial contractor's, bellies, JJ had grown the larger one and I briefly wondered if that qualified him for the top position of spokesperson.

"Good to meet you. I'm Katlin Greene, Project Superintendent, as you already seem to have figured out," I said.

"I don't know anyone else who'd willingly be living in Ol' Blue. Gene tried to talk me into it once, when we were working a job in some dinky town in Eastern Washington. I told him he couldn't pay me enough to stay in that heap of junk. A motel was just fine with me," JJ confided.

"Yes. Well. Glad to see you're so prompt."

"Don and I have done enough of these, we could do them in our sleep. It'll just take a few minutes to get everything lined out for your guys to do the trenching."

"Actually, I've been informed that I'm the guys who will be doing the trenching."

That little bit of information seemed to surprise him. I could see him arguing with himself about whether to say something or not. Finally, he spit it out. "You shouldn't be doing the digging. Gene's got grunts to do that kind of work. I'd never ask a woman to dig a trench. It's just downright undignified," he said with disgust.

I was beginning to like this man. We thought alike.

"Tell you what I'm going to do. I'll have my guys dig the trenches. You don't say anything to Gene about it, though," he said.

"Not to be ungrateful, but that's going to cost you additional in labor, isn't it?" I asked him.

"Yep. And ol' Gene will pay for it, too. He just won't know it. I'll include it in his bill as materials or something. He never looks at the bills and Ginnie don't know what's going on at these jobs anyways," he said.

"Sounds good to me. I wasn't looking forward to that back-breaking work. I can't tell you how much I appreciate this," I said, almost tearful with gratitude.

"Don't you fret about it. Don and I'll enjoy doing this to Gene probably more than you'll enjoy not having to do the ditchwork," JJ said as he winked at me, his co-conspirator.

"I have to leave for a few minutes, but I'll be right back. Do you need me to pick up anything in town for you," I asked, feeling expansive toward this man.

"No, thanks. I'll be gone by the time you get back. I'll have a couple of my guys come over here in a bit to do the digging. Just so happens my schedule is flexible right now and I have a few guys I can spare. They'll be done by noon or maybe even before. It's pretty shallow digging and the soil is sandy, so they shouldn't have anything to slow them down," he replied.

"Thanks, again. I truly appreciate this. Oh, by the way, when will you have the wiring and plumbing in the ground so we can pour the slab?"

"The end of this week we should be done," he said.

"Thank you so much. I can't tell you what a relief it is to have quality subcontractors like you and Don on the job. Do you have a card I can give my concrete guy, just in case he has questions?" I could feel gratitude and relief oozing through my body like hot fudge on ice cream, melting away all my stress.

He handed me a wad of his business cards. "You just never know when you might run into someone who needs an electrician," he explained.

I grinned at him as I accepted the stack of cards and left to get my much-needed coffee. Now that I had three subs who needed to coordinate their work, things were getting interesting on the job site. I hoped it would all work out. I could tell that JJ and Don knew their stuff, but I wasn't quite as confidant about Larry.

As I stood around and watched the guys working for a few minutes, trying out different poses to make me look like a proper Project Supe, I discovered the secret to painting dirt. A modern miracle called "upside down paint" – paint in a spray can that works upside down. Sometimes I'm in awe of the little things people invent that so greatly ease other people's day-to-day life.

I mused about the unknown genius who had invented spray paint cans that painted upside down as I drove to The Oasis. I hoped whoever that clever inventor was, he was well paid for his idea. I wondered if he'd be open to some ideas of mine, like nose tampons for when you have a cold and don't have time to blow your nose a thousand times a day or to catch every little drip. I envisioned them with little decorative pull strings... maybe colorful beads or rhinestones to coordinate with your ensemble.

# Studs

Cherie was the just saying goodbye to a customer as I strolled in. Perfect timing.

"Hi Cherie, what's today's cookie special?" I asked, barely able to speak past all the drool that had suddenly flooded my mouth at my first sniff of the inside of her shop.

"Hi there, Katlin. Leftovers today. Hope you don't mind. I'll give you twofers just to make up for it," she said.

"No, I don't mind. That's fine with me," I tried to act nonchalant. Was it any wonder I loved this place? "Better make the coffee a triple today. I have a big day ahead of me."

"Looks like you had a big night behind you," she said.

"Does it show that much?"

"Well, it's not so bad, except your eyeballs look like a roadmap, the bags under your eyes look like you could carry a week's groceries in them. Oh, and your tongue looks like a little Polar Bear. But other than that, you look just fine. Don't worry about it. Nobody will notice."

*Yeah, like you didn't notice*, I thought. I didn't care. She could say anything she wanted about me as long as she gave me free cookies.

"Thanks, Cherie. I'll see you tomorrow," I said as I grabbed my daily allowance of cookies and coffee. I'd no doubt be fodder for some of her juicy gossip with customers who came after me. Well, like my dear old friend Annie always says, "if they're talking about you, they're leaving somebody else alone".

On the way back to the job site, I took a slight detour by the Lucky Horseshoe just in the off chance the Larry the Lush might be trying to drink away a hangover. There are some devoted drunks who actually believe you can drink yourself sober. I suspected Larry might be one of them. As I cruised slowly by the tavern, I could see the nose of his truck sticking out beyond a ball of dents that at one time had been a Volkswagen bug. I was glad he was better at concrete work than he was at hiding.

Having nothing to hide from the townspeople of Stanville, I parked directly in front of the tavern on the street. As I entered the bar, I could see Larry slouched over the bar, perched on his usual bar stool. I took pity on him and decided not to surprise him this time. I'd save it for a special occasion, when I'd get greater enjoyment out of watching him tip over again.

"Larry," I said in my indoor voice.

He cringed, then turned around slowly, looking like a hen-pecked husband.

"The electrician and plumber are at the job site now, digging the trenches. They said they'll be done laying their wire and pipes by the end of this week. That means Monday you can place your remesh and get ready for pouring the floor on Tuesday. Does that work into your schedule?" I asked, knowing his schedule revolved more around happy hour than it did work.

"Lemme see," he replied, trying as hard as he could to think. "Yuh, that'll work."

"Great. Be on the job first thing Monday. I'll schedule the concrete for Tuesday at 9am. That'll give you time to finish any little details before the trucks arrive. Fine with you?"

"Yeah. Fine, Katlin," he replied obediently.

"Oh. And I'll see you on the job site this afternoon, stripping your forms. Won't I." It was not a question.

"Yes, Katlin."

I turned and walked out, noticing eyeballs following me. I guess I'd made quite an impression on the regulars the last time I had a discussion with Larry while he laid on the floor, tangled in his bar stool. Come to think of it, the tavern had been deathly quiet while I was talking to Larry this time. Fine with me. The other bar regulars would serve as reinforcement for my message that I meant business so Larry wouldn't easily forget.

As I drove onto the job site, happily full of cookies and coffee, I realized something was missing. A garage moving crew, to be exact. *Where was Red and all his little red-topped helpers*, I wondered. I was a little disappointed. He'd seemed so reliable. Well, it wasn't like the garage moving was holding up any other part of the job at this point. A day or so more on that part of the job wouldn't hurt anything.

I entered Casa de Construction and got to work scheduling the pumper truck, concrete delivery, a few other miscellaneous chores. I was deep into the plans Gene had left for me to work on when I could hear someone scuffling around outside the camper by the door. Soon whoever it was began mumbling to themselves. Finally, the mysterious mumbler knocked on the door. Just to be frisky, I flung it open, wanting to see the reaction from this timid person.

I don't know who was more surprised. I expected some normal-sized person, and instead saw a bear of a man jump back, nearly falling over backwards. His head and face were almost completely covered in what appeared to be matted black fur. As he grabbed his cap from his head I noticed his hands more resembled big paws.

"May I help you?" I inquired sweetly, not wanting to anger this bear-man.

"Yes, ma'am, you can. Would you please point me to the Project Superintendent for this job?" he asked very politely in a voice sounding much like a soft, gentle growl.

"I'm the Project Supe. What can I do for you?"

"If you haven't already bid out the framing, I'd like to give you my bid."

"Well, I do have someone who gave me a good number, but I haven't committed to him yet and would be happy to get another bid. Come in and I'll show you the plans. It's a pretty simple building, as you'll see," I said as I stepped back giving him lots of room. I left the door open... just in case.

I spread the plans out on top of the others I'd been working on and opened them to the framing page. "I'll just leave you with these for a bit and you can take a look at them. I'll be out here by the foundation if you have any questions," I said slipping by him quickly. I'd heard bears could get riled up quickly and I didn't want to be alone in Ol' Blue with this guy just in case.

After a while I got bored and wandered back to the camper. "How are you doing with the plans?" I asked from the safety of outside the camper.

"I'm almost done, ma'am," he replied in his deep, raspy voice.

I waited a few more minutes and he emerged from Ol' Blue, blinking his small, beady eyes in the bright sunlight as if he'd just awakened from hibernation.

"Here's my card. My bid's on the back," he said, replacing his filthy cap on his furry head as he turned to walk to his beat-up truck.

I watched him walk away before I remembered I should have said "good-bye" or "thank you" or something. So far he got top prize for being the oddest of all the characters I'd met in Stanville. I looked at his card where his name was printed in big, bold, simple type. Harold "Harry" Ursus Black. His mother must have quite a sense of humor, I figured.

His bid, scrawled on the back of his card, was about twice the amount of Roger's. Now I had to hire Roger. I grabbed the phone and dialed his number. It rang for an eternity before the answering machine began intoning a message in a metallic voice. I left a message for Roger telling him he had the job and to call me ASAP so we could coordinate scheduling.

Tonight was the Project Management class and I was looking forward to it. I could only hope I'd learn enough to help ease me through the never-ending stream of challenges that seemed to come at me like a swarm of mad hornets. I'd no sooner get rid of one challenge then two or three more would take its place. A person would have to be an adrenalin junkie to love a job like this, I decided. Well, I'd find out more about the type of people who became Project Supes at this class.

In the meantime, I had plenty more hornets to swat at. So far I had foundation, electrical, plumbing, and framing subs. It was past time to find out how many other subs I needed for this job. A call to Ginnie would no doubt get me that information. She seemed to know more about this business than Gene.

"G & G Construction," said the Angel of Information.

"Hi Ginnie. Katlin here. Hey, Gene didn't leave me a list of the subcontractors he's already gotten for this job. How can I find out who he's got?" I asked, as if I didn't already know.

"Why, that's easy, honey. I got a list right here in the office," she said. I expected no less.

"I'm meeting Gene tonight at the Contractor's Association and we're going to the Project Management class. Would you give it to him so I can get it tonight? I think it's past the time when I should have scheduled all my subs."

"You're probably right about that. Gene's never been one to take care of the details. He pretty much just leaves all that to me. I think you're going to be better at project management than he is."

I was so surprised at her generous compliment that I didn't know what to say for a moment. Then it came to me. "Thank you. That's very encouraging of you to say that," I said.

"The truth's the truth. Well I gotta get back to work. Like they say, the job's not over until the paperwork's done," she said breaking into hoots of laughter at her reference to a bit of bathroom humor.

"Thanks again for all your help. I really appreciate it, "I said and hung up after hearing her "buh-bye" to me.

Suddenly the camper started shaking – a sure sign that had a visitor in a very large vehicle. I jiggled over to the door on Ol' Blue and jumped over the steps and onto the ground in my hurry to see who the next hornet was. To my delight, it was Mark with his dump truck pulling a lowboy on which sat a backhoe. The truck was dark blue under a generous coating of dust, except where someone had swiped at the dirt on the truck door. Through the smear I could just make out Mark's business name – Hobak's Backhoe and Excavation Services. I wondered briefly if he'd chosen his line of work because of his name.

"Hey Mark!" I yelled waving my hands so he could see me.

He stopped his truck alongside the new foundation and acknowledged my wave with a pull on the cord to his air horn, blasting me with an AOOOOOOOOOGAHH loud enough to deafen anyone within half a mile.

After my teeth stopped vibrating I looked up to see nothing but chrome. While I was holding my ears and squinting my eyes shut to keep the blast of his air horn from getting into my brain and doing untold damage, Mark had crept his truck to within inches of me. Just what I needed. A sub with gigantic machinery and a penchant for practical jokes. Just above the chrome I could see Mark's Cheshire cat grin, indicating his pride in his own immensely clever wit.

I walked around to his side of the cab, jumped up on the running board, and motioned for him to roll down his window. He shook his head as a symbol of his mock fear, then seeing I was not finding much humor in this whole event, chose wisely and rolled his window down.

"Hey, Mark, good to see you... and your truck and backhoe," I said and I meant it. Number one on my list of desired qualities in a sub is reliability. Second is responsibility. Third is ability.

"I'm simply delighted to be here. Do you have a choice spot where I can keep my backhoe for a few days while I'm doing the backfilling and grading? Or can I drop it just anywhere," he said.

"How about you park it over there by the house next to the side street. Would that suit you okay?" I asked.

"Works for me. You wanna hang on there while I do some fancy maneuvering or would you rather watch the show from a distance, where you can see it better?"

Oh great. He had an ego as big as his equipment. His truck and backhoe, that is. "Well actually I have to check on how the electrician and plumber are doing and chase down my concrete sub.

"You must mean Larry. You gotta stay on top of that guy or come Christmas you'll still be without a foundation. A word of advice. Don't pay him a cent until the job's done. Otherwise you won't see him until he's drunk up every cent you give him."

"Thanks for your words of wisdom. I'll tell our bookkeeper and make sure she holds onto his check until we pass all foundation inspections. Well, you probably want to get unloaded and get out of here so you can get to work. Thanks for everything and I'll see you tomorrow, right?"

"Yep. First thing tomorrow morning I'll be here dumping fill. I figure to start with about ten loads and we'll see if that's about right."

"Great. See you tomorrow, Mark. Thanks."

Things were looking up. I had three excellent subs and only one doofus sub that I had to babysit. Maybe I'd make it through to the end of this job without losing my mind after all. Speaking of the doofus, he still hadn't shown up so a trip back to the tavern seemed to be in order.

With a heavy sigh I turned and walked back to the camper to grab my purse and truck keys. Just as I was closing up Ol' Blue I heard a toot-toot from Mark's air horn. Much quieter and more friendly than the previous blast. I looked up and waved at him as he drove off, leaving his backhoe exactly where I'd asked him to park it. Perfect. Either I was getting the hang of acting and sounding like the Project Supe or Mark was just a really nice guy.

Just then the opposite of a guy like Mark drove onto the job site. Larry was actually being responsible enough to show up without me going to the tavern and dragging his skinny ass off the bar stool.

I watched him as he pulled a few tools out of the back of his truck and started pulling the 2x4 bracing and plywood forms off the foundation walls. I was pretty sure that an important part of my job was to inspect my subs' work, so after he'd removed his framing and exposed the outside of one wall, I walked over to examine the quality of his work.

His monster eggbeater had done a fairly good job, with only a few, very small voids – or rock pockets as they're called in the industry. Good enough for me and, I hoped, good enough for Phil.

"You going to be done by tonight like we talked about, Larry?" I yelled at him.

"Yes, Katlin," he replied all docile-like.

"There'll be some guys here in a bit to start digging the trenches for the electrical and plumbing. Try not to drop any lumber on them, will you?"

"Yes, Katlin." He seemed to be taking to his training by me just fine. I'd know more the next morning, when I could see how far he actually got stripping the walls. If he did his job as he said I'd be able to examine all of the foundation walls to see the true quality of his work.

The morning had somehow melted into afternoon, and I had just enough time to freshen up and put on some makeup so I'd look less like one of my subs before driving to the class in Bellevue. If traffic wasn't too jammed up, I'd even have time to grab a quick dinner at one of my favorite restaurants in Bellevue – Kripps Eats. Kripps had the best deep-fried everything you could ever hope to clog your arteries with.

In no time I was on the road to my favorite big city, Bellevue. Driving on the freeway always lulls my mind into a trance-like state, allowing it to drift off anywhere it wants to go. During this particular drive it seemed to want to focus on work, much to my disgust. I found myself wondering what practical tips and little-known secrets of project management I was about to learn. Would they be worth the money Gene had shelled out for this class? Or would the class be a waste of his money and my time? I was soon to find out.

# Chapter 13

The food at Kripp's Eats was exactly like it had been when I worked at Beacon and ate there regularly. Grease dripped off everything. I swear their secret recipe for a hamburger was to put all the ingredients together – bun, hamburger patty, lettuce, tomato, dill pickle coins, mayo, relish, and mustard – and stick it all in the deep-fat fryer. The regulars hadn't nicknamed the place "Kripp's Grease" for nothing. They, in turn, had been nicknamed "Kripp's Creeps" by the owner. Both names sort of fit.

The typical clientele included first-year students at the U of W (by their second year they usually had enough smarts to eat some place healthier) and drunks hoping to sop up some alcohol with the grease so they could continue drinking and remain upright. Once in a while a group of Bellevue yuppies would down a few of Kripp's grease burgers to top off their evening of slumming in the sleazy bars of Old Town. They didn't usually become repeat customers. Something to do with their delicate digestive systems being better suited to the food at places like Dante's and Thirteen Coins.

Luckily I had lived in Bellevue and knew the streets. The saying, "you can't get there from here" perfectly describes navigation in Bellevue. Streets change names mid-block for no good reason, dead end in a parking lot under a skyscraper, unexpectedly become one way going the other way, and other such interesting and creative engineering feats. I made it to the Association of Contractors building with time to spare and even found an empty parking space near the entrance to the building.

Gene was waiting for me in the lobby and handed me a ticket as he grabbed me by the arm to steer me toward the class room.

"Glad to see you're on time. I was wondering how you'd do with this rush hour traffic," he said.

I stopped my mouth from saying something about having already told him about the traffic. Some people have selective deafness and only hear what they want to hear. It appeared Gene was one of them.

"Did Ginnie give you something to give me?" I asked him. I had no doubt she'd given the list of subs to him; I just hoped he remembered to bring it with him.

"Huh? Oh, yeah. Here it is," he said, pulling an envelope from his inside jacket pocket and giving it to me. "You girls got some secret stuff going on behind my back?" he asked, half kidding.

"Oh, right. As if Ginnie would ever keep any secrets from you... or anybody for that matter. She's about the most honest person I know. Besides myself, that is," I replied, bristling inside to think that he'd doubt my trustworthiness.

"I was just kidding. Jeez, can't you take a joke? Come on, let's get to the classroom and get a seat before all the good ones are taken," he said, doing a very slick job of changing the subject.

As soon as we got seated, Gene stood up and started glad-handing everyone around us. Sometimes he even remembered to introduce me.

We were standing together while he gossiped with another general contractor when unexpectedly his face tightened and turned red. I turned to see what could have possibly triggered such a change in him and saw nothing. Just a bunch of guys standing in a circle talking, like we were doing. One of them abruptly turned to look in our direction, as if he was searching for something. His eyes stopped when he spotted Gene.

He excused himself from his group and made his way through the people and chairs toward us. The closer he got, the more tense Gene became. I could feel the heat from his body increasing as he became more agitated.

"Hello, Gene. Good to see you," the newcomer said in a soothing, quiet tone of voice.

"Bruce," Gene acknowledged tersely giving him just the barest of a nod.

*What in the world is going on here? Are these two arch rivals or something? Did one of them steal a job from the other one? Or worse, their woman?* I wondered. These thoughts must have been streaming across my face just as the unidentified man turned to look at me.

"Hello. I'm Gene's little brother, Bruce. You must be his new Project Superintendent. I've heard good things about you from Ginnie," he said, grinning at me.

I felt Gene's agitation turn to anger at the mention of Ginnie's name. Aha. A clue.

"That's very kind of you to say, Bruce," I replied politely, sticking my hand out to shake. "I'm Katlin Greene."

All of a sudden Gene turned around and stomped out of the room. Nobody in the room paid any attention to his abrupt departure. Either this was normal behavior for him and everyone was used to it or no one wanted to get involved.

"What was that all about," I asked, then mentally slapped my hand over my mouth as I realized it was probably none of my business.

"Well, it's probably none of your business, but you'll no doubt hear the story from someone, so you might as well hear the truth from me. Gene's jealous of me. It's a classic case of one brother thinking the other one was better loved by one or both parents. In this case, he thought our dad gave me all the love and attention. In order to get some of dad's love, he's always tried to best me in whatever I did. In school he'd try out for the same sports I did. Unfortunately, he's not much of an athlete. It was rather embarrassing for him at times. When I got into construction and became a general contractor, building residential developments, he tried to outdo me by becoming a general contractor in commercial construction. Like sports, construction is a natural for me. Not so for him. To top things off, I'm president of the state builder's association," he explained.

I was relieved to hear it was no more than sibling rivalry. But still, Gene was an adult now, not a child. His behavior was far less than I'd come to expect from a grown-up. He was proving to be quite an enigma. Kind, gentle, and quiet one moment, then explosively emotional the next.

"Thank you for telling me about this. It must be difficult for you," I said.

"Yes, and I don't want to aggravate the situation and make things difficult for you. He's coming back now, so I'll say my goodbyes to you. Here's my card. If you ever need anything, let me know," he said.

I took his card and nodded my acknowledgment of the situation to him, then turned and sat down in my chair. This added yet another facet of intrigue to my job and I wondered how it might affect things. In the midst of my wondering, Gene plopped down in his chair next to me.

"Looks like you and my brother got along just swell," he growled.

"We talked for a few minutes until you returned. He's okay," I said, not wanting to get him riled up again. His face was almost a normal color and he wasn't talking through clenched teeth anymore.

"Class is going to start. I hope you brought something for note-taking," he said.

"Uh, no. I didn't. I honestly didn't know what to expect," I began to offer lame excuses only to be shushed by someone at the podium.

"Everyone take your seats. We're going to start the class now. Under your seats each of you will find a workbook. This is yours to take with you. You'll find a notepad, too, for those of you who like to take your own notes," the instructor said.

I gave Gene The Look to let him know next time he could give me a little more information so I'd be better prepared. He got off easy this time, The Look implied.

# Studs

A mere three hours later my brain was full. I had no idea there was so much to being a Project Superintendent. I was naïve enough to think all I had to do was schedule subs and they'd all be professional enough to do their work properly and on time. According to this instructor, my job was more along the lines of a glorified baby-sitter. There went my fantasy of being surrounded by gorgeous, muscular studs who efficiently and professionally obeyed my merest commands without hesitation. Instead it sounded like my job was going to be more like riding herd on a bunch of guys like Larry the Lush.

I did learn some practical tools to help me keep my sanity - timeline charts, flow charts, and the elements of a proper contract. The instructor emphasized the importance of having a contract with each sub-contractor.

"That's why the people in this business are called "contractors". If you want to stay in this business, you'll remember this little fact," were his exact words.

I gave Gene The Look again, but he seemed to be paying extraordinarily intense attention to the instructor just at that moment. Either that or he'd gone to sleep with his eyes open.

Luckily, there were sample contracts in the notebook, of which I'd be making about a thousand copies the next day. Roger was going to be the recipient of my first contract. Larry the Lush was beyond a contract, but still I had all the rest of the subs. I couldn't wait to get started being so professional.

After the class was over, Gene grabbed me by the arm and hustled me out of the building.

"Hope you learned something tonight," he said brusquely.

"Yes, I did. Thank you so..." I managed to get out before he muttered a goodbye and spun around, disappearing quickly. Either he was in a hurry to get back to his beloved Ginnie or else to get away from his detested brother. My guess was the latter.

I made it back to my truck at a much more sedate pace, piled the notebook and all the tons of notes I'd taken in the seat, and slid in. The drive back to Stanville was long and it was late. I had prepared for the drive by drinking about fourteen

Styrofoam cups of the free rot gut coffee they so generously provided during the class. I was good to go. In more ways than one. Luckily I knew the exact locations of all the rest stops along the way.

# Chapter 14

Loud voices woke me from an exhausted sleep. Aggravatingly loud. Where, I ask you, was the consideration for the hardworking people of this country, that we were not allowed to sleep past daybreak?

After finally getting back to Ol' Blue in the wee morning hours from the Project Superintendent class the night before, I was in no mood to be rudely awakened so early. In fact, one might say I was exceptionally cranky as I tumbled down to the main floor of Casa de Construction from my lofty bedroom suite.

Somehow I managed to find the pile of yesterday's clothes and yank them on, getting most of my appendages in the correct holes. Shoving open the door, I took a deep breath, the better to screech loudly and irately at the offensive people. My mouth slammed shut when I saw the happy army of walking matchsticks.

Red and his crew had shown up to finish moving the garage!

In a much chirpier mood now, I stuffed my feet into my boots and went out to see how things were going. After all, according to what I'd learned at class the night before, that was a large part of my job description.

"Hey, Katlin! How goes it?" Red greeted me as soon as he spotted me.

"Hi, Red. I'm very happy to see you and your crew *today*," I said, tossing a subtle hint at him to let him know I was a bit disappointed he wasn't on the job yesterday.

"Oh, yeah. That. Well, there was a great tide – one of the best this year. We couldn't pass it up, could we?" this last he directed at his crew, who correctly obeyed by nodding their heads in agreement.

"Tide?" I questioned, not understanding what tides had to do with moving this building.

"Yeah. One of the lowest tides this year. Oh, I brought you a little something," he said lifting a medium size cooler from the back of his flatbed truck. He set it down on the ground and flipped the top open, proudly displaying the contents.

I wasn't quite sure what it was. My guess was some kind of mutant clam. Whatever it was, it completely filled the cooler all by itself.

"I-I don't know how to thank you," I said, my lips quivering from my effort to stop myself from gagging.

"Just look at you... your lips are already quivering in anticipation of this here gourmet delight. I knew you'd love fresh Gooeyduck," he said, proudly grabbing the slimy thing and holding it up so I could fully appreciate all three feet of its total length. The filthy, barnacle-covered shell was the best-looking part. The neck of the thing hung down about three feet and looked like a bull's limp tally-whacker.

"I'm at a loss for words. You're entirely too generous, Red, giving the food from your family's table to someone like me, almost a complete stranger. I really shouldn't take it," I said trying desperately to figure out a tactful way to get the disgusting thing out of my sight. Good thing I didn't have a hangover just then.

"The eating's the best part of Gooeyducks, but we love the whole challenge of digging them. First you gotta have a real low tide, cuz they live the sand in deep waters, even beyond where the clams are. Then you hafta sneak up on them to find their holes in the sand. If you walk too hard on the beach, they can feel it and they start to dig down – and they dig purty fast, too. It takes three of us about half an hour just to dig one of 'em cuz we gotta go down after them as they dig. You should see us in action! We're all elbows and assholes, chasing them Gooeyduck down into the sand, grabbing 'em before they can get away. They dig fast, but we dig faster, right gang?" he said turning proudly to his army of redheads. They all nodded in agreement, looking like a field of red tulips bobbing in the breeze.

"Well, thank you very much. I'm sure I'll enjoy this one especially, knowing you and your family captured it," I said, trying to be appropriately grateful. "I'll just put it in the camper for now and have it for dinner tonight."

"You gotta cook it hot and fast, otherwise the meat gets tough enough you could make tires out of it," Red generously offered his cooking tip, as he lovingly replaced the Clamasaurus back in the cooler and handed it to me.

"Thanks. I'll remember that," I replied. I couldn't imagine anyone actually chewing on this repulsive-looking lump of flesh. I just didn't understand why anyone would work so hard, bent over and digging for hours in wet, heavy sand, just to be rewarded with a revolting clam of monstrous proportions. It was another one of the mysteries of life, one that I ranked right up there with the love of RVing.

I carried the cooler to Ol' Blue and stuck it under the dinette table. What was it with this guy? Didn't anyone ever tell him that humungous, slimy, prehistoric clams with disgusting three foot long necks were not high on the list of gifts that women liked to receive?

After superficially performing my morning ablutions, I hopped in my truck and made it out to the Oasis in time to grab the last two Marble Mocha cookies. Work, it seemed, might potentially interfere with my new tradition of the morning cookie run. I'd have to be alert for any possible impediments to my morning cookie and coffee acquisition.

Back on the jobsite, happily munching on the last of my cookie and sucking on the high octane coffee that Cherie brewed, I decided it was time for me to act like a Project Supe and inspect the work that JJ's crew had done on the trenching.

The flattened dirt inside the footings looked like some sort of Mondrian art. Absolutely straight trenches crisscrossed the area with a precision that would bring an engineer to his knees in teary awe. The sides of the trenches were perfectly vertical and the bottoms were flat as a table top. I grabbed a level out of the tools Gene had left for me in Ol' Blue to check grade and sure enough, the plumbing trenches had just the right amount of fall so the liquid inside of them would drain properly. These guys were not good. They were excellent!

Just then, a white van with faded blue paint on the side proudly announcing "Hobob Plumbing" drove up and three clean-cut guys jumped out. Without even giving me a glance, they threw open all the doors of the van and began pulling materials out and placing them around the footings. Within minutes they were all on their knees, cutting, gluing, and installing the plastic pipes for their plumbing. Only rarely did they talk to each other. They'd been working together so long and knew their job so well it had become like a well-choreographed dance.

I watched them for a while, until I began to feel completely unnecessary. It was one thing to have efficient subcontractors who knew what they were doing. It was another to feel totally useless because they *were* so efficient. I'd need to find the fine balance point between being an unnecessary accoutrement and a full time babysitter.

After watching them for a while, I discerned who the lead man was. Actually, it was quite easy, since he was the one who mostly pointed at stuff and told the others what to do. I walked over to him to see if he needed anything from me.

"We're fine," he said without even looking up at me. "We'll be done tomorrow and ready for rough-in plumbing inspection on Friday.

"Ok. Thanks. You guys are doing a good job," I said, trying to make sounds like a real Project Supe. They knew they were good. I didn't have to tell them. But they seemed to appreciate it anyway. Or at least one guy did. I caught the faintest wiggle around his mouth, indicating a smile trying to escape.

*Egad,* I thought as I walked back to Ol' Blue. *Two more inspections.* I was beginning to think that every tiny thing that happened on this job site needed to be inspected by somebody. I didn't remember the houses I worked on as a roofer and a carpenter needing so many inspections.

A building inspector once told me that the original building code regarding construction quality and safety was created during the times of Ancient Greece. It went something like this: if a building was defectively built and the failure of its construction caused the death of an occupant, then the builder would likewise lose his life, being put to death in some similarly grotesque manner. Simple and to the point. I'll bet there weren't many poorly constructed buildings in those days.

As I pondered this law, I sauntered back to Ol' Blue. First item of business was a call to JJ, during which I discovered that his work was going to be inspected by the state electrical inspector on Monday.

"Will you be here with the permit on Monday?" I hoped fervently he would be. I had no idea where the permit was and was guessing he had it.

"Didn't Gene give it to you already?" he asked, and then before I could stammer a reply, he barked out a laugh or two. "Hell, I was just joshin'. I know Gene isn't that well organized, so I always just go ahead and get the permits and schedule all the inspections. I'll keep you updated."

"Thank you so much, JJ. It's a real pleasure to work with someone as organized and professional as you," I said with great relief. This was more like it. Subcontractors who did their job well and efficiently.

"See you Monday," he said and hung up.

Even better. He was actually going to be here for the inspection so if anything was unacceptable to the inspector, JJ would be able to deal with it directly instead of me being the go-between.

Next on my agenda was a phone call to Roger, informing him that he needed to sign a contract. He picked up on the first ring. *If he was so busy with work, why was he so instantly available for work and almost always in his office?* I wondered.

"Hi, Roger. It's me, Katlin. Hey, you got the job! You outbid the other guy," I said, trying to keep a straight face. Even over the phone, people can hear in your voice if you're smiling, frowning, grimacing or are making any one of a bunch of other facial expressions.

"Yeah, I figured it like that," he said in a tone that I suspect was false confidence.

"Just one tiny, eensy, little detail. Um. Ineedyoutosignacontract," I said just a little too fast, no doubt making it obvious to him that I was nervous about this issue.

"Katlin, I thought we were friends. Friends don't need contracts," he said.

"Well, this friend does."

"In all the years I've been in business, I never worked with contracts. I'm not about to start now," he said defiantly. "Guess this means we won't be working together. I'm real disappointed. I was looking forward to it."

This put me in a very difficult position. I needed him real bad to do the framing. But did I need him more than he needed me? Still, I had no framing sub and desperately needed one quick. Bear Man wasn't going to be it, so that left me with Roger. I made an executive decision to trust him and hire him anyway.

"Well, since we're friends, as you say, I'll go ahead and trust you. I'll get back to you with a definite start date. Just to be clear, you said you'd be complete with your work, which includes framing the walls, exterior and interior, hanging trusses, nailing the sheathing on the roof, walls, and gambrel roof, and siding the building within two weeks. Right?"

"Yep. Just like I said, I'll have my full crew there every day and we'll get it done on schedule. Don't you worry your pretty head about it. I'll take care of the framing," he said.

"Okay. I'm just making a note about that so I can keep my timelines in order." And also in case I needed evidence should we have a disagreement about his work. Another handy little trick I learned in that class – make notes of every discussion you have with anyone doing anything relating to the job. You just never know when you might need to present such evidence in a court of law. "I'll call you in a day or so to let you know exactly when you can start, so plan on being here and starting in about a week or so," I said and hung up.

His work was crucial to the entire project and if it wasn't done on time, the entire row of subcontractors would fall down behind him like dominoes. Well, I couldn't spend any time fretting about him. I had calls to make, schedules to draw up, and other important Project Supe types of work.

I looked over my list of subcontractors – those who had already been contracted or agreed to do the work and added Roger's name next to "Framing". There were only two spots left to fill – flooring and roofing. I knew who I wanted for my roofing sub and hoped he was available.

"Faith Roofing," said one of my favorite people in the whole world. James and I had worked together on many jobs when I was a roofing contractor in Port Townsend years ago. But that's another story. Although I'd moved on from roofing, he was still a roofing contractor - and the best there was in the area. He and his wife, Margie, were two of the most decent people I'd ever known. They were generous, kind, and loving with everyone they met.

"Hi, James. It's Katlin. Remember that job I talked to you about up in Stanville? The one you bid for me? Well, not only did we get the job, I'm the Project Superintendent," I proudly announced.

"Well, that's wonderful, Katlin. It's good to hear from you. Margie and I were just talking about you the other night over dinner, wondering how you were doing. She sends her love," he said.

"Tell her so far, so good," I said laughing with delight at connecting again with his gentle energy. "But listen, the reason I called is to ask if you'd be interested in doing the roof. It probably won't be for two or three weeks, depending on the schedule."

"That'd work out just about right for me. I have a couple of big jobs and should be done by then. It's a hot mop, right?" he asked, referring to the fact that it was a flat roof requiring hot tar roofing.

"Right. Hopefully the weather will cool down some by then. This wonderful summer weather is great for framing, not so great for hot tar. You'll do it then?" I asked hopefully.

"Sure, sounds good."

"Urm. I'll send you a contract. OK?"

"That's fine. It's actually best that way. We'll both have the details in print in case there's ever a question that comes up."

"Great. Thanks," I said with great relief at his willingness to sign a contract. "I'll contact you when we begin framing so you'll have a better idea of timing. Be talking to you soon. My love to Margie and the boys," I said and hung up.

His crew had evolved through the years since I'd first met him from two and a half people - his brother-in-law and occasionally me - to all four of his boys, now all grown up and happily following in their dad's footsteps. Although their mom had a wild bush of blonde hair, all the boys had their dad's thin, straight, red hair. What was it with these red headed guys and all their red-headed git?

Next I decided to lock in my flooring sub. I called one of my other construction buddies, Burt Bumstead. He wasn't home, so I left a message on his answering machine. Probably he was at the local café, drinking that puny, watered-down stuff they called coffee and playing Ship Captain Crew with his cronies to see who'd pay the coffee tab. You'd think that drinking all that coffee, even that weak stuff, would keep him wired and, thus, thin. Not so. He probably could have won the International Butt Crack Contest, if there was such a thing. I'd have to make sure I was outside when he was laying the tile flooring. The sight of him bent over installing floor tile could put me off my cookies for days, and I wouldn't want that to happen.

Now that all my subs were accounted for, next on my agenda was to create a timeline. During the class I'd learned about this nifty thing called a Timeline Chart and thought I'd try it out to see how it worked in real life. It sounded good in theory. After taping several sheets of paper together to create one super wide sheet, I drew horizontal and vertical lines, creating a spreadsheet of some sort. In the first column, I listed all the subcontractors. Across the top I inserted dates by the week, beginning with when I had first started this "wunnerful" job and ending approximately three months later.

Then came the timeline part. I drew lines across the rows, one line for each sub indicating when each of them would be on the job. I made a few notes for clarification, such as "rough in" or "trim out". It looked good on paper. However, the map isn't always the territory. It would be interesting to see how accurate this was and how much help it would give me in scheduling and keeping things straight.

A quick glance at the clock told me it was getting close to quitting time and my stomach agreed. What delicacy would be on my dinner menu tonight? Oh, crap. I had that monster gooeyduck stuffed under my feet in Red's cooler. I hated to throw it away after he and his family had worked so hard to hunt it down and kill it for me. Then a devious thought popped up in my head. Maybe Maude and Henry would appreciate it.

I scooted it out from under the dinette and hefted the cooler onto my shoulder, amazed at how heavy one clam could be. By the time I got to Maude's back door, I was wheezing from the effort of carrying the stupid thing. In the time it took her to finally make it to the door after I'd banged on it a few times, I'd caught my breath and was able to talk.

"Katlin. What a surprise. I haven't seen you around much these last few days," she said rather haughtily. Sheesh. It wasn't like we were best friends, for pity sake.

"Yeah, things are starting to heat up on the job. You probably noticed Red and his crew working on getting the garage moved," I said, trying to distract her from burying me in guilt. "I have something for you. Do you and Henry like Gooeyduck?"

"Like it? We love it! It's a delicacy we don't get very often. Is that what you have in that cooler? It looks kinda heavy. Let me get Henry to help you with it," she said, obviously anxious to latch onto the disgusting clam.

"HENNNNNNRYYYYY!" She shrieked toward the room where her husband was pretending to sleep. Her shrill yell was impossible to ignore. Henry slowly and reluctantly cranked himself out of his ratty recliner and shuffled into the hallway.

"Here, take this cooler from Katlin. She's kindly giving us a Gooeyduck," Maude explained to him.

He slowly nodded his head and grabbed the cooler from my shoulder, where it had probably created permanent dents.

131

"It's quite huge. You'll be able to eat Gooeyduck for a week or more," I said.

Maude must have thought this was a hint to join them in devouring this prehistoric shellfish. "Why don't you join us for dinner? I make the best Gooeyduck steaks in this county," she proudly bragged.

"Uh, thanks, but I have work to do tonight," I said in my lame attempt to escape.

"Oh, but you have to. It isn't every day we get to enjoy such a rare treat, is it Henry?" she said to his slowly disappearing back as he carted the cooler into the kitchen. "You come back in an hour and be ready for a real treat."

There was no escaping this Clam from Hell. I agreed to return for what I was sure would be my last meal on Earth. I had serious doubts about living through the ingestion of such a nauseating entrée.

As I strode back to Ol' Blue I shot a glance in the direction of the old garage, noticing a distinct lack of red-headed house movers. The garage was hanging about eight feet up in the air. I just hoped we didn't get a big wind or it could tumble right into Ol' Blue. Not a pleasant thought. Especially if I was in it. I could see the headlines in the local weekly paper now – "Woman Squished to Death by Mouse-poop Filled, Decrepit Garage".

Red was dragging this out longer than he'd promised and the Gooeyduck wasn't having the soothing effect on me that I'm sure he'd hoped for. If he didn't get that garage out of my sight by tomorrow, I'd let him have it. Right after the crab feed, of course

Just then I heard the deep growl of a Mack dump truck grinding along in "Granny gear" – the lowest and slowest gear. It was Mark bringing the dirt to backfill around the outside of the foundation walls. I watched as he raised the bed and dumped the dirt exactly where he wanted it while slowly and carefully driving along, just an inch or so from the footings. He was goooood. When the box clanged back down, I ran over to him waving my arms so he'd see me and not drive over me.

"Hey, Katlin! Thought I'd get the dirt here so I'm ready when you get the OK from Phil for backfilling. No sense wasting time, I figure," he said.

"Great! You and I are thinking alike here. But it's getting kinda late. Are you planning on bringing all the dirt this afternoon? I mean, it's past quitting time for most of my subcontractors."

"Yeah. So I noticed. Well, I got too much work to be diddling around at the bars like some guys. I'll bring a few more loads until they close the gravel pit for the night and finish it up tomorrow. Then I'll be ready on Monday after your inspections to make it all smooth and pretty for you."

"Well, you're sure on the ball and I appreciate that kind of go-getter energy. Let me know if you need anything. I'll be in Ol' Blue," I said waving my hand in the general direction of Casa de Construction.

"That thing has a name?" he asked incredulously.

"Yeah. Pathetic, isn't it."

He just shook his head, then grinned that face-splitting grin of his, put his truck in gear and roared off to get another load of dirt.

An hour later, I emerged from Ol' Blue, ready as I'd ever be for what was probably going to be the worst meal I'd ever eat. Considering all the mealtime disasters I'd cooked and actually eaten, this was saying a lot about the questionable eating quality of something called a Gooeyduck. After grabbing a bottle of cheap wine that I kept in case of emergency, I walked as slowly as possible back over to Maude's, trying to delay the inevitable as long as possible.

Maude greeted me at the back door, almost vibrating with excitement as I handed her the gallon bottle of rotgut wine. I figured if I drank enough of it, what I was eating wouldn't matter.

"I have to confess, I sampled some of this Gooeyduck before you got here and it's the best ever. So fresh with that special flavor only Gooeyducks have. You're just going to love it," she gushed at me.

Special flavor. Great. It was one thing to have to eat horrid food. It was an entirely other level of Hell to have to pretend to enjoy it. I quickly opened the wine, found a large water glass, and filled it to the brim with wine. I'd gulped down half of it before we sat down for dinner in their cramped living/dining room. Maude dished up in the kitchen, since the table was too small for serving plates.

She and Henry watched me intently as I slowly carved a couple of molecules off the Gooeyduck steak and placed it on the edge of my tongue. After a minute or so I gathered enough courage to chew down on it.

OMIGAWD! It was scrumptious! Delectable! Splendiforous! The best thing that I'd ever tasted! How had I ever missed such a scrumptious eating experience in my life? The meat was tender, sweet, and with just a hint of the sea. Maude had dredged it in flour seasoned with just the right amount of salt and pepper. Anything more would have overpowered the delicate flavor. Then she fried it in butter, hot and quick just as Red had recommended, giving it a lightly crunchy crust.

When they saw the look of surprised delight on my face at my first bite, Maude laughed and Henry actually smiled Then we all dug in and devoured the entire stack of Gooeyduck steaks.

After dinner, I helped Maude clean up the kitchen to show my appreciation for her heavenly cooking. Then I waddled back to Ol' Blue, musing on the wonderful experiences that are missed in life because of preconceived notions and incorrect judgments. I vowed that from now on I'd be less opinionated and more open when new and unusual opportunities presented themselves. Especially those that included offerings of gastronomic delights.

As I settled into my cozy nest in the bed loft, I sent a silent and very grateful thanks to Red for sharing the unexpected delight of Gooeyducks with me.

# Chapter 15

There was no reason for me to be awake at the unholy hour of 7am, but there I was... unable to make my eyes stay shut for more than a few seconds. They kept popping open, much to my disgust. I finally gave up and slid out of my warm, cozy bed, slithered down the ladder and scuffled into the Master Bath.

After enjoying the camper version of a shower, I scrounged through the black plastic garbage bag that served as my dresser and found a clean set of clothes. Voila! I was ready for the day.

Well, almost.

There was one important thing missing. My morning caffeine and sugar rush. I was at my truck, ready to hop in and drive off to the Oasis when I noticed there were several white vans parked around the job site. This could only mean one thing: either the plumbers or the electricians had no good sense. Or maybe both. Who in their right mind would begin the work day so early? It bordered on being uncivilized.

The Oasis would have to wait until I'd done my job, which I now realized pretty much consisted of making sure other people were doing their job. There were guys everywhere, heads down, doing construction-type things in the trenches with plastic pipes and wires. Ah. Wires. That was a dead giveaway to the identity of these guys: Electricians.

I stomped over to the building site in my most business-like manner, expecting instant attention from the workers. No one even noticed me. Obviously they didn't know who I was. I looked around for someone in charge but they all seemed to be of the worker classification.

Just then yet another white van pulled up and Don Hobob jumped out. "Hey, Katlin, you're up pretty early, aren't you?" he yelled loud enough for half the town of Stanville to hear.

"I'm up at the crack of dawn every morning, Don," I replied rather haughtily. Hey, 10am was early I figured, so 7 or 8 in the morning rated as the crack of dawn in my book.

"Yeah, right. Well, anyway, things are going smoothly. My guys should be here soon and we plan on being out of your hair this afternoon. JJ's guys have a good start, I see, and should be done tomorrow. You got the plumbing inspection scheduled yet?"

"Don't need to. The building inspector comes by every day."

"He's not the one you need to schedule. It's the state inspector you want to call. Didn't Gene give you his number?" he asked me. Then, muttering to himself said, "Why did I even ask that question. I should know better by now. Sometimes I wonder if that man has the sense God gave a rock."

"Nope, Gene didn't give it to me. Do you have the number with you? I'll call right away."

"You better let me call. Usually they need two weeks notice, but I'm a friend of the inspector's secretary, if you know what I mean," he said wiggling his eyebrows so I'd know what kind of friends they were.

He grabbed his clipboard off the dash of his van and we trundled over to Ol' Blue. It only took him a few suggestive comments to get the inspector's secretary to rearrange her boss's schedule so he'd inspect the Stanville jobsite on Monday.

Don wasn't the kind of guy I'd expect to have such power over women. He sure didn't look like much. Kinda short and spindly with not much hair on top. Whatever magic he had, it was well hidden. I was curious, but not *that* curious. I was just glad he used his super powers to get the job inspected without delay. I was still two weeks behind schedule and needed to make up time, not lose it waiting for an inspection.

"Thank you so much, Don. You've saved the day. Because of you, this crisis passed by so fast I hardly even noticed it," I gushed at him.

He actually blushed, and the added color in his cheeks made him almost cute. "Aww, you're welcome, Katlin. You're going to have enough problems on this job without added delays," he said looking at me with his insipid blue eyes all innocent.

What did he mean, I was going to have enough problems? What did he know that I didn't, I wondered. I had no time to ask him. Just then there was a yell from the site.

"That's one of my guys. I better go see what he wants," Don said and trotted away.

I watched Don talking with his worker, both of them pointing at stuff as guys are wont to do when they talk. No one was bleeding, so I reckoned things were under control for the time being. I hopped in my truck and made my escape to the Oasis while the getting was good.

"Hi, Cherie. What sumptuous delight did you bake for me today?" I greeted her back. She turned around and I was shocked to see her looking a bit on the haggard side. "Are you OK?" I asked.

"Yeah. I guess. That danged guy I've been seeing lately just up and left the country without telling me about it. I had to learn it from one of my customers yesterday," she sniffled.

"What a rat. What a fool. He must be one of the stupidest men in the world," I said to comfort her.

"You got that right, kiddo. Makes me kinda wonder what I ever saw in the guy to begin with." She took a deep breath, straightened up, put a smile on her face, and chirped, "Well, like I always say.... NEXT!"

"Boy, that's the fastest I've ever seen anyone get over a heartbreak," I said in awe of her quick recovery.

"It's a talent I learned over the years. My first heartbreak was a killer. I truly thought I was going to die from a broken heart, if you can believe that. But two months later I was still alive and I figured that heartbreak wasn't how I was destined to die, so I picked myself up and got on with my life. After that each one got easier than the one before it. Now I get over them so fast it's hardly worth bothering with a pity party."

It was a talent I recognized. These days my suffering with a broken heart over lost loves usually lasted all of two or three hours. Sometimes I dragged them out for a day or so if I had nothing better to do.

"Yep. I know what you mean. Well, I'll have the usual," I said, my mouth already beginning to water in anticipation of the exquisite pleasure it was soon to experience.

Happily chomping on my cookies and slurping up my high octane coffee, I drove back to the job site. Going through town I noticed an odor similar to propane, but with slightly more pungency about it. I rolled up the windows on my truck and pulled the cellophane down a bit more on the tree deodorizer hanging from my rear-view mirror.

When I arrived at the job site, Red and crew were there just standing around. I wanted to get out and ask them what was going on, but was afraid to open the door for fear of the stench getting in and permanently adhering to my hair, skin, and clothing. I rolled the window down half an inch and aimed my nose toward it. One little sniff told me it was probably safe to get out.

"Hey, Red, thanks so much for that Gooeyduck," I said as I exited my truck." I shared it with Maude and Henry and I think they may remember you in their will now. That Maude can sure cook Gooeyduck. By the way, is today the big day for moving this thing?" I said.

"Hi, Katlin. Yep. We didn't get the permit until yesterday afternoon. Some glitch in the paperwork at the Dee Oh Tee. You know, the Department of Transportation. Anyway, we're good to go and our truck should be here any minute," he said, eyes focused on the end of the street.

*Another* permit? Jeez. So far I counted six, including the new one for moving the garage... and the job had just started. If this kept up, I'd have enough permits to wallpaper the entire inside of Ol' Blue.

138

"There it is now," Red broke into my thoughts, nodding toward a cloud of black smoke coming toward us.

The truck looked about as healthy as Henry as it wheezed slowly along. It moved about as fast as he did, too. And, like Henry, eventually it got the job done. By late morning, the garage was setting on the bed of the truck. Sparky and Scarlet were driving the pilot cars with flashing red lights on top. Red, Jr, who was driving the ancient flatbed truck, had turned on the flashing lights that were on top of the truck cab. It looked like an automotive disco. Red walked over to where I was standing far enough away from the truck and garage that I didn't have to be concerned about it falling on me.

"Don't forget the crab feed tonight, Katlin," he said.

"That's something I don't ever forget about – eating," I replied.

"Here's the directions to our house," he said handing me paper with neatly printed instructions on it and decorated like his business cards with glitter and stickers. "We'll see you about six."

"You bet! I'm looking forward to it," I said taking the instructions from him. I stood and watched as their little parade got moving and trundled down the road, slowly moving out of sight.

As I walked back to the building site I noticed there were even more white vans parked all caddywompus. Evidently the plumbers had arrived.

For a while I watched the guys working, but they were so efficient it was quickly obvious that my professional supervisory talents were unnecessary. Feeling as useless as tits on a noodle, I went back to Ol' Blue and worked on the estimate for the plans Gene had given me.

As always, I lost track of time as I immersed myself in the plans. It seemed like only minutes had passed when my stomach began telling me it was noon o'clock, and it was never late when indicating time to eat. Lunch at The Daisy was sounding pretty good. Things were under control for the moment at the job site, so I drove to the café, getting there just before the busyness of the daily lunch crunch.

Disembarking my truck, I noticed that the aroma I'd smelled earlier seemed thicker here by The Daisy. Holding my nose, I ran into the café.

I found an empty stool at the counter and glanced at the blackboard to see the special du jour. It was one of my favorites – hot turkey sandwich. No need to look at the menu. I gave the waitress my order as she was placing silverware, a glass of water, and a cup of coffee in front of me. She wrote it on a tablet, tore the sheet off, stuck it in the whirly-gig thingy and gave it a spin, placing my order directly in front of the cook.

I barely had time to unwrap the paper napkin from my silverware before a platter the size of a car hood was placed in front of me. It was filled to overflowing with slices of white turkey meat layered over squishy white bread and swimming in gallons of light brown gravy, with a mountain of mashed potatoes on the side. A few cooked vegetables of indeterminate color and shape were hiding behind the potatoes. Who cared what they were? With the gigantic quantity of *real* food on my plate, I wouldn't be bothering with any wimpy veggies.

I managed to slurp down less than half of the food before giving up. I had to stop myself from getting overstuffed. I had the crab feed-o-rama tonight and wanted to make sure I had plenty of room for fresh cracked Dungeness crab.

"Want a doggie bag, hon?" the waitress asked with a smirk.

"Yeah, that'd be great. My St. Bernard would love a little snack when I get home," I replied. Somehow I think she didn't believe me. I didn't care. I'd have enough food for another lunch and maybe even dinner before heading home tomorrow. "By the way, what's that strange odor I smelled as I was coming in here?"

"Oh, that. It's the sewage treatment plant. It's just across the highway," she said, nodding in the direction of the highway. "When the wind blows from the south and the tide's high, we get to enjoy the aroma. Only happens about once a month or so."

"I see. Well, thanks for the great service, delicious lunch, and the information," I said, standing up to leave. As I walked out I contemplated Maude's choice of location for the café. It seemed rather unfortunate, but maybe the locals didn't notice it so much, what with the aroma from the rendering plant constantly infiltrating the town.

On my way back to the job I swung by the Lucky Horseshoe, hoping to get lucky and find Larry. I wanted to keep him alert to the fact that he had to be on the job bright and early Monday, getting ready for the concrete pour on Tuesday.

As luck would have it, I spotted his truck amongst those of the other regulars trying to keep their bar habit a secret by parking behind the tavern. I'd seen this trick done too many times behind too many bars, yet I was still incredulous at the degree of stupidity this kind of thinking required.

I opened the door, letting in some of the pungent aroma of the sewage treatment plant. This was greeted with complaints from all directions to shut the %#@&* door. Such a warm welcome. My eyes slowly adjusted to the dimness as I moved toward the general area in which Larry usually hunkered over the bar. I had just enough night vision to see his shape a moment before I might have bumped into him.

"Larry, what a delightful surprise, finding you here," I said solicitously.

He turned slowly around, giving me a squinty look, full of suspicion. "Hullo, Katlin. What are you doing here?" he asked.

"I came to see you, of course. I want to share some good news with you," I said.

His eyes got even squintier. "What's that?"

"The plumbers and electricians will be done with their work tomorrow. Their inspections are scheduled for first thing Monday morning. That means you can be on the job bright and early Monday morning to get your gravel to grade and set your remesh and rebar."

"What's the rush? Why can't I wait until Tuesday? I don't want to be getting in the way of no inspectors," he whined at me.

"The rush is that we're already two weeks behind schedule and you need to get your scrawny ass to my job site first thing Monday morning. Do I need to make myself any more clear?" I said in a deathly quiet voice.

"N-n-no. I understand you just fine. I'll be there by 8... maybe even before," he stuttered.

I turned and walked out without saying buh-bye. When I got to my truck, I took a moment to take a deep breath and slow my speeding heart rate. My macho muscles were getting stronger, but still, it was a bit nerve-wracking to be so "persuasive" with anyone. Even Larry the Lush.

Back on the job site I stowed the remains of my lunch in the little refrigerator in Ol' Blue and sat down at the dinette/office desk to see what other chores I needed to complete. According to my professional Timeline Chart, I needed to schedule gravel for Monday afternoon. That would give the inspectors time to inspect whatever they needed to inspect as well as giving the plumbers and electricians time to backfill the trenches. I didn't know who had the chore of backfilling, but I knew it wasn't going to be me. Concrete delivery and a pump truck would need to be scheduled for Tuesday morning. I knew I was scheduling things kinda close, but I needed to push in order to make up for lost time.

Those little chores done, I went back out to the pad site to see how things were progressing. The plumbers had finished their work and were just packing up their tools and what was salvageable from their materials. Certain trades were typically neat and tidy while others were unbelievable slobs. Electricians fell into the latter group, while the plumbers were tidy and picked up after themselves. As I scanned the site I could see that the electricians had parts and pieces scattered all over the job site. I knew from experience, I'd be the one to pick up after them when they'd gone home.

The electricians were still bent over working and I had no idea who their lead guy was, so I yelled to no one in particular, "You guys gonna be done by tomorrow?"

The youngest-looking member of the crew slowly raised his head. "Yes, Katlin," he said in a voice that bordered between extreme weariness from being nagged constantly and snide sarcasm. He probably used it on his mother, wife, and or girlfriend a lot.

"Hey, it's part of my job to make sure things are staying on schedule," I replied in an only slightly haughty tone. Instantly I wanted to kick myself for offering any justification for my question.

He just shook his head at me in dismissal and went back to work. The other guys had been watching this exchange out of the sides of their eyes and I noticed a few glances being exchanged between some of them. No doubt there'd be a time coming when I'd find out what all this was about. In the meantime, I decided to ignore the undercurrents and be satisfied that things were proceeding on schedule.

I stood around watching for a while, just to let junior know that he didn't intimidate me all that much. After boring myself almost to death watching pipe being glued together and wire shoved through it, I sauntered back to Casa de Construction. Halfway there I heard a very strange sound. As I got closer I recognized it as a phone ringing. My phone was ringing! Somebody was calling me! Luckily I'd left the door open on Ol' Blue, otherwise I'd probably have crashed right through it in my excitement to answer the phone.

"Hello?" I answered breathlessly.

"Well, howdydeedoo to you. I had no idea you felt that way about me. Or did I interrupt something," said my favorite flooring subcontractor, chuckling to himself in appreciation of his great talent for wittiness.

"Oh, hi, Burt. Good to hear from you," I said, a bit less breathlessly now.

"What's up, Katlin?"

"Remember those jobs you bid for me? The Thomas Oil convenience stores? Well, I'm up here in Stanville building one of them. Gene made me Project Superintendent and I get to choose some of my subs. You're it for flooring."

"How soon you need me? You know my schedule is pretty full."

Yeah, right. Full of hunting and fishing trips, not to mention recreation time at the café playing dice. "I'm just now starting the foundation," I said. We spent a few minutes talking about our schedules and getting an approximate start date for him. Then he caught me up on all the latest gossip from the local construction scene and the café – his two worlds. Even though I'd only been gone less than two weeks, it seemed like ages since I'd been part of the local happenings. It felt comforting to touch home, even if it was only through surrogate gossip.

By the time we hung up it was getting late afternoon, and I decided to check one more time on the progress of the electricians. In my absence, they'd packed up and left. I wasn't too concerned, because as I examined their work more closely, I could see they were very close to being done. However, after the little show of machismo from the lead guy, I thought it prudent to check with the true boss, JJ.

A quick call to him confirmed that his guys would be on the job here tomorrow and would finish before end of day. JJ also confirmed that the lead guy was his son. This tidbit of news didn't bode well for me.

Next on my busy agenda was getting ready for the crab feed. What, I wondered to myself, does one wear to a crab feed? Time enough to figure that out during my freshening-up. I even scrounged up an old tube of mascara and swiped some on my eyelashes. After browsing through my vast clothing choices, I opted for jeans (clean) and a sweater (barely wrinkled). Combined with my tennis shoes, I was ready for any and all action of the crab eating variety.

I located the slip of paper with the driving directions on it after a quick search in Ol' Blue, where I'd cleverly placed it somewhere in the pile of papers on the dinette. I had everything I needed for this Stanville soiree, so I headed out the door. There was no need to lock up; no one would believe there was anything of value in the pile of rust and oxidation known as Ol' Blue.

It only took fifteen minutes and two wrong turns to find Red's house. It was nothing like I had imagined it. No rusted out skeletons of vehicles lying around, no stacks of building materials overgrown with blackberry vines and moss, and no junk yard dog. Instead I found a beautiful multi-storied home, set on the river bank in a glade of huge, ancient evergreen trees. The thick, cedar siding on the house was barn red, of course, and it was nicely accented with trim and shutters painted pristine white. There were several very shiny newer vehicles parked around the curved edges of the tidy gravel driveway. I took a minute to appreciate it all before walking up to the house.

Before I had a chance to knock on the deeply paneled wood door, it opened to reveal Red and a herd of mini Reds behind him.

"Welcome to the melee," he said extending his hand and pulling me inward to the kitchen/family room. "Everybody, this here's Katlin," he announced loudly to overcome the volume of the many voices all talking at once.

All heads turned to look at me with smiling faces, and a few shouted out "Hi" and "Hello" before returning to their chores. Some were combing heads of red hair on those younger than themselves. Others were helping with clothing choices or make-up techniques. I watched for a few minutes and then offered to help, but the chaos was somehow under control.

Soon Red herded us all out toward the parked vehicles. There were two vans which I hoped were large enough to carry this crowd of people. As it turned out, a few of the younger ones shared seats or sat on somebody's lap, all with lots of giggling and teasing. We made it to the IOOF hall too soon. I was relishing the warmth and good-natured camaraderie that was so natural within Red's family.

We piled out of the vans and, with Red leading, moved into the hall together as one big multicolored, red-topped amoeba. He found us an empty table big enough for the whole group and we all found places to sit. As soon as that bit of organization was done, Red announced we could commence to getting our food. He pointed behind me and as I stood up, I turned to find a veritable mountain of bright red Dungeness crabs. The sight took my breath away and I spent a few moments just gazing at this wonder... a delay that was almost my demise.

The rest of the table wasn't standing around in awe of this mountain of food – they were galloping toward it. Had I not begun moving precisely when I did, I might easily have been trampled.

When the stampede finally stopped, we were in a line at the opposite end of the hall from the crab. My greatest fear at that moment was that all the crab would be grabbed up by the other hungry people in front of me before I even got there. I had nothing to worry about, as it turned out. The stack of crab had barely dwindled by the time I got my dinner plate, plastic utensils, glob of cole slaw, fluffy dinner roll, and, at long last, my crab.

The feeding frenzy had begun by the time I found my chair and got seated. The noise that seemed a part of Red's family was eerily silenced and all that could be heard was chomping and slurping sounds with an occasional crack as a crab shell was broken apart.

We were encouraged to go back for more, and I didn't need to be prodded into action. That night I broke my own personal record of consuming Dungeness crabs by eating two and a half crabs. Even though the good ladies of the organization had made rich chocolate desserts, I had no room for even a crumb.

"Anybody going back for more, or are we all about done pigging out on crab?" Red asked of no one in particular at the table. His answer came back to him in a chorus of groans and much tummy rubbing. I only hoped Red had overload springs on those vans for the ride home.

Our unloading process was much slower and more stately at Red's house than it had been at the IOOF hall. Everyone was so stuffed full of the rich crab meat they could barely waddle... me included.

"Ohhhh, what a feast. Thank you a jillion times for inviting me, Red. And thanks, too, for including me with your family. They're a wonderful bunch of people," I said gratefully.

"It was my pleasure and my honor to have you as our guest. It's our way of saying "thank you" for letting us haul off the garage and house at your job site," he said kindly.

"I'll let you know when the house is ready to be moved."

"Give me about a week's notice. You just never know how busy things can get in the house moving business."

"Will do. Thanks again," I said, giving him and his wife warm hugs before I turned around to waddle back to my truck.

Back at Casa de Construction, I fell slowly and carefully into bed, lying on my back in order to give my full stomach more room. It was a while before I finally drifted off to sleep, as I spent time reliving every delicious moment of the evening.

# Chapter 16

Oboy. Friday! The excitement of the day had me awake hours before I normally even opened my eyes. Two things were great about today: the plumbers and electricians would be complete with their piping and wiring under the soon-to-be slab *and* I would get to go home tonight after work.

I thought I was up extremely early until I stepped out of Ol' Blue and saw a couple of JJ's vans already parked by the construction pad. The three guys in the trenches were busy shoving wire through pipes and tying big knots in the ends so the wire wouldn't accidently slip back down into the pipe and get lost.

After the crab extravaganza I shouldn't have been hungry, but I was. It didn't seem as if my presence was needed at the job site, so I jumped in my truck and drove to the Oasis for my morning sustenance.

On the way back to the job site with my daily ration of sugar and caffeine, I decided it was too early to stop by the tavern and nag Larry, so I headed straight back to the job site. I'd finished every one of my Peanut Butter Crunch cookies and was on the second coffee as I drove up. Not much had changed in the time I'd been gone, so I went into Ol' Blue to see what administrative chores needed to be done.

First on my agenda was to confirm the gravel delivery late morning to use in backfilling the trenches and for the concrete slab base. With that little chore complete, I made one more quick call and the truss order was a done deal. The truss plant already had the prints and all they needed was for me to give them an estimated date of delivery, which was easy now that I had my spiffy Timeline Chart.

I sure hoped all this scheduling worked out as planned. Otherwise I could have a mess of people mad at me.

# Studs

After those little chores, all I had to do was finish estimating the materials for the lumber package and get it scheduled for delivery. The original estimate for this job was based on the concrete block version of Thomas Oil's standard mini-mart, which somewhere along the line had been converted to stick framing. I wanted things to be ready for Roger when he showed up with his huge framing crew. There was a slight chance that if Roger's crew was as good as he said they could shave a day or so off my "critical path" – the timeline for completion of construction.

I was so engrossed in the plans and figuring the materials for the framing, I barely heard the knock on the back of Ol' Blue. I turned to see the electrical crew foreman standing almost in the camper.

"Hi, what can I do for you?" I asked.

"You got a phone I can borrow?"

"Yes, I do," I announced proudly. "By the way, my name's Katlin," I said, sticking my hand out for him to shake.

"Name's Jay," he said. "JJ's my dad."

*Aha. So you're the one. Thanks for the warning*, I thought to myself. Aloud to him I said, "Nice to meet you. Here's the phone. You can take it outside if you want. There's lots of cord, but not much room in here."

He took it outside with him and as I went back to my plans I heard him talking to someone who I assumed was a supplier. Then things got quiet. I waited for him to return the phone, but it didn't happen. *Maybe he just left it on the ground,* I thought and went outside to find it. But no, Jay was leaning against the side of Ol' Blue with the phone tucked up against his ear and held in place by his shoulder. He looked like he might be taking a nap.

"Jay?" I queried.

"Huh? Oh, I'm waiting for the salesman to check on some materials for me," he said.

I waited with him for a while, then went back to my plans. Some time passed and still no sound from Jay. I stepped outside once more to find him in the same position.

"Jay?"

"Hmm?"

"What's going on with the supplier? Did they find what you want?"

"No. I'm still on hold."

On hold? It'd been half an hour he'd been hanging on hold while the long distance charges piled up. I grabbed the phone receiver and slammed it down on the phone.

"What did you do that for?" he demanded indignantly.

"The long distance charges on this phone aren't cheap. You were eating up the minutes - lots of them - and with no results. Not to mention the time you wasted standing here, asleep on your feet. Now. You call them back and when they ask to place you on hold, you tell them NO. You can call them back later or they can call you. We don't have the budget on this job for you or anyone else to be taking naps on the phone instead of being productive and doing their job."

He glared at me, then snatched the phone back. I stood right in front of him as he called his supplier back. Amazingly, they had the information he needed right away.

*Another pissing match over with*, I thought to myself. I wondered if this one had done the job of letting Jay know that he wasn't the one running this job or if it had just sparked the beginning of a larger battle.

I didn't have much time to think about it as I was watching him stomp back to the trenches because a cloud of dust suddenly obscured my vision. I turned to see who was coming to visit me now. The cloud parted to reveal Ginnie's land yacht. Goodie. A surprise visit from the boss... and just when things were going so well on the job.

"Hey Gene! Ginnie! What brings you up here?" I yelled at them as they disembarked.

150

# Studs

"Hey, Katlin. Figured it was time we came up to see the fabulous job you're doing," Gene shouted back.

I waited until they got closer to Ol' Blue and then herded them toward the building pad. I wanted Gene to look at the work with his sharp eye to see if it was correct. I didn't have a clue if it was done right or not and was relying on the inspectors to determine if the work was acceptable. We stopped at the edge of the footings and I let Gene scan the job undistracted by my chitchat so he could focus.

"Looks pretty good, Katlin," he said after what seemed like a very long while. He turned his back to the job and made his voice quieter so the electricians couldn't hear what he had to say next. "That Jay is a lazy bugger. I've known him since he was in grade school. He thinks that because he's the boss's son he doesn't have to work. I hope I'm outta this business before he takes over the company from his dad because I won't deal with him. Anyway, a word of warning. Stay on him. If he gives you any trouble, call his dad. He's the only one Jay listens to."

Oh great. This meant that most likely the power struggle between Jay and I was just getting started. "Thanks for the warning, Gene. I appreciate it and I'll keep a sharp eye on the boy," I said gratefully... and quietly.

"So, what else ya got for me to look at?" Gene said in his loud, outdoor voice.

"Not much. We can go inside Ol' Blue and sit while I bring you up to date. I've got some cold bottles of lemonade."

"Sounds good to me. C'mon, Ginnie," he ordered, and we all tromped back to the camper.

After I told Gene all the news about the job site, he broke out into a wide grin. "I told you she'd be great at this, didn't I," he said, elbowing Ginnie for agreement. "You just keep up the good work and I'll see you at the office Monday bright and early," he said, getting up. "You ready to head back home?" he asked Ginnie, who silently nodded her head.

I walked them back out to Ginnie's car, Gene chatting happily all the way. As I stood next to the vacant space where the garage had been, waving bye-bye to them, I wondered where

Gene had been all week. Wherever it was, it had had a profound effect on him. Last week he was Mr. Grump, and today he was Mr. Sunshine. Ginnie had been awfully quiet, though. I wondered what was up with her. Was their relationship an emotional see-saw, with one person up while the other was down? Well, I had more productive things to do than analyze someone else's relationship.

As I turned around to walk back to my "office" I noticed that the electricians were packing up. *Better check this out and see if they're done*, I thought to myself. After a quick glance I discovered that there were still pipes sticking up with no wire in them.

"You boys just leaving for lunch?" I yelled at them.

They turned around and two of them had the decency to look sheepish. Jay sneered at me, "We're done for the day. See you Monday."

"Hold up there, pal," I said walking quickly to get within range of normal conversational volume. "This needs to be done today. You know we have electrical inspection on Monday."

"We've done all we're going to do today on this job," he said, still doing his impression of Macho Man.

I walked straight up to him and got nose to nose with him. He was exactly my height, which made it real easy to butt noses with him. He had me on weight, though, being one of those doughy, flabby fat boys. "The wiring under the slab needs to be completed *today*," I said in my deadly quiet voice.

"Hey, we're outta here," he said. "It's beer-thirty and time to hit Happy Hour at the Lucky Horseshoe."

I decided now was a good time to use my power move. "Your dad promised me this would be done today and I don't think he's going to be very happy to hear that you left the job before it was done," I informed him.

I could almost hear the gears grinding under his thick skull as he thought over the two options. Leave early and go drinking with the guys *or* finish the job and save himself from the wrath

152

of his father, which as I understood from Gene was considerable.

"Well, why didn't you say my dad had promised you? Unpack the gear, guys, and let's go finish this job," he ordered. He had chosen well.

I stomped back to Ol' Blue, not saying another word. Anything I would have said at that point would have diffused the power of the moment and might have diminished the delicate bit of face that Jay had saved himself.

Actually, his sense of time was off. It was lunch-thirty, not beer-thirty. My stomach was growling the hour. I debated whether it was a good idea to leave the job site unattended by my watchful presence. After a few more growls from down south, I decided that Jay had had enough of a scare to keep him on the job until he finished it today, and that it was safe for me to escape to The Daisy for another gargantuan country café meal.

The parking lot at The Daisy was full of pick-up trucks and I even spotted a couple of semi rigs. I found a place on the street and hiked the distance to the café, working up an even greater appetite. I was disheartened to find there was a waiting line standing against the wall by the front door. I jumped up and down a couple of times and spotted a single empty stool at the counter and made a run for it. I wiggled onto the stool, wedging myself between two hefty guys who must have been eating at The Daisy for some time.

A glance at the blackboard set my mouth to flooding – Beef Stew in a Cannonball. Actually it wasn't a real cannonball. It was a cantaloupe-sized sourdough roll with the top cut off, the bread inside scooped out, and stew ladled into it. Pure heaven!

Half an hour later, the waitress could have rolled me out the door and down the street to my truck. I was so full of stew that I probably looked like a giant cannonball. That place could be harmful to my girlish figure.

Back at the jobsite, Jay and his crew were still working and it looked like they'd be done shortly. I wanted to say to him, "See? That wasn't so bad now, was it?' But I figured that in the interest of détente I'd better go inside the camper and do something productive.

The framing materials list was almost complete, so I worked on it for a little bit longer and quickly completed it. I couldn't help telling myself, "See? That wasn't so bad now, was it?" It sounded so stupidly funny I couldn't help but break out in laughter.

"What's the joke?" someone said.

I turned around in the dinette and saw my favorite building inspector. "Phil! Your wife's food is deadly to my waistline! I just had the most scrumptious Stew in a Cannonball at The Daisy. She's going to have to place those stools at the counter a little farther apart, I think."

He chortled proudly and said, "Would you believe I used to have a 32" waist when I first met her?"

"Yes, I would." That confirmed what Cherie had told me about Phil being fattened up for the kill by Maude. "I'm glad you stopped by. Larry said he'd be done with the remesh for the slab Monday afternoon. Could you stop by then and inspect it? I just might have some lemonade on ice and maybe an extra cookie from the Oasis."

"Are you trying to bribe an official of the US of A government?" he asked with a twinkle in his eyes.

"I sure am. Is it a date?"

"See you then," he said and half saluted as he walked back to his government issue micro-car.

I glanced over at the building pad site to see that the electrical crew was still at work. So far, so good.

I gathered up my materials list and made a call to Glenn Bob at Beacon Building Materials, Inc. He'd given me his extension number so I didn't need to go through the wait on hold if I didn't want to. Calling the store number connected me to Bobbi, the receptionist, and there were times when I preferred that method... like when I wanted to catch up on all the store gossip. Today wasn't one of those days. Today I was all business.

"Glenn Bob here," he answered as he had for twenty-some years.

"Hi Glenn Bob. Katlin Bob here. Hey, I've got a materials list I'd like you to bid. It's not too long – can I just give it to you over the phone?" I asked.

"Why, shore, Katlin Bob. Go head on 'er. I'm ready," he said. I loved listening to him talk. When we had worked together I often found myself slipping some of his countrified phrases into my normal conversations.

After I finished reading off the list, we chatted for a while about the construction business and some of the contractors who had been my clients when I worked with him.

"Oh, I almost forgot to tell you. I hired Roger for the framing. Thanks so much for giving me his name," I said.

"Hope he works out for you. His dad was pretty good in his day, but I don't know what Roger's like. Let me know when he's done, will ya? I'd like to know if he's good for referring or if he's good for nothing. Haw haw haw," he guffawed at his little joke. His humor said much about him. It was always kind, gentle, and sometimes even funny.

"Will do. I better let you get to work now. Talk with you soon," I said before hanging up.

I stood in the center of my Casa de Construction and found nothing that needed to be done right at that moment, so I took the opportunity to go out to the pad once more to see how the electrical crew was doing. They were once again packing up. This time, though, there were wires sticking out of all the appropriate pipes.

"Good work, guys. Have a great weekend," I said kindly.

They all nodded their acknowledgment but said nothing. Jay looked at me with just the barest hint of a glare before looking away as he finished stowing his tools in the van. I stood back and watched them as they drove off, wondering what my conversation with JJ was going to be like on Monday. At this point I felt more like a mean step-mother than a Project Superintendent.

As I was watching them pull off the job site, Mark's big orange backhoe came careening around the corner of the foundation, skidding to a stop just in front of my toes.

"Hiya, Toots," said a big, toothy grin of a Cheshire cat from inside the dust-filled backhoe cab. As the dust cleared away I could see it was attached to Mark.

"That's Superintendent Toots to you. What are you doing here so late? It's almost quitting time for normal folks."

"Yep, well I guess that tells you a lot about me. I don't drink and I don't have a girlfriend. That frees up a lot of time to do such things as work and make money. I plan on being retired by the time I'm 45. Then I may just take up drinking and chasing women. I might even catch a few."

"Sounds like a plan. I was just about to pack up and leave for the weekend. You need anything from me?"

"Maybe after I'm 45," he said leering at me and looking more like a lovesick leprechaun than a lecher. "If I run out of daylight and don't get the backfilling done tonight I'll get 'er done tomorrow."

"Great. Oh, by the way, what else did Gene have you lined up for on this project?"

"Any and all of the dirtwork."

"Perfect. That's easy, then. I'll be calling you when I need you and your heavy equipment again."

He tried another leer at that last comment and looked so goofy I could only giggle at him.

At last! There was nothing left to do but leave. I quickly tossed my dirty clothes in another garbage bag, locked up Ol' Blue, and jumped in my own truck to head for home-sweet-home. Another week of challenges had been met, with probably only about six or eight more to come in the next week. If, that is, I was lucky.

# Studs

I mused on the upcoming segments of the job as I drove down the freeway to the ferry. Once I was on the ferry, however, I left the job behind as I entered another world – the world where my heart was at home.

# Chapter 17

I didn't think I'd ever get used to my Mondays - getting up in the middle of the night so I could get to G & G Headquarters and then rush to catch the early ferry. It was inhuman.

When I reached the office my mind was still uncaffeinated enough that I wasn't thinking clearly and before I could stop it, my hand pushed The Button, setting off one of the hundreds of whiney, nasal Country Western songs stored in the electronic brain of Gene and Ginnie's doorbell. The sounds of country music have much the same effect on me as does the screech of fingernails on a blackboard.

Ginnie opened the door which thankfully ended the torturous music.

"Hi, Ginnie," I greeted her as I walked past her and into the dining room/office. "What's new?"

"Gene, Katlin's here," she yelled toward the back of the house somewhere.

Gene's muffled voice acknowledged her announcement and soon he appeared, freshly shaven and all smiley-faced. Nothing made me more nervous than a smiley-faced Gene.

"Hey, Katlin. I hear you've been raising a few eyebrows on the job site," he said slyly.

"What do you mean?" I asked. It was way too early and I was way too uncaffeinated to be playing guessing games.

"JJ says you slapped his boy down when he tried to best you."

"I didn't slap him down. I just told him to do his job. That's all."

"Not how he's telling it. Anyway, don't worry about it. JJ was pleased as punch that you didn't kowtow to his boy. The brat tries to throw his weight around and most everyone lets him get away with it. But not my Katlin," he said and his grin got amazingly even wider. I hoped it didn't hurt his face.

"If you talked to JJ then you know I have electrical and plumbing inspections this morning," I started out with that and then gave him the rest of my update of progress on the job. He was grinning like a fool all the way through it.

"You're doing a great job, Katlin. I knew you would. Here's your check and a list of a few things to keep you from getting too bored this week," he said handing me a thick file folder.

"Yeah, like I need that. So far I haven't had much of a chance to get bored. There's a lot happening on the job."

"It won't be like that all the time. You'll be coming up to some slack time soon when the framers get there. Not much else goes on until after the framing goes up. Then get ready for another busy period after that."

"Thanks for the warning. Anything else? I've got to get going and catch the ferry in order to be there for the inspections. Oh, and I've got that bid done for you. It's in my truck. Walk out with me and I'll give it to you," I said, waving bye-bye to Ginnie.

I handed Gene the plans and my estimate, jumped in my truck, and raced to the ferry, making it in plenty of time. I hauled myself upstairs to the snack bar, where I bought a large Styrofoam cup of the rancid brown water they call coffee. I suspect there's some oil from the engines that somehow seeps into the coffee maker and gives it the special flavor known only to ferry coffee. Its sole redeeming feature is that one of the main ingredients is caffeine.

Luckily, after I drove off the ferry there was little traffic, owing no doubt to the obscenely early hour, and I made it to the Oasis in record time. I couldn't wait to wash the taste of that evil ferry coffee out of my mouth with Cherie's rich, dark coffee. As I pulled in, Cherie was busy putting cookies in the glass display cabinet. I don't know why she bothered. They disappeared into her customer's mouths so fast she might as well just have left them on the baking tray.

159

Kathy Wilson

"Hey, Cherie! I'll have my usual three monster size coffees and three cookies, please," I said in a rush.

"Hey, Katlin. Don't you even want to know what kind of cookies they are? I mean, what if you don't like them?" I couldn't believe she'd ask me such a stupid question. How could anyone not love any and all of her fantabulous cookies?

"Cherie, I seriously doubt you could make a cookie I wouldn't like. Just for giggles, though, what is the cookie o' the day?" I asked just to be nice.

"Thought you'd never ask. Oatmeal applesauce with walnut chunks, drizzled with cinnamon sour cream frosting," she said smugly.

"Make that four cookies," I amended my ordered and she smiled knowingly.

"How was your weekend?" Cherie asked as she worked on my order.

"Interesting. I have a couple of friends house sitting for me while I'm up here slaving away."

"Do you own your house?" she asked, ever the vigilant real estate broker.

"No, I'm just renting," I said.

"I'm going to give you some critical advice. There's three things every adult women should have: her passport, at least one good piece of jewelry, and her own house," she said, counting them off with her fingers for emphasis. You need to have financial security, and owning your home is the best security there is. Just ask me," she added.

"I suppose you're right. I've dumped thousands of dollars into rent over the years. I wonder what I'd have now if I'd invested it in a house," I mused.

"Well, you're talking to the right gal. I'm not the top real estate agent in these parts for nothing, ya know. Why, my little Paradise Real Estate office does almost all the home and land sales in Stanville. In case you haven't noticed, my real estate office is right through that door. Yep. I got the two hottest

160

businesses in town. Listen, sometime this week let's you and me have a sit-down and talk about what you can afford. Then we'll take a tour of some of the houses that are in your price range in and around Stanville. I know the best locations and nicest neighborhoods, unlike some of those big city real estate agents who come into town with their clients and don't even know where the main street is," she sneered.

"I appreciate your offer, Cherie, but if I'm going to buy a place, it's going to be on the Olympic Peninsula, where my heart already has taken up residence," I said. "If it wasn't for that, I'd surely be tempted to look around here. I like Stanville – it's a nice, friendly town."

"Well, here's your order. If you change your mind, you know where I'm at," she said graciously.

"Thanks, Cherie. I appreciate that," I said with sincere gratitude. It was always nice to be wanted, even if it was by a real estate agent who wanted to sell me a house.

When I arrived at the job site, JJ and Don were already there, inspecting the work of their respective crews. From all the nodding that was going on between them, I gathered that the guys had done a good job. I unlocked Ol' Blue and tossed my sturdy garbage sack full of clean laundry inside. Just to be safe, I put one of the cookies in the refrigerator. I'd promised Phil a cookie and if I left it out where I could see it, the sugary concoction would be history.

Armed with one of my gargantuan coffees and another cookie, I sauntered out to the pad to see what the professionals had to say about their guy's work.

"Hi, JJ. Don. How's it look to you?" I asked nonchalantly. I held my breath for their answer. It was vital that the work be done correctly so that it passed inspection by the official state and local inspectors. If it didn't, every portion of the job that was scheduled behind it would fall down like tightly packed dominoes.

They turned in unison, as if they were performing a choreographed dance. JJ once again elected himself to be the spokesperson.

"It's looking excellent, as usual, Katlin. Did you expect anything less?" he asked only half kiddingly.

"I expected exactly that, JJ... excellence. Everything I've heard about your work would lead me to believe that we'll have no problems on this site with the quality of your work," I said, tactfully not mentioning the poor quality of his son's behavior.

"The inspectors should be here in a few minutes. They said they'd be here at ten to nine, and being ex-engineers, they're very precise about everything they do," Don warned me.

"I'll just hang out with you guys until they get here, if you don't mind. I'd like to see what they look for and hear what they have to say," I said.

"We're glad for your company, aren't we, Don?" JJ said, smiling. It was a nice smile, gentle and open.

We didn't have long to wait before two grey government-issue compact cars drove slowly and carefully onto the job site. The men who got out of them could have been twins, except one had more hair and less girth than the other. Both men wore white nylon shirts, the kind you can see through, tucked neatly into their khaki permanent press slacks. The pocket in each man's shirt was lined with pens, organized by size and color, all safely contained in a plastic pocket protector. Each of the inspectors took a few moments to make notes on their respective forms on their clipboards before walking carefully over the untidy ground to the job pad.

"Good morning, John. Howdy, John," JJ greeted them. They were both named John? I looked at JJ with the question in my eyes and he winked. I smothered my giggles with another bite of cookie.

The inspectors led the way to the job, with JJ and Don following them. I tailed along behind them all. Suddenly both Johns abruptly stopped and turned around, causing the choo-choo train of people behind them to bump into the person in front of them. The Johns both stared at me curiously.

"Oh. Sorry. I should have introduced you. This is Katlin Greene, the Project Superintendent on the job," JJ said.

Both Johns scrutinized me carefully, no doubt looking for code infractions, and finally deemed me satisfactory... but just barely I suspected. I'm certain that in their world, women belonged in kitchens, not on construction sites getting all dirty and everything. After a terse nod from both of them to acknowledge me, they turned and we continued on.

All went well with the inspections, and within minutes everyone drove off in their respective vehicles, leaving me in a huge cloud of dust with two permits that were freshly inked with the inspectors' initials on them. Two more inspections down, only kajillion more to go.

As I stood there reveling in the success of the inspections, it dawned on me that something was missing. Larry. Of course.

I stormed back to my truck, ready to find the little weasel and blister him with some choice language. Luckily for him, just at that moment his truck pulled in with him in it. He had no idea how near he'd just come to death by tongue lashing. He and two very bedraggled guys piled out of the truck and walked over to the pad, not talking, just looking. I waited for a while to see what they'd do next and soon discovered it was just more of the same. Standing and staring.

Shaking my head in disgust, I began walking toward them. "LARRY!" I yelled, startling all of them out of their stupor. Watching them all jump like puppets whose strings had been jerked was almost as rewarding as having the electrical and plumbing inspections pass.

"Oh hi, Katlin," Larry said blandly. "Just checking out the job site. I don't see any gravel or remesh here yet. We'll come back later."

"No. You won't come back later because you're not leaving now. The gravel will be here within the hour, so I suggest you get your shovels out and get to backfilling those trenches," I informed him.

"Okay. I guess we could do that," he said, looking at his guys apologetically. Odds were he'd promised them free drinks at the tavern just for showing up with him and pretending to be workers.

Just then the dump truck full of gravel turned into the job site. I ran over the truck so I could direct the driver where I wanted him to back it in. He was very compliant, probably due to his having heard from the other driver about the hellion female Project Supe on this job.

Larry and his crew shifted into high speed and began tossing dirt into the trenches to cover up the plastic pipes. The trenches didn't need to be completely filled, but they did need to have enough dirt on the pipes to cushion them from the gravel as it was dumped from the truck. Without the protection of the dirt, the pipes would shatter as the rocks hit them. Then we'd have to start all over laying new pipes – a delay of several days which, at this point, made me want to take up nail biting.

I talked with the driver to keep him amused long enough for Larry and crew to sufficiently cover the pipes, then stepped back and let him dump the gravel inside the footings. He drove off with the dump bed still up in the air, finally releasing it to fall into place with a loud CLANG that got everyone's attention as he drove down the street. Another grandstander, like many of the truck drivers I've known.

Just then a delivery truck with several rolls of remesh appeared and I let Larry direct the truck where he wanted the load dumped. Larry and crew now had plenty to keep them occupied. Raking the gravel to grade would take them several hours, after which they'd have the remesh to lay.

"Remember, Larry, the cement will be here at 9 tomorrow morning, so you need to have everything ready *today* for the pour," I reminded him, just in case he having fond thoughts of happy hour and planning on leaving before the job was done.

"Yes, Katlin," he said in a voice sounding much like Henry when he answered Maude.

He ordered his workers to shovel and rake gravel while he began to measure and cut the remesh to length. They didn't need me to stand watch over them, so I went back to Ol' Blue.

I had a lot of subcontractors to get scheduled, starting with Roger. Although we'd set up an approximate start date, I wanted to give him a specific date and confirm with him that he'd actually be here with this crew to start work on that date.

# Studs

Two hours later my phone ear was numb from having the phone constantly pressed against it as I contacted all the subs. Each one of them had been able to put my job on their schedule when I needed them, which was a miracle of the highest degree. After rubbing some feeling back into my ear, I sent my thanks heavenward to the Construction Gods for their assistance with my scheduling.

A sudden growl from my stomach alerted me to the time. I could hear The Daisy Café calling my name. The calls I'd planned to the suppliers, ordering materials and scheduling their delivery, would just have to wait until after lunch. Otherwise, I'd never be able to hear what they were saying over the noise my demanding stomach was emitting.

On my way out to my truck I detoured to the building pad and was gratified to see Larry and gang still at work. Larry had his transit set up and was checking the grade with one of his guys while the other one finished cutting the remaining pieces of remesh to length.

"Hey, Larry!" I yelled, diverting his attention from the hand signals his partner was giving him. "I'm going to The Daisy. Do you want me to pick up lunch for you and your guys?" I asked. After the smooth scheduling session I'd just had, I was feeling kindly toward all living things, including Larry.

"Naw. We'll be done here in another hour or so. We'll just work through lunch, right guys?" he looked at the two guys working for him, asking their permission with his eyes. They nodded and he turned back to me, nodding as if forwarding on their approval to me.

"Okay. I'll be back quickly," I said, not wanting to give Larry enough time to escape before he finished the job at hand.

It looked like I was just a few minutes behind the lunch crunch at The Daisy, which meant I had to drive around the parking lot several times before giving up and enlarging my search area to the entire block. Even so, I considered myself lucky to find a spot on a side street. It seemed The Daisy had been discovered by more than the local townsfolk. There were several motorhomes and travel trailers hogging more than one parking space. I gave them an appropriate blessing as I walked by on my trek to the café.

The line of people waiting for a table was almost out the door, but I managed to squeeze by and grab a stool at the corner of the counter. I plopped down, ignoring the frowns and pointed glares directed at me. Hey, it wasn't my fault all those people standing in line weren't quick enough to grab the last seat available.

"Hiya, honey. Be with you in a sec," said a harried waitress as she sped by me.

She was back before I'd had a chance to look at the menu. Not that I needed to. It was identical to the menu in every country café I'd ever been in. I was more interested in the lunch special – the Deluxe Seafood Platter.

"What'll you have?" she asked, multitasking by pouring coffee, whether I wanted it or not, and setting my paper napkin and a wad of eating utensils in front of me.

"The special, with extra tartar, please," I ordered.

"You got it, honey," she said in between chomps on her gum. "What kind of salad dressing you want?"

"What are my choices?"

"White or red."

"White." I didn't know what it was but it sounded safer than the red. I figured you can't hide much in something that's white.

She scribbled something that looked totally unreadable to me on her order pad and stuck it in the whirleygig for the cooks. Before I got half my unordered coffee drunk she slapped my lunch special down in front of me.

A delectable selection of fresh seafood showed up in front of me. Clam strips, Halibut strips, scallops, and an oyster had been dipped in perfectly seasoned beer batter that had just a hint of dill. It was cooked to perfection - the crunchy crust a delectable contrast to the tender, fresh seafood. The pile of salad greens was fresh, too, without that pink tinge around the edges that says "Beware. These veggies have been sitting in a bucket of chemicals since last Christmas."

# Studs

As hungry as I'd been when I first walked through the door, I'd have bet there would be room for pie after my main course. I'm glad I didn't make that bet. One of these days I was going to order only dessert so I wouldn't feel like I was missing out.

I happily paid my bill and waddled out past the line that now ended outside the door. I could have sworn that some of the same people were still standing there, glaring at me as I held in my stomach to make enough room to slide by them.

Back at the job site, I was amazed to see that Larry and crew were still there, bent over as they tied the pieces of remesh together with tiewire. As I got closer to the pad, I saw the gravel was neatly raked smooth and to grade... or close enough. It looked like Larry was going to be ready for the cement when the truck arrived tomorrow morning. What a surprise. What a relief.

I left them to finish up and went into Ol' Blue. Now I needed to call the suppliers and order the materials, starting with the framing package. I was looking forward to talking to Glenn Bob again. Just hearing the sound of his voice and the slow cadence of his drawl was as soothing as a lullaby to me. I dialed his phone direct, using the number he gave out only to special people like me... and everyone else he knew. He had never met anyone he didn't like and we were all special to him.

"Glenn Bob here."

"Hey, Glenn Bob. Katlin Bob here. Must be a slow day at Beacon Building Materials, Inc., you picked up so fast."

"Naw. I knew it was you. You're looking real purty today, too, I might add. What can I do ya for?"

"Remember the lumber list for this job I gave you? I'd like to schedule delivery Thursday so it'll be onsite when Roger shows up Friday."

"Works for me. We'll go head on 'er."

"There may be some doo-dads that I overlooked, but Roger can just pick up anything he needs. Tell Ernie it's easy to find the place. Just tell him to go straight through Stanville like he's

167

heading toward Camas Island. It's the last place on the right just before the bridge."

Ernie was the oldest living employee of Beacon. Even the founding owner couldn't remember a time when Ernie hadn't been the head truck driver. His status afforded him the luxury of his co-workers overlooking some of his idiosyncrasies, such as not talking to anyone who hadn't worked there for at least two years. After I'd been there for two years, I asked him about this. He said he'd seen too many people come and go to be bothered with the short-timers.

"Got it. Everyone here says 'hi'," Glenn Bob said, as I heard a chorus of male voices yelling assorted versions of greetings, some more descriptive than others.

"Tell them I said thanks and ditto," I laughed, hanging up. I missed the camaraderie of the guys in that office. Working there had been one of my more colorful experiences. But that's another story.

It didn't take long for me to order the rest of the materials and, thanks to my shiny new Timeline Chart, schedule approximate delivery dates. Everyone I talked to was most impressed with my organization and the ability I had to plan things way in advance, like delivery dates. According to most of the suppliers I talked with, the majority of contractors just called in their order at the last minute, expecting next-day delivery no matter what. Having worked at Beacon in contractor sales, I could empathize. The typical organizational methods of construction people seemed to be, at best, quite messy. I was beginning to think it was a miracle that anything ever got built from what seemed to be a constant pile of total chaos.

Within a short time, I'd managed to work myself right out of having anything to do. Wasn't I just little Miss Efficient. Now what was I to do?

I needn't have been concerned.

A loud "harrumph" caught my attention. I looked up and saw my favorite building inspector standing just outside the open door.

# Studs

"Phil! Good to see you," I greeted him. "Did you come to inspect the remesh?"

"That, and something else," he said as he gave me a conspiratorial wink.

*What was that about?* I wondered. Aloud I said, "Good timing on your part. I need to go see how Larry and his crew are doing. Let's walk over there together."

"And when we come back, perhaps we can have a cool drink and something else," he said with another of those winks.

Ah. A clue. A cool drink and something else. Of course! The promised lemonade and cookie from The Oasis!

"We'll see," I said, playing along.

When we got to the pad, Larry and crew were just packing up their tools. I was so amazed he'd actually gotten the work done before I had a nervous breakdown that my face almost fell off. "How's it look, Phil?" I asked. To me, it looked great, but it was his initials that went on the permit.

He was quiet as he gazed around, every once in a while his eyes stopping for a better look at something. He was taking an awful long time and it was making me nervous. Finally he turned to me, and rubbing one of his chins, gave me a serious look and said, "Well. It's like this..." and my knees turned to Jell-o. He was going to fail the inspection. I knew it. "It looks fine. Let's go back to your camper and I'll initial the permit and we can have our lemonade and the other, too," he said, his eyes twinkling with his little joke.

I blew the breath out that I hadn't realized I'd been holding onto. "Phil, you scared me. I thought you were going to fail the inspection," I said.

He just chortled and began moving toward Ol' Blue. I trotted after him, amazed at how fast he could move when food was the destination. He climbed into the Formal Dining Room/Office of Ol' Blue and squeezed into the dinette, then turned expectantly toward me. He was like a little boy getting an after-school treat.

We sat and enjoyed our lemonades, talking like old friends, as he munched happily on his cookie from The Oasis. Its sinfulness probably made it even sweeter to him. In too short a time he announced he'd better be getting home and wiggled out of the dinette.

"I guess your next inspection is the framing, right?" I asked.

"Yep. I'll stop by when I see your framers have the walls up," he said.

"Great. It'll probably be a couple of weeks or so. The concrete for the slab is coming first thing tomorrow and the framers can start just as soon as the concrete's had a couple of days to cure."

"Good golly, girl. You sure don't waste any time, do you?"

"I can't. We're already a couple of weeks behind schedule and I need to get back on schedule, or at least not add to the delay," I informed him.

"Well, you're doing a great job. Your boss should be proud of you," he said.

I was so overwhelmed by his kind words that I couldn't move. Tears began to flood my eyes, embarrassing both of us. He gave me a casual wave as he turned to walk to his car, saying something about seeing me soon.

Phil was one of the many surprises of this job. One of the few good surprises.

I hoped tomorrow would bring another good surprise – a smooth and efficient concrete pour with a sober, non-hungover concrete sub and his crew.

# Chapter 18

I was getting the hang of camper life and could now hustle through my shower before I used up the cup or two of hot water from the miniscule water heater. The briefness of camper showers saved me enough time that I could usually make it to The Oasis and back before anyone needful of my professional supervisory talents showed up on the job.

This morning, as I arrived at The Oasis and opened the door to my favorite breakfast spot, the aroma of something unbelievably marvelous hit me, jolting awake my salivary glands.

"What's that delicious smell, Cherie?" I asked, suddenly ravenous with cookie-lust.

"It's a new cookie recipe I'm trying. Chocolate Ginger with chopped Macadamia nuts on top. Here, have a taste," she said handing me a sample in a wax paper square. "Wha'cha think?" she asked.

"I think I'll have about fourteen of them," I answered, my mouth swooning in ecstasy.

She giggled, delightedly. "You're my most appreciative customer, ever since Phil was stolen from me by that Mavis. You have a good taster. If *you* like it, I know it's gonna be a good seller," she said, snapping open a white paper bag and inserting my regular order of three cookies into it. "How many coffees today?"

"Just three. I've got a busy morning and won't have much time for my customary tranquil enjoyment of my morning repast."

"Sometimes you talk funny," she said, looking at me sideways. "But I like you anyway."

"Me, too, you. You're one of the best parts of Stanville. You and the Oasis," I said, meaning every cookie-crumb covered word.

On the drive back to the job site, I was hit with the realization that I was beginning to make friends here. That was the good part. The bad part was that in a very few weeks I'd be leaving the job... and my new friends. Oh, sure, I could always come back and visit. But how often does that happen in real life? If I was going to stay in this profession, continually moving from job to job, I'd need to come to some sort of agreement with myself about how to accept short-term friendships.

By the time I drove back to the job site, the concrete pumper had arrived. The driver, who'd been appropriately named "Pigpen" by his coworkers because of his quirky personal hygiene, was the same one as before. He was parked on the side street, waiting obediently for me to direct him onto the job site. *Good boy*, I mentally congratulated him.

I parked my truck out of the way next to Ol' Blue and walked over to the pump truck where Pigpen was standing, making sure I was upwind of him. After a brief discussion of his needs as truck driver/crane operator and my needs as Project Supe, we came to an amicable agreement as to where he'd park while pumping the concrete.

It wasn't long before the concrete truck showed up.

"Hi there. I'm Katlin, the Project Supe," I said as I hopped up on the running board, hanging onto the side mirrors as I directed the driver to his parking spot.

"Mack, here," he said with a warning look on his face. He probably had heard all the jokes about how much he looked like the hood ornament on his Mack truck and wasn't particularly open to hearing another one.

Doing my best to keep my face from breaking up with hilarity, I asked, "What happened to the other driver who was here last time?"

As he maneuvered the huge truck deftly around the cramped job site he responded, "Aw, he asked to be transferred to another job. Sumthin' about the Project Supe on this job giving him the hives. You shoulda seen him backin' up to anything that would stand still so's he could scratch his back on it, just like an ol' bear." His face lit up with a huge, yellow-toothed grin at the memory.

"Guess they don't make truck drivers like they used to," I said innocently and jumped off the running board, leaving him to wonder about his own prowess.

All that was missing now was Larry. As all three of us stood around waiting for Larry, I began to feel an urge to jump in my truck, hunt Larry down, and cause him massive public humiliation and possibly a bit of physical harm. Nothing that would leave permanent scars, of course. I was just about to give in to my urge when he drove up. He had no idea how lucky he was that I needed him in full working order right then.

Like a trapped animal, he could sense he was in some pretty deep dog doo-doo. He scurried nervously about, being careful not to look directly at me while he pulled tools out of his truck and yelled at the two guys who had ridden with him. From the looks of them, I suspected that his crew consisted of whoever he could find in the bar that morning that was semi-sober.

In a scant few minutes he gave a thumb-up signal to the two waiting drivers and they moved into action. The slow, choreographed dance of cement truck driver, pumper operator, and concrete finisher began. The concrete truck driver had to feed the wet concrete slurry to the pump struck smoothly and at just the correct volume. Too little and the concrete pumper would run dry and need to be re-primed. Too much and the concrete pumper couldn't handle it, ending up with concrete slopped all over the place. As Pigpen moved the crane back and forth across the inside of the footings, he was careful to move it at the same speed and in the same direction that Larry was moving. Concrete spewed out of the nozzle at the end of the hose hanging off the crane arm as Larry held onto it, walking slowly back and forth. He was using every ounce of strength he could find in his scrawny body to hang onto the hose, aiming the flow exactly as it was needed.

I stood by Pigpen, safely out of the way of everyone as I watched the show. I was surprised to see how evenly Larry was distributing the "mud". It gave me hope for the quality of the end result.

There must have been a hundred levers and things on the pumper truck control panel. I was fascinated, watching how easily Pigpen moved them without even looking at his hands. His expert ability to operate this machine as if it were an extension of his body was intriguing. It was like watching a concert pianist's fingers flying over the keyboard. I was completely engrossed.

Suddenly I heard something that sounded like a gigantic toilet plunger, followed by the shrieks of some little girl screaming. It seemed to come from the general direction of the slab area. I turned to look and immediately spotted Larry swinging in the air above the slab, holding desperately onto the end of the hose. As he swung back and forth high over the pond of fresh, wet concrete, he was singing high C like an opera soprano. He began kicking his legs, as if walking in mid-air was going to get him back to ground level. When that didn't work, he began cussing, using some new phrases I'd never heard. I made note of them, just in case the occasion should arise when they might be useful.

A strangled sound from Pigpen pulled my attention away from Larry. His face was red as a tomato and all scrunched up. He looked like he was in horrible agony.

"Bwahhhhhhh haaaaaaaaaw haaaaaaaaaaw," exploded from his mouth as his face became almost normal again.

"Trying to contain all that hilarity must have been very painful," I commented sarcastically to him. "Now, how about putting my concrete sub back on Planet Earth?"

"Huh? Oh. Uh. Oops. My fingers must have slipped. Sorry. I'll put him down right away," he said, reluctantly turning his attention to me and the real job at hand.

"Do so without damaging him, or else you may be the one out there mucking around in that slime while I'm the one fiddling with these levers. That might prove to be a whole lot more fun," I threatened, making my eyes into mean, narrow slits. It was one of the power looks I'd been practicing in the mirror each morning as I showered in my one-size-fits-all bathroom.

# Studs

The sound of a hoarse donkey braying came from behind us. I turned to see the cement truck driver hysterical with laughter, hanging on to the concrete chute to keep from falling over.

"Uh, Mack? How's the concrete? You got enough or do we need another truck?" Pigpen asked, nodding his head toward me in warning.

Mack wiped at his tears of laughter, trying to clear his vision... all the better to see the laser beams shooting from my eyes at him. "We're fine, Pigpen. Got plenty. Let's head on 'er," he said, making a huge effort to put his face back to normal.

Even with all the fun and games, in less than an hour the entire form for the slab was filled with concrete and all the machinery was shut off.

"That Larry sure is great to work with. He's always on the job in time, ready to work," Mack said just before I was going to voice my thanks to him for a job well done. "And he sure knows how to figure concrete. He got the yardage so close I almost ran out. I don't even have a bucketful of concrete left."

For the span of a New York second I was speechless at this guy's incomprehension of the situation. Quickly, though, I found my voice. "As has been his typical modus operendi, Larry got here late today. He arrived just barely in time to stop me from having to hunt him down and do him harm that would leave him scarred for life – physically and emotionally. I intend to inform him of that fact just as soon as he's done finishing the concrete. And for your information, he was *not* the person who estimated the concrete. That would be me you have to thank for being so knowledgeable and efficient," I said in a quiet voice sounding much like the low, warning growl of a Doberman about to attack.

Mack slowly and carefully backed away from me, his eyes big and fearful. "Oh. Yeah. I get it. Thank you. Thank you very much," he said very respectfully, glancing over at the pump truck driver in a silent plea for help.

I slid my eyes over to Pigpen and caught him just straightening up, holding his hand over his mouth as tears streamed out of his eyes. His sides were in spasms as he tried to control his laughter at the sight of the big, beer-bellied cement truck driver fearfully backtracking away from me, a mere woman. I squinted my eyes into a look that said, "Be careful, Buster, or you're next," and walked away to watch Larry and crew begin the tedious process of working the lumpy concrete into a smooth finish.

As I watched, I pondered on how easy it had just been for me to scare the beejeezuz out of a big, burly, macho truck driver. It *was* kinda funny, now that I thought about it. It was also kinda scary. Was I turning into some horridly frightening monster? Or was that what it took to be a good Project Superintendent and get the job done? Bad Ass 101 wasn't something that had been covered in the Project Management class I'd gone to with Gene.

Pigpen and Mack took a few minutes to rinse the wet concrete from their respective machines before driving off. Not because either of them was naturally tidy. If they dripped concrete as they drove down the highway, their company and possibly themselves would be paying a hefty fine. They gave me a quick salute from the safety of their truck cabs before roaring off. Maybe I was overdoing this tough Project Superintendent thing.

Larry, being the boss of his crew, had taken control of the gas-powered concrete finisher. The childhood rules made by little boys on the playground seemed to still be honored by big boys in the working world. It was Larry's toy, so he got first dibs using it. It looked like a lawn mower motor on top of a giant fan. The blades of the fan moved slowly around, smoothing out the concrete in circles about four feet in diameter... much faster than the old fashioned way of using a small hand tool. And a lot easier on the body, too. No bending over for hours, tediously working the concrete into a slurry and then smoothing it with a mere 12" trowel.

His two employees were working in front of him, moving from one end of the slab to the opposite end. Each one was at the opposite end of a 2 x 8 board, one that was long enough to span half the width of the slab. As they held the board on edge, they pushed and pulled it back and forth, slowly seesawing it as they moved the mushy concrete into some general semblance of level.

# Studs

When they were done with that portion of the concrete smoothing process, they tossed the board on the ground and dug around in the tool box in Larry's truck until they found some rusty hand tools. Not too happily, they once again waded into the middle of the concrete pond, this time to begin slowly hand-finishing it. Only occasionally did they look wistfully at Larry, who was having all the fun.

I was relieved to see that Larry was following his crew as they moved down the slab. I wasn't all that confident about the professional quality of the work his so-called crew was capable of doing.

It looked like things were temporarily under control, so I decided to take the opportunity to drop in on Maude and Henry. I wanted to make sure they had made plans for moving soon to another living space. Red was going to be hauling their current home-sweet-home down the road sometime soon and it would be nice if they weren't in it when that happened.

But before I went a-visiting, I needed to make a very important phone call to Roger and let him know that his start date was Friday.

After several rings he answered the phone. Did the man ever work? "O'Donnell Construction. Roger here."

"Hi Roger. Katlin here. I've got a start date for you. Friday. The guys just finished the slab and I want to give it a couple of days to cure before your crew starts whamming away on it. The framing lumber will be delivered Thursday."

"Monday would work better for me. I've got stuff to do," he complained.

"Well, it won't work for me. I'm already two weeks behind on this job and can't let the job sit. Besides, we already discussed this and you agreed to be ready to start this week." My teeth were starting to gnash.

"Things happen."

"Yes. They do. Like framing contractors getting fired before they even start the job, for instance," I threatened.

"Now, let's not get too hasty. Lemme see here. Yeah. I can rearrange my schedule and have my boys there first thing Friday."

"We're talking about the whole crew, right? All eight of them and your dad? All day?"

"Yep."

"Splendid. I'll see you and your full crew on Friday no later than 8am."

Whew. I hadn't expected him to try another power play so early on. First refusing to sign a contract and now this attempted delay. Good thing I'd had lots of practice strengthening my macho muscles with Larry. I had a hunch I was going to be needing them with Roger.

A few deep breaths calmed me down enough to walk over to Maude and Henry's. After a few minutes of banging on their back door, I heard Maude's loud complaining as she slowly thumped her way through the narrow alleys of accumulated junk. Before she got to the door, Fuzzles decided to join in the fun and yipped along with the Maude's grouching.

"Well, hi there, Katlin. Haven't seen you for a few days," she greeted me.

"Yeah, this job is keeping me hopping. But I've got some time now and thought I'd come over and say 'Hi' to you," I said, sidling down the hallway behind her. There must have been some magical phenomenon of physics that allowed her to squeeze her bulk exactly to the size needed to navigate through the narrow aisles of ceiling-high piles of newspapers and magazines. I could barely make it and I was half her width.

"I've got coffee made, if you have time. I might even be able to find a couple of your favorites – my famous chocolate chip cookies," she offered.

"Oh, don't go to any trouble on my part," I replied, hoping she wouldn't be able to locate her Cookies from Hell. "I have to be back on the job in a short while to make sure that the concrete contractor finishes the job right. Just coffee will be fine."

# Studs

I sat down in one of the two tired and beaten old wooden chairs at the kitchen table while Maude poured me a cup of coffee and refilled her own cup. She settled herself in the other chair, wiggling and squirming her butt into place as the chair screamed for mercy.

"Well, what's new over there?" she asked.

"Today the concrete slab for the floor is being finished. By Friday the framer will start. I think I'm getting the job back on schedule, slowly but surely," I began, gently beginning to touch on the subject of when their house would be moved. She beat me to it.

"That means this old house is going to be moved purty much on schedule, don't it, hon," she didn't so much ask as make a statement.

"Yes, that's right. I figure a couple of weeks and Red will be here to move it. Where are you and Henry going to go? Do you have a place?" I asked, genuinely concerned. I didn't want to be responsible for tossing two elderly people out of their house, making them homeless waifs. I could just see the headlines in the local Stanville paper – "Mean, Heartless Project Superintendent Found Guilty of Elder Abuse: Moves House with Old Folks *Still Living In It!*"

"Oh, we can't wait to get out of here. Henry and me already bought a place just a ways down the road in a real nice trailer park. I guess they call them mobile home estates nowadays. Anyways, they got a recreation building with Bingo every Wednesday night and a potluck every Sunday. We got us a good deal on our trailer because the previous owner was taken off to prison for making some kind of drugs in the house. So anyways, the state confiscated his trailer and sold it real cheap and we got it. It just needs a bit of fixing and it'll be better'n new. Henry can patch the bullet holes in the walls so's you'll hardly notice them. And I can cover up the blood stains on the linoleum with some scatter rugs," she said proudly.

"It sounds very nice," I said, relieved that I wouldn't have a homeless old couple on my conscience.

"It's even got a view of the river. Ya just stand in the bath tub on your tippy toes and crane your neck a little to the left so's you can look out the little window," she said, getting more excited about her new place the longer she talked about it. "I'll give you our address and directions. After we get moved in and settled, you can come over and visit," she invited.

"Yes. A visit sounds nice," I said, hoping my lack of enthusiasm wasn't obvious. "Well, I better get back to the job and make sure that concrete sub is doing what he's supposed to," I said standing up quickly, startling Fuzzles who had been napping on Maude's ample lap and setting him off on a yap rant.

She walked me to the door and we said our good-byes over Fuzzle's excited yipping and doggie dance. As I walked back to the job, I mused over Maude and Henry's new home and hoped they'd be very happy in it. I knew Maude would enjoy the socials and Henry would enjoy his TV programs, never again to be interrupted by another gas customer.

Larry and crew were still hard at work and it looked like they'd be done within an hour or so. That big finishing machine sure sped things up. I went back to Ol' Blue and sat down at the dinette/office desk to check my timeline chart just in case there was some official duty for me to perform. I was running out of work. After the hectic, frantic pace of the last couple of weeks, it was unnerving to not have umpty-ump things to do.

For want of anything better to do, I looked through my notes from the Project Management Class and discovered that I'd forgotten to start a job diary. The teacher had stressed that this was as important, if not more so, than updating the plans with the "as-builts", plans that are the original plans drawn by the architect with additional notations made as to how the project was actually built. Just as the map is not the territory, the plans are not the building. These would come in handy when, sometime in the future, such things as buried plumbing, in-wall electrical, or studs needed to be located.

I'd already measured where the plumbing and electrical lines were in the trenches and marked them on the plans. My as-builts were up to date. It was my job diary that was not only sadly out of date, but non-existent. I didn't even have a notebook to start my diary.

Once more I checked on Larry, and sure enough, things still looked to be under control and moving towards completion quite nicely. I caught Larry's attention and made the slicing-across-the-throat motion. He turned the machine off and looked at me attentively. He was coming along nicely in his behavioral training.

"Larry, how are you doing? Do you need anything from me? If not, I'm leaving now to get some supplies," I said.

"Nope. I think we've got everything covered here. We'll be done in another hour or so. Then it's just clean up and we're outta here," he said, taking off his baseball cap and wiping imaginary sweat off his brow.

"Great." What a relief it would be when he was done and I wouldn't have to babysit him anymore. As far as I knew, this was the end of his work on this project.

I smiled at him and gave him a thumbs-up. He smiled and nodded his head in acknowledgement, then waited for a moment to make sure I was done with him before starting up his big toy again.

I watched him for a while, then walked around the edge of the slab and surveyed the quality of the finishing. So far, so good. It looked almost mirror smooth. I was amazed and delighted at the quality of this piece of Larry's work. The finished condition of the footings and foundation walls wasn't as critical as that of the slab, so the few rock pockets he'd left in the walls was acceptable. But the vinyl floor tile would be applied directly to the slab so it needed to be extremely smooth – no lumps, bumps, or holes.

As I walked back to Ol' Blue, my stomach began telling me it was way past time for lunch and if I didn't feed it soon, it was going to tell everyone in Stanville how I neglected its welfare.

I found some green leafy stuff in the little refrigerator in Ol' Blue, chopped some cheese and tossed the chunks on it, then drowned it in Goddess Dressing. Years of eating my own cooking proved that any food I prepared would have a greater chance of being edible if I didn't actually cook it. Cheetos, potato chips, and the occasional green salad were fairly safe for human consumption when prepared by me. Microwaved popcorn had about a 50/50 chance of being edible.

Since the dinette was covered with plans, I ate my sumptuous early dinner on the back bumper of Ol' Blue, watching Larry and crew finish up. I just love live entertainment when I dine.

By the time Larry and the other Stooges were done washing concrete off the tools, they were all half drowned. The backwash and overspray had entirely drenched them. They threw the tools in the back of Larry's truck and roared off, no doubt to the tavern where they'd become beer-soaked in addition to being water-logged.

After my fine repast, I took a few moments to do the dishes, which consisted of tossing my paper plate and plastic fork into the garbage. Water conservation is high on my list of environmental concerns, particularly where it applies to housework. You won't catch me unnecessarily washing dishes or mopping the kitchen floor and wasting all that water.

I'd just finished that little bit of housekeeping when I heard Phil calling me.

"Katlin? You in there?" he yelled loud enough for half the entire west half of the town to hear.

I threw open the door and feigned a surprised jump backward. "Phil! I didn't hear you," I said innocently.

"But I yelled... oh. You're just having a little joke, aren't you?"

"Yep! Good to see you Phil. Have you had a chance to look at the slab yet?"

"Not yet. I just got here, ya know. How about we take a little walk over there and see how old Larry did?"

"Sorry, I don't have any cookies for you. I didn't know you'd be here today," I apologized as we walked the few steps to the foundation.

"That's okay. My wife's getting suspicious anyway. I had to let my belt out a notch and that always makes her eyes get all green. Well, here we are. Larry and crew did a mighty fine job, looks like. Let's go back to your office and I'll sign off on it. Got any lemonade or anything? It's mighty hot out today, isn't it?"

# Studs

he chattered on as we made our short journey to the slab and back to Ol' Blue.

"I think I might have something in the fridge for you, Phil. Can't let my favorite inspector go away thirsty now, can I?"

I found a couple of cans of some kind of fruity, sweet tea drink and we sat inside where it was cooler. The end of summer was always hotter than the rest of it for some bizarre reason.

"This is the weirdest foundation I've ever seen. I know it was engineered and drawn up by licensed, accredited architects and engineers, but it still doesn't make sense to me," I said.

"What part of it doesn't make sense?"

"The part about the slab not being connected to anything. Every structure I've ever estimated or built was connected to the foundation by bolts. This one just sits there, free to move around."

"It's another of those engineering wonders that people of my kind are so fond of," he said, gently reminding me that before he was an inspector, he had a long career as a structural engineer. "The soils here are very unique and require some very creative and unusual construction techniques."

"I know the soil's a bit soft, but that's not very unique."

"It's more than a bit soft. We're now sitting on Puget Sound tidal flats between two rivers that converge in the bay just under that bridge to the island. You may have noticed that when those trucks from the rendering plant roll past here the ground shakes."

"Yeah, I had noticed that. Especially when they all go roaring by first thing in the morning. It almost shakes me out of my bed," I said nodding toward the upstairs Master Bedroom Suite in Ol' Blue.

"Yes, I'll bet," he said, chuckling. "This soil consists of river silt, and when the tide comes in, the ground becomes saturated like a sponge, and actually rises. If your slab was solidly connected to the foundation it would buckle and crack like a dried mud pack on a woman's face. Not a pretty sight, I can tell you from experience," he said, giving a small shudder.

"Interesting. That explains why there are other things like cabinets that are connected to either the floor or the walls, but not both."

"There's some other odd construction ideas that architects and engineers have come up with in the past. Some of 'em worked. Some didn't," he said grinning.

"Thanks for the education, Phil," I said gratefully. He was more valuable to me than he probably knew. "Well, we have a bit of a break for a few days until framing starts. At least, that's the plan. So I probably won't see you for a few days."

"I might just stop by to see how you're doing anyway, he said as he pried himself out of the dinette. He walked his XXL body over to his XXS car, squeezed himself into it, and buzzed away to his wife and a good home cooked, country meal.

With nothing else to occupy my time, I decided to pop into town and get a notebook at the local drug store and start my jobsite diary. I raced into town and quickly netted a spiral bound notebook, which would be the source of my entertainment for the evening. Revisiting all the experiences I'd had so far on this job – good, bad, and everything in-between – would probably be enough to amuse me for several evenings to come.

# Chapter 19

There was nothing like the promise of Cherie's really good, really strong coffee and one of her massively scrumptious cookies to coerce me out of bed in the morning. But before I scurried out to the Oasis I needed to take a shower. It had been a couple of days since I'd had time for more than a quick spit bath and I was ripe for a complete shower.

In the midst of the first wet-down I noticed that water was starting to creep up around my ankles. I was pretty sure this hadn't happened before, but the 15 second showers didn't given me much time to pay attention to the water drainage. The water seemed to be of a slightly brownish color... and it didn't smell very nice, either. This couldn't be good.

I quickly finished my shower, threw some clothes on, and called my personal RV expert, Ginnie.

"G and..."

"GINNIE! There's brown stinky water in the shower. What do I do?"

"Hon, do you remember that little conversation we had about the trailer dump?" she said slowly, as if she was talking to someone whose second language was English.

"Oh. That."

"Yes. That. And you better do it soonest. Or else."

I didn't want to know what the "or else" was.

After the big concrete pour yesterday and all the frolicking by Pigpen and Mack I needed a nice, quiet catch-up day. Now Ol' Blue was telling me he needed to go to the trailer bathroom. This was not making me happy.

Before I tackled *that* ordeal I needed some cookie and coffee fortification. Swinging out the door, I silently promised Ol' Blue we'd go to the trailer dump as soon as I got back and in the meantime to just hold it. I mean, what else was the poor thing going to do?

Speeding toward the Oasis I noticed that the wind had shifted and the aroma of the sewage ponds was once again drifting across downtown Stanville, making it easy to recognize the weekenders from Seattle who had beach cabins on Camas Island. They were the ones with the watering eyes and noses covered with whatever they could find to block the stench. The locals had become immune to the smell and thought those city folk must be kinda wimpy to be so overly sensitive to the aroma of eau de sewage.

The instant I arrived at The Oasis, I threw open the door and sucked in the wonderful cookie smells. What a wonderful antidote to the nose-hair curling smell in Stanville.

"Hey, Cherie! What sumptuous repast have you conjured up today?"

She just looked at me for a minute or so, squinting her eyes as if it would help her hear a little more clearly what I'd just said. "What?"

"What's the cookie of the day?" I said a little slower and more carefully.

"Oh. That's what I thought you said. My hearing isn't too good today. I think it's caused by Fuzzy Navel poisoning from last night. I think the Peach Schnapps in them makes your brain go deaf," she said

"Where were you imbibing these concoctions?"

"What?"

"Where were you drinking?"

"Oh. At my new boyfriend's apartment. They're delish! I'm thinking of creating a cookie in honor of Fuzzy Navels. Maybe a orange flavored sugar cookie with a hint of ginger and topped with some shredded coconut."

186

"Sounds yummy. For now, I'd like three of those Mocha Monsters and two giant coffees. I have a nasty chore and need to fortify myself first."

"I can't even begin to imagine what horrid thing you might have to do with the job you have. That's not a job for a sissy," she said stuffing my breakfast into a white bakery bag.

"It's not exactly job related. I have to take Ol' Blue – that camper I've been staying in on the job – to the trailer dump today."

"Oh gawd. That's the worst ever. Here. Have a cookie on me," she said, her entire face puckering up at the very thought of my upcoming household chore.

It wasn't exactly the encouragement and support I was looking for, but hey, a free cookie is always a good thing.

On the drive back to the job site, happily munching on my second Mocha Monster, a dire thought passed through my brain. Maybe I should have waited until *after* my ordeal to eat. Oh well. If I lost my cookies, so to speak, I had two more in the bag.

Back at the job site all was quiet. Unless some unexpected surprises jumped out at me, nothing would be happening until at least the next day when the framing package was scheduled to be delivered. Then on Friday when Roger and his crew were scheduled to begin framing, I'd probably go back to being busier than a one-armed wallpaper hanger. For now, it seemed safe for me to leave the job site and take care of Ol' Blue's personal business.

After disconnecting the water hose and extension cord and putting the phone in the bushes behind a tree where I hoped no one would find it and no dogs would pee on it, I jumped in Ol' Blue and prayed to the God of Dilapidated Vehicles that he'd start. After only eight or ten times cranking on the starter, Ol' Blue coughed to life. I let him run for a bit to kind of warm up and get all his parts working, then shoved the gearshift into D and off we went to the RV Potty.

As a result of Ginnie's "or else" warning, I was afraid to look in the mirror on the side of the camper with the door that hid the poop chute hose as we rocked 'n rolled down the road. I didn't want to know if brown liquid was splashing out, leaving a tell-tale trail of slime behind me and Ol' Blue. Besides being potentially illegal, it could be excessively humiliating.

Once at the Camas Island State Park Official Trailer Dump, I began getting dressed in my brand new protective gear that I figured was just perfect for this type of event. Knee-high rubber boots. Check. Plastic industrial weight elbow-length gloves. Check. Rubberized rain pants with bib. Check. Rain jacket with hood. Check. Full length plastic poncho. Check. Sou'wester hat. Check. Goggles. Check. And last but certainly not least, three layers of surgical masks. Check.

I was ready. I could do this.

As I walked around to the poop chute door on the other side of Ol' Blue I felt the close presence of someone. I stopped, spun around, and almost knocked Mark over.

"Wah ah oo doig er?" I asked him.

"What? Take those silly masks off. I can't understand what you're saying through them," he ordered.

Pulling them down below my chin I asked again, this time slowly and with exaggerated pronunciation just to make sure he caught my sarcasm. "What. Are. You. Doing. Here?"

"Ah. That's pretty much what I thought you said. Well, after working my tail off for several months, I'm taking a couple of days and going fishing at my secret spot up by Mt. Baker. Got my trailer all packed and ready to go. I just need to empty the black water tank and I'm set. What are you doing here? No, never mind. Stupid question."

He looked at me for a few beats without saying anything.

"I know this is probably another stupid question, but would you like some help?"

Oh... only all I could get. "Well, actually I was kinda looking forward to this. It's all part of the RV experience, you know."

"Sure. I understand. Well then, I won't hold you up any longer. You just go ahead and I'll get out of your way," he said taking a step backward.

Before I could stop them, my hands shot out and grabbed his shirt front and began pulling him toward me.

"Do I detect a change of mind here?" he said with that adorable twinkle in his eyes.

"Maybe. Um, okay. Yes. Please." Sometimes it's better to save face by retreating than to have said face all covered in brown icky poop chute slime.

I watched as he deftly opened the little door on Ol' Blue, pulled the hose out and stuck it in the official Trailer Dump Hole. I could almost hear Ol' Blue give a big sigh of relief as brown liquid gurgled out of him and into the underground septic tank.

When Ol' Blue was finally empty, Mark shoved the hose back inside the little door, turned a little lever, closed the door, and smiled at me with one of his world famous Cheshire cat grins. He hadn't gotten a drop of brown icky on him. "See? That wasn't so bad, now, was it?"

"Nope. It looked pretty easy. You handled it like a true pro. But I think I might have missed one or two important steps in the process. Maybe you could show me again sometime. Like maybe the next time Ol' Blue needs to come here."

"That might just be a possibility. But if you're really so anxious for my company, why don't you let me take you out to dinner after I get back from fishing? Better yet, how about if you come over and I'll fix you dinner – fresh Trout as only I can do it... dredged in tempura batter for the lightest, crispiest coating, seasoned with my special secret spices, sautéed in butter..." he stopped, looking at me with concern. "Are you okay?"

"Um, yeah," I said coming back to Planet Earth. I'd kinda drifted off while envisioning the delectable dinner he was describing. I hoped I wasn't drooling. "Do you think it's appropriate to consort with upper management?" Now that the dreaded trailer dump experience was behind me, I was feeling a little frisky.

"Oh, I'm sure any consorting between you and me would be just fine. I'll stop by the job site or give you a call when I get back. In the meantime, you might want to remove that gear you've got on and hide it where nobody will ever find it. People might think you're a bit touched in the head if they see you wearing it," he suggested.

Right now he could say anything he wanted to me. I was so grateful I almost kissed his hands, until I remembered where they'd been – too close to the poop chute for my comfort. "Thank you so much, Mark. I can't begin to tell you how much. It's beyond words. Well, talk to you soon," I said stripping layers of protective outerwear off as I stumbled around Ol' Blue to the driver's side door.

After throwing the mini-mountain of protective gear on the seat next to me, I started Ol' Blue and pulled out of the trailer dump as Mark pulled in after me. I honked and waved as I drove by on my way back to the jobsite.

After getting Ol' Blue settled once again in his spot and hooked up to everything, I figured it was time to do something productive and earn the big bucks I was being paid. Time for a review of the plans and specs to see how I was doing on getting the project built as it was designed. Or close to it.

After what seemed like a short time later my eyes were glazed over and I realized my stomach had been telling me it was way past time for lunch. Two cookies and a quart of coffee wasn't enough to keep me going all day. The other two cookies were in the refrigerator, saved from any danger of me eating them in case my favorite building inspector came by.

A quick check in the micro-fridge told me that The Daisy Café was my best bet for something edible. So off I drove to my favorite spot in Stanville... other than the Oasis.

For some strange reason the parking lot was almost empty. I spotted only a few of the regulars' cars and pickups. As I opened the door to my truck I understood why. I'd forgotten that the wind had shifted to its most unfortunate position for the town of Stanville. This was good news for me. I wouldn't have to fight the hoards of tourists and week-enders for a place to sit.

Half an hour later I waddled out the front door of The Daisy, packed within an inch of my life with a triple-decker bacon cheeseburger, smothered in onions that had been fried to a tender golden brown in bacon grease. Oh, and don't forget the mound of French Fries, coated with flour and seasonings to make them extra crispy-crunchy and spicy on the outside. And just to appease the US FDA's MDR, there was a glop of cole slaw somewhere on the plate. Not that I cared.

Back at the jobsite once more, I immersed myself in the plans and specs, checking off all the work that had been completed so far and comparing what still needed to be done on my handy-dandy Timeline Chart.

With that little chore done, next on the agenda was figuring the finish lumber and accompanying materials that needed to be ordered. As was my habit, when I listed each item on my estimating sheet I colored it with a specific color of highlighter pen, using my own secret code on the plans. It was on the framing page that I discovered an item with no color coding. This was odd. I'd gone over these plans a kajillion times. How could I have missed something?

Holding the plans up to the miniscule window so I could get more light and see a bit better, the item became clear. It said on the plans that it was a flood gate. The name seemed familiar, whatever it was. According to the detail inset, it consisted of 1 1/8" thick plywood and had steel-reinforced edges. That would be a heavy bugger. After studying this newly-discovered contraption I could understand how it was built. But what the heck did it do? This was worth a call to G and G headquarters.

"G and G Construction. Ginnie speaking."

"Hi Ginnie. Hey, is Gene there? I have a question for him."

"Nope, he's not here. Say, how'd the trailer dump go?" she deftly changed the subject.

"Better than wonderful! Mark, the dirt sub just happened to pull in right behind me with his travel trailer and he did it for me. We have a hot date the next time I need to take Ol' Blue to the trailer dump," I happily shared with her.

"Boy, some gals sure know how to have a good time."

"Yeah. That's me all over. Well, the reason I called wasn't to regale you with the marvels of my love life, but to ask Gene a question about something I found on the plans. It's kinda weird and I don't get it. When will he be back?"

"He'll be here probably tomorrow. He had some business to take care of. Maybe I can help you with your question."

"Ginnie, I hate to bother you. You're always the one who answers my questions, knows who I should call, and gives me support when I need it. If it wasn't for you I don't know how G and G would stay in business," I said gratefully.

"Those are often my thoughts, too. But Gene does some of the things I can't do, like the heavy lifting. So I guess it's fair. What's your question?"

"What's a flood gate?"

"Well, this is one time I can't help you. I don't have a clue. That's the strangest construction job I've even seen in all the years I've been in construction... and that's a long time. My dad had a construction business and I helped him out. But I've never run across a flood gate. Now if you want to know what a Flitch plate is, I can help you there."

"Okay. Thanks. Just have Gene call me when he gets back," I said and hung up, just as mystified as ever about this doomaflinky. And now also wondering what in heck a Flitch plate was.

Even though I didn't know what the flood gate was for or how it operated, the plans were specific enough that I could get it manufactured. Then hopefully someone else would know what to do with it.

Next call was to Glenn Bob.

"Hey Katlin Bob, you're lookin' good today. You musta got some last night," he teased when I identified myself on the phone.

"No such luck. You'd think that with all these studs up here I'd find at least one to share some romance with. But so far they're either married, have butt cracks the size of the Grand Canyon, or have more alcohol in their veins than blood."

"Sounds like you're experiencing a bit of a dry spell. Maybe I should come up there and help you out," he offered. We both knew he was just kidding. He was totally devoted to his wife. One of the really good guys.

"Thanks for the offer but I'd like to live to a ripe old age and not be murdered to death by your wife for messin' around with you. Hey, the reason I called is I want to add a couple sheets of 1 1/8" CDX plywood to my order. That okay?"

"Sure 'nough. I'll get right on it. You want it on the top or the bottom?"

All lumber deliveries, and especially the framing packages, were loaded with the materials that would be needed first on the top. That saved the framers from having to dig through a huge pile of lumber before they could start to work.

"Top, please. And put some protective corners on it. This is for a special project and I need the edges clean."

"You got it! We're still set for delivery tomorrow and Ernie's got it scheduled first thing. I think he's anxious to see what you're doing up there. We expect to get the full report when he returns," he said.

"Well, tell him the plywood is for a flood gate. That ought to keep him guessing until tomorrow," I added.

After he told me the latest gossip we hung up.

*Now to find someone to manufacture the metal parts of this flojobber*, I mused to myself. Then it came to me. When I'd had horses, I'd needed someone to manufacture some metal parts for my horse trailer. Aha! I knew just the guy to call. My friend Gig, the welder and metal artiste.

"B and B Welding," said a familiar voice when I called his welding shop and art gallery.

"Hey, Gig. This is Katlin. I've got a small but unusual job for you. Interested?"

"Gal, anything ya'll have goin' is almost sure to be unusual. Ah've never knowed anyone as crazy or dumb ass enough as you to get into such oddball predicaments," he said in his soft, slow drawl.

"Glad to be able to make your dull, boring life more interesting," I countered. We were good friends, although anyone listening in on the conversation might wonder. "I'm building a little mini-mart gas station up here in Stanville and I've just found a foobar on the plans that needs to be manufactured. You're the only one who can do it right."

"Flattery will get ya'll everywhere. What is it exactly?"

"It says here on the plans it's a flood gate," I figured that would pretty much confound him.

"Oh yeah. Ah've done them lots of times," he counter-countered. I suspected he was probably killer at poker.

"Oh, yeah. Then I'm sure you know *all* about it."

"Actually Ah do. Where Ah come from in Loosiana, lots of the commercial buildings have 'em. 'Specially the ones on flood plains. I've probably built 20 or 30 of the buggers. Most of 'em are pretty basic. Unless yer's has some surprises Ah can probably get 'er done in a few days or so. That suit?"

This was amazing news. "That'd be fabulous! How about if I drive down to your shop later this afternoon and you can take a look at the plans?" I asked excitedly.

"Lookin' forward to seein' ya, darlin'," he said and abruptly hung up. His phone manners often left much to be desired but I didn't care because he was about to perform a miracle and create something no one around this area had ever heard of before.

Half an hour later I burst into the dark, grimy office of B and B Welding. I banged on the bell thingy on the front desk and a few minutes later Gig sauntered in from the shop in back.

"Katlin, darlin'! C'mere and give me a big ol' hug," he said chuckling and holding his arms out to me. He was black all over with soot and grime.

# Studs

"Uh, maybe I'll take a rain check on that. Like after you've gotten cleaned up enough for polite society," I said backing up a step or two.

"Hunh. My feelin's is hurt," he said, slumping his shoulders and dropping his arms in an exaggerated pose of deflation.

"Oh, I've no doubt you'll get over it. Here's the plans for that flood gate. Wait! Don't touch them! I'll unfold them so you can see it," I yelled, not wanting him to smear black crud all over the plans, making them illegible.

He just stood still and grinned at me, his mouth half filled with yellowed teeth. The other half was empty spaces. "Dang, it's good to see ya, gal! Now, whatcha' got here?" he said, bending over the plans to take a closer look. Like a good little boy, he put his hands in his pants pockets so he wouldn't be tempted to touch the plans and leave grimy black streaks and smudges.

"What do you think?" I asked a little nervously. After all, this was my first flood gate.

"Hmmm. Uh huh. Mmmm mmm mm," for a few minutes he made noises like a doctor examining a patient.

"WHAT?" I couldn't stand the suspense any longer.

"Huh? Oh, nuthin'. It's real simple. Ah can have it done in a couple of days if ya'll want to pick it up. This here's just channel metal for the door frame and there's some metal bracing for the plywood. Ya'll can bring me the plywood or install it yerself."

"I'll bring you the plywood and have the framers install it all, if they can figure it out. By the way, what does this thing do?"

"Well, it's like this. When a flood's a-comin' a guy just slides the plywood into these-here channels on the doorway. Then he just runs a bead of caulk inside the frame on both sides. It's supposed to stop flood water from gittin' in the building."

"Why, that piece of plywood must weigh close to 100 pounds, with the metal bracing," I surmised.

"Yep. Purty much. And then some, I figger."

195

"Well, if there *is* a flood in Stanville, I'm wondering what minimum-wage employee is going to linger at the store long enough to install this flood gate in order to keep the potato chips from getting soggy. And in the process, possibly jeopardize their life while attempting this behemoth task. Besides, it'll take two or more people just to lift the plywood and there's usually only one person on duty in these kinds of stores."

"Yep. Purty much."

"If it were me, at the first word of a flood warning, I'd be grabbing the money, locking the door, and speeding to higher ground. You wouldn't catch me endangering my life for Cheetos, Ding Dongs, and stale pepperoni sticks. This is one of the stupidest things I've ever heard of. Probably some engineer from Colorado or New York City where they don't have floods decided this would be a fine thing to add into the plans."

"Yep. Purty much. Well, Katlin, it's been fun but Ah gotta git back to work now. It'll be done on Monday. Ya wanna pick it up then?"

"Yep. I'll pick it up in the morning on my way back up to the job site. Thanks, Gig. By the way, in all your years of building flood gates, have any of them ever been used?"

"Nope. They's been a few floods, but it's purty much like you said. People just git out and the hell with the store. Well, see ya Monday, darlin'" he said as he returned to his world of red hot metal, black sooty smoke, and noxious welding gases.

Neither of us were the type to bother with any big, gooey, emotional good-by scene, so I jumped in my truck and scurried back to the job site.

# Chapter 20

There was no telling what time Ernie was going to show up with the framing lumber, so I jumped out of my cozy bed earlier than I like and did the 15 second version of my morning ablutions. I also postponed my daily sojourn to the Oasis until later. Besides, it wasn't like I was going to suffer from cookie depravation. I had two Mocha Monsters in the micro-mini fridge. Of course, I'd sort of branded them as Phil's, but this might be an emergency. I'm sure he'd understand.

I'd barely begun munching on the first Mocha Monster when I heard the rumble of Ernie's truck. As a life-long employee at Beacon, he had special privileges. One of which was that the company paid to customize the semi truck he, and he alone, used for deliveries. He'd opted for iridescent orange paint on the body with yellow flames around the front fenders, chrome on everything that could be chromed, and a special exhaust system that sounded like a dragster roaring down the track.

I crammed the last hunk of cookie in my mouth and jumped out of Ol' Blue to direct Ernie where I wanted the load dumped.

**HONNNNNNK** greeted me as soon as I hit solid ground. Ernie had evidently spotted me. I'd forgotten about Ernie's custom Sonicblaster air horn with seventeen levels of ear-busting sound blasts. Good thing he had it turned down to the Temporary Deafness setting.

"Hiya, Katlin! Good to see you," he yelled from the safety of his truck cab. I think he could tell I wasn't delighted to have my eardrums shattered so early in the morning.

"Hey, Ernie. I was wondering if you were ever going to get here. You must have gotten lost trying to find the place," I said jokingly. He prided himself on a perfect record of always being early or on time for his deliveries. And he never got lost.

"Now, Katlin. No sense getting all prickley over a little happy horn honking. I was just trying to let you know how delighted I am to see you," he said giving me a lopsided grin.

"Yeah. Me, everyone in Stanville, and half of Camas Island now know you're happy to see me. Go ahead and back up over on that end of the building and dump the load alongside it. Okay?" That last part was just to humor him. He and I both knew it didn't much matter if it was okay with him or not. But I wanted to appease him so he'd give me a neat drop rather than a nasty, messed up pile of wood.

I watched as he deftly slid the bundle of framing lumber off the truck bed without so much as breaking one of the metal bands that held the package together. He wasn't just good. He was *gooooooooood*.

"That work for you?" he yelled as he pulled the truck out from under the load.

"Yeah. I guess that's gonna have to do," I didn't want to make his head any bigger or it wouldn't fit inside the truck cab. "You got time for coffee? I'm buying," I said as I jumped on the running board and hung onto the side mirror.

"Thanks, but I gotta get back. We just got real busy. Seems all our regular contractors have houses in the latest Street of Dreams this year. I'll take a rain check for next time. "

"Okay. The offer's always good. Give the guys back at the office a big, sloppy, wet kiss for me."

"Oh, sure. You can just bet I'll do that. See ya, Katlin." He shoved the truck in gear and I jumped down, watching in amazement as he performed a mini wheelie after he hit pavement. I honestly didn't think a semi truck was capable of doing such a trick, especially with a flatbed trailer hooked up to it. I wondered what other custom work Ernie'd had done to his baby.

Now that the big event of the day was over, there wasn't much to get in my way of making a run to the Oasis for my daily coffee infusion. In a scant few minutes I was gratefully inhaling the rich aroma of deep, dark, delectable coffee and fresh-baked cookies. Heady stuff.

198

"Have you thought about what we talked about?" Cherie interrupted my reverie.

"What?"

"You know. About buying a house for yourself."

"Oh. Actually, I have. I'm going to investigate what's available when I go home this weekend."

"Good deal. Of course, I'd much rather you bought a place up here. But since that's not likely to happen, I'm glad to hear that you're going to buy one on the peninsula."

"Well, it's not a done deal yet. I'm just investigating.

"Yep. And that's the first step. You'll be all settled in your own home sooner than you think. What'll you have today?"

For a few beats I couldn't think of cookies. The thought of me actually owning my home was so beyond my comprehension it made my mind freeze.

"You in there?" Cheri asked, bringing me back to cookie reality.

"Oh. Yeah. I'll have a couple of those Chocolate Mountains and three giganto coffees. It's going to be a long day."

"Lots going on?"

"No. Just the opposite. I'll need lots of caffeine just to keep me awake."

She giggled as if I'd said something hilarious. "Here ya go, honey. That'll be $17.42."

"And here you go," I said handing her a $20. "Probably see you on the morrow unless something unforetold blunders along."

"What?"

"I'll see you tomorrow probably."

"Oh."

She was a great person with a heart as big as an extra giant coffee, although sometimes I wondered if her brain was the size of a demitasse. I was really going to miss her when this job was over.

Happily filled with coffee and chocolate cookie, I cruised onto the jobsite and was greeted with a sight I never expected to see... Henry wearing rubber work boots and holding a shovel. I was so engrossed with the sight of Henry I almost drove into the side of Ol' Blue.

"Katlin!" he yelled at me. "Come over here."

I didn't need two invitations to go over to their house and find out what could possibly motivate Henry out of his recliner and away from his TV.

"What's the trouble?" I asked.

"We got a leak in the water pipe coming into the house and it's flooding around the gas pumps and running out into the street," he said breathless with the exertion of actually digging a few shovelfuls of mud.

"Call Thomas Oil and have them send someone out to fix it. This is their property, after all," I offered.

"We already did and they told us to fix it ourselves. Some twerp in their office told me they ain't plumbers. They're in the oil business, he said."

"I see. Well, let's go give them a call again and I'll explain how things work in the real world to him. Did you happen to get the twerp's name?" I asked, walking toward their back door.

"Yep. It's Eldon," he said, surprising me by opening the door for me like a gentleman.

"Give me the number and I'll call them. There can't be too many Eldons working there," I said.

Minutes later I connected with Eldon at the main office of Thomas Oil. "Hello, Eldon. You're just the man I want," I began, even though from his high-pitched voice I had doubts about the man part. "This is Katlin Greene at the Stanville project..."

"Yes, I know about you and your operation. I already told that Henry that we aren't sending anyone out to fix his little leak.

You can just have one of your people fix it. Go ask your foreman to assign someone to the task," he squeaked at me.

"Eldon. I AM the foreman. And I have no intention of performing plumbing work on a city water main. I'll need you or whoever has the authority to give me permission to hire a plumber and have them fix it. Immediately," I said as calmly as I could. Henry was right about him being a twerp.

"I can't allow that," he retorted in a snotty voice.

"I see. Well then, just connect me with Van Payne and we'll see what he has to say about this situation. If you can't figure out how to transfer this call to him, don't worry about it. I have his private number right here," I figured insinuating a little bit of power into my end of the conversation wouldn't hurt.

"Oh. Um. Just a moment, please, and I'll connect you directly," he said, suddenly very polite.

"Van," said a familiar voice.

"Hi, Van. Katlin here. We have a small problem up here. I just need an authorization for us to call a plumber so we can get a leak repaired in the water main to the house. Do you have the authority to do that?"

Through experiences similar to this one, it had become my habit to ask the person I was dealing with if they had the authority to do what I wanted them to do. They'd always say, "of *course* I have the authority", in a tone that insinuated it was insulting to question the scope and power of their clout.

So, *of course* Van said he had the authority.

"Wonderful! Thank you so much, Van. We'll get this taken care of right away," I said in a voice contrived to simulate awe and gratitude. I hung up and turned to Henry.

"Call a local plumber and have him come out right away to fix it. Then send his bill to Thomas Oil and make sure you mark it 'Approved by the authority of Van Payne'," I ordered Henry.

He stood still, staring at me with his mouth hanging open for a few seconds. "Th-thank you, Katlin. That was quite a piece of work," he said grinning at me.

"Yep. One of my finest, if I do say so mydamnself," I said sending a grin back at him.

Maybe I *was* strutting a bit as I walked back to Ol' Blue, but I figured it was permissible, given the mini-miracle I'd just wrought.

It may have been because my nose was just a tish too much in the air that I didn't see the huge cardboard box with something very solid inside of it. "Yeeouch!" I said a little loudly as I bounced backward after hitting the box with some rather soft spots of my anatomy. "Who put this dang thing here right in my way? What the heck is it? And who is the idiot who ordered it delivered weeks before I need whatever it is?" I asked of no one in particular.

After my nose quit stinging and my eyes quit watering enough for me to see clearly, I read the big, bold, bright red lettering on the side of the box. "Bigger's Best Chicken Broaster," I said to myself... mostly because no one else was around. "Whoever delivered it couldn't have put it in a worse spot. Right where everyone drives onto the jobsite. Well, I'll just have to drag it out of the way. It couldn't be too heavy. Those things are usually made of aluminum, aren't they?" I didn't really expect an answer, but I got one anyway.

"Actually, they're stainless steel and this one says it weighs 279 pounds," a manly voice said behind me.

"Crikey!!" I yelled, jumping straight up in the air and turning around. "Oh, Mark. You scared the livin' bejeezus out of me," I said rather breathlessly, once I'd landed on solid ground again.

"I was just driving by on my way to look at a job and give them an estimate when I noticed you sort of scratching your head and looking a bit consarned at this box. So I thought it was time for me to put on my superhero suit and rescue my favorite damsel again," he said with that lop-sided grin I was beginning to like... just a little.

"Yeah, evidently I received a delivery when I was over at Maude and Henry's taking care of one of their problems."

"Now I get to rescue the rescuer. Great! This thing's too heavy for the two of us to lift and I'm not going to drag it over this rough ground. I'll go get my hand truck and we can wheel it where ever you want it. Be back in a sec," he said as he wheeled around and trotted back to his pickup.

*Too bad he's not a little taller. Then he'd sure fit my criteria of a potential boyfriend. If he was about a foot taller...maybe even just six inches...,* I mused to myself while Mark was getting his Superhero stuff together.

Before I could get a clear vision of Mark being 6' 4" tall, he was back with the promised hand truck. And a bonus – another guy. They loaded the huge chicken broaster box onto the hand truck and wheeled it toward where I pointed. Within a scant few minutes they were done, and before I could blink they'd hopped in Mark's truck and were driving off. All I could see of them was their hands waving buh-bye out the truck window as I shouted "Hey, thanks!" in their direction.

*"If only all my problems could be solved so easily and quickly,"* I thought wistfully letting out a sigh. *"Well, I guess I'll just be grateful for the easy ones and thankful the problems I do have aren't so bad I can't solve them. So far, anyway,"* I continued, crossing my fingers and looking for some wood to knock on.

"Now where was I before all this fun happened?" I asked myself. Oh yeah. Going into Ol' Blue to enjoy my coffee, which was probably stone cold by now. And my cookies. Or had I already enjoyed my cookies? The two surprises had temporarily knocked me off balance.

Stepping into Ol' Blue I was ever so grateful to see my three quart containers of coffee and my two Chocolate Mountain cookies on the dinky counter top. I took a sample swig of the coffee and discovered that it was still fairly hot. Life was good.

I'd just settled down in the dinette booth when there was a tentative knock on the side of Ol' Blue.

"Enter, if you dare," I invited whoever it was. Now that I was once again in possession of my daily C & C (cookies and coffee) *and* I'd solved not one but two problems already and it was still morning, I was feeling pretty smug.

"Hi there, Katlin. Henry and me want to thank you again for helping us with that little water main problem. I brung ya some of my famous chocolate chip cookies," said Maude as she handed me a paper plate with tin foil covering gawd-knew-what-kind of inedible gorp. Every cook had their specialty, and while she cooked what was probably the world's best gooeyduck, her cookies belonged in a Hazardous Materials waste site.

"Why, Maude. You shouldn't have," I said as tactfully as I could. "After all, you let me use your phone when I didn't have one. Not to mention some other little problems you generously helped me with."

"Well, we appreciate your help anaways," she said holding the plate out to me.

I had no choice but to take it. "I'll just put them in the refrigerator for now and enjoy them after dinner," I said but what I was really thinking was, *"After dinner I'll really enjoy tossing them into the garbage."*

"Yuh, okay. Well, I gotta be gettin' back. No tellin' what kind of trouble Henry's got hisself into while I'm over here, chitchattin' with you."

"I understand. Well, thanks again for the cookies. I'm sure I'll really enjoy them," I said to her retreating back as she waddled back to the old house. *"Heart of gold, that one,"* I thought to myself as I watched her to make sure she didn't trip and fall on the rough ground. *"Too bad she commits the mortal sin of destroying the most sacred of all cookies – chocolate chip."*

For a few minutes I allowed myself the decadent pleasure of a container of Cherie's dark, scrumptious coffee and one of her Chocolate Mountain cookies. That done, there was nothing else to do but get back to work.

The rest of the day I worked on some more plans for another Thomas Oil Mini-Mart Gas Station that Gene had given me to estimate. I was beginning to hope I wouldn't do a very good job on the estimate so he'd lose the bid. According to Ginnie, he already had too much work going on and couldn't handle it. After all, that's why he'd given me this job. I wasn't fool enough to believe that it was because I had such incredible qualifications as a Project Superintendent. Although it seemed I was starting to get the hang of it pretty good, I thought.

# Chapter 21

Another day, another cookie fest at the Oasis. After my semi-quiet day on the job yesterday, I was feeling quite benevolent toward all living things... including Gene and certain framing subs. The fact that at day's end I'd be heading home added to my buoyant emotions. And thoughts of the cookie or two along with some high-octane coffee that were in my near future didn't hurt, either.

"Hey, Cherie," I said swinging into the Oasis. "How's my most favoritest cookie chef this glorious morning?"

"Well, ain't you just the frickin' Bluebeard of Happiness this morning," she grumped at me.

"Um, I believe that's Bluebird, not BlueBeard. What's got your tail in a knot so early in the am this morning?"

"Oh, that dang guy I been seein'. We were gettin' pretty regular. Every couple days he'd be at my place or I'd stay with him. I thought he was real serious. Turned out he was real serious... about keeping his options open. I was standing in line at the Superette behind Lulu from the Puff and Pouf Beauty Salon and overheard her tell Shirley, the checker, that she was dating this guy and things were heating up between them. Shirley asked who it was and when Lulu gave her my guy's name my face almost fell off."

"Ohhh, Cherie. I'm so sorry. What a way to find out that your dreamboat was really a garbage scow."

"Come to find out, she was seeing him on the days I wasn't. Wonder who he was seeing on Sunday. Maybe he needed that day to rest up. Poor baby," she started to giggle. Soon we were both wiping tears off our cheeks from laughing so hard at the vision of the poor, bedraggled guy trying to rest up for another onslaught of keeping two of Stanville's finest females contented.

"Well, she's welcome to him. I don't want sloppy seconds. Besides, I deserve better," she said straightening up, pulling her shoulders back, and raising her head in a posture of pride, strength, and courage.

"You got that right. Way mo' bettah, baby," I yelled sticking my fist in the air as a symbol of well fought battles and much deserved victory. It must have looked pretty stupid because it set her off on another laughing hoot.

"Oh, hon, you're just what I needed this morning. Here, have a couple extra cookies on the house. You're way better'n any shrink... and you work real cheap, too," she said and chuckled for a bit, winding down from her laughing fit.

"You underestimate the value of your cookies. They, too, are better'n any shrink. Better give me a couple giganto coffees, too. The framers are showing up today and I think I'm going to need extra energy to deal with that crew," I said, grabbing the bag of life-giving C and C and waving bye-bye as I turned and swung out the door.

Luckily it was all mostly good news on the job. Roger and his crew had arrived while I was at the Oasis and were busy setting up generators, compressors, cords of various types and sizes, and other implements of construction. That was the good news. The bad news was that the huge crew Roger had promised turned out to be two guys and him. Not exactly what he had promised me that last time we talked. Eight was the number I remembered hearing him say when referring to the size of his framing crew.

"Roger!" I yelled to get his attention over the noise of the generator and compressors.

He turned with a frown on his face, but quickly plastered a big happy smile on his face when he saw me. "Katlin! We're here, darlin', just as I said we'd be."

"This is good. However, you led me to believe your crew was much larger. The number you quoted me was eight guys, not two. Are you still going to be able to complete the framing in two weeks like you promised with such a small crew?"

"There may not be a lot of them, but they work like hungry beavers," he replied with that shiney smile still on his face.

"Well, that's good. I know you want to get right to work, so I won't keep you from it," I said beginning to step away from him.

He was too quick for me. Before I could move, he'd snaked his arm around my shoulder and dragged me closer to him. "Don't you worry your pretty li'l head, darlin'. I'll make sure this job is done on time, just as I promised," he said giving me a knowing wink.

Gak. I ducked under his arm, escaping the confines of his ghastly attempt at wooing me. "Well, we're wasting daylight. I'll let you get to work," I mumbled as I back-peddled away from him.

Back in the safety of Ol' Blue, I sprayed a cloud of disinfecting aerosol and walked through it, like the models do in those fancy perfume commercials on TV. I repeated this process a couple more times, just to make sure all the Roger cooties were obliterated.

I'd no sooner settled down in my dinette office with the second half of my Oasis breakfast when there was a polite knock on the side of the doorway. I turned around, expecting to see Roger but was surprised and delighted to see it was... LANCE!!

"Hi there, sugar. Just thought I'd drop in and see how the job's progressing," he drawled. His voice always sounded like warm caramel syrup to me.

"Oh, Lance! I was expecting you to be the framing sub. They just got here and I thought it was their boss with some questions about the work or something," I said lamely hoping I didn't have cookie crumbs all over my face, down my front, in my hair, and stuck between my front teeth like I usually do.

"Sorry to disappoint," he teased.

"I'd much rather talk to you," I said quickly, my face turning red. *How did he always manage to get me all flustered,* I wondered.

"That's good news. Not to interfere with your job or anything, but is that all the guys the framer has in his crew?"

"Evidently. He promised me more but that's all he showed up with. He says he'll be done as per our agreement. I intend to keep a close watch on him."

"Not too close, I hope. You'll be makin' me all jealous."

Despite my efforts at controlling my reactions to Lance, he made my stomach feel all squiggly and warm. On the other hand, being around Roger made my stomach feel like throwing up. My body worked like a dowsing rod when it came to studs of the manly man type, I guess.

"Y-you don't have to worry, Lance. Roger's not my type," I stuttered. Oh gawd. Could I *possibly* say anything dumber?

"I see you got the chicken broaster that I ordered," he announced proudly.

*He* was the one who ordered that monstrosity to be delivered weeks before I'd need it? So it was because of Lance that I'd probably be wasting time and potentially hurting important parts of my body by dragging the dang thing around the jobsite multiple times just to get it out of the way. His rating on my Stud-o-meter slipped just a notch.

"Yes, I certainly did receive it. We don't actually need it for several weeks yet," I tried valiantly to be diplomatic and yet let him know that, while he might be a great Regional Manager, he sucked big time as a Project Superintendent.

"Well, when you need it, you won't have to worry about whether it'll show up on time or not cuz it's already here," he said, beaming with huge pride in how helpful he'd been to me.

"Yes. That is true. Well, besides checking on your chicken broaster, what brings you up to Stanville today," I asked in an attempt to change the subject to a less inflammatory subject.

"Besides it being my regularly scheduled day to be here, I was looking forward to seeing how the job's going."

"Oh."

"And I was kinda looking forward to seeing you again, too."

"OH!"

Just then I heard the finely tuned serenade of the horns in Ginnie's land yacht. *How did Gene always manage to time his visits to coincide with Lance's visits?* I wondered to myself. Some inner sense must have told him it was time once again to screw up any potential I might have for a love life.

"Sounds like Gene and Ginnie are here for their weekly visit," I said, trying but not succeeding in keeping the disappointment from my voice.

Lance looked at me for a couple of beats. "How about if I go say Howdy to them, make my manager noises, and leave. They usually don't stay long, I've noticed. I'll circle back around after making another stop up the road a piece. Be back about noon-thirty to take you to lunch. From the looks of things, you could use some proper nourishment," he said pointing his eyeballs at the pile of cookie crumbs on top of the plans I'd left lying on the dinette table.

A lunch date? With Lance? He could say anything he wanted about my dietary habits. He could even order more stuff to be delivered. "Sure. That'd work for me," I said hoping it sounded more normal to his ears than it did to mine. What I sounded like to my own ears was more along the lines of a teeny bopper shrieking at her favorite movie idol.

"Great. See you then. And you don't need to mention this to Gene and Ginnie. No sense starting rumors," he said quietly so they wouldn't hear him.

Actually, I wouldn't mind a few rumors about Lance and I... especially if they were true. "Sure. Fine. See you later," I said.

He folded himself up enough to fit through Ol' Blue's door and I followed him out to see what "wunnerful" surprises Gene had for me now.

"Well, what have we here? What hankypanky have you two been up to in Ol' Blue? Huh?" bellowed Gene, loud enough that all of Stanville could hear him.

"Oh Gene, shut up," said Ginnie elbowing him in the belly hard enough to knock air out of him.

"Nice love tap, Ginnie," I complimented her.

"Yeah, well, sometimes I gotta get his attention so I can remind him to be mannerly. Say, what *is* goin' on between you and Lancie anyhoo?" she said quietly, taking my arm and pulling me aside.

"Nothing. Yet. Why?"

"He only drives his classic Shelby Mustang when he wants to impress somebody. My guess is that'd be you."

"His WHAT?" I shrieked in a whisper. This is not easy to do, and I don't recommend that you try it at home.

"Yep. You heard me. It's one of his toys. He's got about a dozen or so in his collection of classic muscle cars. It's one of his more pricey hobbies."

"He has pricey hobbies? I thought all he had was a big, um, belt buckle. Where does he get all his money? Regional Manager for a small-time oil company like Thomas can't pay enough to collect expensive cars."

"Guess you don't know about him, do ya, honey? His family owns half of Oklahoma. Mostly the half with oil wells. He's just playing at Thomas Oil to see if there's anything he can learn before he takes over the business from his daddy. Honey? Katlin? Are you all right?" she asked worriedly.

I think I stopped breathing somewhere in her Lance story because my vision was starting to fade to black. And Lance's rating on my Stud-o-meter had just risen again... waaay past where it was before.

"Here, sit down and put your head between your knees," she said quickly pushing me into the passenger side of her land yacht.

# Studs

The world came back into view and I sat up. This was impossible. Lance wasn't only adorable, he had money too! None of the guys I'd dated ever had both. Cute and poor. Dorky and rich. Historically those were the two major types of men in my life.

"Oh gawd, I hope he didn't see me almost faint," I said quietly to Ginnie.

"No, I got you out of the line of sight before he noticed anything. He and Gene are over there kicking dirt and pointing at manly stuff. You ready to get up?"

"Yeah, I'm fine. Let's go over there and say Howdy, as Lance says," I grinned as I leveraged myself out of the cushy seat and strolled over to where the two guys were going through yet another male bonding ritual – spitting in the dirt.

"There you are. What have you two been talking about? Us?" Gene asked, looking hopefully at Ginnie. I was kinda getting the impression he'd just emerged from being in deep doggie doo-doo with her.

"Actually, we were talking about the job," Ginnie said rather haughtily, throwing Gene off the scent of our true conversation.

"Katlin's doing a great job, isn't she?" Lance put in. I could have kissed him for that. Or for any reason, actually.

"Told ya she'd do a great job," Gene added his voice to the rest.

"You guys are embarrassing me. Truth is, the job has barely started. Wait until we get a little further along, or better yet, wait until the end before you judge my professionalism," I said. Too much gushy stuff makes me squirmy. "Gene, let me introduce you to Roger, my framing contractor," I said, grabbing his arm and propelling him toward where the framing crew was busy making lots of noise and sawdust.

"ROGER!" I yelled to make myself heard over all the noise.

He heard me and took his time unhooking his toolbelt and dropping it to the ground. Then he slowly sauntered over to me.

"Roger, this is Gene. Gene is my boss, the general contractor on this job. Gene, this is Roger, your framing sub," I introduced them to each other.

For a few seconds they just stood and looked blankly at each other. Then Roger stuck his hand out for Gene to shake. It was as if they'd never been around anyone with the manners to properly introduce them to someone before and they didn't exactly know what to do.

"Glad to meet you, Roger," Gene said jovially as he shook the hell out of Roger's hand. It was one of those subtle power plays that are so eloquently expressed during the ritual of two men shaking hands.

"Same here, Gene," Roger replied doing his best to ignore the increasing pressure on his hand as Gene slowly ground the bones in Roger's hand around.

After Gene had caused Roger enough pain and showed him who was top dog, he dropped Roger's hand. "You do my girl here a good job," he said throwing his arm protectively around me. Somehow it felt kinda good to be protected from Roger.

"That's my intention, Gene," Roger said, trying to hide his nearly crippled hand behind his back in order to save it from further abuse by Gene. "We're gonna do our darnedest to do the best job we can for her," he said. I'm sure he intended his words to sound sincere, but somehow they came out sounding like he'd read them off a cue card.

"Atta boy. Well, nice meeting you. We'd better get back to Ginnie before Lance charms her away from me," Gene said, making a small joke that no one laughed at. I think Roger was in too much pain to feel humorous and I didn't want Lance charming anyone but me.

As we walked back toward Ginnie's car, Gene kept his arm around me. He leaned over and quietly said in my ear, "You watch that guy. I don't like his looks. Untrustworthy sort, I'd wager."

"Thanks, Gene. I pretty much agree with you. Unfortunately I didn't have a lot of framers to pick from. They're all busy right now. You should have seen the ones I tossed back," I said.

He smiled kindly at me and said, "I know this isn't the easiest job for you to start on as a Project Supe, but once you're done here you'll be able to handle anything that comes at you."

Wow. I didn't know what had caused this turnaround in Gene, but I liked it. I mean, he'd always been supportive of me, but not like this. This was from the heart. "Thank you," I said and from the smile on his face, I knew he could tell how sincere my gratitude was.

By the time we'd gotten back to where we'd left Lance and Ginnie, only Ginnie was there. Just as Lance had told me he would, he'd left to visit another store in the area. I was certain he'd be back as soon as Gene and Ginnie left. I was looking forward to spending some time with him and, hopefully, learning more about him. This time from the source.

"Did you find out if Katlin got the canopy permit when you were over there having your little power struggle?" Ginnie asked Gene. *She had to have really sharp eyes to be able to see Gene use his power grip from a distance like that*, I was thinking. Just then, she turned to me and gave me a wink that said "He always does that, honey."

"Um, no. I sorta forgot," he said, actually looking embarrassed.

"Another permit? Sheesh. Will they never stop coming at me?" I whined a bit.

"You gotta get this one right away. Go ahead and leave early today so you can stop at the Building Department and pick it up. Van said he sent the paperwork to them a couple weeks ago, so it should be signed and ready," Gene said to me.

"Oh, by the way, Gene's going to a reunion in Utah next week, so you'll get the divine pleasure of dealing with me," Ginnie informed me.

"A reunion? That sounds like fun. What is it... high school? College?" I asked Gene.

"Nah. It's just a bunch of fellas I once knew. We get together like this every so often," he said rather evasively.

"Well, have a good time," I said to the both of them as they dropped into the soft leather seats in Ginnie's luxurious car. They waved as Gene slowly and sedately drove off the job site, trying not to raise any dust. *Not his usual style,* I thought. *Zooming out into the street, creating a dust cloud and screeching the tires on the pavement is more Gene-like. Wonder what's going on with him.*

I didn't have much time for wondering. As Gene and Ginnie drove out one side of the job site, Lance drove in from the other.

"What were you doing, hiding and watching until they left?" I asked him jokingly.

"Thought they'd never leave. C'mon, jump in and let's go eat. I'm starvin'," he said.

"Let me tell Roger that I'm leaving and then we can go," I said, even though I doubted Roger gave a fig whether I was there or not.

Thirty seconds later we were at The Daisy Café. I briefly wondered if the upholstery in his very expensive, very hot car had the outline of my body permanently imprinted in it due to the G force of Lance's racetrack style of driving.

"You must be pretty hungry. Or do you always drive like that?" I asked after I began breathing again.

"Aw, I can't help but show off a little bit. This is one of my favorite toys and it's a real hoot to let 'er loose," he said, giving me just a hint that his personal fortune Ginnie had talked about was actually real.

"So, how many speeding tickets have you gotten with this red beast?" I'm noted for exercising my extreme curiosity and for putting my foot in my mouth - usually at the same time.

"Not as many as you'd probably think. I'm usually a conservative driver. Guess I was just feelin' like showin' off to you."

Must be the cowboy method of wooing a damsel. "Well, you've impressed me. Maybe on the way back we can take it a little slower. I'd like very much not to lose the lunch I'm about to enjoy."

"Yes, ma'am," he said with that adorable lop-sided grin as he opened the door for me. Gad. No one had opened a door for me since my dad was fruitlessly trying to teach me how to be a lady.

The lunch gods were smiling down on us as we walked into the café with no waiting line and an empty booth. It just didn't get much better than this. Neither of us had to look at menus, since we both knew they were the same here as in every country café in the United States.

"Two bacon cheeseburgers with fries. No onions. Black coffee," he said, ordering for both of us without even asking me what I wanted.

If he hadn't gotten it so perfect, even the coffee part, I might have gotten a little perturbed. Instead of being irked, I was impressed. "How did you know what I wanted?" I asked him incredulously.

"I know you better than you know yourself, Katlin," he said after a few beats of looking deeply into my eyes.

Yikes! "If you know me so well, then why are you still here? Why haven't you run screaming into the foothills? Or more appropriately, driven a zillion miles an hour in your Shelby Mustang in any direction away from me?"

"See? That's one of the things I like most about you. You're a great little kidder, you are," he said.

Try to tell a man the truth and he thinks you're kidding. Fine. In this case the best move is to change the subject. "Did you know that besides having some of the greatest food I've ever eaten, this café is owned by the local building inspector's wife?"

"Well, now, ain't you one smart li'l cookie? Gene was right to put you on as Project Supe. I'll be honest... I had my doubts at first. But you just keep getting' better and better."

*As do you, my big ol' rich cowboy,* I thought. I just smiled at him, hoping he couldn't see what was going on in my brain at that moment.

I was getting uncomfortable with the direction this conversation was taking. Luckily the food came just then.

The waitress seemed to take quite a while making sure everything was just perfect for Lance. After her fussing over him began to border on being embarrassing, for me if not for him, she briefly asked if I needed anything. "Eating utensils would be nice. And some ketchup, if it's not too much of an effort for you, dear," I said extra super sweetly.

She sniffed, grabbed some paper napkin-wrapped silverware from a nearby table and a half-used bottle of ketchup, slammed it down by my plate, and flounced off. I heard a choking noise across the table and turned my attention to Lance. His face was purple with the effort to hold his laughter from bubbling out of him.

"You sure do have a strange effect on waitresses, Mr. Lance," I said.

That was all he needed to burst into guffaws. "You sure do have a strange way of showing when you've got a mad on, Miss Katlin," he said when he could once again talk.

We laughed together for a bit and then dug into the food. Not a word was spoken until both plates were clean – except for the glop of soggy cole slaw.

Lance threw some money on the table to pay for our lunch and the entertainment provided by the waitress and we waddled out of The Daisy. The drive back was a smidge slower, but even so it was all too soon that we were back at the job site. Now he would leave.

"Thanks so much for lunch, Lance. It was delightful," I said, climbing out of the car.

"The pleasure was all mine, Katlin. I'll be seein' you real soon," he said putting his Mustang in gear.

There was nothing else to say, and after a few uncomfortable minutes in which we both were searching for something to prolong the moment, it had to end. He pulled out of the job site, hit pavement, and roared off. I just stood there looking at his taillights, musing about how my romance prospects had transformed so quickly from zilch to two guys who were morphing from just the usual pain-in-the-ass types of guys to really nice guys. In the few short weeks that I'd been on this job, both Mark and Lance had become waaaay more promising in the love department.

*What's next?* I asked myself. Since I had no good answers handy, I decided it was time to get back to reality. I still had work to do.

There were still construction-type noises coming from the building site. It was time for me to make an appearance and check on Roger and crew. The closer I got to the building, the more tension and anxiety I felt. "Roger?" I said quietly. No response. *Just let the man work*, said my common sense self. For once I decided to listen to that voice. Some of my executive decisions are better than others.

Back in Ol' Blue I stuffed whatever dirty laundry I could find into a garbage sack I'd designated specifically for that purpose. Taking a last look around my Casa de Construction, I grabbed my purse, my dirty laundry, and jumped out of Ol' Blue. Just in case any of the local Stanville drunks decided they wanted Ol' Blue for their very own, I locked him up tight. No sense tempting those who are half a bubble off level and who might actually lust after a rusted-out rig like Ol' Blue.

I needed to make two stops on my way back to my own personal Paradise. One, I had to go to the court house in Everett to get the canopy permit, if it was there. Two, I had to drop off the plywood at Gig's so he could create a flood gate for me.

To my amazement and astonishment, not only was the permit completed and waiting to be picked up, someone had actually put it in an envelope with my name on it and laid it on the counter in the Building Department. If only life in construction were always this simple.

Dropping off the plywood at Gig's took no time at all, giving me nothing else to do but enjoy my journey home.

# Chapter 22

It had taken me only a few tortuous experiences with Gene and Ginnie's doorbell before I remembered to knock on the door rather than experience the horror of yet another whiney Country and Western tune blasting at me from their doorbell. Despite my cleverness in avoiding the doorbell serenade, I was doomed to hearing the complaining melody and depressing lyrics of some nasally-voiced cow herder who'd lost his one true love to the raptures of city life. It was blaring at full volume from the stereo as Ginnie opened the door to greet me. It was pretty obvious that she *loved* C&W music.

"Please, Ginnie, tell me you have coffee brewed," I begged her. It was the one thing that would offset the pain my ears were enduring.

"Sure, honey. You know where the pot is in the kitchen. Just go help yourself," she said, waving me into the house and toward the kitchen.

"What do you hear from Gene?" I yelled at her from the kitchen. Yelling was necessary in order to be heard over the ear-drum blasting volume of the so-called music.

"Wait a sec while I turn the music down," she yelled back.

*O thank you Music Angels*, I sent my silent gratitude toward the heavens.

"Here's the paperwork he said to give you for this week. I won't be hearing from him until Saturday when I pick him up at the airport, so it's just you and me, kiddo," she said, handing me a fat file.

"Where'd he go for this reunion?" I asked.

"Out in Utah somewhere. It's a ranch of some sort where they do guy stuff, I guess," she answered vaguely. "How are things up on the job?"

"You were just there on Friday. Not much has changed since then."

"No. I mean, you know. With Lance and all."

"What do you mean, 'with Lance and all'? All what?"

"I saw how you two were looking at each other. Sparks were flying."

"We just had lunch. No big thing. He just took me out to lunch to talk about the job. That's all. He's just interested in seeing this job go smoothly. No sparks. Just work."

"Yuh huh," she said, hand on hip and knowing look in her eyes.

"Yep. Well, I better get going or I'll miss the ferry. Thanks, Ginnie. I'll call you later this week unless something comes up before," I said, rushing to escape her prodding into my romantic interests.

Ginnie's coffee, while not as good as Cherie's, was whole bunches better than the insipid stuff on the ferry. I'd slugged down enough of her brew while we were chatting to save me from ferry coffee. It would hold me until I got to Stanville and my favorite breakfast stop – the Oasis.

Before I began the drive up the freeway to the job site I had one more stop to make - B & B Welding, where I'd pick up one of the world's weirdest construction bejabbers - a flood gate.

No one was in the front of the shop when I arrived, so I meandered toward the back. "Gig? Hey, GIG!" I yelled as loud as I could so as to be heard over the roar of the super-hot fire in the kilns.

"Ya'll don't have to yell," said a quiet male voice directly behind me.

"Yipes!" I yelled, jumping almost straight up in the air and somehow managing to turn around before I landed. "Don't be sneaking up on me like that, Gig. You scared the beejeezus out of me."

When he could control his hysterical laughter, he wiped the tears off his face, leaving a black streak that made him look like a masked bandit. "Ah just couldn't hep m'self. Ya'll looked so funny tippy-toeing in here like you wuz gonna rob the joint."

"I wasn't tippy-toeing. I was simply walking in a lady-like manner. Anyway, is the notorious flood gate done?"

"Lady-like. Yuh huh. Well, anyways, your flood gate's right here," he said pointing to the two sheets of plywood, now with metal trim, and some pieces of channel iron that were spray-painted with black primer. "Ah didn't know what color ya'll wanted it, so Ah used the universal color. Goes with everthin'," he said, cracking himself up with his cleverness.

"Great. Do you have someone to help load them into my truck?"

"It's me and you, babe. Just pull around into the alley and we can scoot 'em into the back of yer truck easy as eels slide down yer throat."

Urk. "It's a little early in the day to be thinking of eels sliding down my throat, if you don't mind. I'll just move my truck so we can do this deed," I said side-stepping by him and trying not to think of slimey eels slithering around in my mouth and throat.

The metal and plywood combo must have weighed over 200 pounds, but we somehow levered it into the bed of my truck, along with the trim pieces for the door jamb. More importantly, we managed to avoid dropping it on any toes even once.

"Thanks, Gig. You've been of immense help, once again. If you have the invoice handy, I'll take it and give it to Ginnie next week when I see her. I'll tell her to pay you right away."

"Got 'er right here," he said handing me a paper splotchy with black finger marks all over it. " 'preciate you gettin' this paid quick. Ah moved yer project in front of some others."

"Well, I truly appreciate that. I'll be seeing you – probably the next time I have some kind of metalish challenge," I said backing out the door before he could offer to give me a "big ol' hug" again.

The drive up to Stanville whisked by as I let my mind wander over, under, around, and through various subjects – Lance, the job, Lance, Gene's volatility, Lance, the flood gate, Lance, buying a house, Lance...

Before I knew, I was at the Oasis. "Hey, Cherie! Howzit going?" I inquired of her butt.

She straightened up from leaning out the drive-by window where she had been chatting with another satisfied customer. "Katlin! Glad you're back! I've got a new cookie I want you to try out... ChocoBerry. It's a dark chocolate cookie with raspberry filling inside and frosting made from cream cheese and raspberry jam. Here, try one," she said shoving one at me.

"I really don't need to test out your cookies, you know. They're all super delish. Where do you find the time to do all this creative baking, anyhow?"

"Well, I'm a little short on my supply of men right now. You know how much time they take," she said, shaking her head in wonderment.

"Actually, no I don't know how much time they take since my supply of men is rather low right now, too. And when I did have a goodly supply, it was so long ago I've forgotten what it's like. Wouldn't you think with all those studs walking around the job site all day, I'd be able to snag at least one?"

"I heard you did snag one. That Lance guy."

"Criminy! Does everyone in the English speaking world think we're having some kind of affair or something? *We just work together. That's all. Nothing else. Nada.*" Was that my voice that was rising into screechiness?

Cherie looked at me for a few beats... then burst out laughing. "Oh, honey. You got it bad."

# Studs

I blew out a big sigh, traded her some money for the bag she was holding out to me with my daily ration of calories and caffeine. "Well, it seems everyone but Lance and I know about this hot romance. Thanks for the goodies. I'll see you tomorrow, most likely," I said and scuffled to the door.

This was getting embarrassing. I hoped Lance wasn't getting the same guff that I was receiving.

It was a relief to arrive at the job site, where there was no one around to harass me about Lance. *So nice and quiet... no one around.* I mused to myself as I threw my contractor's suitcase of clothes up into my Master Bedroom Suite. *Wait a minute. Nice and quiet? No one around?* Suddenly I realized why it was so quiet on the job site. *Where's my framing crew?*

If anyone was looking closely as I stormed over to the construction site, they might have seen actual flames shooting out my mouth as I was describing the particular hell I was going to treat Roger to when, and if, he showed up. I did notice, as I was stomping around and flailing my arms to accentuate my meaning, that the framers had actually managed to get some work done on Friday. The two end walls were up and braced. Of course, those particular walls were of the most simple framing – no windows, doors, angles, or anything else even remotely creative and time-consuming.

In the days when I was working as a framer I could have done these two walls all by my lonesome in an hour, so I wasn't real impressed with the speed of their work. The quality of their work remained to be seen, especially once they got to the roof where there were some tricky framing areas around the HVAC units and chicken broaster vent.

After a few laps around the building site I'd pretty much used up my tantrum and was just about to head back to Ol' Blue and call Roger, when I heard truck doors slamming. Peeking around the corner of an end wall I saw Roger's entire framing crew - Pete and Dave - pile out of their truck and head for the tool box in the back.

"Glad to see you boys could make it," I said, my voice pitched at the level of attack dog growl.

They stopped dead in their tracks, looked at each other with their eyes opened big and wide with surprise. "Busted," said Pete to Repeat through unmoving lips. In the micro-second it took for him to spin around and face me, he'd re-arranged his face with a crinkly mass around the area of his eyes accentuated by a slash of a smile. "Katlin. So good to see you," he smarmed.

The thought instantly crossed my mind that he must be taking acting lessons from his boss. "Pete. Dave. Good to see you. I see you got started on the framing. Looks good. I'm looking forward to seeing a *lot more good work* out of you two," I hoped the emphasis of my comment wasn't lost on them.

"Sorry we're late, but we had a meeting with Roger this morning and it went longer than we thought it would. It won't happen again," said Dave.

"Excellent. Well, I won't keep you any longer. Please..." I said, sweeping my arm in a grandiose manner toward the building site, as a butler might when showing an honored guest into his master's home.

They looked at each other again with big, questioning eyes, grabbed their toolbelts, and trotted into the building.

No doubt they were wondering if the Project Supe here was a little batty. That was fine with me. I'd found that it was best sometimes to keep certain people off balance, unsure of themselves, and wondering about me. People who were cocksure of themselves were typically more difficult to deal with than those who were dubious as to their position of power in any given situation. I preferred to have certain people who worked for me in a dubious and unsure mindset.

Halfway back to Ol' Blue I turned around and saw them on the other side of their truck, watching me as they grabbed extension cords, Skil saws, and other implements of construction. When I reached the door to Ol' Blue, I turned around again to see that they were still watching me carefully. I gave a little finger-wave, to which they hesitantly finger-waved back, and jumped inside. The sight of those two big gallunks finger-waving almost brought me to a fit of the giggles.

# Studs

I suddenly felt the need for a phone call to Roger. "Roger," I said curtly to his answering machine. "Katlin here. Your two guys showed up on the job this morning. That's the good part. The *not*-good part is that they just now arrived on the job. The morning's half gone. The two end walls that were completed on Friday are a pathetic beginning. At this rate it's going to take you far longer than you promised to get the framing done on this job. I want to see MORE guys here tomorrow... *and* on time."

Even if my call to Roger wouldn't get a bigger crew up here, at least I'd feel better knowing it would probably irritate him to be nagged by me. To my way of thinking, if he didn't like it he could get the job done sooner and end his misery all that much quicker.

I settled into the work of updating my paperwork and before I knew, it was noon-thirty. After rummaging around in the dinky kitchenette it became obvious to me that I needed groceries. Either that or another diet-blasting lunch at The Daisy. Since it was becoming more difficult to button myself into my jeans, I wisely chose the grocery store.

Deciding what to buy didn't take much time. Given my limited cooking talent, a salad seemed the best bet. Cabbage was easy. Just whack it a bunch with a big knife and you had cole slaw. Add some kind of protein and a flavor in the form of salad dressing and voila! Dinner was served! Or lunch. Or whatever. Some BBQ potato chips and dip rounded out my dietary needs. Too much healthy stuff could upset the delicate balance of my digestive system.

"You must be Katlin," a woman's voice brought me out of my inner dialogue of whether to add a six pack of beer or a box of wine to my delectables. I looked up and realized I was already at the checkstand.

"Yes. How did you know?"

"My boy, Mark, told me about you. He speaks very highly of you and the job you're doing over there at the mini-mart," she said. Even if she hadn't told me he was her son, I might have put the two together. She looked just like him, but with longer hair and more curves.

"He's been the greatest guy, helping me out and coming to my rescue a couple of times."

"That's just like him. He's so good-hearted and generous. I just don't know why some smart young lady, such as yourself, hasn't snatched him up," she said with one of those sighs that only mothers with adult, unmarried sons are so good at doing.

"Well, he certainly deserves someone as great as himself. That's hard to find. I'm sure she'll come along and you'll have grandkids before you know it," I said grabbing my groceries the instant they were bagged. "Tell him I said 'Hi'," I chirped as I backpedaled away from the checkstand and out the door.

Once in the safety of my truck I allowed myself to breathe easier. *That was close*, I acknowledged to myself. There's nothing that gives me a case of the heebie jeebies like a mother who's determined to get her only son married off to some nice yet unsuspecting girl. Someone like myself for instance. Mark *was* a nice guy. He just didn't ring my bells. Maybe if he was taller...

As I drove onto the job site I noticed that Pete and Dave were hard at it, making lots of noise and sawdust. I just hoped they were also making some walls.

After stocking my shelf and micro-mini refrigerator with groceries, I found a semi-sharp steak knife and whittled some cabbage into a bowl. Then I dumped a can of tuna on top, drowned it in Goddess salad dressing, and set it on the dinette. After grabbing a serviette, in this case a paper towel, and a fork I was set to enjoy my delectable repast.

Tap. Tap. Tap.

Dang. My gourmet lunch was being interrupted. In my frustration, I swung the door open just a little too fast and was greeted with the hilarious picture of Pete sprawled in the dirt, holding his nose.

"OH, P-p-pete," I stuttered in between hiccups of laughter. "Are you okay?"

"Yeah. Nothin' broke and I guess my nose will quit bleeding soon," he grumped at me.

I grabbed a paper towel and handed it to him as he dusted off his back side. "What did you want to see me about?" I asked, full of contriteness.

"We got a question on the framing, is all. The plan calls for fire blocking but we aren't sure if it's supposed to be in the middle or at 8', like it is in residential construction."

"Just leave it out for now. That wasn't specified in the plans or specs and I'll need to ask the architect about it," I said. "Anything else?"

"Nope. That's it. I'll be getting back to work now," he said, sounding kind of funny as he held his nose to keep it from bleeding all over the front of his shirt.

"That's not an injury you can claim on Industrial Insurance, you know," I called after him.

He just waved his hand at me, as if to say, "Don't sweat the small stuff. I'm a man and can take it." Amazing how guys who work on noisy construction sites can get so good at the language of hand signals that one wave can speak whole paragraphs.

After quietly enjoying my lunch I tossed the dinnerware into the garbage. I love how modern technology makes housework so easy and quick. In my humble opinion, whoever invented paper plates and plastic forks deserves the Nobel Prize or an Academy Award or something.

Next on my agenda was finishing up one of the bids Gene had given me for yet another Thomas Oil mini-mart. It seemed like I'd been working on the plans for only a short time when I was suddenly jolted into awareness of truck doors slamming and an engine cranking over. A quick glance at the clock shocked me – it was almost 6pm! I jumped out of Ol' Blue to tell the guys thanks for a good days work but all I could do was wave at their dust cloud as they exited the job site.

Time for me to put on my Project Supe hat and inspect their work.

I was not especially delighted to find that all they'd accomplished was to frame up the back wall, which was another simple framing job – no windows, doors, etc. They did manage to actually get the T1-11 siding on the walls they already had framed. I had hoped they'd at least get all four exterior walls framed up and braced for plumb, level, and square within the next couple of days because roof trusses were coming Thursday morning first thing. If the walls weren't up there were only two choices, neither of which I found appealing. I could cancel the delivery and hopefully reschedule as soon as the framers were ready OR I could have them delivered to the ground, in which case the framers would need to figure out how to lift the heavy, bulky things up on the 15' high walls.

I began to think it was too bad I'd sold or given away all my horse equipment. I could use a couple of my old whips right about now. The crack of my long lunge whip would certainly grab the attention of any slacker framers. Movies began playing in my head – movies that included scenes of me playfully scaring the framers into action by cracking my whip over their head. This kept me amused the rest of the evening.

# Chapter 23

The familiar sounds of wood screaming as it was being severed in two with a Skil saw woke me. Gawd, I missed the peace and quiet of the farm where I was gently serenaded awake by my Bantam roosters.

My constant bitching about the lack of framers that Roger had promised me for this job must have been preying on the consciences of Pete and Dave because they were getting to the jobsite and actually starting work before lunchtime. Today they snuck onto the jobsite and were busy before I'd even fallen out of bed. Their extra effort gained some much needed progress, but a lot more needed to be gained.

It helped that they had worked later yesterday, too, before charging off to join the others in the giant parking lot known as the evening commute on I-5. If it was guilt from listening to me whine about Roger's broken promise that was causing them to increase their work hours, I was all for it. Whatever it took – whining, threats, pleading, begging, badgering, nagging, bribes – I'd do it to get the job done.

The timing was going to be close for them getting the work done when I needed it to be done. If the framing portion of the job was held up then everything else had to be rescheduled. Most of my subs were busy and if I tried to reschedule them now, there was every possibility they'd not be able to slide into new slots in my snazzy Timeline Chart for a long time. This, in turn, would mean that the subs and suppliers following them would also have their schedules fall apart and would no doubt reschedule at a much, much later date. I wanted to avoid that mess with all my heart.

I reached into what I hoped was my bag of clean clothes and found some jeans and a Tshirt. I pulled them on, figuring I had a 50/50 chance they were from the clean bag. If not, maybe I'd be lucky and get some that didn't have food dribbles on them.

Quickly I performed my ablutions in the only bathroom I'd ever seen that allowed one to multitask in such a unique manner. A glance in the mirror at my face and hair told me I was probably not going to scare anybody too terribly much on the job site today. "Good enough," I said aloud to my reflection, before throwing open Ol' Blue's door and stumbling on over to the building site.

"Hey, Pete. Repeat," I yelled my greeting so as to be heard over the hammering and sawing noises. I'd discovered Dave's nickname yesterday and I rather liked it. The nickname suited him well since all he ever did was repeat what someone else said to him. Ask him a question and he'd repeat it before answering, as if he was in a spelling bee in grade school or something. Tell him something and he'd repeat it back to you, sometimes being clever enough to actually change a word or two so it sounded almost original.

All construction sounds quit as my two framers turned to look at me. "Hey, Katlin. What gets you up so early in the morning?" Pete teased.

"I've been up for hours, waiting for you to slackers to show up," I retorted.

"Musta been real dark when you got up and got dressed," Pete said, trying to keep from laughing.

I looked down at my attire and discovered my Tshirt was not only on inside out, but backwards. "Yes. Well, I had to get dressed all by myself this morning."

That was all it took for the two of them to fall all over themselves hoo-hawing. *Some people are sure easily amused,* I thought to myself. "When you're done having your little fun time, maybe we could talk about your higher purpose in life? Like getting some framing done on this building?"

"Sorry, Katlin," said Pete.

"Yeah, sorry, Katlin," echoed Repeat.

"Forget it. I'm just getting a little tense here because we've got trusses coming tomorrow first thing and you still have a lot of work to do to be ready for them."

# Studs

"We'll have the front wall done by noon and after that all we have to do is square the building, brace it, and we'll be set," Pete informed me.

"Yeah, we'll easily finish the front wall and have it all ready for trusses by the end of work today," Repeat paraphrased Pete.

"Let me know as soon as you're done with framing up this last wall. I'll help you mark on the top plate where the doubler trusses go for the HVAC and chicken broaster vent," I said.

"Will do," came from Pete, echoed almost instantly by Repeat.

"I have to leave for a meeting now, but I'll be back in a little bit." I sorta lied. Well, I *did* have a very important meeting with an Oasis cookie or three and at least a half gallon of coffee.

Pete and Repeat continued to stand in place, as if they were waiting for something. After a few beats, I brushed my hands toward them and said quietly, "Shoo." They jerked as if they'd just woken up. They turned back to their tools and went back to work. Being a self-propelled person, I find it strange that there are people who need to be told what to do and when to do it.

I could hear my cookie and coffee calling me. I trotted back to Ol' Blue, grabbed my purse, jumped in my truck, and drove as fast as I could without attracting the attention of either one of Stanville's finest and only cops.

"Hey, Cherie. Got any cookies left?" I greeted my favorite cookie chef.

"Well, hush my puppies. What are you doin' here so early this morning?" she asked.

"It's only because you're the world's greatest cookie cooker that I won't take umbrage at that aspersion on my character. What's the special?" I asked.

"How does a person learn to talk funny like you do? Oh well. The Oasis Special O' the Day is Harvest Gold. It's my new pumpkin cookie with tiny pieces of candied ginger in it, slathered with sour cream frosting, and topped with a giant chocolate chip."

"Did I die and go to heaven? I'll take three of them. And three ginormous coffees, high octane of course."

One of the Harvest Gold cookies disappeared before I even got in my truck. The other lasted all the way back to the jobsite. I was saving the last one for my mid-morning break from the dreaded paperwork. Until the framing was done, there was little else for me to do.

Actually, as I was catching up on my daily journal, I discovered that I was beginning to enjoy the process of writing. Instead of brief notations of who showed up on the job site, their purpose, and what they did while there, I found my writing becoming very descriptive. My daily journal was beginning to read more like a novel than a business form.

The morning flew by. It was only when I stopped to shake the writer's cramps out of my fingers that I realized it was very quiet on the job site. This was not a good sign.

Two jumps and I was out of Ol' Blue and running toward the building site. I blasted through the doorway expecting to find my two framers gone. Instead they were sitting on sawhorses, staring at me with their eyes all huge and googley. They each held a sandwich in a hand that had stopped in midair on way to a mouth, which was hanging wide open.

"Oh. Hi, guys. Just checking to see if everything's all right," I managed to blurt out.

"Yeah, we're fine. Just takin' a lunch break, if that's alright with you," Pete said after he took a few beats to gather his wits.

"Okay. You're doing a good job. I'll leave you to your lunch. Let me know when you're ready for me to help you mark the top plate," I said, backing out of the building.

Lunch. It was lunchtime already. I'd been having so much fun writing in my journal that I'd lost all track of time. Since my fingers were all crampy from writing, I figured it was best if I let the pros at The Daisy fix my lunch. In my condition, any cooking on my part could be disastrous. Actually, any cooking on my part *always* had a good chance of being disastrous.

# Studs

Since my jeans seemed to be shrinking in the wash lately, I decided a salad was a good choice. Probably walking to The Daisy was a good idea, too, but I didn't want to stress my body with too much healthy stuff all at once.

After finding a parking space only one block from The Daisy, I walked all the way, not even breaking into a sweat by the time I reached the open door. I spotted a seat at the counter and squeezed by all the tourists waiting in line, ignoring their dirty looks.

"What'll ya have, honey?" asked one of my favorite waitresses. I once saw her carry eight platters heaped with food from the kitchen to the back of the dining room without spilling one drop of anything while dodging knee-high children that were running around like marbles in an arcade game. Me, I would have dropped a couple of the plates of food down somebody's back and tripped over a kid or two, kicking them (accidently of course) and sending them howling back to their mommy.

"The Chef's Salad, please," I replied.

"Will that be the half plate or the full plate?" she asked.

"Full, please. I've been working real hard on the jobsite today," I justified unnecessarily to her.

"Uh huh." It's amazing how some people can throw so much meaning into a couple of sounds. She knew, I was sure of it by the tone of her uh huh, that all I did was sit at my dinette/desk and write all morning as I munched on cookies and glugged coffee from The Oasis.

"And a cup of your high octane coffee."

"You got it, doll," and she whisked away to stuff the slip of paper with my order on it on the little whirligig, turning it so the cook could see it.

Within nanoseconds a platter appeared in front of me, piled so high with veggies, several kinds of meat, white cheese, yellow cheese, and white and yellow cheese that I could only see the waitress' forehead. "Enjoy, darlin'," she said, her voice a little muffled by the mountain of food between us.

233

Kathy Wilson

If this was dieting, I was all for it.

Somehow I didn't feel much thinner as I waddled out of The Daisy toward my truck. Maybe it was all the water in the lettuce. Yeah, that was probably it.

I was gratified to see Pete and Repeat back at work when I drove up along side Ol' Blue and parked my truck. They'd made good progress and I was feeling hopeful that we'd be ready for trusses tomorrow. I sauntered over to the building to take a closer look. Well, okay. Maybe waddled is a more accurate description.

"Hey, you guys ready for me to mark the top plate for the doubler trusses yet?" I yelled at them.

Without stopping, Pete yelled back, "Whenever you are."

Grabbing the set of plans, I turned toward them and we climbed up the ladder to walk the top plate and mark it for these special trusses.

This is the thing I hate about setting trusses – walking the top plate. It was like being a tightrope walker except there was a couple more inches of width underfoot. Also it was solid wood, not bouncing, wiggly wire. But hanging on to one end of a heavy, bulky truss that's flexing back and forth while walking high up in the air on a 2 x 6 with someone on the opposite wall doing the same thing can be real scary. And no *real* framer would be caught dead sitting on the top plate, straddling the wall like it was a horse and scooching along. Nope. Better by far to fall off the wall and be mangled or killed dead, your ego intact, than to be safe.

"You okay there, Katlin?" asked Pete.

"Yeah, you look a little peaked," said Repeat.

"I'm fine. Just fine. Let's do this and get it over with. I have more work to do," I said, trying not to stutter in fear.

It only took a few minutes and we were all climbing back down to the safety of Mother Earth.

"You guys good to go now?" I asked. I could almost feel the blood coming back into my face as I breathed more freely.

"Remember that trusses are being delivered at 7am. That's in the morning. Tomorrow."

"Yep. We'll be here before they're delivered. And if we need you the rest of the day, we know where to find you," said Pete.

"Yeah, we can always find you in that rusted-out old camper," echoed Repeat.

"Do not talk badly about Ol' Blue. He may be old but he's still got a lot of years left of good service in him." Did I really say that? Did this mean I was starting to like and appreciate Ol' Blue. Cripes. This job was beginning to make me think in strange ways.

I strolled back to Ol' Blue, settled myself into the dinette/desk and lost myself once again in the daily journal. Before I knew it the jobsite had gotten quiet again. When I peeked out the teensy window over the sinkette I saw Pete and Repeat driving off into the sunset. They had worked almost until dark. These were two good guys and I hoped that Roger appreciated them. I suspected he didn't.

# Chapter 24

There'd be no sleeping in for me today. The trusses were being delivered at 7am, which meant I had to be on the building site before then, looking and acting like a Project Supe. Luckily for me the early morning parade of rumbling trucks from the rendering plant shook the ground under Ol Blue like it was Jell-o, making it difficult to sleep in. It still didn't make getting up so early any less painful for me. Only a gallon or two of coffee would open my eyes all the way in the morning.

Somehow I made it to the building site, where I was greeted by Pete and Repeat. It was a good omen that, just like they said they would, they got on the jobsite before the trusses did.

"Good to see you boys here so early," I said to both of them.

"We got here a little early and didn't want to start bangin' around making noise and waking you up," said Pete.

"Yeah, so we're just settin' here quietly waiting for you," this from Repeat.

"I've been up for hours, doing paperwork," I lied, but I had my fingers crossed behind my back so that neutralizes the bad karma, right? "Well, now that you can see I'm not sleeping, you can get to work and do something until the trusses arrive." I could almost hear a bullwhip cracking after I said that, making me feel like a real slave driver.

"We was plannin' on doin' just that," said Pete, getting up and dusting his pants off with abrupt motions.

"Yeah, we're gettin' to work right now," said Repeat.

"Right. Well, I'm going back to Ol' Blue. When the truss truck arrives I'll be back," I said as I turned and walked back to my Casa de Construction.

# Studs

Until the trusses arrived there was not much for me to do but start another of the estimates on the plans Gene had given me. I'd gotten into the mind state that always happens to me when I'm doing a materials take-off from a set of plans. It's almost a hypnotic trance in which I can visualize the project in 3D. Suddenly, a loud rapping on Ol' Blue's door shocked me out of my state and brought me back to the real world.

"Come in," I said loudly.

The door opened and Pete stuck his head in. "Katlin, it's gettin' late and the trusses still aren't here," he said with a worried look on his face.

A quick glance at the clock sent waves of alarm through my body. It was almost 8am. "Thanks for alerting me. I'll call them right now and find out what's going on," I said.

Tossing papers aside, I found the business card with the phone number of the truss manufacturer and quickly dialed it.

"Walker Truss Company," said a chirpy female voice.

"This is Katlin Greene. I have a truss order that was supposed to be delivered to my job an hour ago. It's still not here. I'd sure like to find out what's going on with it," I said, trying to keep my voice calm.

"What's the company name on the order, please"

"G and G Construction."

I could hear the sound of paper being ruffled and I hoped she would be able to find my order. Visions of a desk piled high with a mountain of papers floated across in front of my eyes. If that were the case, finding my order would be a hopeless task.

"Oh, yes. Here it is. We have it scheduled for production tomorrow, on Tuesday and delivery the day after, on Wednesday," she informed me.

"Honey, you better take a look at your calendar. Today IS Wednesday." I never call anyone "Honey" unless I'm stressed out of my mind... much like I was at that moment.

"Oh my goodness," she chirped. "How did this happen?"

"I don't know and I don't care. I just want those trusses. Now," I said, somehow still managing to keep from shrieking at a decibel level that could shatter windows for several blocks in all directions.

"Well, I'll see what I can do," she said.

"Unless you can start manufacturing them right this minute, put me through to Frank," I growled. Frank was the owner and had been my prime supplier of trusses when I'd worked at Beacon. I'd made him a lot of money – not only from all the business I gave him but from all the referrals I'd sent his way - and he owed me. It was time to call in a favor.

"Frank here," said a familiar raspy voice. He smoked way too many cigars.

"Katlin here," I said back to him.

"Why Katlin, what a delightful surprise. To what do I owe this pleasure?"

"Well, you can start manufacturing my trusses that were supposed to be delivered to my jobsite an hour ago now. And then you can deliver them today," I answered, a bit brusquely I admit.

"I saw that order and I'm mighty appreciative, Katlin."

"Yes, well like I just said, I'll be mighty appreciative if you can get those trusses manufactured and delivered today. I've never had a problem with any of your orders and this one is especially important. It's not for one of my customers. It's for me. I'm the Project Supe on this job up in Stanville and I've got the framing crew sitting here waiting for your truck with the trusses on it." I was rather proud of myself for keeping the volume of my voice nearly normal.

"Oh, golly, Katlin. I had no idea. I don't know what went wrong, but I'll make it right. We'll pull the job off the line that we have going now and get your job on it. Let's see, as I recollect it was a pretty simple order, wasn't it?"

"Yes, it's a flat roof and all the trusses are the same, except for four doublers. What time can I expect them on the jobsite then?"

"I'd say about mid afternoon. I'll call you later and let you know when the truck heads out of the yard here."

"The faster you get them to me the more grateful I'll be. I'll be doing more of these jobs, and I'd sure like to give you all my truss orders."

"Well, who else would you get them from," he said with a nervous chuckle. "I'll talk to you later today."

"Thanks, Frank." I hung up and blew out some breath I'd been holding onto in case I needed to scream or yell or something. Turning to Pete I arranged a smile on my face. "Everything's fine. There was a slight glitch at the truss plant but it's being taken care of now. We should have the trusses this afternoon."

"That's kinda late, Katlin. It could take hours to set them," whined Pete.

"I'll help. We can at least get them started and have them on the roof. Or would you rather just go home now and I can have them delivered on the ground? Then you and Dave can hoist them up to the top of the walls by yourselves," I threatened.

"When you put it that way, I guess it'd be better to set some of them this afternoon. Well, I'll go tell Dave," he said backing away from Ol' Blue.

"I'm sure you two can find something to do to keep yourselves busy and productive until the trusses arrive," I said to his back. He waved back at me to acknowledge what I'd said and kept walking. I made a mental sticky note to check up on those two later and make sure they weren't just taking a nap or something.

As I returned to the set of plans I'd been working on, I realized my hands were shaking just a wee bit. Either that was caused by the intense drama of the last few minutes or it was a sign that I was about a quart low on caffeine.

I made it to the Oasis in record time, screeched to a halt and threw the door open. I ran into the coffee shop like I was competing in an obstacle course race.

"Wow! What's got into you this morning?" Cherie asked me

"Sorry. I'm just a miniscule iota stressed out."

"It's a little early in the a.m. for that, doncha think?" she said shaking her head as if to clear cobwebs out of it. "Where can a person learn to talk funny like you do?"

"Hang around with me a lot. Cherie, I absolutely agree with you 10,000% about it being too early for stress of this magnitude, but there are others who would disagree. There are actually homo sapiens on this planet who seem to derive much joviality from screwing up my day before most sane humans are even out of bed."

"Well, lucky for you I have a special treat today. I'm thinkin' it'll put a smile on your face quicker than greased lightnin'."

"So, don't keep me in suspenders, what is it?"

"Chocolate fudge cookie dough wrapped around a Reese's Peanut Butter Cup and topped with a dollop of raspberry jam."

"Holy shamoly! I think I gained 10 pounds just listening to you describe this new concoction. Better give me four of them. And at least four Godzilla-sized coffees. High octane, if you please," I said, wiping the drool from the corners of my mouth.

"See? You're feeling better already. I could sell my cookies to the people who take those pills to get happy. What do you call them?" she said, snapping a large white paper bag open and stuffing my order into it.

"Drug addicts."

"No, I mean normal people. Oh yeah. Antidepressers or something like that," she said with a charming giggle.

"Oh. Those people. Yep, I agree. Your cookies definitely make me real happy. Thanks, Cherie," I said turning to walk out the door to my truck in a much more normal manner.

# Studs

Two of her new creations somehow disappeared by the time I got back to the job site. As if by magic I was suddenly feeling very cheery.

In the interests of keeping up my façade of Super Project Supe, I looked in on Pete and Dave. In my absence, they'd actually been working and had caught up on much of the detail work they'd skimmed by in their rush to get ready for the trusses.

"Good work, guys," I hollered at them with a big, happy smile on my face.

They looked at me cautiously. "You feelin' okay, Katlin?" asked Pete with a worried look on his face.

"Yes I am. Why do you ask?"

"Oh. Just wondering. You look kinda funny," he said in a nervous voice.

"I'm just a happy kinda gal," I retorted, widening my smile even more and enjoying how it seemed to scare them just a bit.

I spun around and flounced to Ol' Blue, sneaking a look at them just before I dove into the innards of Casa de Construction. They were still staring at me with astonished looks on their faces. Keeping men just a little off balance seemed to be something that came naturally to me. Or possibly it was simply that I was a little off balance anyway. There are many who would agree with that last part.

After I'd been working on the plans for some time, my stomach told me it was lunch time. A quick glance at the clock surprised me – it was way past lunch time. The clock showed 2:30, which meant today I'd be grabbing something within arm's reach rather than taking time to go to The Daisy.

A quick look in my mini-fridge and micro cabinets showed that my lunch was going to be a potato chip and aerosol cheese sandwich on white bread. One of my favorite gourmet meals. While I was munching on this tasty morsel, I thought it might be a good idea to call my friend Frank at the truss company and find out how my order was coming along.

I'd just finished swallowing the last mouthful of my sandwich when I heard the familiar growl of a semi truck pulling into the job site. *Oh miracle of miracles, could it possibly be my trusses?* I asked the Construction Gods.

Jumping out of Ol' Blue I was rewarded with the beautiful sight of a truckload of trusses, fresh off the assembly line, brought to me personally by my favorite truss guy, Frank.

He blew the air horn a few times, just to let me and half of Stanville know he'd arrived. "Hey, Katlin! Just like I promised!" he shouted at me after I pulled my hands away from my ears.

"You are the most beautiful thing I've seen in days. Weeks, even," I yelled back at him.

"Where do you want them?"

"Oh, I dunno. How about up on the top of the walls?"

As he maneuvered his truck around so he could lift the trusses from the truck bed up to the wall top I rousted Pete and Repeat. We all climbed up on the top of the walls and got in position to set the trusses as Frank lifted them up to us with the built-in crane on the truck bed.

We all worked like ants on speed and within three hours all the trusses were in place and braced, ready for the plywood.

"Thanks, you guys. All of you. Because each of you gave it your all today, we didn't lose any time on this already-behind-schedule project. I deeply appreciate all you did today," I said to them as we were standing on the ground admiring our work.

This little display of gratitude produced a bit of scuffling in the dirt with the toe of their boots from all of them. Finally, Frank spoke, "It isn't every day we get to rescue a pretty lady, is it boys?"

Pete and Repeat agreed with vigorous nodding of their heads in unison. Abruptly, Pete turned away but not before I could see him wiping his eyes on his shirt sleeve. I guessed they didn't get much praise from Roger and it shook them up a little.

"Well, thanks again for rescuing me. Frank, you're probably anxious to get back to the plant, so I'll let you get on the road.

# Studs

Pete and Dave, I'll see you first thing tomorrow morning. You can get started on the plywood decking for the roof."

Things were back to normal, with the Project Supe barking out orders. The guys seemed to be relieved that the little emotional moment was over and they could relax back into their normal comfort zone, where girly-type emotions weren't allowed.

I was relieved too, but for another reason. Now that yet another crisis had been averted, I could breathe easily for a bit. I made a mental note to get a couple extra cookies tomorrow for my framing crew. They'd worked over and above the call of duty and deserved a little treat

Later that night, as I climbed into my cozy bed, I was reminded by my body that I wasn't used to the physical – and mental – stress of setting trusses. Optimally, both people moved in unison but typically there was a lot of counter-balancing going on, mingled with great quantities of cussing. It had never been one of my favorite parts of construction and now I was reminded of how much it still wasn't.

Especially as I began finding parts of my body that were complaining about the extreme work by getting all achy.

# Chapter 25

Until I'd started this job I didn't even know there *was* a 6am in the morning. Now here I was, starting to get used to getting up at that ridiculous hour. I wasn't sure if this was a good thing.

By now I'd gotten the hang of multi-tasking in the miniscule bathroom and it took me five minutes or less to make myself socially acceptable in the personal hygiene department. I had no doubt there was much lacking in the make-up, hair, and clothing departments, but after all, this was a construction site and not a fashion show.

Today was Friday and that meant I'd get to go home. But first I had some important business to take care of. Before Pete and Repeat arrived on the job I wanted to get them each a cookie surprise from the Oasis.

A quick look toward the job site assured me that my framing crew wasn't here yet, and I probably had time to get to the Oasis and back before they showed up. Just in case, I drove as fast as I could without breaking any of Stanville's speed limits... whatever they were. I'd never seen a speed limit sign within the city limits. I guess it was one of those things that all the locals just knew, and if they didn't, they probably were informed by one of the two cops in the local police department at the appropriate moment.

There was nothing I could think of this early in the morning that smelled as good as opening the door to the Oasis and stepping inside. I sucked in as much of the delicious aroma as I could without exploding my lungs.

"What *are* you doing? You puff yourself up like that, you'll bust something. And it could be something important," Cherie said, concerned and astonished at the same time. That's no easy feat, by the way.

Studs

"I just can't help it. It smells so fantasmagorically wonderful in here. If you could bottle this and sell it as perfume you'd be richer than God," I said after expelling the used-up cookie smells. "What's the special of the day?"

"In honor of your favorite day of the week, I've gone and created the TGIF cookie. Thick Gooey Icing Filled. Of course the icing that fills the cookie center is your favorite - chocolate fudge. I chose cinnamon snickerdoodles for the cookie and topped it with a few red hot cinnamon candies."

"You are truly Divinely inspired... the Da Vinci of cookiedom. I'll take six. No make that eight. And add two coffees to my regular order. I'm treating my framing crew today for being such good li'l boys and working so hard this week. Plus it's time for Phil to stop by and check out the framing."

"If Mavis ever caught him eating one of my cookies she'd hike his suspenders up so high he'd be singing soprano at church on Sunday," she said giggling at the thought.

"I don't think we need to worry. He keeps some peppermint breath mints in the glove box of his car and sucks on a few on the way home so she won't smell cookies on his breath," I said, sending Cherie into a hysterical fit of hoots.

She helped me load my order into the truck, remnants of giggles bubbling forth from her lips now and again, and gave me a hug. "See ya Monday," she said waving bye-bye as I drove off.

All the way back to the job I schemed upon how I might get Cherie to move over to the Peninsula. And open another Oasis, of course. How was I ever going to live without her and her cookies to make my mornings worth getting out of bed for?

By the time I drove up to Ol' Blue, Pete and Repeat were unpacking their tools, getting ready for another busy day. I pulled a couple of cookies out of one sack and stuck them on top of two coffees in another sack. As I piled out of my truck, I hid the sack behind my back and sauntered over to the building.

"Hey, boys. How goes it this morning?" I said nonchalantly.

245

"It's a little early to tell, Katlin," Pete said rather warily.

"Yeah, we just got here," said Repeat.

"Well, maybe this will help you figure it out," I said handing the sack to Pete.

He opened it, peered down into it, then looked at me with his eyes wide and a little teary. "You didn't have to go and do that," he said as his way of saying thanks. He pulled out a cookie and coffee then handed the sack to Repeat, who just looked into it with disbelief.

"I like this job. You gonna have any more?" Repeat said and then bit into the cookie.

Further conversation was impossible, since they both quickly stuffed their mouths to maximum capacity with the gigantic TGIF cookies.

"Remember, the roofer is coming Monday, so I need all that plywood nailed on today," I figured they'd be receptive to whatever I had to say, now that they were blissed out with Cherie's masterpieces. The way to a man's heart and all.

They simply nodded their heads in agreement to what I'd said. If I had told them to go up on the roof and jump off, they'd probably have done it right at that moment.

"Okay. Well, I'll be in my office if you need me," I said and started walking back to Ol' Blue. They didn't even bother snickering at me calling that huge piece of scrap metal my office. I'd have to remember this cookie trick. It might come in handy sometime in the future when I needed to prompt a work crew into working harder and longer.

I'd just settled into enjoying my very own TGIF when there was a light tapping on the side of Ol' Blue. Cookieus Interruptus. Damn.

Not being too happy at having my private time with my cookie disturbed, I flung the door open, hoping to catch the rude person on the other side of it and knock them on their keester. No such luck. It was the plumbers and they already knew about my camper door trick, having watched me fling it open and charge out of Ol' Blue on previous occasions. They were smart enough to knock and then jump back out of the danger zone.

"What's up guys?" I greeted them.

"Well, it sure ain't the interior walls. We're scheduled to do the rough-in plumbing today, but there's no walls for the plumbing to go into," explained the Head Plumber. That was his title. Seriously. It said so on the little embroidered name thingy on his shirt front.

"I thought you weren't supposed to be here until next week. Let me check my Timeline Chart," I said ducking back into Ol' Blue. "Yep. It says right here that you're supposed to be here Monday," I yelled out at him.

"Unh uh."

"Uh huh," I countered. "I talked to Don earlier this week and we agreed on Monday."

They looked at each other, communicating silently with their eyes as only two types of people can - those who have been together for a long time and aliens from other planets.

"Don must have gotten his scheduling mixed up. Can I use your phone to call him?" the main guy asked.

"Sure. C'mon in," I said backing up so he could step into Ol' Blue.

He slid into my dinette/desk and dialed the number. "Hey boss. I'm up here in Stanville to do the rough-in, but the framers aren't ready for us and Katlin says we're scheduled for Monday. Uh huh. Uh huh. Okay," he said, handing me the phone.

"Hi, Don. Looks like we have a schedule miscommunication going here," I said.

"Yeah. I screwed up. Will your framers be ready for us on Monday?"

"I'll make sure they are. These guys are pretty good and even work on the weekend, if they have to," I said, determined that they'd better work this weekend if I needed them to. Else I'd cut off their cookies.

"Okay. Just go ahead and send my guys back here to the shop. Thanks, Katlin," he said and hung up.

"Well, I guess you guys get the rest of the day off. He said for you to come back to the shop."

"I doubt that we'll get the day off. He'll come up with something else for us to do," the Head guy said almost dejectedly. I could empathize. After all, it was Friday and one couldn't get started too early on one's weekend, could one?

The Timeline Chart had certainly come in handy. It made me think that maybe I was beginning to get the hang of this Project Superintendent stuff.

Just in case, I thought it prudent to talk to Pete and Dave about the plumber issue. The sounds coming from the building site indicated they'd gotten some plywood up on the trusses and were starting to nail it down. *This part of the job should go fast*, I thought to myself. *Of course, it would go a lot faster if Roger had the crew here that he'd promised me*. This additional thought made my teeth start grinding.

Locating the ladder and then climbing up to the roof took my attention away from the tooth-grinding thoughts. When I'd been a roofer most of the accidents I'd had, which wasn't a great number, involved ladders. This had resulted in making me especially mindful of what I was doing as I climbed up or down on them.

"Hey guys," I yelled when I reached the top of the ladder. I found ladder dismounts at the top most precarious and avoided them if at all possible.

They stopped and turned, looking at me expectantly. *Oh, crumb. I hope I haven't created the framer equivalent of Pavlov's dogs*, I thought as I saw them wiping their mouths.

"What's up, Katlin? Besides you, of course," Pete chortled and slapped Repeat on the back, signaling that he'd just made a funny. Repeat chortled along with Pete for a bit, absolutely clueless about what was so funny.

"The plumbers just showed up to do the rough-in plumbing and the interior walls aren't up, so they went home. It's okay, though," I said quickly when their happy little faces fell. "They're coming back on Monday, which is actually when I had them scheduled to be here. Can you get the roof sheathing down and the interiors walls up by Monday morning?"

They looked at each other as if expecting the other to come up with an answer to my question. Finally Pete said, "Well, yeah, if we work tomorrow."

"Would you do that for me? I'd really be grateful," I said, mentally sending them visions of more cookie treats.

It only took Pete and Repeat a couple of minutes to figure out that they were more or less committed to working tomorrow... and that they'd been bought off with cookies. "Yeah, we'll do it, Katlin," Pete said with a bit of reluctance. Repeat just nodded in agreement.

"Oh, thank you so much, guys," I beamed them the biggest, widest smile I could make on my face. My work there was done, so I climbed back down the ladder.

The plumbers had actually done me a great favor. I wasn't so sure Pete and Dave would be able to get all the plywood for the roof nailed down so it'd be ready for the roofers on Monday. By pressuring them into working Saturday, I was more confident that the roof really *would* be ready on time.

Back in Ol' Blue I'd settled down once again to enjoy my TGIF and high octane coffee, when the phone rang. It was so rare that anyone called me I jumped and almost spilled the better portion of a quart of coffee down my front.

"G and G Construction, Stanville," I answered. It had only taken me a few weeks to come up with that snappy greeting.

"Hi, Katlin, it's Bill Graves here."

"Hi Bill. Uh oh. You're still coming up here Monday to install the glass, aren't you?"

"Heh heh. Well, not exactly. Uh, to be exact... no. My delivery truck broke down and won't be fixed until next week some time. Your glass is loaded on it now, and as soon as the mechanic fixes the truck, I'll be on the road bringing the glass to your job so I can install it. I hope this doesn't mess you up too bad."

"No, actually it's fine. The framers are just now getting the plywood on the roof and the roofer's due here Monday. So they should all be done and out of your way towards the end of the week. That work for you?"

"Yeah, that's great. Thanks, Katlin. I'll call you as soon as I'm ready to roll."

It was amazing to me the amount of flexibility that was required in a construction project. I'd barely started this job and already my finely tuned Timeflow Chart was all caddywompus. I pulled it off the wall where I'd taped it and began painting in some of the squares with my new bottle of white-out. Then I got out my colored pens and penned in the adjusted scheduling. I put the bottle of white-out where I could get at it quickly and easily. I had a hunch I was going to be using it a lot. If this rescheduling stuff kept up I might need to stock up on a six-pack of the giant economy size.

Next on my agenda was a call to the roofers to let them know about the delay.

"Faith Roofing," Margie and James answered the phone in unison.

"You two certainly are in synch," I said laughing. And so they were. So much so that they went way beyond finishing each other's sentences. They could carry on entire conversations, both of them talking at the same time, saying the exact same thing. It was almost spooky.

"Hi, Katlin," they said, again in unison.

"What's up on the job?" James asked, heh-hehing at his little roofer joke.

"We've had a slight change of schedule and I hope it won't inconvenience you too much. My framers are about a day behind, so I'm wondering if you could maybe start the job on Tuesday instead of Monday. They've promised me they'll have the plywood down for the hot mop, but I'm not too sure. Their boss promised me a huge framing crew when I hired him and I guess he thinks two is a big number because that's the total amount of guys in this crew."

"Actually, that'll work fine for me because it'll give me time to take care of the tail end doo-dads on a job we're just finishing here," Jim said. "Look for us on Tuesday, then."

"Great. Thanks, James... and Margie," I said, knowing she was still on the line.

"Bye, Katlin," she said.

Well. Another change to my Timeline Chart. I was beginning to think that maybe I should have used pencils instead of pens to create it.

The rest of the day passed without any more surprises. It was getting close to quitting time and I was still hearing the hammering and sawing of my industrious little framing crew. Emphasis on the "little" part. Since it was part of my job description to oversee the work of the subs, I did my duty and strolled out to the building site to see how Pete and Repeat were coming along.

There was a lot of scrap on the ground – more than I thought there should be for a simple rectangular building. This was an indication that I needed to perform a closer look at the roof. Carefully I crawled up the ladder, did my girlie-style dismount at the top of the ladder, and stood for a moment examining the work these two had done. Actually, it looked pretty darn good.

"Hey, guys," I yelled to be heard above all the noise of the Skilsaw, the country music they had blaring from their portable radio, and the air compressor that was powering their nail guns. I especially wanted to be heard above the whine of country music. It sounds bad enough on a good stereo system, but on a cheap little radio it was almost more than my ears could stand.

They both gave a little jump and turned toward me. Pete reached behind him and turned the volume down on the radio so he wouldn't have to listen to me shrieking in order to be heard over the nasally singing of some rhinestone cowboy.

"How's it going?" I asked in an almost normal tone of voice.

251

"We're almost done with the plywood decking. Just a couple more pieces and it'll be done," replied Pete.

"Great. How much plywood do you have left?" I asked him.

"Just enough to finish the roof."

"I hope your definition of 'the roof' includes the mansard roof that spans the entire front and part of the ends of this building."

"Uh, no. We figured that all the ½" plywood was for the roof decking."

"I see. And what, then, did you figure on using for the mansard? Do you see another stack of plywood anywhere on the ground?" I asked, my voice beginning to rise toward screeching tones. Okay. I was getting snarky, but I didn't need the hassle of a problem now... at the very end of the work week just before I left for my treasured two days at home. The last thing I wanted was for problems to follow me home and ruin my whole weekend.

"Oh. Um, I guess we did get a little careless about salvaging the scrap plywood and using it."

"I guess."

Pete and Repeat looked at each other helplessly. It was getting pretty obvious, even to them, that they were in deep doggie doo-doo with the cookie-supplying Project Supe.

"When you get done with the roof, I want you to go through all the scrap and salvage every single piece you can to use on the mansard. It had better be enough to finish it," I growled at them. "I want the interior walls framed and the sheathing for the mansard *and* this roof finished when I come back on Monday. Do you understand me?" I threatened. I could almost feel flames from my eyes burning through the two of them. The way they had sort of shrunk themselves down, it looked like they could feel the heat, too.

I climbed back down the ladder and turned to walk back to Ol' Blue, but was stopped by a large object in my way. A step or two backwards and I could see that I'd run into Roger. I briefly wondered if he'd been lurking down there long enough to hear what I'd told his crew. No matter. I was in the perfect frame of mind to have a little chat with him right now.

"Well. I see you managed to find the job site finally," I said with enough acidic sarcasm to peel the skin clean off his face.

"Hello, there, Katlin. It looks like my guys are doing a fine job, as always," he said with a smarmy smile that didn't hang around on his face for long. Especially after I grabbed him by the lapels of his polyester plaid shirt and dragged his face down to my level.

"You promised me a huge crew. A very, very large crew. Eight guys was the exact number you quoted me. Does this look like eight guys to you?" I said in a low voice that held unmentionable threats as I pointedly darted my eyes toward the roof and back to him. He started blinking his eyes quickly - a sure sign a lie was forming in his reptilian brain. I pushed him backward, releasing my grip on his sleazy shirt. The sudden release surprised him so much he almost fell over backward, but caught his balance just in time.

"Now, Katlin. These guys have been doing just fine, haven't they? There's no need to get all upset. Calm down," he blathered, verbally back-pedaling in order to give himself time to regain his typically bullshit-laden state of mind.

"Here's how it stands, Roger. You committed verbally to finishing the framing on this job by next Wednesday. Your guys still have to frame up and sheath the mansard PLUS frame the interior walls. Right now you're holding up my plumber, my glass guy, and my roofers." Okay. So this wasn't exactly the truth. But they did all need to reschedule because of the framing not being complete. He didn't need to know that they all had been relieved to have a day or two reprieve.

"We'll get it done. Don't you worry your pretty little head about this. You just let me take care of everything. That's what we men are for," he said trying to placate me with what he probably thought was a soothing voice.

*Pretty little head?* His sleazy, slimy, condescending words only added to the fiery anger I already had built up. "You agreed to have the job done within a certain timeframe. That timeframe ends this Wednesday. I expect that come Wednesday you and your guys will have all the framing done, and I mean ALL the framing. Do I make myself clear?" I said, speaking slowly and clearly so he wouldn't miss one word.

Not waiting for Roger to reply, I turned and stomped back to Ol' Blue. I hoped he didn't notice that I was shaking so hard I could barely walk.

I hated confrontations. Especially I hated confrontations with guys who were a lot bigger than me. Like Roger, for example. It scared the beejeebers out of me. Confronting a wimpy guy like Larry the Lush was nothing compared to standing up to Roger, who towered over me and probably outweighed me by 75 pounds. Not to mention Roger was in top shape from playing on a Rugby team, unlike Larry who never lifted anything heavier than a beer bottle.

I made it safely back to the interior of Ol' Blue, slamming the door loudly as a message to Roger of my intense anger. Quickly, I slid into the dinette before my shaking knees gave way and I collapsed on the floor. Two or three deep breaths later I heard Roger's truck dig out as he left the job site. Whew. I hoped he never found out what a wimp I was. If that ever happened, I'd lose what little status I had with him and he'd really walk all over me.  And his crew, too.

Just when I'd managed to calm myself enough so I'd pretty much stopped shaking, there was a loud bang on Ol' Blue's door. *Please don't let this be Roger,* I prayed silently to the construction angels. I was momentarily terrified that he might have turned around to come back and threaten me. Or possibly something worse.

Timidly I opened the door and was greeted by my favorite building inspector.

"Phil! What a delight. Please, do come in. I have a little surprise for you," I said with deep relief.

"Happy to see you too, Katlin. I thought it might just be a good idea to check up on you and see how you're doing. It's been pretty quiet for a while on your job site," he said stepping into Ol' Blue. The overload springs creaked as he heaved himself into my so-called office.

# Studs

"Have a seat while I get your surprise," I said, reaching into the mini-mini fridge for his cookie and lemonade. "This is a special cookie Cherie concocted just for today. She calls it a TGIF, which stands for Thick Gooey Icing Filled. Wait'll you try it. It'll make you swoon," I said handing him the giant sugary treat.

His eyes went all wide and for a second or two I thought he just might swoon. He bit into it and rolled his eyes heavenward. "How does she do it? This is fantastic. You know, I dated her once upon a time. I think it's probably a good thing I didn't marry her or I'd never fit through that little door of your camper," he said winking in conspiracy with me.

"I think you made a good choice with Mavis," I said diplomatically.

While he munched on his TGIF, taking sips every so often of his sweet lemonade, I caught him up on all the happenings on the job site.

"Guess I better stop by on Wednesday to sign off on your framing," he said through a mouthful of cookie.

"Make it Thursday. I'm not too sure the framing contractor will live up to his commitment and have his work done as he promised."

"Okay. We have a date on Thursday, then," he said winking again, this time with meaning. I was beginning to think I'd created a cookie monster. Or maybe I'd just let the cookie monster free from its bondage. I hoped Phil had enough breath mints to get him home safely.

I'd had enough of this job for one week. It took me precisely 37 seconds after Phil left to pack my dirty clothes into a garbage sack, lock up Ol' Blue, and bounce my truck out of the job site and onto the highway to heaven... my home on the farm.

# Chapter 26

The torture of hearing the whiney sounds of some cowboy singing through his nostrils as he laments his lot in life, accompanied by a shrill steel guitar, was more than I could handle this early in the morning. Especially in my caffeine-deprived state.

I rapped on the door and waited. Not having had the time to learn patience, I knocked again after two seconds... this time much louder. I was rewarded with the sounds of big, heavy boots clumping toward the door and some muffled comments. Probably it was best that I couldn't hear the comments too clearly.

The door was yanked open by none other than Gene himself.

"Wow. What a surprise! I haven't seen you for years, it seems," I greeted him.

"Not nearly long enough, if you ask me," he greeted me back. Then he surprised me by pulling me into the house and giving me a huge bear hug, almost squeezing all the air right out of me. "Good to see you again, girl."

"You, too," I wheezed. He released me and I took some deep, gasping breaths. "How was the reunion?"

"Couldn't have been better," he said all smiley-faced.

This wasn't the Gene I was familiar with. Whatever happened to him during his time away at that reunion, it had done wonders to improve his attitude. In all the time I'd known him he'd never hugged me, and I wasn't quite sure it was something I wanted to experience again. Ever. "Got any coffee?" I asked him, backing away and out of his reach.

"You betcha. Ginnie just made it," he said.

I turned toward the kitchen and saw that Ginnie had been watching us. Odd. She'd never paid much attention when Gene and I were talking before.

"Hi, Ginnie," I greeted her. "Gene says you've got some coffee ready. How about a cup?"

"Help yourself, honey. You know where the cups are," she said, still watching Gene.

As I fortified myself with my first coffee of the day, I updated Gene on the progress at the job. He listened intently to me without interrupting. Another first for Gene.

"You're doing a great job, girl. Didn't I tell you she'd be great at this?" he said, turning toward Ginnie who was still watching from the kitchen.

"Yep, Gene, you sure did," she said rather tersely.

My eyes went from Gene to Ginnie and back again a few times, but I couldn't pick up any clues about what was going on, other than the tension that seemed to fog the air like an invisible stench.

"Well, I better get going so I don't miss the ferry," I said after gulping down the last dregs in my coffee cup and grabbing the file with the week's paperwork and my check.

"Okay, girl. I'll be up Friday with a couple of guys. By then the framers should be done and outta the way so we can start forming up the sidewalks. You need me, you just call," he said with a big, happy smile.

All the way up to the jobsite I pondered this new, changed Gene. Whatever had happened at that reunion, it had sure made a big difference in Gene's outlook on life. Happy Gene might take some getting used to, but he was sure going to be a lot more pleasant to work with than the old unpredictable, Gruff Gene.

I was so busy musing about the changed Gene that I almost drove right by The Oasis. That would have been dire. No cookies or coffee meant I wouldn't be able to start my day right. Plus I'd promised myself I'd talk to Cherie about the house I was potentially thinking about buying.

"Hey, Katlin! How as your weekend?" she greeted me.

"Glad you asked. I've got something I'd like to run by you and get your professional opinion."

"Professional cookie-maker or professional real estate agent?" she asked.

"It's a real estate question. I looked at a house for sale this weekend and I'd like to have you take a look at the paperwork and tell me what you think. If you don't mind, that is." I was feeling a bit uneasy about asking her to help me buy a house from another agent. But not uneasy enough to stop me from asking anyway. I trusted her and valued her real estate savvy.

"For my best customer, I'd be happy to help," she said, taking the wad of papers from me.

After a few hmmms, tsks, and uh huhs as she glanced at all the papers, she looked up at me with a big grin. I wasn't sure if this meant she thought this was a big joke or a good thing.

"Well? Don't keep me in suspenders. What do you think?" I asked.

"It needs some work, but I think you can handle it. This is a good price and the location is good – close to downtown but hidden away behind the park and lagoon. And the house is kinda cute. I'd snap it up if I was you," she announced.

"Oh, whew. Thank you so much. I've talked to a few people this weekend but the more advice I got, the more I became confused. You made it simple and clear. I'll call the agent today and get her started on the paperwork. Now. How about some cookies and coffee?"

On the way back to the job site, happily munching on another of Cherie's unspeakably delicious concoctions, I felt about twenty pounds lighter. I couldn't wait to call my friendly real estate agent, Sheila, with the good news.

When I arrived at the job site, I was relieved to see Pete and Dave busily working. After I unlocked Ol' Blue and threw my wardrobe for the week inside, I trundled over to the building site to take a closer look at their progress.

"Howdy, boys," I drawled at them.

They looked up from their work and nodded at me, then quickly returned to what they were doing. Fine with me. My priority wasn't chit-chatting with them. It was inspecting the work they'd done on the roof sheathing.

I found a ladder laying alongside the building and propped it against the building, inspecting and testing it for stability. I really hated falling off ladders. I usually ended up hurting myself. As I climbed upward I felt eyes watching me. Pete and Dave were both watching me carefully with semi-worried looks on their faces. This didn't bode well.

After a slow and careful dismount from the ladder, I turned around and was delightfully surprised that the roof was actually clean. Framers are one of several types of subcontractors noted for being job slobs. Finding the roof clean of debris and actually swept of sawdust was pleasing, yet shocking. Just to make sure Pete and Repeat didn't get all diabolical and clean up just to keep me from inspecting their work, I took a slow walk around the roof. I discovered that they'd actually done a very good job... so far.

I walked to the front of the building where they were working on the mansard, leaned over, and yelled to be heard above their construction noises, "GOOD WORK YOU GUYS!"

Suddenly there was silence.

"What did you say, Katlin?" asked Pete.

"I said, you guys did a good job up here. I'm really impressed that you actually cleaned up the roof when you were done. Thank you."

They looked at me, stunned. I'd forgotten that Roger's managerial method ran more toward abuse than appreciation.

"You can go back to work now."I said after they'd not moved for a few minutes.

"Huh? Oh, yeah. Thanks, Katlin," said Pete.

"Yeah, yer welcome," from Repeat.

"Just remember that the mansard needs to be finished today so the roofers can start tomorrow, as scheduled. If it looks like you're going to run out of plywood, let me know *before* it's too late to run to the lumber yard and get more."

"Yep. Will do," said Pete as they returned to making sawdust and noise.

Carefully, I climbed back down the ladder and laid it back down on the ground. An unwatched ladder can become troublesome. The wind can knock it down, which is especially annoying if you happen to still be up on the roof. Ladders also have a trick they do in which they blend into their surroundings, causing people to walk smack into them.

With the world now safe from the untrustworthy ladder, I walked into the building to check on the interior walls the guys had promised to frame up. It was a quick inspection since there were no walls to inspect. Evidently the little talk I'd had with them on Friday wasn't very effective. They hadn't kept their promise to work on Saturday and complete the interior walls so the plumbers could do their rough-in. *What was it going to take to light a fire under these two so they'd get the job done*, I wondered silently to myself. Heaving a giant sigh, I trundled back outside.

"EXCUSE ME!" I yelled in order for Pete and Repeat to hear me over their hammering and sawing noise.

When there was silence, I said in a dangerously quiet voice, "And what about the interior walls that you promised to complete this weekend?"

After they looked at one another a while, searching for the answer to my question, Pete, the more intelligent of the two said, "Oopsie."

"Oopsie? That's the best you can come up with? I've got plumbers scheduled to be here today. THEY NEED THOSE WALLS." I heard my voice shrieking like a fire engine siren.

Pete and Repeat continued to just stand still, looking blankly at me. Their eyes had glazed over and I suspected that they'd both gone catatonic. It's a protective technique I've seen men use before when threatened by a hysterical woman screaming in their face.

"Oh, never mind. Just get back to work and finish that mansard. TODAY. Do you understand the words that are coming out of my mouth?" I screeched at them.

In unison they nodded and then returned back to their work, happy not to have to listen to the wigged-out Project Supe anymore.

I stomped back to Ol' Blue, threw the door open so hard it bounced back and slammed closed again. "Well, isn't this just perfect?" I grumbled to myself as I opened the door once again, this time more sedately.

Rummaging through the piles of paperwork on my dinette/desk, I found Don Hobob's phone number and reluctantly called him. His secretary put me right through when I announced myself.

"Hey, Katlin. How ya doin'," Don's cheery voice greeted me.

"Hi, Don. Not so good. My framers are behind schedule and I'm wondering if I can reschedule or something," I said lamely.

"Sure. When do you want us up there?"

"I'm not sure. They were supposed to have the interior walls done this weekend and instead they finished the roof. They said they'd get both done, but that didn't happen. Actually, I'm not sure exactly when they'll get to those walls."

"How about this: you give me a call the day before you want us up there."

"You can do that? Get your crew here so quickly?"

"Oh yeah. We've done a ton of these stores and the rough-in will go fast. I can squeeze you in just about anywhere."

"You are an angel," I said, so grateful I almost cried.

"Not a problem. Happy to do it for you. Gene dumped a lot on you with this job, and that's not right. I don't mean to talk bad about the guy. I've known him and worked with him for years, and I like him alright. But he seems to be getting pretty flaky lately. This job was a lot to settle on your shoulders. You're doing a good job, considering the circumstances, and I'll help you out as much as I can."

Oh gawd. Now I was going to get all teary-faced. "Th-thank you, Don. I'm very grateful. Thanks. I'll call you as soon as those guys get to framing on the walls," I said and hung up before I started boo-hooing all over the place.

I was beginning to understand that a construction project was a microcosm of the real world... the good and the bad. After a bit of thought in this direction I realized that without the contrast of the bad, I probably wouldn't appreciate the good to the extent that I did. Without the Rogers I likely wouldn't appreciate the Dons as much.

"Well, that's enough philosophizing. I need to get back to earth and get this project moving ahead faster," I said aloud in an effort to prod myself into action. It was time to call Roger again and remind him of his promise to have the framing completed tomorrow. This was one of the bads in the world of construction – confronting subcontractors who were not keeping their commitments. Especially the ones who were lots taller and way more muscular than me.

Just as I grabbed for the phone I heard the deep rumbling sounds of a very large truck pulling onto the job site. *What now?* I asked myself. Nobody answered, so I decided to go outside to find out.

Rounding the corner of Ol' Blue I was stunned to see a double trailer semi backing toward me. My greatest hope at that moment was that the entire contents of both gigantic trailers were not meant for this job site. Before I could send my customary prayers to the Construction Gods I realized I'd better get out of the way before I became part of the tires.

With much screeching of metal and whooshing of air from the brakes, the truck finally stopped... just inches from where I'd been standing next to Ol' Blue. As I watched, one of the hugest butt cracks I'd ever seen appeared from the driver's door and swung from side to side as the driver who owned it climbed out of the truck cab. I had to turn away and compose myself before I could face the front side of this apparition.

"Hey, where's the boss around here?" I heard a little girl ask.

I turned around and looked directly at a belly so big I wondered how it fit behind the wheel of a truck. Then I looked up... and up and up. Not only was this guy wide, he was high, too.

"Excuse me," I said trying to peer behind him to find the little girl.

"I said, where's the boss?" the little girl asked again. It was then I realized it wasn't a little girl. It was the giant-sized truck driver.

"Uh, th-that would be me," I said trying not to break into guffaws. I couldn't help but stare at him. A guy that big with such a tiny voice.

After a few seconds I realized he was staring at me, probably with the same shocked look on his face that I had on mine. Guess he didn't run into women Project Superintendents very often. We were even. I didn't run into gigantic men who sounded like Betty Boop very often either.

"I got a present for ya, little lady," he said when he recovered.

"You can call me boss or you can call me Katlin, but never, ever call me little lady again," I said narrowing my eyes into mean little slits. It was another threatening look that I'd been practicing in the mirror lately.

"Yeah. Sure. I've got a delivery of some refrigeration equipment. Where do ya want it?" he asked in his soprano voice, much more politely this time.

"Oh gawd. That wasn't supposed to be delivered for another couple of weeks yet. Let's take a look, shall we?" I asked, moving toward the building site. "How big are these things?"

"Well, I was told you'd have a fork lift here. Either that or we'll need about eight gorillas," he squeaked, giggling at his superior sense of humor.

"Tell you what. How about if you back up over by that house next to where those long boxes are. I'll call someone who might be able to help us," I said.

*Please oh please let Mark be available*, I prayed to my favorite Construction Gods as I climbed back in Ol' Blue. Scrounging around through the mess of papers on the dinette/desk, I found his card and called him.

"Hoback Construction," said the man who was my most favorite person in the whole world just then.

"Hi Mark, it's me, Katlin."

"Well, hi there darlin'. Where you been hiding lately?"

"As if you didn't know. I hear you go by and honk at least once a day. You could stop and say hi, you know."

"I don't mean to be ignoring you, honey, but this is my busy season. What blessed event prompted you to call me?"

"I need help from my favorite White Knight."

"What kind of trouble did you get yourself into now?"

"I just got a surprise delivery of some refrigeration equipment and the truck driver says we need either a fork life or eight gorillas."

"Well, since I've only got five gorillas on my payroll, how about if I bring my fork lift over there? See you in a few," he said and hung up.

"My hero," I said to the dial tone.

I hung up the phone and strode out to where the truck driver was just finishing maneuvering his ginasaurus rig exactly where I'd told him to park it. Maybe I'd forgive his calling me "little lady" just this once for being such a good boy and doing exactly as I said. Remembering the last time he exited his truck, I quickly looked down at my feet. I wasn't sure my eyes could take the vision of him climbing down from his truck and exposing his version of the Grand Canyon again.

"Help is on its way," I said in his direction. I wasn't sure if it was safe to look at him yet.

"What ya got?" he said, his voice so close I realized I'd almost run into him.

"Oh, a friend of mine is bringing his fork lift over. He'll be here in a few minutes."

"I'll get things ready for him. Only take me a few minutes. By the way, is there a good place to eat around here?"

"You bet. The Daisy Café. You're going to love it," I said, thinking how Mavis was going to flip out when she saw this stomach on legs squeeze through her front door. By the time I'd finished giving him directions, Mark drove up in his monster pick-up towing a lowboy trailer with a fork lift on it.

"Hiya, baby!" he called to me, knowing he could get away with talking to me like that when he was being my White Knight.

"That was fast," I said. I was so happy to see him I could have hugged him right then and there, but that wouldn't have been appropriate behavior for someone of my exalted position.

"You call, I come," he said wiggling his eyebrows to emphasize the double meaning.

"There's the truck and there's the trucker. He can tell you what needs to be offloaded from the truck. Just set it down somewhere near those other long boxes."

"Your wish is my command," he said, taking his cap off and placing it over his heart.

"You're a goof, but I sure do appreciate you," I said.

"I'll take that for now," he said with a big grin.

I left the two of them to do their manly stuff and I returned to Ol' Blue. I was hoping to find something else important to do besides call Roger. Most of the estimates Gene had given me to do were done.

Oh yeah! I'd almost forgotten! Call Sheila, the real estate agent. Grabbing my purse, I pulled her card out of the top layer of stuff and dialed her office. The receptionist put me right through to her.

"This is Sheila," said a sweet voice.

"Hi, Sheila. This is Katlin Greene. We looked at a house this weekend. Do you remember?"

"Of course I remember. Have you more questions or have you come to a decision?"

"I've made a decision. Let's write up an offer. How do we do that?" I asked, blatantly showing my ignorance of all things real estatey.

"Can you come into the office today?"

"Um, no, actually. I'm working up in Stanville and won't be back until Friday night."

"Oh, that's right. Well, tell you what. I'll write up the offer in my name with you as assignee. That means that I can transfer this offer to your name anytime. We can take care of making that change this weekend."

"What's the rush? Why can't I just come in on Saturday and make the offer?"

"As often happens in real estate, a property will sit with no action for months, even years sometimes. Then suddenly it becomes a hot property and everybody wants it. There's been a lot of showings on that house this weekend and I hear that other offers may be coming in. It would be in your best interest to get an accepted offer before anyone else decides to also make an offer."

"Okay. Whatever you think is best."

"I'll write the check for the earnest money and you can repay me when you come in on Saturday."

"What's earnest money?"

"It's upfront money to show that you're in earnest about buying this house. It's deducted from the final closing costs so you won't lose it."

Studs

"Okay. Well, if you need me, here's my phone number," I said and gave it to her twice, to make sure she got it right. "See you Saturday. I'll call before I come into town."

"Let's make an appointment now so that I'm sure to be available for you," she countered.

We set the appointment and hung up. There. I was now officially on my way to becoming a proud home owner.

It took a few minutes for this concept to sink in, and when it did, I started shaking. This wasn't fun and games. This was responsible grown-up stuff. And it was scary.

Just then there was a gentle rap on the door and Mark appeared.

"The driver left this for you," he said handing me the bill of lading. "You okay?" he asked, concern all over his face.

"I th-th-think so," I said between chattering teeth. "I just made an offer on my first house I ever bought in my whole life."

"There, there," he said, putting his arm around my shivering shoulders and patting my shaking hands. "You'll be fine. It's not so scary. I've bought and sold lots of property and it didn't hurt a bit."

"Really?"

"Really."

He sat with me for quite a while until I'd finally calmed down. Then he got up, kissed me gently on the cheek, gave me a grandiose bow, and left. In his wake, I wondered if maybe I should re-think my opinion of him as just a friend and consider that he could become someone more... well, just more. He had so many of the qualities I appreciate in a man – kindness, sensitivity, generosity, sense of humor, honesty. I wondered if he also had a big, um, belt buckle.

When my thoughts came back to reality, I realized I couldn't find one thing to stop me from calling Roger. Drat.

"Yeah. Roger here," he answered on the first ring.

"Roger? This is Katlin. The two guys you sent up here are working, but far too slowly. You remember that you promised to have the job done by a certain time? Well, that time is tomorrow," I said.

"Don't worry, Katlin. I keep telling you it'll be done on time."

"You also told me you were going to have a huge crew up here. Two is not huge. They're behind schedule now. As you may recall from a previous conversation we've had, so far I've had to delay the plumber, the glass installer, and the roofer. Your guys maybe, possibly will barely finish tomorrow, but there's a good chance they won't. Plus there's no additional time available to take care of things on a punch list."

"I told you don't worry. The job'll be done tomorrow. Now stop bugging me."

And he hung up on me.

That was not a wise move on his part. For one thing, such acts tend to fuel my very volcanic temper. For another, he hadn't been paid yet.

I waited until the steam was no longer shooting out of my ears, and then stormed over to the building site. Pete and Repeat were still working on the mansard, part of the framing that should have been completed two days ago. And they still hadn't framed up the interior walls. A part of me knew that if I started in on them now they might not live through it. *Just turn around and go back to Ol' Blue* said a much wiser part of me.

Releasing a heavy sigh, I turned around and trundled back to my Casa de Construction. Tomorrow, after I'd cooled down somewhat, I'd deal with Roger and his so-called huge framing crew.

# Chapter 27

Boy Howdy, did I need a cookie and coffee injection... and I needed it *now*. I'd not slept well due to a non-stop series of fantasies in which I brought excessive harm to Roger in places where it would hurt him most. It was the wee hours before I'd finally cooled down enough to sleep. And then I was abruptly awakened from a wonderful dream, just at the precise point where I was running over Roger with one of Mark's backhoes. Repeatedly. It must have been his loud screaming in my dream that woke me from all the fun I was having.

After completing one of the world's fastest showers in the one-size-fits-all bathroom, I grabbed some clothes that I hoped were from the clean bag, threw them on, and jammed out the door to C&C heaven.

Cherie's eyes got all big and round when I stumbled through her front door.

"What happened to you last night? You look like something a raccoon got hold of. You sure don't have that special glow, so you must not have gotten lucky. Here. Take a bite of this. Quick," she said, pushing something chocolate in my face.

I did as she said and, sure enough, I felt better almost at once. "Thank you, Angel of Cookiedom. I didn't get much sleep last night due to... what else... a man."

"Oh, honey. There'll be another stud come down the road real soon. Don't you worry. Who is the rat? One of my exes, prolly. I got 'em all over the place," she said.

"It's not like that. It's one of my subcontractors. He's not doing the job as he promised, which is holding up all the other subs from doing their work. And I'm already behind schedule on this job. In fact, I started behind schedule. Just when I was beginning to catch up, this yahoo tells me he's gonna have a huge crew on my job and get the work done fast. His idea of a huge crew is two guys, whose combined IQ is less than their body temperature. Yesterday I called him and got rather stern with him. The son of a bitch hung up on me. Now all I can think of is how and where I could hurt him the most."

"Well, if you need any help coming up with ideas, I've got a few I've used over the years," she said with a very satisfied smile as she momentarily relived the memories of some of them.

"Sometimes you scare me... but in a good way," I said.

She poured me a cup of coffee and we sat down at one of the little tables she'd crammed into the teensy space. After she shared a few stories of men who had not treated her right and the retaliations she'd used to get her revenge on them, I was in a much better mood. There's nothing like a little girl-talk to brighten one's spirits.

"Well, I guess I'd better get back to the job site and see what new surprises await me. Thank you a kajillion for your helpful hints. I may just use one or more of them on Roger. Make me up a cookie and coffee care package and I'll be on my way," I said.

She stuffed some of my favorites in a bag along with several giant coffees, and sent me on my way with a hug. I didn't know which was sweeter – her cookies or her hugs.

By the time I returned to the job site and Ol' Blue, there had been another surprise package delivered. Rolls of black tar paper, boxes of nails, and paper-wrapped cylinders of hard tar had been dropped off right in front of the building. All the materials needed for the roof.

Good thing James was going to be done with the roof by Friday because the entire roofing package was smack-dab where Gene and boys were going to be setting up forms for the sidewalks. Having to coordinate the placement of all these deliveries was beginning to make me feel more like a parking lot attendant than a Project Supe.

Pete and Repeat still weren't on the job yet and I was a little concerned. What if Roger had been so mad that he pulled them off my job? Actually, at this point it wouldn't be such a disaster.

# Studs

Framing up walls was simple and there wasn't much left to do. I'd done it a lot when I'd worked for a local contractor as a framer, finish carpenter, laborer, cement worker, painter, and whatever else was needed. It just wasn't anything I was excited about having to do, now that I held the esteemed position of Project Supe and all.

My cookies, coffee, and I went into Ol' Blue where I devoured most of what was in the sack from the Oasis. It was amazing how much chirpier I felt after gobbling three giganto cookies and two quarts of coffee.

Adding to my chirpiness was the sound of Pete and Repeat's truck driving onto the job site. Life, for the time being, was getting better.

I let them offload their tools out of the truck and get all set up before I sauntered out to greet them.

"Hi there, boys. How goes it this morning," I asked all cheerified.

They looked at me rather fearfully, eyes darting around to spot the nearest escape exit.

"Sorry we're late, but Roger wanted to talk to us and we missed our regular ferry," said Pete.

"Yeah, by just two cars," filled in Repeat.

"What are your plans for the day?" I asked.

They looked at each other as if I'd just spoken Martian. "Plans. Yeah. Uh, I guess we'll finish the mansard, if that's all right with you," offered Pete.

"That's fine. What about the interior walls? Think you might be able to get them done today too?" I asked Pete.

"We'll try," he answered pathetically.

"Oh, I think you'd better do more than try," I said narrowing my eyes at them in an attempt to look threatening.

In answer, they looked at each other again, helpless to say anything that wasn't a lie. We all knew they wouldn't finish everything today. I was okay with that, now that I'd had my little chat with Cherie. I'd made an executive decision that Roger and I were going to have a little business meeting the next day. Roger wouldn't have any clue of what was coming his way. He was going to find himself in a very uncomfortable position and he wouldn't be able to worm his way out of it. I'd have him by his nuggies.

I smiled at my framing crew as if everything was fine, which only served to confuse them more. They knew that things on the job were far from fine.

With the uplifting thoughts of what was in store for Roger, I strolled back to Ol' Blue to take care of my regular Project Supe duties. And to call Roger.

Boring as I find paperwork, today it was serving to calm me so I could think more clearly about how I was going to handle Roger during our little meeting. I was beginning to get fairly immersed in writing my daily journal and had almost completely lost contact with the real world when a new sound began to enter my awareness. It was men talking. Lots of them.

My first hopeful thought was that maybe a party of handsome studs with a truckload of beer had landed on my job site. I rushed outside to investigate. It was James and his roofing crew. That was the second thing I was hoping for.

"Hey, James! Good to see you," I greeted him, walking toward him and his crew.

"Hi, Katlin," he said grabbing me and giving me a big hug. "You ready for the best roofing crew in the entire state to start putting your roof on?"

"Modesty has always been one of your better qualities," I teased him. "I'm so glad to see you. The roof is ready for you. I checked it out personally and gave it my stamp of approval."

"Good enough for me. Looks like our materials got here okay. I'll just start the pot while my guys get the first layer of paper down."

# Studs

"I'll get out of your way so you can do your magic. If you need anything, I'll be over there in Ol' Blue," I said doing a Vanna White impression.

"Deluxe accommodations, eh? Can't say as I envy you much."

"Yeah. Me too. It ain't much but it's a real dump. Well, have fun," I said turning around to walk back to Ol' Blue.

I abhorred hot tar. The stench of it made my nose want to slam shut. I especially hated the little droplets of molten tar that hit my skin and burned my flesh down to the bone. You could tell a hot tar roofer by the white scars on his arms where the 450° tar had hit his skin.

Before I got back to updating my daily journal, I decided it was time to call Roger.

"Hullo?" he sounded like the epitome of a hangover. I could almost feel his head throbbing.

"Roger. This is Katlin. How are you?" I asked more for entertainment purposes than out of genuine caring.

"Oh, I'm just dandy. I'm a little tired from working late last night."

Yeah. I bet.

"Listen. You need to come up to the jobsite tomorrow. Early. There's something I need to talk with you about and we can't do it over the phone. You can catch the 7am ferry and be here by 8. See you then". I hung up, not giving him a chance to weasel out of it.

Oboy. This was going to be goooood!

I returned to my daily journal and became so immersed in it that quite a bit of time had passed before I noticed some extra loud grumbles from south of my belt line, alerting me that it was past my lunch time. Since things were going so swell on the job I decided to treat myself to a lunch at The Daisy.

Even though it was mid-week, tourist season had arrived. I could tell by the number of RVs, campers, and trailers that were parked everywhere within two blocks of The Daisy. It took only two circles around the block before someone pulled out of a space right in front of the door. I wheeled into the space, ignoring the complicated hand signals from the driver of a car stopped in front of the vacant spot. Translated, I think the message would have been something like "#!@&, you %$*, for taking the &!#% space I was ^*@!+#  backing into."

"Scuse me, pardon me, scuse me." I mumbled as I slid past the line of hungry tourists that was out the door. Their hunger was making them mean. A few of them even used the same hand signals as the driver of the car to communicate their opinion of me.

There was one empty stool at the counter and it was mine. I slid onto it and grabbed a menu to hide from all that unwarranted hostility.

"You sure do have a knack for getting people all excited," said a familiar voice.

I peeked around the edge of the menu to see Mark's twinkling eyes laughing at me. "Yeah, it's an acquired talent," I said. "What are you doing here? I thought you worked day and night."

"A fella's gotta keep his strength up," he said wiggling his eyebrows at me in an attempted leer. He was just too darn cute to carry off a good leer. "Actually, I'm doing some work for Mavis out back, enlarging her parking area... something she can certainly use. Word is getting out about our secret – the world's finest eating establishment. Well, Stanville's finest anyway."

"I'm not going to argue with you. I've seen the evidence. Phil's waistband on his pants seems to be getting tighter and tighter."

"You sure it's not the waist on *your* jeans that's shrinking?" He waited for me to get done rolling my eyes before continuing. "Actually, I think you're just right. I don't find skinny women attractive."

"Oh puh-leeze. You're turning my head." Thankfully, the waitress poked her head between us to take our orders. That little bit of business done, we carried on with our teasing banter until the food arrived. Then it became very quiet, except for the chomping and slurping.

"That was mighty good. Well, I've gotta get back to my work. This is your lucky day. Not only did you get to enjoy my terrific company, but lunch is on me today." he said as he stood up, threw some money on the counter, and began to walk away.

"Wow. Thank you! Does this count as a date, then?" I said teasingly.

That stopped him. He turned around, walked back to me and stuck his face this close to mine. "Honey, you'll know when it's a date because I'll treat you so right you won't want to ever go home." He held my eyes with his for just a moment too long and electricity began crackling between us. Then he turned around and vanished into the hoard of hungry tourists still lined up at the door.

Somebody must have turned the heat up in the café because it sure got hot all of a sudden. I fanned myself with the plastic coated menu until I stopped sweating and then walked out of the café on shaky legs.

*What just happened in there?* I asked myself repeatedly all the way back to the job site. I wasn't prepared for sparks to fly between me and nice, friendly, helpful Mark. Up to now I'd thought of him more like he was a little puppy dog. Now he seemed more like a ravenous wolf... and I think he was eyeballing me as his meal. Yikes!

When I returned to the jobsite, I decided that helping Pete and Repeat nail some of the plywood on the mansard was just the thing I needed to refocus. Plus it was far enough from the hot tar pot that I felt pretty safe. I grabbed my trusty old toolbelt and sauntered over to them.

"Howdy, boys. Have a nice lunch?" I said with a smile.

Evidently they still didn't quite know where they stood with me. I could tell by the way their eyes slid from side to side when I talked to them, as if they were looking for someone to rescue them. Finally Pete spoke. "Yep."

"Excellent. Would you like some help? I seem to find myself in need of some physical exercise. Mind if I strap on my tool belt and finish nailing some of the plywood on the mansard?"

"Nope."

"Great. I'll just get to work, then," I said buckling my toolbelt behind my back and walking over to the box of nails.

Good thing they were only 6d nails. It had been a few years since I'd actually done any nailing and I didn't want to embarrass myself by taking thirty swings with the framing hammer to pound one dinky nail into plywood. The best framers prided themselves on tapping a 16d nail on the up-stroke to set it, then driving it in completely with one down-stroke. At one time I'd been one of those framers. But that had been years ago and now I just hoped I'd be able to pound in the little 6d nails with five or six strokes and not bend them over in the process. I didn't want to make a fool of myself in front of these guys.

The sound of an air horn stopped me before I climbed up the ladder to the mansard. Oh goodie. Another delivery. No doubt something huge. Something I wouldn't need until the end of the job. Something I'd get to move a zillion times.

I dropped my tool belt to the ground and walked over to the semi. The driver leaned out his window and slapped the outside of the door a couple of times with the flat of his hand. It reminded me of certain male animals who use various materials to amplify their mating calls.

"Hiya, honey. What can I do for you?" he said, moving a well-used toothpick around the corners of his mouth.

"For starters, you can refrain from calling me honey. Next, you can tell me what you're doing on my job site," I said.

"*Your* job site?" he asked incredulously.

"Yes. *My* job site. I'm Katlin Greene, the Project Superintendent here," I said, very much enjoying the vision of his toothpick falling out of his gaping mouth after I'd introduced myself.

"Yes sir. I mean ma'am."

"Now, do you have a delivery for this project or are you just lost?"

"I do have a delivery. A couple of purty big boxes. Where would you like them?" he asked, properly contrite now.

"May I see the Bill of Lading and then I can tell you," I said reaching my hand out for the documents. A quick scan told me that he had brought the HVAC vents. Perfect timing, since they'd be going up on the roof right after James and crew were done.

"You can place them over there, in front of the building," I directed him pointing to where they were to be off-loaded.

He maneuvered his truck around so the back of it was exactly where I'd indicated I wanted the parts delivered. I watched him to make sure he didn't damage anything as he slid it carefully off the tailgate and onto the ground. He handed me some paperwork to sign, then jumped in his truck cab and roared off.

With no other excuses readily available, I went back to where I'd dropped my tool belt. It wasn't there. I looked all around and it still wasn't there.

"Hey, Pete. Have you seen my tool belt anywhere?" I yelled up at him on the mansard.

"Nope," he said and then turned around quickly so I couldn't see his face.

Something was going on. Oh yeah. It took me a few minutes to remember the old framer game of Hide the Toolbelt. Usually it was nailed to the highest part of the building or hung from the highest tree branch or telephone pole in the area.

"Okay, guys. Where's my tool belt?" I asked of no one in particular. Then I heard some smothered laughing coming from the roof. "Okay, James. What'd you do with it?"

Nothing but more laughs and a few hoo-haws. I scanned the top of the building. Nothing. Then I noticed my tool belt hanging from one of the pegs on the telephone pole next to the building. Great.

"Mind if I borrow your ladder for a minute?" I asked, pulling it off the side of the building and leaning it against the pole. "You guys are real funny," I said as I unhooked my belt and climbed back down the ladder.

Again, nothing but laughter. This time it was more raucous and much louder.

I wasn't planning on taking their tool belts in retaliation. But they might get a surprise when they went to get off the roof one of these times. Their ladder might just have disappeared.

After an hour or so of pounding nails, my hammer hand was about numb. Years of lifting nothing heavier than a pencil had taken its toll.

"Well, I'd better get back to the office. More paperwork to do. I guess you two can handle the rest of this on your own, now that I've gotten most of the work done for you," I said to Pete and Repeat.

They just looked at me with mouths agape, not knowing whether I was joking or seriously delusional.

In the hour plus that I'd been hammering away, I'd gotten four small pieces of plywood nailed up. Much of my time was spent pulling out bent nails or trying to straighten them enough to finish pounding them in all the way. I suspected my days of swinging an eighteen ounce framing hammer all day were pretty much over.

"I'll be in my office if you need me. Go ahead and keep working," I said to them.

I hunkered down in Ol' Blue to finish my paperwork. Hours later, I became aware of silence. Sometime while I'd been doing my administrative chores, the roofing and framing crews had called it a day. That meant I should do the same.

# Chapter 28

Today was a big day, and for once I couldn't wait for it to start. This was the day I was going to take care of the Roger problem.

After taking another of the world's fastest showers, I threw my clothes on and sped out to the Oasis.

"Cherie this is it!" I announced as I flew through the door. "Today I'm taking care of the problem I'm having with my framing sub and it's going to be great!"

"What are you schemin' on?" she asked with a gleam in her eyes.

"Well, he sweet talked me out of having a contract, a mistake I'll *never* make again. That means I don't have his signature on any kind of agreement as to the finish date. Howsomever, I do have an ace up my sleeve. I took a Construction Project Management class a couple of weeks ago and they said to keep a job diary in case you had to prove something in court. So I've been doing just that. I've got everything he promised me written down. Every word. He'll have to live up to his word now. The weasel."

"Well, wahoo! You've gotta tell me how it works out. Call me when it's over and tell me all the gory details. To give you some extra go-power, here's a free Death by Chocolate cookie along with your regular order. Go get 'em, girl!" she practically yelled.

With half a gallon of her high octane coffee, my regular order of her massive cookies, plus a Death by Chocolate cookie, I couldn't help but succeed in my evil plot.

James and crew were already hard at work when I returned to Ol' Blue. Soon, I heard another truck pull in next to Ol' Blue. A quick glance through the teeny kitchen window showed me that Roger and crew had arrived.

Before Roger could come inside Ol' Blue, I stomped outside to meet him. I wanted this to be a public meeting, so that he couldn't change the story afterward when word got out and people would ask him about it. Especially others in the construction business. Especially others that I knew.

"Morning, Pete. Dave. You two go ahead and pick up where you left off yesterday. Roger and I have a few things to discuss," I said, taking command of the situation right off the gitgo.

They wasted no time getting out of the line of fire. I turned to face Roger.

"Roger, when we agreed that you would be the framing subcontractor on this job, you said you'd have your entire crew of eight guys up here and it would be finished within a specific time period. Neither of those things have happened. Your crew is several days behind schedule and I'm having to help them in order to keep the rest of the subs on schedule," I stated loud enough for everyone else on the jobsite to hear.

"Now Katlin," he began in a condescending tone, "let's not get all fired up about this. According to my figuring, there's plenty of time for my boys to finish this little framing job of yours.

Wrong. Wrong attitude. Wrong figuring.

"Are you going to get the rest of your crew up here and finish this by tomorrow or not?" I asked him.

"Well, if you remember correctly, we don't have a contract so I'm not obligated to any time line here. My guys will get it done when they get it done. And that's that," he said, stepping toward me, close enough so that we were belly to belly with him towering over me. I had to crane my neck all the way back so I could look him in his eyes.

Although this was a great technique for intimidating someone smaller, namely me, it wasn't the first time a big guy had tried to use this scare tactic on me. I'd had bikers, loggers, roofers in my employ, and other such gentlemen who were a whole lot bigger and meaner than him try it. I'd learned to stand my ground, which almost always made them back down. What else could they do?

So I stood my ground and calmly said, "Fine. Then since we have no contract, you're fired. Get your crew and get off my job site."

For all of a minute he stood there with his mouth hanging open. Then he gathered what few wits he had and said, "You can't fire me. Where's your boss? He's the only one who can fire me."

"Not true. I hired you and I can fire you."

"Let me talk to your boss. Where is he?"

"He's in his office. Allow me to call him for you," I said sweetly. In just a few steps I made it into Ol' Blue, grabbed the phone, and quickly brought it out to where he was standing. I didn't want him to follow me into the confines of Ol' Blue. Keeping this confrontation public was part of my scheme. Quickly I dialed the G and G office.

"G and G Construction," Gene answered.

"Hi Gene. Katlin here. Roger, the framing sub, is here and wants to talk to you." I confidently handed Roger the phone. Gene and I had already discussed the issues I was having with my framing sub and I had several possible solutions and outcomes already prepared.

"Hi Gene," Roger said in his most smarmy voice. "Katlin here just tried to fire me. She can't do that."

"Actually, Roger, she can. She's my Project Supe and whatever she says goes. So if she said you're fired, you're fired," Gene's voice boomed through the phone loud enough for everyone within half a mile to hear. "She has informed me of the promises you made regarding the size of your crew and the completion date of your work."

"But we don't have a contract, so I can't be legally held to what I said to her," Roger whined.

"Yes. You can. She's keeping a job diary and whatever you told her, she's written down. That's considered proof," Gene rebutted.

281

"Oh," Roger said quietly. I watched him as he seemed to physically deflate. "Well, I'll get a bigger crew here tomorrow and we can finish it all up by the end of the day. Would that be all right with you?" Roger asked in a much more humble tone of voice.

"If it's okay with Katlin, it's okay with me," Gene confirmed.

"Th-thanks," Roger said, but Gene had already hung up.

Roger returned the phone to me, eyes focused on the toes of his boots. "Okay. I'll stay here today and work with the guys, and tomorrow I'll bring more crew so we can finish the job. Is that okay with you, Katlin?"

"You've got two days. You better get your tool belt on and join your crew," I stated. He wasn't moving, just looking at the dirt as if he didn't understand what had just happened. "NOW!" I yelled at him.

He jumped, quickly turned around, and began moving toward his truck and his tool belt.

I turned and sauntered back to Ol' Blue, carrying the phone and feeling smugly satisfied with my performance and how things had turned out. So far, this had been one of the biggest challenges on the jobsite, and I was relieved that it was almost over.

Just as I was getting my mind back to my paperwork, another truck pulled into the jobsite. A quick glance out the teeny window let me see that my glass sub had just showed up with the front door.

"Hey, Bill! Good to see you," I shouted at him from the steps of Ol' Blue.

"Katlin! Back at ya!" he yelled in my direction as he got out of his truck.

We walked together to the building as he updated me on the local gossip in the construction trades at home.

"Before I unload that monster off my truck, I'm just gonna check to make sure we have the correct dimensions here," he said as he took his tape measure off his belt.

# Studs

"Um hummm. Huh. Well, I got bad news for ya," he said after checking the measurements. "This opening is ½" too tight. You're gonna either have to tear it out and rebuild it or take your Skil saw and back blade it. Luckily it's rough opening, not finished, so it doesn't have to look good. I'd go with the back blading. I'll come back tomorrow and install the door."

And he drove off.

I stood there, feeling my anger towards Roger and his framing crew growing by the second. Quickly, before it got to lethal proportions, I turned to Roger, who was trying to hide behind some 2 x 4 studs he'd just installed in the bathroom wall.

"Drop whatever you're doing and get over here and correct this. NOW," I ordered him.

As he meekly tip-toed past me, I repeated what Bill had said. "Take your Skil saw and back blade ¼" off each side of that doorway. And make it look good."

I stormed back to Ol' Blue to continue with my paperwork, but was too upset to keep my mind on it. Probably it had something to do with my empty stomach complaining to me so loudly. Not wanting to leave the job in fear of Roger sneaking away, I opted to cook my own lunch. Well, "cook" may have been a bit of an exaggeration. "Throw together" was more like it. I decided that a tuna and potato chip sandwich was just exactly what I needed.

After dining on my gourmet lunch, my head was much more capable of staying focused on my paperwork. I became completely absorbed by it and was surprised when I heard the sounds of vehicles leaving the job site. A quick look at the clock showed that it was way past quitting time.

I took the short jaunt out to the building site to check the progress of my framer and my roofer.

James' crew had finished everything except the metal trim – scuppers and drains.

Roger's crew had almost finished the plywood on the mansard roof, half the T1-11 siding, and the walls for the bathroom. Still to go was the wall for the coolers, which covered the entire width of the store on the side wall, and the rest of the mansard and siding. It looked just possibly like the framing might be done tomorrow.

Something looked a little off with the bathroom wall, though. The studs looked like they were too far apart. I grabbed my tape measure and, sure enough, the studs were on 32" centers instead of the required 24" centers. Evidently Roger was trying to save time by using fewer studs. That was the bad news. The good news was that I caught it before they framed the entire wall for the cooler.

Tomorrow I'd have them add studs between the existing ones and also make damn sure they built the cooler wall to the dimensions on the plans and in the specs. If I had to, I'd stand there every minute and measure between each and every stud.

Yep. Being a Project Supe really was a lot more like babysitting than the high falutin' management position I had imagined it to be. The reality wasn't even remotely close to the vision I had of me pointing at the project and my studly workers racing to do my bidding.

# Chapter 29

I was beginning to suspect that Cherie had some kind of powerful electromagnetic tractor beam that took hold of my body and pulled me to the Oasis every morning. Either that or her cookies were highly addictive. Whatever it was, it got me out of bed in the morning and for that I was grateful. Usually.

"Do you have any more of those magical mystical Death by Chocolate cookies? I'm in deep need of something powerful to get me through this day," I whined to Cherie.

"Things not so hunky-dory at the job site, hon?"

"Yesterday I almost fired my framer. Luckily for both of us, he made the right decision. He actually strapped on his tool belt and went to work with his crew yesterday. And he's promised to show up today with them and finish the job that he had committed to doing, but wasn't. I'll be eternally happy to see the backside of that man for the last time."

"You just let me know when that happens and we'll have a little celebration," she said. "Cookies and champagne. Howzat?"

"Marvelloso idea! I'll bring the champagne! What a great way to start off the day – cookies and champagne! It could easily replace bacon and waffles as one of my favorite breakfasts," I chirped at her, as I went out the door with my bag of C and C.

My happy mood continued, even after I arrived at the job site. Roger's truck had arrived and I heard the glorious sounds of multiple hammerings and sawings. Life was getting better by the minute.

After depositing my extra coffee and cookies in Ol' Blue, I strode out to the building to see what Roger and crew were doing. He was framing up the refrigeration wall while Pete and Repeat were outside, finishing up the siding and trim. If they stayed on the job all day they'd likely get it all finished, and I'd make damn sure they stayed. Like all macho contractors, Roger left his keys in the ignition of his truck. I quietly removed them and stashed them in the refrigerator in Ol' Blue. For safe keeping, you understand. I didn't want anyone to steal his truck or anything.

I hooked my tape measure on my belt and went out to the building. I wanted to make sure Roger wasn't pulling another sneaky move by spacing the studs too far apart. If he was, I wanted to catch him now, at the beginning, rather than later when he was nothing but a cloud of dust as he drove down the road away from the job.

He watched me with wary eyes as I measured the spacing of the studs where he'd been working.

"Good work," I said, turning to face him. "Keep going. And when you get done here, you can correct the framing on the bathroom walls by adding another stud centered in between the existing studs. If you look at the plans you'll notice that it calls for the studs to be 24" on center, not 32" as your guys framed it. Instead of having you tear out the walls and do it all over, just add another stud in between the existing studs. It'll give us 16" o.c. spacing, but that's okay. I'll just note it here on the as-built plans."

He stood looking at me with a dumbfounded look, as if he couldn't believe that a woman could possibly be smart enough to catch him cheating. I was quite sure this wasn't the first time, nor was it necessarily under the same sort of circumstances, that he'd been caught cheating. As someone much wiser than me once said, "How you do anything is how you do everything." I've found this to be true so often and in so many ways.

I heard stomping and yelling over my head. Apparently the roofers had arrived to finish their job.

"You guys wanna keep it quiet up there? I'm trying to have an intelligent conversation down here," I yelled at them.

"C'mon up here and say that," James challenged me.

# Studs

I walked outside and looked roofward just in time to see several gleaming white butt cheeks greeting me in the morning sun.

"Good one, guys. Funny. Oh wait. What's that? I think I hear the siren from one of the local police cars," I shouted at them, watching all those morning moons quickly disappear like magic from the rooftop. Soon I heard only the sounds of roofing materials being applied.

Well, it appeared that my work there was done, so I ambled back to Ol' Blue. Next on the agenda was to call the plumber to tell him he could begin his rough-in tomorrow.

After listening to his five minute monologue on his answering machine, I left a ten second message telling him that I'd be ready for his rough-in tomorrow first thing.

Next was a call to one of my favorite people, Red. Just as I was dialing his number, there was a yoohoo just outside of Ol' Blue. I stepped outside to be greeted by Maude with a plate of her infamous cookies.

"Hi, Katlin. I brought you a going away gift," she said almost shyly.

"I'm not going anywhere," I replied.

"Well, we are. We're moving out this weekend and will be gone by Monday," she said.

"Oh. I didn't think it would be so soon. Come on in and set for a spell. I don't have any coffee, but I do have some lemonade. Let's have us a little going away party," I offered, and waved her ahead of me.

"Maybe you could give me a little push," she said over her shoulder as she wedged herself into the doorway. "I have a little difficulty with stairs."

Stairs. Right. Even with me pushing her from behind, she barely squeezed through the doorway. I got her settled and pulled out a couple of icey lemonades to accompany our cookies. Amazingly she had managed to bake these to perfection - brown and crunchy on the outside while remaining soft and gooey - yet fully cooked - on the inside.

She rambled on about the new place and their new neighbors, most of whom they'd met during the weekly Bingo game. After we downed all the cookies and lemonade, I got up first. I didn't want to be stuck inside Ol' Blue just in case she'd added more girth to her existing mass with all the cookies she'd just consumed, making her bootie too big to get through the doorway opening.

Pulling her through the doorway and down the steps was actually much easier than pushing her up. We hugged and then she turned and walked away. I'd probably never see them again and to tell the truth, I'd miss them. Yes, they were real oddballs, and they were also kind, generous, and honest folks. They were the kind of people you can count on to help you when you need it, even if you don't ask them. Their new neighbors would no doubt find out just how lucky they were that Maude and Henry were moving in to their neighborhood.

After those deep thoughts it took me a while to remember what I was doing before Maude showed up. Oh yeah. A call to Red to tell him to begin moving the house next week.

"Red's House Moving and Demolition," his cheery voice answered the phone.

"Hey, Red. This is Katlin. I'm just wondering, is the moving and demolition combined in one operation or are they separate?"

"Haw haw! I never heard that one before," he chortled.

"I suspect there's a bit of sarcasm there. Well, it's deserved. Hey. I just want to tell you that Maude and Henry are moving out this weekend, so can you move the house next week?"

"Wal, we've got a job we're doing now, but we should be finished on Tuesday. We could start Wednesday next week. Is that too soon for ya?"

"Sounds good. Wait. Start? How long will it take to actually move the house off the lot?" I was hoping it would go faster than the garage had.

"Ohhh, it oughta be off the lot in a couple of days. That okay?"

"That's fine, Red. Do you call the utility companies to get the disconnects or do I?" I asked, since this was yet another of those things I'd never before encountered in my entire life.

"Ya'll do it, since you got the utility info. You know, account numbers and all," he answered.

"Okeedokee. I'll take care of it and will see you on Wednesday. Say hi to all the family for me," and we hung up.

Now all I needed was the utility information. Who would have it, I wondered, and how would I find out.

Just then the phone rang.

"G and…"

"Hey, girl," Gene bellowed into the phone before I could finish my greeting. "I got a sooprise for you tomorrow. I'm comin' up there with one of my guys. I figure it's time to start forming up the sidewalks and the gas tank hold-down pad."

My eyes rolled so far back in my head I almost fell over. Just what I didn't need now was Gene coming up here and confusing things. It seemed like I had just gotten things under control one second ago.

"Okay. Good. About what time do you think you'll be arriving?" I asked through clenched teeth.

"We'll catch the early ferry and be there about 7 or 8. You got your tool belt with ya, doncha?"

"Um. Yes. Why would you ask me that?" I felt my stomach go south.

"Whaddya think? You'll be working with my guy. No sense in there being two bosses on the job at the same time. See ya tomorrow." And he hung up.

I was too stunned to move. In a flash I had been demoted from Project Superintendent to laborer.

Slowly I hung up the phone, and as I did so, I remembered that right now, at that moment, I was still the Project Supe and I had more work to do. Pulling myself up by my theoretical bootstraps came easy for me, having done it many times before in a zillion or so previous situations.

I figured Thomas Oil would have the information I needed about the utility companies. I found their phone number under the growing stack of papers on what used to be the Dining Room table and called.

"Thomas Oil. How may I direct your call?" a mechanical voice answered. I guess I'd get pretty mechanical too if I had to do nothing but answer the phone all day long and direct calls.

"Accounts Payable, please," I answered. I figured the people who paid the bills should have the account numbers and contact information I needed.

"Accounts Payable," said a nasally, bored voice.

"Hi, I'm Katlin Green from the Stanville project and I need to get some information about the utilities. Do you have the authorization to give me the account numbers and contact information for the utilities on the existing house on this job?"

"Honey, you don't have to use that old tactic on me about having the authorization. I do have it and I don't care who I give it out to. Whaddya need to know?"

I was so relieved that I wouldn't have to go through the usual layers of corporate protocol that I actually giggled. "Thank you for your honesty and your help. Here's what I need..." and I gave her the utilities that I'd be having disconnected next week.

She quickly and efficiently gave me what I needed and then, almost as an afterthought, asked "Have you gotten permission to disconnect and move the house yet? You probably should do that."

"Um, no I didn't think I needed to. Who do I talk to about that?"

"Van Payne. I'll transfer you. And by the way, you're quite the talk of the company here. We all admire you for the job you've taken on. That's the most difficult and complicated project we've ever attempted," she informed me.

"Oh. Thank you," I didn't know what else to say. I was pleased to be so complimented and at the same time shocked to learn it was such an unusual project. I thought it was just business as usual. Now, knowing it was such a huge, difficult project somehow made it intimidating. I liked it better when I believed it was just a simple little nothing project. Now I felt overwhelmed.

"Van here," a pleasant male voice interrupted my whiny thoughts.

"Hi Van. Katlin Green up here on the Stanville probject. I guess I need to get your permission to disconnect the utilities from the house and have the house moved off the lot," I explained.

"True. All of it true. I thought we were going to keep that house connected until the store was built," he sort of questioned.

"Well, that would probably be ideal from a financial perspective, but from the construction viewpoint it's just not feasible. The lot is real tight and already I'm running out of room to store the equipment and materials that are being delivered. The canopy is already here and it's taking up a lot of space. We're starting construction of the hold-down pad for the new gas pumps tomorrow. Aside from all that, Maude and Henry are moving out this weekend, so there will be no one to sell gas there," I informed him.

After a long pause in which I wondered if he'd gone to sleep or maybe fell into a catatonic state, he said, "Well, then I guess I better give you my permission, hadn't I?"

"Thank you!" I said with great relief in my voice. What a hassle, what a catastrophe it would have been had he said no. "You'll have to come up and visit the job site and see what's going on here," I invited him. "Just give me a call and let me know when. I'll let you take me to lunch."

"Sounds good. I'll take you up on that," he said with a smile in his voice, and with that we hung up.

Whew. Another close call and trouble averted. This job never failed to keep my adrenalin pumping.

The rest of the day I spent calling the utility companies and scheduling their disconnects.

Suddenly I noticed it was quiet on the job. A quick trip over to the building site showed me that Roger and crew were gone... and that he had actually finished framing the refrigeration wall and added the studs to the bathroom walls. As I walked around the outside, checking the siding, I discovered there were a few small pieces missing and some trim that needed to be added. If they never showed up again it would be no big deal. I could finish that little dab of work myself. Of course, if I had to complete their work for them I'd backcharge Roger substantially. Very substantially.

"Katlin! Oh Katlin! Where are youuuuuu?" a voice called. I walked around to the front of the building to discover James.

"I thought you were gone, it was so quiet up there on the roof," I said.

"My crew left already and I'm just finishing the clean up and giving you my bill," he said, handing me his invoice.

"Thanks so much, James. I'll give this to Ginnie at the office and tell her to pay you right away. It's always a pleasure to work with a professional such as yourself," I said.

He blushed a brighter red than his hair. "Thanks, Katlin. Ditto," he said, giving me a quick hug before hopping into his truck and driving off.

And just like that, my work day was over. Things had turned out quite well this day and tomorrow was Friday. Life just kept getting better and better.

# Chapter 30

There I was, sleeping soundly and in the middle of a very pleasant dream about the kind of guys whom I'd originally imagined would be working on my job - gorgeous, muscular, tanned, shirtless studs – when suddenly Gene appeared in my dream, getting in my face and telling me he was coming up to the job and I'd have to work on forming and finishing concrete.

Still half asleep, I sat up so quickly I forgot the ceiling was only inches above me. The force of hitting my head on it was enough to complete my wake-up process. It was a perfectly horrid start to what was promising to be a perfectly horrid day.

There was no time for a coffee and cookie run to the Oasis this morning, since Gene seemed to be one of those obnoxious people who likes to start his day in the middle of the night, like around 6am or so. When he'd called the day before, he'd threatened to be here bright and early. I couldn't even begin to imagine a bright and early Gene, especially without any coffee in my system. Maybe I could just make a real quick run to the Oasis, I thought.

Throwing on some clothes I found laying around and swiping a brush over my hair was going to be the extent of my beautification this morning. I was on a mission to get some life-saving sustenance.

I got to the Oasis in record-breaking time and threw open the door. I was relieved to see no lines of waiting customers in front of me.

"Quick, Cherie! Coffee and cookies. Any kind," I practically shrieked at her.

"Wow, hon, what's got your tail in a knot this morning?" She asked as she began assembling my order.

"My boss just announced yesterday that he's coming up here with one of his workers and they'll be here bright and early. I think that means very soon, if not already."

"You might just want to take a look in a mirror before you go meet him. You don't want to make him wonder if you've turned into some kind of crazy woman," she gently advised me.

I looked at my reflection in the window. Eeep! She was right. "Okay. Here's what we do. In case he's there on the job already, give me another coffee and cookie in a separate bag. I'll distract him with that while I rush into Ol' Blue and freshen up."

"Good plan. Here ya go. Have a good weekend, and let me know on Monday how it goes today."

"Oh, that's right. It's Friday. Well, that's one good thing to look forward to," I said to her as I ran out to my truck.

Arriving back at the job site in a cloud of dust, I was relieved to notice no other trucks on the job site. Whew. I'd made it before Gene and his guy got there. I was just finishing brushing the knots and snarls out of my hair when I heard a truck drive up next to Ol' Blue. A quick peek out the tiny window showed Gene exiting the driver's side and a scrawny young guy getting out of the passenger side.

"Mornin' Gene," I said as I stepped out of Ol' Blue. "Welcome to Casa de Construction."

He chortled, while the his passenger looked at me with blank eyes. "Meet Lennie. You and he are going to be working together now," he happily announced.

Lennie looked about as excited as I was about this prospect. "Nice to meet you, Lennie," I lied.

"Yuh," he lied back.

Just then Don Hobab drove up in his van. "Um, excuse me for a minute. I need to consult with my plumber about some, uh, plumbing stuff," I said backpeddling as fast as I could over to Don.

# Studs

"Let's get this stuff unloaded," I heard Gene say to Lennie, who just stood in place, not moving. "Today would be good!" Gene howled at him.

Lennie began moving in slow motion toward the back of the pickup. After carefully lowering the tail gate, he pulled one 2 x 4 out of the pile of materials in the truck bed and carried it over to the front of the building, carefully placing it just so on the ground. Then, gradually turning around, he began the ever-so-slow journey back to the truck for one more board.

This was going to be interesting,

Turning around I saw Don nearly doubled up trying to hold his laughter inside. "And I thought Jay was a rotten worker. This guy's got him beat all to hell. Haw! Haw! Where did Gene find him?"

"From the looks of him, I'd say in a bar somewhere," I said with a smile. It was kind of funny, especially if you weren't the one who was going to have to work with him.

"Well, anyhoo. What can I do ya for this fine mornin'," he asked.

"I was just going to ask you the same thing. Let's take a walk over to the building and see what the framers left you," I said, grabbing his arm and walking alongside of him. I needed to keep my subs happy, and if that meant a little flirting now and again, I didn't mind.

"Looks just fine from my house," he said, using one of the jokes that had been going around construction sites since the Egyptians built the pyramids.

I laughed appropriately and had him take a closer look. "Notice that the studs in the bathroom walls are 16" o.c. That's because the idiots originally framed them at 32" o.c. so they could save a couple of bucks in labor costs. Instead of having them rip the walls out, I had them add studs. I hope that's okay with you."

"Yeah, that's fine with me. No problemo," he said. "I'll be outta your hair in a couple of hours. The rough-in for these stores is a breeze."

"Okay, then. I'll be around the job site all day if you need me for anything. Thanks, Don." And I turned to walk out and face the Gene and Lennie show.

As I was nearing Gene's truck, I heard the sounds of a bigger truck entering the job site. A huge two-ton van pulled up alongside the underground gas tanks. The guy who jumped out of the cab was so covered in black grease and oil that all I could see was the whites of his eyes and the gleam of a gold front tooth as he grinned at me.

"Howdy. I'm your handy dandy tank tester," he announced. "I go by the name of Jim, but you can call me Jim."

I couldn't help but like this character... at least as long as I stood upwind of him. He was rather, um, aromatic. "Howdy back at ya. I'm Katlin, the Project Supe here. How can I help you?"

"You mean, how am I gonna help you! I got a call from Thomas Oil to come and check the tanks. They have to be tested before the new pumps can go up."

"We're a long ways from that," I informed him.

"Not so's you'd think. They have to be tested before you place the hold-down pad on top of them, and I understand Gene thinks you're about to do that starting next week."

"You're right about that," said the booming voice of Gene behind me. "Girl, you go help Lennie and I'll deal with Jim," he said, abruptly dismissing me.

Even though I shouldn't have been, I was shocked at Gene's rudeness and insensitivity. In a few words he had diminished me from Project Supe to a mere laborer in front of a Thomas Oil representative. Jim looked at me with understanding in his eyes. Evidently he'd had workings with Gene before and knew how thoughtless and crude he could be.

"Nice meeting you, Katlin," Jim kindly said by way of letting me know he understood the situation.

"You too, Jim. I hope I get to see you again," I said to let him know in our secret code that I appreciated his understanding.

I turned away and walked over to Gene's truck, moving as slowly as Lennie. When I got there I noticed that, even though Lennie was slower than a slug, somehow he'd managed to unload everything from the truck.

"Lennie, do you like cookies?" I asked him, already knowing the answer.

"I sure do, Katlin,"

"Do you like coffee?"

"Yes ma'am."

"Come with me then," I said walking over to Ol' Blue where I'd stashed the goodies from my morning Oasis run. I gave Lennie the coffee and cookies I'd originally intended for Gene. I felt great satisfaction in knowing that I'd given them to the right person, someone who would appreciate the thoughtfulness of a little kindness. And I felt even greater satisfaction knowing that Gene would have loved the cookies and coffee.

"Well, that was delish" Lenny said as he licked the last of the crumbs from around his mouth.

"Yeah, we better be getting to work before Gene blows a gasket," I said just as Gene threw open the door on Ol' Blue.

"What're you two up to? Why aren't you up at the building site, starting the framing for the sidewalks?" he growled at us.

"We were just having a little go-juice and were about to go up there," I said. "Grab the plans, would you Lennie?" I said, getting up and moving toward the door, effectively pushing Gene backwards by intruding in his personal space.

"Oh," Gene grumbled. "Well, I got the tank tester all straightened out. He'll be taking samples of dirt around the tanks today and then this weekend Thomas Oil will send a truck in to fill the tanks. Monday Jim will come back to do another test to make sure they're holding the gas and not leaking it. After that, we'll be good to go as far as installing the new pumps and having the canopy installed."

"Well, Gene, that should work out well with the schedule. Maude and Henry are moving out this weekend, so Monday all utilities to the building will be disconnected and Wednesday Red and crew will be moving the house."

For a couple of beats Gene was stunned into silence. I don't think he quite understood how much work I'd been doing as far as organizing and scheduling various phases of work on the project.

"Well, that's just fine then," he said, unable to come up with any curt or demeaning remarks.

"Okay then. Lennie, lets get to work," I said as I stepped out of Ol' Blue and began walking toward the building.

Lennie and I had just begun framing up for the sidewalk when Don came out of the building.

"I'm all done with the rough-in.... wait! What are you doing?" he asked in a panicked voice.

"Uh, forming for sidewalks," I answered. "Why? What does it look like we're doing?"

"It looks like you're going to build your sidewalk right where J.J. and I have to dig a ditch. He has to run his wires out to the pumps and I have to run some lines out there too."

"Well, you guys better get on the stick," I said smiling, so he wouldn't know I was entirely serious. "You can do it this weekend or on Monday. We probably won't be pouring until Tuesday or Wednesday, depending on how many interruptions I get."

"I'll let J.J. know and he can get Jay out here first thing next week to do the ditching," he announced.

"Fine with me," I agreed. I wasn't looking forward to any more encounters with that spoiled brat son of J. J.'s but I guess that was just one more reason why I was getting paid the big bucks. "I'll give him a call in a bit and let him know that you're done so he can come in and start his rough-in on Monday."

"Oh, don't bother. I'll see him tonight and will let him know. We always have beers on Friday with a few of the other guys," he announced with a twinkle in his eyes.

"Thanks. See ya next week probably," I said and went back to work with Lennie, thinking how tasty a beer would be right about now.

It seemed like only minutes had passed when a dark shadow fell over where I was working. I looked up and saw Gene's big belly blocking the sun before I looked higher and noticed the rest of him.

"I'm takin' Lennie and we're going now. I won't be back on Monday, so you'll have to be the boss," he said, throwing another subtle insult at me. As if I hadn't been the boss the entire time I'd been on this hairball job. I'd already straightened out enough of his screw ups in the time I'd been on this job to last me a lifetime. And I would have bet good money that there'd be more in my near future.

"Okay. See ya Monday at your house," I replied and went back to work on the forming. I used the excuse of working on the framing a little more in order to miss the same ferry as he'd be on. I didn't want to have to sit with him and be polite. I wasn't feeling very sociable toward him right at that moment.

After a suitable amount of time, I picked up the tools and hauled them over to Ol' Blue. I threw my dirty clothes in a sack and carried it out to my truck. After locking up Ol' Blue I jumped in my truck and drove off the job site, away from this crazy job and Gene and toward my weekend of freedom.

# Chapter 31

I could hardly wait to share the great news with Cherie. Gene and Ginnie had been rather ho-hum when I told them about it as I was picking up and delivering paperwork during my usual Monday morning stop. Screeching to a halt inches away from the wide open door at The Oasis, I jumped out of my truck and ran up to the counter.

Cherie was not at her usual place, behind the cookie display. *Maybe she's in the back*, I thought to myself. "CHERIE!" I yelled toward the back of the store, leaning over the counter.

Suddenly she popped up in front of me, so close she almost hit my nose on the way up.

A surprised "Yipes!" escaped from my mouth as I jumped backward, almost hitting one of the little tables.

"Ya don't have to yell. I'm right here," she said with just a bit of huffiness.

"Sorry. I'm just so excited to tell you my good news that I'm jumping up and down inside of me."

"Well, don't keep me in suspenders. What's your big important news?"

"Ahem," I cleared my throat importantly. "You are now looking at Katlin Green, proud homeowner."

"YAHOO! That *is* good news," she said, breaking into a smile that stretched clear across her face. "Cookies are on me this morning! C'mon, sit down and tell me all about it."

She was one person I could count on to give me the happy response I wanted to my news. Like Gene, most of the guys on the job couldn't possibly understand how scary it is for a single woman to make such a huge purchase and take on the gigantic responsibility of buying a home. So for the time being, Cherie was the only one in Stanville who knew.

We sat and chatted for quite a while as I told her all about the deal and how Sheila, my real estate agent, had been so kind and patient with me during the transaction. She'd even loaned me some money because I didn't understand that I'd be paying half the closing costs and wouldn't have the funds to cover those costs until my next paycheck.

"Well, sounds like you got yourself just the right agent and a nice home too. Congratulations," she said, giving me a warm hug.

"Thanks, Cherie. Well, I better get to work before I get fired and won't be able to make my first house payment," I joked. Little did I know as I drove off how prophetic those words would prove to be in the very near future.

After unlocking Ol' Blue and tossing my clean clothes somewhere, I headed out to the job site to see who was there and what was going on.

As he'd promised, Don was starting his plumbing rough-in and was on his hands and knees, gluing some drain pipe connections together.

"Glad to see someone is on the job bright and early," I said by way of greeting.

"Katlin!" he said jumping up a bit and falling over backward. "Now look what you made me do. You could at least give a guy some warning when you're coming sneaking around."

"What's the point in that? I sneak around to have a little fun, and there's nothing funnier than seeing you jump a mile high," I said, laughing.

"I did NOT jump a mile high. And don't you dare tell anyone, either," he said, trying to stifle his laughter. "I've just got a couple more things to do and my rough-in will be done. Then I'll need to fill the pipes for the pressure test. Where can I hook up my hose to water around here?"

"Water's still on at the house and there's an outside faucet by the door."

"Okeedokee. I'm all set. Now, what can I do ya for?"

"Exactly what you're doing. I just wanted to let you know I'm here and to see if you need anything."

"I sure will let you know, honey," he said wiggling his eyebrows at me in a meaningful way.

"Keep on hoping, Don," I said, laughing as I walked back to Ol' Blue.

I had phone calls to make, but before I got settled into that little chore, I wanted to make sure that Maude and Henry were actually completely moved out of the old house.

As I walked quickly through the old empty house, opening up doors and drawers, it was apparent that the old folks were gone. Really gone. The only things left were some old invoices, which I gathered up and took with me to Ol' Blue. Someone at Thomas Oil might need some of this paperwork. As I walked away from the house for the last time, I turned and looked back at it. Even though we weren't exactly best of buds, I was going to miss them.

As I climbed into Ol' Blue I heard the phone ringing. *Now where the hell did I stash that thing,* I wondered to myself as I followed the sound. Finally I found it under one of the seat cushions in the Dining Room.

"G and G ... "I began, but was cut off

"Hey girl, I forgot to tell you that I won't be up there today. So you'll have to be the boss. Lennie should be up there soon. You'll know where to put him to work," the familiar rasp of Gene's voice came through as loud as always.

"Yes, you mentioned that last..." I began, but was cut off by the sound of the phone being slammed down.

Although Gene had done some strange and weird things, he'd never forgotten what he'd told me. This was very strange.

# Studs

My thoughts about Gene and his unusually odd behavior were cut short by the sounds of a visitor in a rather large truck. I Jumped down from Ol' Blue in time to see Jim, the tank tester, driving up to where the gas tanks were buried.

"Hey, Jim," I yelled at him as he jumped down out of his truck.

"Hey Katlin. As you can see, I'm as good as my word," he said turning to me and beaming with self pride. It appeared that neither Saturday night nor Sunday go-to-meeting held any special meaning for him, since he was just as black with filth as he had been on Friday. "Someone from Thomas Oil called my office this weekend and confirmed that they'd filled the gas tanks, so I guess we're good to go for the testing."

"Great. Let me know if you need anything. I'll be in my office," I said pointing to Ol' Blue.

I watched his face as it followed his thoughts from disbelief to outrageous hilarity. He finally settled on a blank stare, so I guessed he couldn't find a suitable response and was going for neutral.

"It's okay, Jim. You can guffaw if you want. I'm way beyond being sensitive about it anymore," I said.

He was kind enough to not fall on the ground and roll around hoohawing at my so-called office. "I'll be sure to let you know if I need anything. And I'll stop by when I'm done with my testing," he said gently. "Oh, and by the way, remember to call them at the office to send someone out to disconnect the old gas pumps from the house before you move it."

Another nice guy. So far the only negative this morning was Gene. All the rest of the people in my world seemed to be quite pleasant and helpful, actually.

Since I had no other excuses, I headed back to Ol' Blue and my phone calls. I got the gas pumps scheduled to be disconnected by Wednesday and even confirmed with Red that he'd have his crew here first thing that day to begin lifting the house off the foundation in preparation for moving it.

My stomach was beginning to tell me it was lunch time. But wait a minute. Where was Lennie? According to Gene, Lennie should have been here shortly after I arrived.

A call to G and G didn't help me find Lennie. Oddly, no one answered the phone. Even if Gene wasn't available, Ginnie was always at their office during business hours. Things at G and G were getting very strange lately.

My stomach was talking to my brain, telling it that if food wasn't on the way pretty soon, it was going to start growling loud enough to let everyone within several miles that it wasn't being properly fed. I hadn't done any grocery shopping, so it was off to The Daisy Café for me and my stomach.

Luckily I arrived before the lunch bunch and quickly found a stool at the counter. I was becoming a local, which meant I got to enjoy the special benefits, one of which was being waited on before any of the tourists.

"What'll ya have, hon," said my favorite waitress. "The special, if you're interested, is Deep Fried Snot, otherwise known as oysters. It comes with garlic fries to kill the flavor of the slimy beach boogers."

Obviously she was in alignment with me on oysters. I just couldn't imagine the first person who thought that a big hunk of slime in a shell looked good to eat. "The Daisy Burger with onion rings, please. Extra tarter," I ordered.

"An excellent choice," she said ripping the notes she made for my order off her little notebook and sticking on the round wheel, to be discovered and fulfilled by the cook.

After once again gorging myself almost to oblivion at The Daisy, I waddled out to my truck, stuffed myself behind the steering wheel, and belched my way back to the job site.

For dessert, I was treated to the sight of J.J.'s van nosed up to the building. Just as he'd promised, he was here to start the electrical rough-in today. Since it was such a simple job, he'd be done with his part sometime tomorrow.

I parked my truck, scooched myself out, and walked into the building to be further treated to the sight of not only J.J., but his son, too. This would be interesting. I wondered briefly how Jay would treat me, now that daddy was present.

"Hey, J.J. I'm sure delighted to see you here," I greeted him. I looked around and noticed that Don had finished his plumbing rough-in and was gone. "Looks like you missed your buddy, Don."

"Hey, Katlin. Good to be here, too. As I always say, every day above ground is a good day," he responded.

"Words to live by. Anything you need here?" I politely asked him. Of course he'd have everything he needed. Like his plumber buddy, Don, they were some of the best in the trades, and showing up for work without the tools and supplies they needed would be a mortal sin to either of them.

"Nah. We're good. I'm gonna start the rough-in here inside the building and Jay's gonna be digging the trenches for the computer cable and electronics out to the pumps."

I quickly glanced over at Jay to see how he was taking this news, but he wasn't facing my direction. It seemed there was something totally fascinating about the studs in the bathroom wall that was grabbing his complete attention just at that moment.

"Okay then. Sounds like you're good to go, so I'll just get out of your hair," I said, somehow managing to not even crack a tiny smile at the thought of Jay bent over, digging in the dirt all day. Sometimes the construction gods seemed to see fit to bless me and mete out a little karmic justice.

I headed back to Ol' Blue, smiling one of my biggest smiles all the way.

I'd just gotten settled in my "office" when there was a knock on the door. I slowly opened the door, careful not to smash it into whoever was standing in front of it.

"Hi, Katlin," said Jim. It was hard to believe, but he had actually added yet another layer of dirt to his existing caked-on filth. I could tell, because in spots some of the older, black dirt was showing through. "I'm done with the testing and so far the results look really good. They'll keep those tanks filled now, so they don't go floating off."

"Yeah. Right. Big, heavy gas tanks floating off. You really think I'm dumb enough to fall for that?" I said sarcastically.

"It's the truth. If those tanks were emptied, with no hold-down pad on top of them they'd float to the surface. Especially in this ground. Haven't you noticed that in the lower areas on this site, water appears and then disappears for no logical reason?"

Actually, I had. Especially in the neighbor's back yard. Before we began construction, they'd drained their excess water onto the job site, where it sometimes soaked in and other times just stayed on the surface in puddles. Now our water drained onto their yard, with the same results. I nodded my acknowledgement.

"Well, that's because every time the tide comes in, it saturates this loose, sandy ground. When the tide goes out, the water drains out of it. If those tanks weren't weighted down with the gas, they'd float to the surface at high tide. Wouldn't that be a sight," he informed me.

"This is the strangest job site I've ever been on," I mused, not to Jim as much as to myself.

"Gotta agree with you there," he said. "Well, when you've completed this project, you can pretty much do any job, what with all the challenges you're having here, and the challenges you're going to have." He turned and began to walk to his truck.

"Wait! What do you mean, 'the challenges I'm going to have'," I yelled after him, but he'd already begun driving off.

Oh crikey. What was coming next?

Just then my favorite building inspector pulled onto the side.

"Hi, Phil," I greeted him as he pushed and pulled his large and substantial body out of a car built for small, skinny people.

"I just thought I'd drop by and check out the framing. If you've gotten as good quality out of your framer as you have the rest of your subs, I'll okay the framing for cover," he announced.

# Studs

"Okay, go to it. I'll be here in my so-called office," I told him.

With his clipboard in hand and five different colored pens and markers in his shirt pocket, he plodded into the building.

As I was watching him, grateful for such a nice, kind building inspector, I heard a truck roar up behind me, sounding like it stopped just inches from my butt. I jumped and turned around to see my glass guy, Bill, laughing at my response to his idea of humor.

"I didn't know an old bag like you could move so fast," he said.

"Good thing I like you," I said, placing my boot on the front bumper, "else I might be tempted to scrape my dirty boot around your fancy chrome bumper a bit. His truck was his pride and joy, his baby, and nobody even dared to touch it without incurring his wrath. To me, it was just another one ton flatbed, but to him it was the epitome of redneck status. Go figure.

"Now, now, Katlin. I brought you a present. A nice big front door and two big front windows. If you're nice to me, I might even install them today."

"Okay. You win. I'm always a sucker for a guy who brings me presents like doors and windows. I'm glad to see you, Bill. Do you need any help getting those things off your truck?" As near as I could tell, he hadn't brought any help.

"Nah. I got me a fancy doo-dad that works like one of those cranes on a big ship. 'Course, it's not quite that big," he chortled at his own little joke.

"I'll leave you to it. If you need anything, I'll be in my office or whatever," I said, and walked to Ol' Blue.

It wasn't two minutes before I heard a "Yooo hoooo" outside Ol' Blue. I'd left the door open but evidently someone was too polite to just walk in. I stuck my head out to see Bill. "Well, that didn't take long. What now?" I asked him.

"Seems your framers forgot to put the window stop in. If you have any laying around, I'll nail it in for you," he offered.

"There should be some inside the building. Look around the area where the checkstand will be. If it's not there, let me know and I'll go get some. And be sure to bill me for it. I'll be happy to backcharge the framing sub."

He nodded his agreement and went back to the building while I made yet another note for Ginnie to backcharge Roger for additional work not done. After a few minutes of growling about lousy framing subs, I thought I'd better check on Phil and see what he thought of said framer's work. As I stepped out of Ol' Blue I ran smack into Phil.

"Ooof! Oh, I hope I didn't hurt you," I said. It was like bouncing off a big marshmallow for me.

"Nope, I'm fine. And so's your framer's work. I signed off on it and you can go ahead and schedule your insulation and drywall whenever your plumber and electrician get their work approved."

"Wow. That's great news. Thanks. I'd offer you a cold drink, but I haven't had time to get to the store yet. There's so much going on with this job now."

"Yes, you'll find that it's like that in construction. Once the sheet rockers and painters are inside, you'll find things will slow down a lot," he said.

"I hope so, but with all the outside stuff, that may not happen. I've got gas tanks, concrete sidewalks and hold-down pads, the house is being moved this week, and painting is going to start on the outside of the building. Oh, and the electrician has wiring to do for the new pumps. Plus my boss thinks I should be the one to install all the metal roofing on the mansard," I informed him.

"Well, I hope you'll still have time for your favorite building inspector," he said hopefully. I think there was more to it than him just wanting a cookie from The Oasis. I hoped anyway. He was a nice man and a good ally to have on this crazy job. And he was becoming a dear friend, like Cherie.

"I'll make the time," I said, watching a smile grow on his face.

After he left, I called the insulation company and updated them on the schedule. The manager guaranteed that his guys would be on my job tomorrow afternoon.

# Studs

It was getting late so I trundled up to the building to see how the electrical was coming along. Amazingly, Jay had almost completed his ditch work. I made a mental note to request that Jay always be accompanied by his father on my jobs. Always.

"How ya doing, J.J.," I asked as I entered the building.

"It's coming better than I thought. We'll be done for sure tomorrow," he said confidently. "I've scheduled the electrical inspection for the rough-in on Wednesday and Don said the plumbing inspection is scheduled for then, too."

"Good news, that," I said. "And I see that Jay almost has his ditching done."

"Well, today it's been ditching and bitching, but he's doing it," J.J. said, looking at me knowingly.

Either Jay whined to daddy about the mean old Project Supe on this job or someone else wised J.J. up to his son's behavior. Either way, J.J. was a good dad, making sure the punishment fit the situation. A little hard work would go far to teach Jay a lesson in humility.

I looked over at the front of the building to see that Bill had already installed the doors and was working on the windows. "Do you need any help?" I asked him.

"Nah, I've almost got this one done and the next one will go even faster, now that I've got the hang of it," he responded without even looking up from his work.

"When you're done, stop by Ol' Blue, my sort-of office, and give me your invoice. I'll make sure that Ginnie pays you right away."

"Thanks. I appreciate that," he said.

"I appreciate your patience in dealing with my flaky framers," I said.

"It was easier on me than it was on you," he said understandingly.

I almost got all teared up, from that unexpected bit of sensitivity. Quickly, before any of the guys could see my girlieness, I retreated to Ol' Blue.

The world of construction was just one surprise after another. Mostly they were not nice surprises, which made the nice ones all that much more appreciated.

# Chapter 32

There was no need for an alarm clock on this job. Right on schedule, the trucks from the rendering plant woke me up as they rumbled past, shaking me awake. After my usual quickie shower I jumped into my uniform of jeans, tshirt, and OSHA approved work boots. All that was left to officially start my day was a run to the Oasis for my life-sustaining cookies and coffee.

"Mornin' Cherie," I said as I stumbled half-awake into the haven of good smells. "Don't make me think this morning. Just fill me up"

"Looks like somebody had herself a late night out," she said slyly.

"No. Just lack of sleep. There's so much going on with the job right now that my brain just won't shut up at night. It keeps reminding me of all the stuff I have to do the next day. I just hope I can keep up with everything. There's so much going on it's getting confusilatin'. Eighteen different subcontractors on the building, ninety-seven of them outside on the gas pumps. Or so it seems."

"This'll fix ya up. It's your favorite. Oh. Wait. They're all your favorites. I forgot there for a sec," she said handing me a bag that seemed just a bit heavier than normal.

"Thanks. You're a life saver. Really," I said as I gave her a bunch of money and stumbled out to my truck.

On the way back to the job site I dove into the bag and discovered she'd given me an extra of everything. What a sweetie. I was sure going to miss her... and her cookies and coffee... when this job ended.

When I got back to the job site, J.J. was already there, unloading his van. There was no need for me to check on him.

311

He was totally self sufficient and completely reliable, as I wished all my subs were.

I'd just climbed back into Ol' Blue to enjoy a bite of my breakfast ala The Oasis when I heard another truck pull onto the job. Soon there was a timid knock on the side of Ol' Blue. Sloshing down what was left of my first cookie of the day with what was left of my first coffee, I stepped out to greet my newest visitor.

"Howdy, ma'am. I'm Clyde McNabb from Thomas Oil," he said pointing to his truck, a one-ton van with "Thomas Oil" proudly painted on the side in two-foot high bright red lettering.

"Nice calling card you've got there," I dead panned. "What can I do for you?"

It took him a few moments to register what I'd said before he responded with, "I'm here to disconnect the gas pumps from the house. Bob said so."

I assumed he meant Bob the Architect at Thomas Oil. "Well, there's the house and the gas pumps are right in front of it. You can just pull up over there and do whatever it is you need to do. Please let me know when you're done. I'll be somewhere around here on the job site. You should be able to find me... it's not a very big job."

Again there was a time delay before he responded, as if he existed in another time zone. "Yes, ma'am. I'll let you know when I'm done. I'll just go over there now," he managed to say as he slowly turned around and trundled back to his van.

I watched as he moved his truck closer to where he'd be working, just to make sure he got it right. It was almost scary that someone who seemed to have such limited brain power was working with gas lines. Well, maybe he was one of those genius-type people who can do one complex thing amazingly well but can't tie their shoes to save their soul. Like Einstein.

I turned to walk back to Ol' Blue and almost got run over by a cloud of dust. After it stopped and the wind blew the dust away I could tell that it was Lennie in his own car. Evidently Gene wasn't going to make it up to the job again today. But lucky me. He sent Lennie.

After Lennie finished his breakfast of cigarettes and coffee, he climbed out of the wreck and scanned the job site, stopping when he spotted me.

"Morning, Lennie. And what brings you to this delightful location so early in the day," I asked him, maybe with just a little bit of snideness.

"Oh, hi Katlin. Gene sent me up here to finish the forming for the sidewalks," he said glumly. "Gene wants to pour concrete for the sidewalks tomorrow."

"It would be nice if he'd consult with me first. That's not going to work. I have too much scheduled. I'll call him and cancel. You can still finish the forms but the concrete will have to wait until next week." And with that I turned to go back to Ol' Blue and call the missing Gene.

"G and G Construction," said a way too cheery Gene.

"Hi Gene. This is Katlin. Up in Stanville. Remember me? Well, I've got Lennie here and he tells me that you told him to finish forming the sidewalks today so you could pour concrete tomorrow. That's not going to work. Tomorrow I've got electrical and plumbing inspections, insulation is going in today over where the refrigeration will be, and sheetrock is being delivered tomorrow afternoon. You'll have to reschedule the concrete for next week some time. By then only the sheetrockers will be inside the building."

"Oh. Well I guess I can do that. You just keep up the good work, Katlin," he said and slammed the phone down without saying buh-bye. As usual.

It was beginning to appear as if I was not only babysitting my subs but also my boss. Thankfully Lennie mentioned Gene's plans or I would have had a real circus on my hands the next day.

I went back to where Lennie was still standing by his car. "Its okay, Lennie. You can go to work and finish the forms. Gene is rescheduling the concrete and you'll be back up here next week to play in the mud," I joked with him. In the trades, "mud" is a nickname for concrete.

No response. Either he was half brain-dead or he just simply didn't think my little joke was funny.

After a few minutes, he began to move. Grabbing some tools out of the back seat of his car, he trudged up to the job site to finish the forms. The dynamics between us were rather strained, despite the cookie and coffee I'd shared with him. I was supposed to be the Project Supe, but Gene had hired Lennie, not me. So Lennie's loyalties were with Gene. He did what Gene told him to do while usually ignoring any orders I gave him. At some point, it was likely that there was going to be a meeting of our minds, and it probably wasn't going to be a pretty sight.

I went back into Ol' Blue to check my Timeline chart and see if there was anything I had missed. Nope. All was well, so I performed a job site inspection, just to make sure everything on the job was hunky dorey.

So far I hadn't heard any major explosions from the direction of the old gas pumps, so I decided Clyde was doing his job just fine.

By the time I sauntered up to the building, Lennie had all his tools out and was actually starting to work. Everything in the sidewalk forming department looked just fine. Because of the hostility I got from Lennie, I wasn't going to offer to help him. Actually it was pretty difficult to screw up something as simple as nailing a bunch of 2 x 6s together and bracing them so they'd hold 4" of concrete.

Walking inside the building, I saw J.J. was almost done and was beginning to clean up the scrap material around where he'd been working. "Looks like you'll be leaving me soon," I said in J.J.'s direction.

"You can't get rid of me that easy. I'll be here for the inspection tomorrow. And so will Don. If the inspectors have any issues we can usually clear them up on the spot instead of waiting to go through the usual channels. Makes life a lot simpler."

"Well, good then. I'll see the two of you tomorrow. Anything you need between now and then? Jobwise, I mean," I said as he began wiggling his eyebrows suggestively.

"Nah, I'm good."

"See you tomorrow then," I said. With nothing else to keep me there I began walking back to Ol' Blue.

But as had become the norm, there was not to be a lack of activity on the job. The insulators had just arrived and were backing their van up to the building. I waited until they hopped out of the truck and went to talk with them.

It was a brief conversation. They spoke Spanish. I didn't. I pointed to where they were to install the insulation. They nodded. I left.

The rest of the day was thankfully quiet except for the sounds of Lennie's sawing and hammering and the banging of the insulators staple guns.

Later, after everyone had gone, I performed my last inspection of the day. I didn't even have to look at the electrical to know it was done correctly. Not that I would have been able to tell anyway. Plumbing and electrical were two aspects of construction I knew nothing about, except as the old joke goes, it all runs downhill. The insulation above and behind where the refrigeration was to go looked like a clean, tight job.

I didn't bother looking too closely at the sidewalk forms. I'd find out how good that forming went next week when the concrete was delivered. Hopefully Lennie was coming back to the job before then to finish the forms and install the remesh. Remesh is the construction code name for reinforcing wire mesh, used to strengthen the concrete and keep it from breaking up in case of earthquakes or other such movements.

I didn't mind working with remesh since it didn't involve wet concrete. But I was going to have to find some other really important work to keep me away from the back-breaking job of hand-troweling concrete next week.

# Chapter 33

*Electrical inspection. Plumbing inspection.* My eyes popped wide open as my brain reminded me of those two very important events that were happening today. Although I had confidence in my two subs, every inspection was nail-biting time for me. Especially with this job, because I was still way behind schedule. Anything that wasn't approved by the inspectors would mean additional time spent making corrections plus more inspections. Right now I just didn't have the wiggle room for that.

To make this day even more fun filled, Red and his crew were going to begin moving the house off the lot. The garage was a piece of cake. The house might prove to be a bit more difficult since it was larger and at one time a couple of rooms had been added to the house, making it a kind of odd shape in the back.

I was going to need an extra cookie this morning to get me through the day.

Cherie was just stocking the shelves with a generous selection of cookies as I whipped into the shop. "I'll take one of each and an extra coffee," I said, already getting my mouth set to wallow in all the delicious flavors of all the cookies.

"You must be having quite a time on that job of yours," she said, stacking cookie after cookie into a large sack.

"Today is going to be very busy and quite possibly very stressful. I've got two inspections – electrical and plumbing. Plus Red is going to start lifting the house off the foundation so he can move it away."

"I'd like to see that. If I get time later I'll take a drive by. Here's your goodies," she said handing me a huge shopping bag full of everything I'd need to get me through the day.

# Studs

Two of the cookies disappeared on the drive back to the job site. I was so caught up in my thoughts about the work today that I didn't even notice what they were.

As I pulled into the job, I saw Red and his crew offloading the equipment and materials they'd need for this job. Before I went over to chat with them and make sure everything was set, the phone rang in Ol' Blue.

"G and G Construction, Stanville," I answered using my very most business-like voice.

"Hey girl, I'm not going to be up there today, but I'm sending Lennie up to finish the framing for the sidewalks and install the remesh. You keep an eye on him and make sure he does it right," he blared into the phone.

"Are you sending him up here with the remesh and tie wire, because I don't have any here on the job," I warned him.

"Oh yeah. I'll have him stop at the lumber yard here and pick some up. How much do you think he'll need?"

The man was oblivious. Clueless. I was beginning to wonder how he could ever run a construction business. "Send him up with a couple of rolls of remesh and four rolls of tie wire. And remember to give him the wire snips so he can cut the stuff."

"Okay. Will do." And he hung up, signaling that our conversation was over.

Oh goodie. I'd have Lennie to babysit again today. Just for giggles, I decided to measure his sidewalk. After double checking the plans to make sure I got the correction dimensions, I grabbed my tape measure and sauntered up to the building.

Wonder of all wonders, he'd actually gotten the width and height correct. The length was obvious, since the sidewalk ended where the building did.

Just then a parade of vehicles entered the job side. It looked like two of my favorite subcontractors and their inspectors had arrived.

"Hey, Katlin, we made it!" J.J. yelled at me as he jumped out of his van.

"We woulda been here sooner but you-know-who made us stop for coffee and you-know-whats at the Oasis," Don yelled, jabbing a thumb in J.J.'s direction.

The inspectors were still in their cars, making sure they had every form they might possibly need on their clipboards and that they were in sequential order. Finally they emerged and I had to turn away before they saw me starting to laugh. Just like the previous inspectors, one was bald and one was fat, but otherwise they looked like twins. From the ground up, they were identical. Both wore black cop shoes with white socks. Their trousers were permanent press polyester in Navy Blue. They both wore those white nylon short-sleeved shirts that were transparent enough you could see their white undershirts. And to top off their ensemble, their requisite pocket protectors were filled with a multitude of pens and pencils. They were appropriately and properly attired in the uniform of engineers the world over.

They marched up to the building and each one handed me their card by way of identifying themselves.

"Welcome, gentlemen. Please, make yourselves at home," I invited them with a sweeping gesture and an almost-bow.

They gave me a look of disdain and stepped into the building.

"You shouldn't be like that with these guys," Don quietly warned me. "They have a birth defect. They were born without a sense of humor."

Don, J.J., and I stayed outside, out of the way of the two ever-so efficient inspectors, chatting and laughing about them.

Within minutes both the inspectors exited the building and walked up to us. One handed J.J. a signed form while the other one handed Don a form with his signature on it.

"You'll be pleased to know that your work passed inspection," one of them said. And with that, they turned and marched back to their respective cars and sedately drove off.

# Studs

"Yahooo!" I hooted. "Two more inspections completed and passed. Only five gazillion more to go."

"You got that right," agreed J.J. "Well, I'll take this back to the office and make a copy for you and get it to you later this week or maybe next week. Don'll probably do the same," he said while Don nodded his agreement.

"So I guess I'll give you a call when we're ready for the finish work, huh?" I asked.

"Nope. You're much luckier than that. You'll be seeing us next week when we start our work setting up the plumbing and electrical for the new gas pumps," J.J. informed me.

"But they're *gas* pumps, not water pumps," I said to Don.

"True. But Don here is a licensed gas plumber too, so he'll be laying all the pipe for the new gas pumps. Before you pour the concrete for the sidewalks, we'll be installing the electrical conduit in the trenches that Jay dug from the building, through where the sidewalks will be, and out to where the gas pumps will be installed. I'll be doing the electrical conduit for the lights, pumps, and computer wires," J.J. said, answering for Don as well as himself.

"This sure is one complicated job," I replied.

"Oh, you'll get used to it, after the first hundred or so," Don joked.

"It may just take me that long," I said.

And with that they both took off, leaving me to deal with the rest of the job.

I didn't have long to wait for yet another visitor. This time it was a *very* welcome one. Lance was paying me an unscheduled visit. I tried to act nonchalant by slowing my steps as I walked down to where he'd parked to greet him.

"Hey, Lance. What brings you to this part of the world?"

"It's my job to check on all my stores, honey. And this one is the best part of my job," he said moving just a little closer to

319

me than was really needed. As his energy field collided with mine I could almost see the sparks and fireworks going off.

"Well, let's start your tour with the new building," I said moving backward and out of the magnetism of his energy before I got sucked completely into his force field.

I gave him the grand tour, pointing out what was done, inspected, and approved. Then I began telling him about what was scheduled for the near future, but he stopped me.

"What's going on down there by the old house?" he asked, pointing to it as if I didn't know where it was.

"The house is getting lifted off the foundation today and they're probably going to be able to move it tomorrow. It looks like they've got a good start on it and already have about a two foot lift," I said.

"WHAT? NO! That's wrong! That house isn't supposed to be moved until the very last. We planned on selling gas there until we switched over to the new store and pumps. We're going to keep the business going, selling gas and making a profit," he almost shouted at me.

I was stunned. Where had Mr. Nice Guy disappeared to all of a sudden?

"Well, while I'm sure that's desirable, it's not possible. Let me explain..."

"NO. You let me explain. You better go down there right now and tell those people to put that house back on the foundation," he ordered.

I took several deep breaths and in the calmest voice I could manage yelled back at him "That is NOT going to happen. Here's why. Maude and Henry have already moved out. They're gone. You have no one to run your so-called gas station. Additionally, the utilities have been disconnected. All of them. And finally, the gas pumps were disconnected from the house yesterday by a guy from Thomas Oil."

"Who authorized this?" he challenged me.

# Studs

"*I* authorized this. It's my job. I'm the Project Superintendent here and *I'm* making the decisions," I said, leaning toward him so he could more clearly see the angry fire in my eyes and hear the threatening growl in my voice.

"Where's your phone? I'm calling Van at the main office and get this straightened out."

For one stunned moment I stared at him, astounded that he seemed to not have heard what I just told him. Or if he did, he was giving me zero credibility by not honoring my authority and my position. My deepest, darkest thoughts were that he believed me to be just a pretty little placeholder that Gene had installed on the job in order to appease those who held the *real* authority at Thomas Oil.

In seconds I recovered from my shock and motioned for him to follow me as I stomped over to Ol' Blue. Stopping in front of the door, I jabbed my arm straight out and pointed toward the phone inside Ol' Blue. Then I spun on my heels and went back to the building. I was so furious I could have spit 16d nails. I needed something to vent my anger on instead of yelling at Lance. After all, he *was* management from the oil company and someone I should show respect to. Plus, there was no denying that he was drop-dead gorgeous and so sexy he made me dizzy when I was around him. Except for now. Now he was making me dizzy with pure, high octane anger.

I looked around the building and remembered that the framers hadn't installed the fire stop – 2 x6's nailed horizontally at a specific height between the studs. The theory was that it would stop fire from running up inside the wall, should the building happen to catch on fire.

Grabbing my tool belt, I strapped it on as I looked around for the pile of fire stop. I stuck one between the studs and positioned it where the framers had made their marks. Then I began slamming nails into the fire stop. I was so fueled by fury that I was almost driving the sinker nails halfway through the studs. Each nail head had Lance's face on it. A few had his, um, belt buckle on them. After I'd almost finished one wall my anger had dissipated to a mild rage. There was nothing so satisfying as working off anger by hitting something. And hitting it as hard as possible. Repeatedly.

It was then that I heard a quietly cautious "Ahem."

I spun around and saw Lance standing just inside the door, positioning himself for a quick escape should the need arise.

"I owe you an apology, Katlin. I called Van and he told me you'd been in contact with him about shutting down the operation here and that he approved your decision. He also told me to butt out of your job because you are going a great job here, better than Gene has ever done," he said extremely meekly.

What could I do? The guy was adorable, standing there with his cowboy hat in his hand, head bowed, shuffling his feet nervously in the sawdust on the floor.

"In the future, kindly have more confidence in me and what I'm doing here. For now, apology accepted, Lance," I said in a rather stilted manner. I didn't want to let him off the hook too easily or quickly.

"Yes'm," he said contritely, then turned around and walked back to his car.

I let him go for the time being. There'd be another opportunity for me to let him apologize in a manner more appropriate to the offense. Besides, I wasn't done being angry with him just yet.

The morning had been so busy that I hadn't yet checked in with Red, although he and his crew seemed to be doing just fine without my professional management abilities. Just the same, it was part of my job to make sure that every phase of the project was running smoothly. Or at the very least, that things weren't going in the can.

"Hey Red," I yelled from a safe distance. I didn't want to end up like the Wicked Witch from the North with a house on top of me.

"Hey, Katlin," he responded from around one side of the house. "Come on over here and see how we're doing," he invited.

I walked around to where his voice was and found him and most of his crew jacking up that side of the house. When they got it lifted a tiny increment they'd go to the other side and repeat the process, being very careful not to raise one side too much. None of us wanted the house to break in half or fall over or anything like that.

"How's it going?" I asked him.

"Purty dang good. Not to be nosy or anythin', but I couldn't help hearing a bit of your conversation with that cowboy. Is everything okay?" he asked, showing true concern.

"It is now," I replied, giving a definitive and quick nod to emphasize that any conflict that may have been was now most certainly resolved to my satisfaction.

"That's my Katlin," he said proudly. Coming from him that was high praise. "Well, to answer your question, we'll probably have most if not all the lifting done this afternoon. Tomorrow we'll be able to slide the truck under it and drive it away to its new home. I've already got a place to set it. Some guy just bought a lot upriver from me and he's going to remodel this old house and use it as a little getaway place."

"That sounds like a happy ending for it. Glad to hear it. Well, I'll let you get back to work. I'll be around if you need anything. And thanks again for everything," I said gratefully.

He had done me a huge favor by hauling off these two dilapidated buildings. One of the upper management guys at Thomas Oil was irritated that I didn't make Red pay for the buildings. I pointed out to him that we were getting the buildings hauled off at no cost instead of having to pay some moving company a huge amount of money and then paying even more money for dump fees. Not to mention the fact that they were an oil company, not a used building outlet. He quickly saw the wisdom of my thinking and agreed.

While I'd been talking to Red, Lennie had finally showed up and was beginning to cut the remesh into workable sizes. I'd check on him later. For now I needed to make some phone calls.

I also needed lunch. And since things were going so well on the job site, I figured I deserved a real lunch... one at The Daisy.

Just as I was getting in my truck to leave, however, another visitor pulled into the job. Whoever he was, he looked official. I waited until he got out of his truck and then walked over to him.

"Where's the Supe for this job," he demanded.

"That would be me. What can I help you with?" I politely asked him. He didn't disappoint me in his response. His mouth dropped open and he looked stupidly at me for a few moments before coming to.

"Are you sure?"

"Yes. Positive. Now, what can I help you with," I repeated.

I'm here from the Washington State Department of Weights and Measures, Energy Division, to inspect the gas tanks and certify that they are in suitable condition to be used with the new pumps. Where are the tanks?" he asked.

I couldn't resist playing with him a bit. "We hid them." I leaned toward him and whispered, "They're in the ground.'

"Oh,' he said as he looked around. "That must be them over there with the pipes sticking out of the dirt. Thank you, ma'am," he said as he scurried away to do his inspecting.

*No sense of humor*, I thought. *Must be a requirement in order to become an inspector, with certain exceptions of course, like Phil.*

I looked around and no one else seemed like they needed my superior project management talents at the moment, so I jumped in my truck and took off for the delicious lunch I knew was awaiting me.

Stuffed to the gills with fish and chips made from fresh Cod caught the previous day, I returned to the job with a happy tummy and high hopes for a productive rest of the day. I was not disappointed.

A quick scan of the site showed me that Red and crew almost had the house up high enough for them to drive the truck under it, which they'd be doing tomorrow.

Lennie was still cutting and placing remesh, and was almost at the other end of the building from where he'd begun. It looked like he'd be done today, also. With any luck, Gene wouldn't find any more work for him to do up here for a while.

The gas tank inspector was still there, making notes and muttering to himself. I left him alone to do his job, not wanting to interrupt any important conversation he might be having with himself.

The rest of the day I spent wallowing in paperwork and making phone calls to schedule the next round of subcontractors – sheetrockers, and the insulation installers who needed to finish their job. As usual, it wasn't long before I was interrupted by timid knocking on the door of Ol' Blue. Carefully opening the door so as not to knock over who ever was standing out there, I discovered the gas tank inspector.

"Just thought you'd like to know that the gas tanks passed inspection and you can go ahead and use them with the new pumps," he informed me.

"Thanks for the good news. May I have a copy of that report?" I asked.

"Oh sure. I'll send one to Thomas Oil and I was going to give you one as well. So, here," he said handing me a carbon copy with barely visible writing on it. He must have especially selected the one near the bottom of at least eleven copies just for me.

I took it and nodded my thanks. If I needed a clear copy I could probably get one from Thomas Oil.

The day was drawing to a close and it had been a good and productive day. I hoped the next day would be the same.

# Chapter 34

There'd be no trip to The Oasis for me this morning. I still had enough goodies in the bag to keep me happy until next week sometime. I decided to enjoy my breakfast al fresco, since it was such a warm, sunny day already. Cherie had given me extra coffee, too, and I decided that iced coffee was the perfect accompaniment to enjoy with day-old cookies.

It wasn't long before my delightful little meal was interrupted by vehicles spewing dust all over my Chocolate Cinnamon Pecan cookie. Some people have no respect for the cookie.

These particular people turned out to be the insulation guys. Evidently they wanted to get an early start so they could finish their job before the heat of the day crept into the store. There's no kind of hell I can think of that's as bad as hanging fiberglass insulation, especially when you're all hot and sweaty. Miniscule filaments of fiberglass get stuck in the pores of your skin and itch like a bad case of hives. And it's nearly impossible to get the fiberglass out of your skin.

"Glad to see you so bright and early this morning. I guess you'll be finishing up today, huh?" I greeted several of the guys as they piled out of some very fancy pickups.

No response.

"Let me know if you need anything – phone, water, beer, that sort of thing. I'll be here in my, um, office or else around the job site somewhere," I added.

No response.

"They don't speak English," said a deep voice behind me.

I jumped and turned around to find a tall, heavily muscled, completely bald man who seemed to be tattooed all over. At least the parts I could see were all inked up. "Oh. Thanks. And who are you?" I asked.

"I'm Mitchell, the foreman of this crew. And to answer your question, yes, we will be done today," he said tersely.

He turned to the pack of men who were standing behind him in a clump, smoking cigarettes and trying out some macho poses. He yelled something in Spanish at them and they immediately stomped out their smokes and scurried up to the big van that was parked in front of the building. Soon they were hauling huge rolls of insulation out of the van and into the building.

"We'll be done early afternoon, if that's soon enough for you," he growled at me.

"Yeah. Sure. Fine," I said and returned to my cookies and iced coffee, wondering as I munched and crunched what could possibly keep a person in a job they obviously hated as much as Mitchell seemed to hate his. He sure wasn't making his working conditions any better by being mean and grumpy to everyone around him. Maybe he'd be happier if he started off his day with a Chocolate Pecan Marshmallow cookie from the Oasis. I know it sure improved my outlook on life.

Soon I was enjoying the bam bam bam sounds of their staplers, confident in the knowing that the insulation would be finished today. As a bonus, I knew that Mitchell was getting all sweaty and soon would be itching all over.

I'd barely finished my C & C when another truck arrived. This time it was a semi with a load of sheetrock. Not the best of timing, since there was a bunch of guys in the building rolling out insulation on the floor so they could cut it, while other guys were installing it in the walls and ceiling. I walked out to where the truck had stopped and waited for the driver to come down to earth.

"Where's the Project Supe on this job?" the driver asked as he was climbing backwards down from the cab.

"That would be me," I said, and then waited for his response.

I always loved this part, where I got to tell men who were used to dealing only with men in the world of construction that I, a mere woman, was the Project Supe. The looks on their faces were always entertaining. This guy didn't disappoint.

"Oh," was all he said for a few moments as his eyes went blank. Finally, his brain began to function again and he spoke, "Well, where would you like this load?"

"How about inside the building?"

There actually are people who think that leaving sheetrock outside in the Pacific Northwest for more than a few minutes is an okay idea. If he was one of them, then either he wasn't from these here parts or he had the IQ of a fence post. There was a very good reason why this area was called The Wet Side of Washington.

"It would appear that you currently have a crowd of vehicles parked directly in front of where I need to back my truck."

"That's easily corrected. Just wait here for a few minutes," I said, walking toward the building.

"MITCHELL!" I yelled to be heard above all the banging of staplers and the blaring of Mexican music on the tinny boom box.

The stapling stopped and a bunch of fingers pointed toward where Mitchell was busy cutting insulation. I walked over to him and tapped him on his back, causing him to jump.

"Damn, lady, you're lucky you didn't make me cut my fingers off with this knife," he yelled at me, waving a razor knife in my face.

"I need you to move all your trucks," I said.

"What?" he yelled.

"I NEED YOU TO MOVE ALL YOUR TRUCKS," I yelled.

Pulling massive ear plugs out of his ears, he explained, "I can't stand their music, but it keeps them happy and working so I just shut it out with my own music. The real stuff. Rock n roll. Now what is it you want?"

"Let me show you," I said and grabbed his arm and propelled him out of the store. "You see that big semi parked behind your trucks? He needs to back up to the door so that all that sheetrock can be offloaded inside this building," I explained.

"This ain't a good time for you to be havin' a sheetrock delivery," he pointed out.

"Yes, I realize that but I didn't order it. The sheetrock sub took care of that little detail and I had nothing to do with the scheduling. This isn't the first screwed up delivery I've had. See that pile of boxes over there?" I said pointing to the parts and pieces of the new canopy. "I won't be needing that material for two months yet. I do what I can with what I've got. So, will you please be so kind as to have your men move their trucks over to that area?" I said pointing to an area that was currently vacant and probably large enough for all their trucks. "And also kindly move your van there as well."

"Yeah," he grumbled and went back in the store to tell his crew.

Soon I was playing Traffic Control Cop and motioning the guys where to park their trucks, then signaling the semi driver with the sheet rock as he backed up to the store front.

After Mitchell and crew went back to work, I walked over to the semi driver to find out how he was going to get his entire heavy, bulky load of drywall into the building.

"They told me you were going to take care of that part," he deadpanned.

"Heh heh. *Wrong*. Seriously now, how?"

"I got a crew coming to offload it. There they are now," he said pointing to a pickup truck with two guys in it.

"Your crew is two guys? And they're going to offload all this sheetrock today? Most of it is twelve feet in length and probably weighs about 5,000 pounds per piece."

"They can do it. You'll see," he said moving off.

He slid a couple of metal ramps out from under the truck bed. When he'd pulled them all the way out, they just barely reached inside the building. They were like little bridges from the truck bed, over the framed-up sidewalk, and into the store.

His two crew members slid out of the pickup, threw their jackets off, and my hopes for getting the semi offloaded in one day collapsed into the dust. They were miniature men who looked like they shopped for their clothes in the children's department. Not exactly the big, hairy, muscled-up studs I expected to be unloading a semi truckload of 4' x 12' double sheets of drywall.

"Hi there. You got any place in particular you want this sheetrock stacked?" one of them asked me as they walked into the building.

After the few seconds it took to get my brain to working again, I replied, "put it toward the back but leave enough room for the insulation guys to finish up that wall."

They took a quick look around the inside of the building, shed their shirts, and went to work. They each grabbed four sheets off a stack, carried the weight on one hand and balanced their load with their other hand overhead, and began trotting down the ramp and into the store. Quickly they flipped the sheets onto the floor and went back for the next load. I watched them for several minutes, astounded at their strength and endurance. Had it been me, I'd have been panting, sweating, and barely able to take another step after a couple of loads. These guys were like machines, never stopping, not even hesitating long enough to take a brief rest.

I couldn't stand watching them any more for fear that one or both of them was going to keel over from a heart attack or heat prostration, so I trundled back to the cool safety of Ol' Blue. I had paperwork to do anyway.

Soon there was a knock on side of Ol' Blue. "C'mon in," I yelled at whoever it was, keeping my attention on the blueprint in front of me.

"Hi. You must be Katlin," said a woman's voice.

I looked up in surprise. Women were a rarity on a construction site. I should know. "Yes, that's me. And who might you be?" I queried.

# Studs

"I'm Gigi and this is Flossie. We're Gene's painters. He said you'd be expecting us to start the exterior paint," she said ending with a questioning tone in her voice.

"Obviously you know Gene. He did not mention that he was sending you up here. But that's fine. You can get started on the back of the building. There's just too much going on in the front right now for you to try to paint that area. You did bring the paint, didn't you?"

"Yes. We're Gene's subcontractors, not just his workers, so we're all self contained," she said looking a little annoyed that I could possibly think she was anything but the epitome of professionalism. "We do need water though, to wash out our tools when we're done for the day."

"Okay, then, go ahead and get to it. Water's over there where that house is being moved," I said nodding toward it. "If you need anything else, I'll be here in Ol' Blue or around the job site somewhere."

Gigi walked and Flossie bounced along beside here. Flossie was very appropriately named and I could only hope she wasn't as dingbatty as she looked. Painting doesn't require a Mensa IQ, but it does require *some* brain power – or at least common sense.

I quickly glanced at the old house to see how Red and crew were doing and was surprised to see their truck maneuvering into position under the house. It was time to check in with my house-moving crew.

"Holey Schamoley, you guys work fast," I said to whichever one of them was under the house. Whoever it was had the important job of making sure the truck didn't back into something and knock the house over.

"That's true. We're not only fast, but we're really good, too," said the familiar voice of Red. "We'll have this honey off the lot in the next hour."

"Excellent! Just out of curiosity, why is it that you don't have your usual crowd of sidewalk superintendents this time," I asked him.

"Well, for one thing it wasn't so long ago we did the garage. Remember?" he said as he walked all hunched over out from under the house. "It was all new and exciting then. Now it's the same ol' same ol'. We do have a couple of the old guys watching us to make sure we get it right. See them over there across the street? The ones pointing thisaway and thataway? They're my regulars. They come to all my house moves."

"While I'm glad to be rid of this old dump, I'm going to miss you and your family. It's been a real pleasure working with you and I appreciate all you've done for me. That includes educating me about gooeyduck," I said smiling at the memory.

"Happy to oblige. We may run into each other again, especially if Gene keeps getting more of these jobs. We may be doing a lot of moving for him... and you."

"I hope so," I said and gave him a big hug. "Thanks a bunch for everything and bye for now," I said as I quickly turned and walked away. I didn't want him to see the big, tough Project Supe get all teary-eyed.

It was too early for lunch, so I went back to Ol' Blue to work on the take-off for the latest set of plans Gene had given me. Soon I heard the coughing and wheezing of a very sick and ailing car. I hoped whoever it was didn't think we still sold gas here. I stepped outside and was dismayed to see Lennie pile out of a very crumpled, very old pickup truck.

"What's up, Lennie?" I asked when he'd landed.

"Gene wants me to begin putting the forms together for the pump pads. I've got the pieces in the back. Care to give me a hand unloading them?" he asked sarcastically.

"Sure. No problem," I replied sweetly, hoping to shift him out of his nasty attitude toward me. Even if it was just a tiny bit, any improvement in his demeanor toward me would be a relief. His gratitude for the cookie and coffee I'd shared with him lasted about as long as it took him to gulp it all down.

We lugged the metal forms over to where the new gas pumps were going to be installed. They were easy peasy to install, since they were preformed pieces which, when assembled, would create an elongated oval. Then concrete would be poured into the form and hand troweled to a nice smooth finish. The metal form remained in place to protect the concrete edge from damage by careless drivers.

Lennie would be the one troweling the concrete to a smooth finish. Or so I hoped. The quality of his work depended upon several things, such as how hung over he was and how close it was to payday.

I helped him lay the parts out on the ground in sequential order. Someone at the supplier had thoughtfully crayoned numbers on the parts and pieces so it was simple for us to lay them out in numerical order. Then all he had to do was put tab 1 into slot 1A, insert the bolts in the correct holes and screw the nuts onto the ends of them. I figured he could handle that and left him to it while I returned to the plans I was working on.

After what seemed like only minutes, I once again heard a tapping on the side of the door. When I got up to see who it was, I was surprised to see Phil, my favorite building inspector.

"Hi, Phil. To what do owe this honor?"

"I was just passing by and I noticed that your insulators are gone. If they're finished, I can check out their work and hopefully OK it on the building permit," he informed me.

I looked at the building and sure enough, their pickups and the van were gone. And so was the semi truck of sheetrock. I'd been so preoccupied with the plans I hadn't heard any of them leave.

"Let's go see how they did," I said. "Looks like Red got the house out of here okay, since I don't seem to see it anywhere."

"Yep. He's good, that one is. Let's see how good your insulators are," he commented as we walked into the building and meandered around, checking this and that.

As I followed him I was instantly struck by the visage of HUGE piles of sheetrock. Those two scrawny little guys had lived up to their reputation. There were three stacks of sheetrock positioned strategically where it would be handiest for the installers. The two little guys had neatly stacked that entire semi-truck load, and it only took them half a day. It would have taken me two months to offload that much sheetrock.

As I stood there, looking around in awe and thinking humbling thoughts of not being so quick to prejudge someone by their physical appearance, Phil's voice brought me back to reality.

"Well, it looks good. I'll initial this phase and we can go have a lemonade. Or something," he hinted.

"While you're doing that, I'm going to check on my painters. I'll meet you at Ol' Blue," I said starting to walk around the building to the back.

What I expected to see was two painters painting. Evidently their work day began at noon and ended shortly after that, because they were gone. They'd managed to get paint on about one third of the siding on the back of the building, but only as high as they could reach. Gigi's definition of professionalism must not have included having her own ladders.

With a sigh, I walked around to the front of the building, where Phil was patiently waiting for me... and his cookie and lemonade.

Luckily, I hadn't gorged myself on all the cookies that Cherie had loaded me up with. There were still about five left. We wandered back down to Ol' Blue, talking about how things were progressing on the job and I gave him his little treat. *Did cookies count as bribery*, I wondered as we sat and chatted like old friends.

Soon he said his goodbye and stuffed his extra large body into his extra small car and drove off to yet another home-cooked masterpiece, created by his beloved wife.

I pulled out a bag of Jiffy Pop, stuck it in the microwave, and sloshed down a beer as I waited for my dinner to finish cooking. As I munched on my popcorn entrée, I reflected on how things were getting really busy on the job site and how much more interesting this commercial stuff was than plain old residential construction. But the best part of my wandering thoughts was the realization that tomorrow was Friday.

# Chapter 35

On rare occasions I do wake up early, ready to bound out of bed and start my day. *Very* rare occasions. This was one of those eventful days. Visions of packing all my worldly belongings and moving into the house I'd bought were the last thoughts I remembered having as I drifted off to sleep at night, and the first thing I thought of as I came out of my world of dreams and began my day.

I was thinking it was going to be difficult to keep my mind on the job today, when suddenly I realized I was parked in front of The Oasis. Evidently it was going to be difficult to keep my mind on more than just the job. I had no idea how I got there.

"I was wonderin' if you were going to just set there all day," said Cherie as she began stuffing a bag with my usual order of cookies.

"Yeah. Wow. I don't remember driving here. I'm so excited about moving into my little house that it's all I can think of," I said, amazed that I could even talk.

"Well, this batch of cookies ought to bring you back to reality. It's a new flavor – Mocha Mocha Mocha. I combined three kinds of chocolate and three flavors of finely ground coffee. When you come back down to Earth from the first rush of sugar, you'll be wide awake and ready from the caffeine rush for this here reality," she said with a nod and a knowing wink.

Whoo doggies.

I barely had time to scarf down one cookie on the drive back to the jobsite. Another one disappeared while I sat my mini-micro office in Ol' Blue, facing the beginning of yet another day in my life as Project Supe.

The roar of a rather large truck coming to a halt right next to Ol' Blue, doors slamming, and a loud voice shouting orders at someone brought me completely back to reality. A quick peek out the mini window alerted me that Gene and Lennie had arrived.

For reasons unknown to anyone, including himself probably, Gene had evidently decided to show up on the job site today. He'd given me no warning about why he was here, what he was planning on doing, or the current state of his mental and/or emotional condition.

Throwing open Ol' Blue's door, I barely missed hitting him and knocking him on his keister.

"Well, that's a fine way to greet your favorite boss," he bellowed in his normal volume.

"Hi, Gene. Come on in," I invited him.

"Got any coffee in this dump?" he asked, looking around hopefully.

"Nope. I go up to The Oasis and get my coffee."

"Well, I'll send Lennie up there in a little bit. Right now what I want is to know how you're doing up here," he said as he sat down at the dining table, scrunching his big belly so it would fit in the tight space.

"Well, tell me where you left off reading my weekly reports," I countered.

"Hell, girl, I ain't got time to read reports. Just tell me how you're doing and what's going on," he said, starting to act a little agitated.

To calm him down, I repeated what was in my latest reports, filling him in on what was currently being done and some of the high points of the past couple of weeks. When I was done he was tapping his fingers on the table and looking around distractedly.

After a few seconds of dead air time, he realized that I was done talking. "Good. Good. Sounds like you got everything under control. I knew you could handle it. Didn't I tell ya? Let's go take a walk around," he said squeezing himself out of the dinette.

"I brung Lennie up here with me to do the concrete work on the sidewalk in front of the store today," he said proudly as we headed toward the building. "And you can help him"

"What exactly do you mean, 'help him'?" I questioned. I hate concrete work. The stuff is corrosive to skin and the work requires being on your hands and knees or bent over. It's a back breaking, skin eating, horrible part of construction and I hate it more than installing fiberglass insulation… if that's even possible.

"I mean you'll be working with him, troweling the concrete. The truck should be here in a few minutes."

"Gene, there are a few things you should know about me. One is that I don't hang insulation. Another is that I don't do electrical or plumbing work. The other is that I don't do concrete work. *Especially* I don't do concrete work. If you want a Project Supe who will do that, you'll have to find yourself someone else," I said turning to walk back to Ol' Blue. I was ready to pack up and leave if he insisted that I join Lennie in one of the worst jobs possible in the construction trades. At least in my humble opinion.

Gene grabbed my arm and spun me around. "You don't have to get all uppity about this," he growled at me. Then quick as lightening, he put a big, smarmy smile on his face. "Lennie is capable of doing this hisself, I'm sure. We'll just let him get to work. Let's you and me continue our tour of the wunnerful job you're doing here," he said, all happiness and cheer.

The man could change his emotional temperature in a New York second. He was absolutely stunning in his ability to quickly shift from an intense anger to higher-than-a-kite happiness to deep, dark depression. And back through several other mood shifts and changes in the process.

I hadn't noticed this about him when I was doing his estimating, but then I rarely saw him either. I'd pick up the plans at his office, then work up the estimate and fax it to him. Not much opportunity there for lengthy gab fests.

Probably he was just under a lot of pressure because of all the jobs he had going. Yeah. That was it.

"Lennie, you just go ahead and handle the concrete there for the sidewalk," he sternly ordered.

Lennie didn't look all that pleased to be working by himself on the concrete, but it could have been worse. He could have had me next to him for hours, bitching, whining, sniveling, and complaining. As I see it, I did him a favor and he could have at least shown his gratitude to me.

Gene and I walked around the outside of the building and I showed him the work his painters had done, what little there was of it. "Oh, those girls are good. Really good. They're hard workers and probably just had to finish up another job somewheres," he said, explaining away their lack of progress.

Yes. Well.

"Let's go inside and you can see what's been done there," I suggested, ignoring his comments about the painters. So far, I wasn't impressed with their work ethic. The quality of the painting they had managed to do looked okay, but then it's pretty hard to screw up painting T1-11 siding.

We moseyed inside the building and he began looking around with what seemed to be very sharp eyes all of a sudden. "Looks like you had to do some adjusting around the front door," he said casually.

"Yes. The framer made the opening ½" too small, so I made him backblade it. The trim will cover it up." I explained.

"Looks like the studs in the bathroom wall are set purty close together," he commented.

"Yes. The framer tried to save time by putting them on 32" centers instead of 24" centers like the plans called for. So rather than have him tear out the wall, which would have taken more time, I just had him install another set of studs so now they're 16" on center. I was running short on time, as you know."

"How do you get along with the building inspector?"

"Great! He's like my patron saint. He lives on the island and stops by on his way home to do my inspections. I don't even have to call him. And so far he's signed off on everything."

"Hmmmm. Well. I guess you're doing okay. We'll keep you for another week or so," he said chuckling at what I hoped was his little joke.

I didn't think it was all that hilarious, but joined in his laughter to keep him happy. They didn't cover this type of situation in the Project Management 101 class I took, and I think Brown Nosing the Boss should definitely be added to their class subjects.

"Well, things look just fine here, so I'm going to leave you with Lennie. Give him a ride back to my place on your way home tonight, will ya?" he asked without really asking.

Then he just stood there, staring off into the distance. I figured he was thinking about something profoundly important and waited for him to speak. After a few minutes he sort of woke up, shook his head, strode over to his truck, got in, and took off in a cloud of dust and dirt.

"Well, that was just weird," I said to no one in particular.

"Yeah," said Lennie's voice right behind me. "He's been acting real strange lately. He's not on top of things like usual. One minute he's Mr. Nice Guy, the next he's ranting and raving about some stupid thing. I try to stay out of his way as much as possible anymore."

"What do you make of it?" I asked Lennie, turning to face him.

"I dunno. But I've been talking to some guys I know about going to work for them. It's just getting too strange at G and G lately," he announced.

"Well, Lennie. Thanks for the info. I don't know what to make of it either and maybe I should be following your lead. I won't say anything to anyone about you looking for another job."

"Thanks. I appreciate that. Well, for now I have a job so I better get back to it," he said. "The concrete truck should be here any minute now."

Just as he said that, another truck pulled up. However it wasn't the concrete truck. It was the sheetrockers. The two of them just sat in the pickup, looking at the front of the building. I knew how they felt. Toward the end of my career as a roofing contractor, there was always a few moments just before I started to work each day that I'd sit and stare at the roof, wondering just how much longer I could keep on doing that body-breaking labor. And then, just like these two guys, I'd heave a big sigh, get out of my truck and start to work.

I waited until they had their toolbelts on before introducing myself.

"Oh yeah. We heard about you," said the taller of the two. "The guys who loaded the store for us - the Midgets we call them - were still drooling when they got back to the warehouse. Something about an Amazon woman running the job."

I was speechless. Those guys were so busy loading sheetrock I didn't think they'd had time to even look at anything but the loaded truck and the inside of the store.

"Well, I guess when you're only three feet tall, any woman would look like an Amazon to you. When you see them tell them thank you for me, and also tell them I appreciate their ambitious goal setting," I said smirking. What was it with short guys and their lofty, pardon the pun, ideas of dating a women twice as tall as them?

"Oh, by the way, my name's Vern and his is Ernie. People call us Vern and Ern. You can too, if you want," said the tall one, smiling in understanding of the tall woman/short man situation.

"Well, okay then. Just let me know if you need anything. For your work, I mean. If I'm not around the job site, I'll likely be in that old camper. That's my office and home for now," I explained.

They grinned at me as they made their way into the building. As I stood outside the building, wondering what was coming next, I heard the zzt zzt zzt sounds of sheetrock being screwed to the ceiling with electric screwguns. These guys didn't waste any time starting their work.

# Studs

While the sheetrock part of the project was going on, nothing else would be worked on inside the building. After Vern and Ern got all the sheetrock installed, then the mudders and tapers would come in and put the finish on the sheetrock in readiness for painting. Next the trim would go up and interior painting would be done.

As I was musing about the progression of work, the sounds of a *really* big truck got my attention. Lennie's concrete had arrived.

I let Lennie deal with getting the truck backed up into position. He seemed to know all the appropriate hand signals to direct the driver as the concrete spewed out of the chute and slopped inside the forms. Lennie had thought ahead and stapled plastic sheeting to the siding so it wouldn't be accidentally splattered with concrete. It seemed that he actually did know what he was doing. I happily left him to his concrete and walked back to Ol' Blue to make some phone calls and take care of other, less concrete-y work.

One of the calls I wanted to make was to get Gigi's phone number from Ginnie. The two painters hadn't shown up yet and it was getting close to noon. No doubt Ginnie had their number.

"G and G..." began Ginnie.

"Hey Ginnie, do you happen to have the phone number of Gigi, that painter of Gene's? Those two women haven't shown up yet today and yesterday they only got about 20' of the siding painted, and then not even all the way to the top. Evidently they don't own a ladder."

"Oh? Isn't that interesting. I'll be sure to tell Gene all about it when he arrives," she said, sounding all too pleased that I was having trouble with the two women painters. "Gene likes to think of himself as their mentor, but he lets them get away with too much. The one time I met them I was surprised to see how little protective clothing they wear while they paint. I mean, cut-off shorts and a halter top don't protect the skin much from getting all painted, do they?"

*Mentor, my ass*, I thought to myself. *There's some hankying and pankying going on here.*

"Uh, you're right about that, Ginnie. Do you have their number so I can call them?" I asked again. I didn't happen to mention that Gene had seen their progress on the job, or lack thereof, and thought it was fine.

"Gene didn't ever give it to me and they've never given me an invoice. I think he pays them in cash. Sorry I can't help you, but I will definitely tell Gene when he gets home just how unsatisfactory their work is," she said happily and hung up.

Since it was none of my business what was going on between Ginnie, Gene, and his two painters, I turned my attention back to what *was* my business - getting this mini-mart gas station built.

So far, everything seemed pretty much under control, so I went back to Ol' Blue to update my handy dandy Time Chart. It was beginning to look like I might be gaining a bit on the time lost. Although it was too early to celebrate, I felt a small sense of relief. And pride.

My stomach was telling me loud and clear that it was lunch time. A trip to The Daisy was in order, I decided, after a quick check on Lennie to see how he's doing.

"Hey, Lennie. I'm going to the local café for lunch. Can you break and come with me?" I asked, feeling rather kindly toward him now.

"Can't, Katlin. I have to keep working this mud and finish it before it starts to set up. Thankfully, the driver ran out and I only got half of the amount Gene ordered. He had to deliver to a pour close by here and they just added the small amount we needed onto his load. The first pour took more than they figured. I should be done here in another couple hours, though."

I was feeling a bit guilty about not helping him with the concrete finishing. "How about if I bring you back a burger. Can you take a few minutes to cram a Daisy Burger down your gullet?"

"Sure, I guess I could do that," he said, sounding grateful.

# Studs

"I'll be back in about half an hour. Try not to pass out from starvation before then," I said and trotted off to my truck.

The Daisy was, as usual, packed. As I was scanning the café for a place to sit, an arm went straight up in the air. It was attached to my favorite Knight in Shining Armor, Mark. I wiggled and scooched my way through the crowd to where he had his arm draped over an empty stool at the counter.

"Might I interest you in sitting next to one of Stanville's most elegible, attractive, and sexy bachelors?" he asked, wiggling his eyebrows at me.

"You might," I said and gratefully sat down next to him.

"What's new in that zoo you're working at?" he asked.

I filled him in the job stuff, interrupted only twice – once to give the waitress my order and once to munch and crunch my way through it.

"Oh. I almost forgot to tell you. I bought a house," I announced proudly.

"I hope it's in Stanville," he said.

"No, it's not. It's close to where I live now," and I told him all about it. "Once I get settled you're more than welcome to come visit," I offered.

"All you gotta do is call, and I'll be there," he sang off key.

The waitress brought my burger-to-go care package for Lennie and I got up to leave. Mark looked so sad about me buying a house that wasn't in Stanville I couldn't resist giving him a quick little hug to cheer him up.

"*Definitely* you'll see me at your new home," he said all smiley-faced.

When I arrived at the job site, I noticed yet another truck parked where the old house used to be. I delivered lunch to a very grateful Lennie before strolling over to investigate the activity by the old gas pumps.

As I passed by the truck I couldn't help but notice the Thomas Oil logo plastered on the door and tailgate. *What now?* I wondered to myself.

After looking around, I finally found the visitor from the oil company. Someone in filthy, greasy coveralls was monkeying around the gas pumps.

"Excuse me," I said.

No response.

"EXCUSE ME," I yelled.

BANG! "Yeouch! You don't have to yell," said a gravelly voice from behind one of the old gas pumps. "My hearing works just fine. Not so's my head, which you caused me to hit with yer dang yellin'," said a dirty, grungy face as it appeared from behind the pump. As he came toward me I couldn't help but notice that the rest of him was just as grungy.

"Yes, well I'm Katlin Green, Project Superintendent on this job. I'm guessing you're from Thomas Oil, since you're driving one of their trucks. But what exactly are you doing?" I said, stepping backward in case he wanted to be friendly and shake my hand.

"I'm the guy who's going to get rid of these old pumps for you. Name's George, but you can call me Geezer like everyone else does," he replied with a grin that showed me all three of his yellowed teeth. "I'll have these babies out of here in an hour or two."

"That's just, um, great," I managed to croak out. *Where did the personnel department at Thomas Oil find these people*, I wondered. "I'll be up in that camper truck if you need to use the phone or anything," I said backpeddling towards Ol' Blue and away from the dirtiest, greasiest, filthiest, stinkiest man in the world.

Getting rid of the old gas pumps was something that hadn't occurred to me, so I was actually grateful to whoever sent Geezer to take care of that item.

# Studs

On my way back to Ol' Blue I decided to perform an inspection of the work being performed on the site, as any professional Project Supe would do.

Lennie was still on his hands and knees, smoothing out the concrete where soon people would be spitting, stomping out cigarette butts, and just generally defacing all his beautiful work. But I wasn't going to point that out to him. "Looks great, Lennie," I said as I passed by on my way inside the building to see what the sheetrockers were doing.

Vern was just taking off his stilts while Ern was fastening the last screws in the last piece of sheetrock on the ceiling. In the olden days before someone got smart, they used to have to use planks on sawhorses to reach high ceilings like the one in this store. Then someone came up with nifty mechanical stilts that allowed the installers to walk around and reach ceiling heights of up to 12' without the need for sawhorses, planks or even a ladder.

"You two are really fast," I said looking around at how much progress they'd made in such a short time.

"You think this is fast, you ought to see Vern at closing time at the bar," Ern said. "He can sweet talk a girl into going home with him before the barkeep is done yelling 'last call'."

Vern said nothing, but his ears turned red.

"Well, you're doing an amazing job here," I said.

"We'll come back tomorrow and then we should be able to finish up the nailing on Monday. Usually we don't work on Saturdays, but we're backlogged now and need to catch up. Your mudders and tapers will probably be here on Tuesday, so don't plan on doing anything in here for the rest of next week," Vern warned.

"Oh, I think we have enough outside to keep us busy, but thanks for the advance notice. I'll let you two get on with your work now. If I don't see you before I leave, have a great weekend and I'll see you on Monday," I said and began walking back to Ol' Blue.

"We'll be sure to tell the Midgets that you said to tell them hello," Vern teased.

When I got back into Ol' Blue and sat down to do paperwork, I found it impossible to concentrate. Even though the Big Move wasn't until next weekend, all I could think of was getting into my new house. My main concerns were what to pack first and who did I know with a truck and lots of muscle.

As thoughts of moving circled around and around in my head, I was becoming anxious and confused. There was only one way to overcome this common mental craziness. Write it down. Make a list.

I pulled out a pad of paper and began making notes of what to pack, where to get boxes, who to call for muscle and trucks, utility companies to call, and all the other millions of details that need to be completed.

After what seemed like minutes, I heard the sound of vehicles starting up and leaving the job. Dashing out of Ol' Blue, I discovered that everyone was leaving for the day. According to the construction worker's clock it was way past beer-thirty.

This meant I was free to leave! In two minutes I had all my clothes thrown in my contractor's suitcase – the black plastic garbage bag – and was out the door. I could hardly wait to get home and begin the exciting transition to my new home – my own house!

I opened the door on my truck and when I tossed my bag o' clothes on the seat, it made a funny "oof!" sound and then wiggled around some. Terrified that some wild animal had somehow found its way into my week's laundry, I quickly backpeddled out of the attack zone. The bag rolled on the floor, revealing a sleepy Lennie on the seat, stretching and yawning as he went through the process of waking up. I'd forgotten that I had to give him a ride back to G and G headquarters, where his car awaited him.

He slid once more into Dreamland and stayed there all the way back to his car, leaving me to enjoy the rest of the drive as I made my plans for the Big Move.

# Chapter 36

The drive to G and G Headquarters this particular Monday morning was spectacularly awful. All weekend I had spent packing and preparing for the Big Move the next weekend. It wasn't only the packing of my household belongings into what seemed like a thousand and forty-seven boxes that had drained my life force energy. Mostly it was the excessive amounts of beer I'd been forced to drink with my friends of the more muscular species. Especially those who had a pickup truck.

From various past experiences I knew that beer was the currency paid to friends who turned into moving crews, and these guys didn't come cheap. Plus they expected pre-payment, which, of course, I was expected to share with them. The only reason that I joined them was just to be polite, you understand.

I was thinking about the next weekend, and what it would be like during the actual move. It would seem to be wiser and more prudent to hide all the beer until everything was safely in my new house and *then* begin the celebration.

And that was about the extent of my thinking ability, as I drove up to Ginnie's. Blessedly, somehow I remembered to knock rather than ring the doorbell so I wouldn't have to suffer through some whiney cowboy's lament about his girl, horse, dog, or pickup. Especially in my delicate condition.

"Come on in," I heard Ginnie yelling from somewhere inside the house. I hoped it was the kitchen and that she had coffee ready. Lots of coffee.

"Hi, Ginnie. It's the Monday Morning Gang, all together again," I said, sounding much chirpier than I felt.

"Looks like you had yourself some kind of weekend," she said as she handed me a life-giving cup of coffee.

"You might say that. Here's the paperwork from last week. Where's Gene?" I asked, looking around for him.

"Gene's not here. And here's your paycheck for last week. Sorry to say it's your last check," she said sadly.

"Thanks. Huh? Wait. What do you mean, my last check?" I was stupified. Gene had given me no reason to think that he wasn't happy with my work and was going to fire me. I looked up at Ginnie in shock. It was then I noticed that her eyes were red and swollen, like she'd been crying. A lot.

"What happened?" I asked her. "What's going on?"

"Well, hon, I tried to keep it from you, but Gene has what you might call a health problem. The docs say he has something called Manic Depression, which causes him to be, well, volatile I guess you'd say. He has mood swings. As long as he takes his medication he's okay. But sometimes he gets all bullheaded and thinks he doesn't need the drugs. Then he goes off on a tangent. He did that this weekend... and then some."

"What did he do?"

"Well, he got kinda in a tizzy. He'd been drinking a bit, which he's not supposed to do, and it just fired him up. He trashed all the equipment and materials he had stored out in my barn. Then he took off and nobody's heard from him since. We don't know if he's even alive," she ended with a sob.

I went over to her and put my arms around her for comfort – hers and mine.

"So the end result is that there is no G and G Construction any more. I'm sorry, hon, but you're out of a job," she said and began some serious crying.

I was ready to join her in a sob fest. Normally losing a job and going on unemployment compensation wouldn't be such a big deal. But I'd just bought a house. And now I didn't have a job. How was I going to make the payments? Pay for the taxes and insurance? The utilities?

Suddenly my legs wouldn't hold me up and I had to grab onto a chair to keep from sinking to the floor.

# Studs

"How long has he been like this?" I asked.

"Forever, it seems. At first it wasn't so bad, but it's been getting worse and worse. I had to commit him to a special place where they keep people like him. We told you he was at a reunion, but it was that place. They did lots of tests on him and got him on some new medications. They also give their patients a lot of therapy to teach them how to deal with the emotional issues that come up. It did him some good for a while, but then he just got worse," she said.

That explained why he seemed to switch from Mr. Nice Guy to Mr. Wacko in less than a nanosecond.

Just talking about it seemed to help her feel better. She'd stopped crying and looked more calm. I, however, could feel a huge bout of mass hysteria building up inside of me.

"Did I tell you that I just bought a house? Yeah. I closed on it last weekend. I'm moving into it next weekend. I was counting on this job and the ones after it that Gene talked about so I could afford to buy this house. No job, huh?" I just sort of drifted off, unable to fully comprehend the entire reality of the situation.

"Well, I'm sorry, hon, but that's how it is. But don't you worry about me none. I talked to Thomas Oil and they have a couple of other contractors who are gonna take over the job and finish it. So at least I don't have to fret about the legal stuff, like them suing me for breach of contract and causing me to lose my home."

"That's nice," I mumbled.

"Are you gonna be okay, hon?" Ginnie asked me, finally noticing that she wasn't the only one whose life had been turned upside down by a crazed maniac named Gene.

"Dunno. Probably," I managed to say as I shoved my last paycheck into my pocket and stumbled out the door.

This sure was putting a damper on my excitement about my new home. *But something better always turns up*, I thought to myself as I drove slowly back home. And it was true. Just when things seemed to be at the lowest, always something or someone appeared just in the nick of time to save me.

Gene was a prime example of this principle. I met him when I'd been working at a local lumber yard. Gene became a customer there while he was building a mini-mart/gas station nearby for Thomas Oil.

To say I was unhappy working at that particular lumber yard would be a monumental understatement. The manager of the lumber yard, who I later discovered had a mental problem made worse with the huge quantities of alcohol he drank, had been harassing me and sabotaging my efforts in order to get me fired. I saved him the trouble by quitting after one last unforgivable incident in which he made wild and vastly untrue accusations of me in front of several of my contractor customers.

Gene was one of several of my contractor customers who called me minutes after they found out that I'd quit. They all pretty much knew why. Several of them offered me jobs, and I opted for Gene's tantalizing offer of the job of estimator. I could work from my home and on my own time. Plus the pay he offered was much better than what I'd been getting at the lumber yard... and much better than what the other contractors were offering. Once again, something better had turned up for me and just in the nick of time.

Even though working for Gene hadn't lasted forever, it was a step up from my previous job. As I was driving back home after hearing Ginnie's devastating news, I mused about how for the most part each change in my life had been for the better... even if I didn't think so at the time. Given my history, then, this totally unexpected change would no doubt somehow be better, another step up, from where I had been.

Mentally I looked around at my prospects and found them to be greatly lacking. Most of the jobs around where I lived paid minimum wage or close to it. Unless, of course, you had become college or university educated as a doctor, dentist, lawyer, or other such professional. I was lost somewhere in between.

Then an inspired idea struckitheth me. Real estate agent! I already knew almost everything about houses and how they're built. I was very good at sales, as my experience at Beacon Building Materials proved. And I heard that real estate agents made good money. Yeah. *Maybe I'll check into selling real estate,* I thought.

As I drove, my thoughts coalesced. I could talk to Sheila, the real estate agent who sold me my house, and find out from her what it's like to work in real estate. She seemed to like it and she made good money at it, judging by her car and clothes. She'd been one of the top agents in the area for many years and you didn't get that good if you didn't like what you were doing. If anyone knew about working in real estate, it would be her.

*After I've moved into my new house,* I thought, *I'll go talk to Sheila. Yeah. I have a feeling this is going to be the beginning of a whole new bigger and better phase of my life.*

By the time I got home I couldn't wait. I jumped out of my truck and burst into the house, grabbing the phone to call Sheila. After talking with her for a few minutes, she got me an appointment with her broker, the first of many steps I was to take as I began my new career as a Realtor.

And that's another story.

# About Kathy Wilson

Kathy Wilson's life journey has meandered down many diverse paths, each one offering a vast variety of life experiences. A few of her work experiences include pea tester, bartender, motel maid, clam digger, logger, construction superintendent, roofing contractor, Realtor, landscaper, Certified Professional Coach, snowmobile clothing manufacturer, website designer, Tai Chi instructor, and author.

She currently lives on the Olympic Peninsula with her husband and their cats, Jezibel and Silver Cloud.

Check out her website at **www.Warrior-Priestess.com** for more of her books as well as other offerings.

Made in the USA
Columbia, SC
08 June 2019